W9-BVG-488

THE
ELIMINATION
THREAT

ALSO BY MICHAEL LAURENCE

The Extinction Agenda

The Annihilation Protocol

THE
ELIMINATION THREAT

MICHAEL LAURENCE

ST. MARTIN'S PRESS
NEW YORK

First published in the United States by St. Martin's Press, an imprint of St. Martin's Publishing Group

THE ELIMINATION THREAT. Copyright © 2021 by Michael Laurence McBride. All rights reserved. Printed in the United States of America. For information, address St. Martin's Publishing Group, 120 Broadway, New York, NY 10271.

www.stmartins.com

Designed by Omar Chapa

The Library of Congress Cataloging-in-Publication Data

Names: Laurence, Michael, 1973- author.
Title: The elimination threat / Michael Laurence.
Description: First edition. | New York : St. Martin's Press, 2021.
Identifiers: LCCN 2021006974 | ISBN 9781250158536 (hardcover) |
    ISBN 9781250158543 (ebook)
Subjects: GSAFD: Spy stories. | Suspense fiction.
Classification: LCC PS3612.A94422775 E45 2021 | DDC 813/.6—dc23
LC record available at https://lccn.loc.gov/2021006974

Our books may be purchased in bulk for promotional, educational, or business use. Please contact your local bookseller or the Macmillan Corporate and Premium Sales Department at 1-800-221-7945, extension 5442, or by email at MacmillanSpecialMarkets@macmillan.com.

First Edition: 2021

10 9 8 7 6 5 4 3 2 1

For my mom

PART 1

Behind the ostensible government sits enthroned an invisible government owing no allegiance and acknowledging no responsibility to the people.

—Theodore Roosevelt, twenty-sixth president of the United States,
Theodore Roosevelt, An Autobiography, *1913*

1

Slate Langbroek woke from a sound sleep and sat up in bed. He was certain he'd heard something. A thudding sound, like someone dropping a heavy object onto the floor above his cabin. He concentrated and listened.

The yacht rose and fell gently on the still sea. Waves broke softly against the hull. A gull cried in the distance.

He glanced at the clock. 4:12 A.M. The sun would be rising soon.

The chef was already at work in the galley. It smelled like roast pork. Or maybe a whole pig, if the faint scent of singed hair were to be believed.

A minute passed.

Two.

Maybe the sound had been part of his dream, which was always the same. He was standing on top of a ruby red staircase, a tower of digital billboards behind him. Each displayed his image, larger than life. The crowd filled the streets below him. Their eyes were upon him, their cheers as loud as thunder. A woman emerged from their ranks, dressed in samurai armor and wearing a conical straw hat that concealed her face. She extended her arms to either side and spoke without moving her mouth. A single word cut through the roar, penetrating his very being.

"Quintus."

His heart pounded in his chest and he couldn't seem to draw a breath. The voice hadn't been part of his dream. He'd definitely heard it, spoken aloud from just outside his range of sight. And there were only twelve people who called him by that name, eight of whom would sacrifice their firstborn to claim it as their own. He'd prepared for this contingency though, planned every detail so meticulously that there was no way—

Thump.

The sound originated from beyond the foot of his bed, right outside the sliding glass door. The curtains billowed on the gentle breeze. He suddenly regretted leaving the door open so he could fall asleep with the cool air on his face.

Langbroek jumped from his bed, the marble tiles cold against his bare feet, and darted for the door. Slammed it closed and locked it. Finally caught his breath.

His hands were shaking so badly he could barely draw back the curtains.

The body lying on the deck outside of his cabin looked like it had been cooked. He recognized his private captain by the epaulettes on the shoulders of his uniform shirt, which was still burning in places. His hair was gone and the upper layers of his skin were charred.

"Jesus," he whispered, letting the curtains fall from his hands.

He staggered backward. Clipped his bare heels on the tiles. Landed on his rear end. Kicked at the ground to propel himself up against the bed.

"Quintus."

A creak of transferred weight on the deck outside the door.

Langbroek climbed onto his bed and hit the button to engage the electromagnetic locks. He stepped back down to the floor and walked to the center of the room. The walls were reinforced with steel plates, the windows made of bulletproof glass. His cabin was even equipped with a self-contained air supply in the event the boat sank. There was no way anyone could get to him in here, especially not in what little time they'd have once he triggered the emergency transponder and private military contractors stationed on both sides of the Yucatán Channel converged upon his location.

He felt a surge of anger. How dare the other twelve make such a brazen move against him. If they wanted a war, then by God, that was exactly what he was going to give them.

Langbroek strode to the door and ripped open the curtains. The body of his captain was gone. In its place stood a figure wearing a full-body metallic silver suit and clutching an apparatus that looked like an underwater camera in its gloved hands.

Quintus saw a distorted reflection of himself on the golden face shield of the intruder's helmet.

"Tertius Decimus sends his regards," the assassin said.

The aperture opened and a greenish blue light bloomed from behind the lens of the device.

Quintus shielded his eyes.

Felt the heat, even through the glass.

Screamed as his skin blistered.

And started to burn.

2

DENVER, COLORADO
July 2

Special Agent James Mason emerged from the elevator onto the fortieth floor of a building that resembled a giant obsidian stake driven into the heart of downtown Denver. He'd thrown on a plain white T-shirt, jeans, and a baseball cap, covering his sandy blond hair and shielding his blue eyes from the rising sun, which glared through the wall of windows to the east and made the surrounding skyscrapers appear to burn. It was surreal to think that the last time he was here he'd nearly died, when a helicopter crashed into the penthouse suite and turned the building into a towering inferno. While the National Transportation Safety Board's investigation had ruled it an accident—a combination of mechanical failure and pilot error—Mason knew that their explanation was the furthest thing from the truth. Had a hacker known as Anomaly not alerted him to the impending attack at the last possible second, his entire team would have been killed, right along with the pilot, whose body had been so badly burned that the medical examiner had been unable to identify him.

"Pretty freaking unbelievable, right?" Ramses Donovan said. He wore a button-down shirt open to the chest, his ebon hair slicked back, and an expression of pride as he gestured to his private nightclub, which offered a stunning 360-degree panoramic view of the entire front range of the Rocky Mountains. "I was starting to think they might never finish."

Mason took in the room around him. Everything looked just as it had before, and yet different at the same time. The leather of the seats was a slightly darker color, the lighted terrariums built into the support columns subtly altered, and the freestanding wet bars not quite where they'd been before, or perhaps his recollection was tainted by the memory of the chopper's spotlight turning them into silhouettes in the seconds before impact.

"I don't know how you can move back in here after what happened," Special Agent Jessica Layne said. She walked between the tables, tracing the contours of the booths with her fingertips. Her raven black hair was pulled up from her slender neck and her sapphire eyes betrayed nothing of the thoughts playing out behind them. "It's only a matter of time before they take another shot at you."

"Let them," Ramses said. He'd never even considered living anywhere else. It would have been a betrayal of everything that made him who he was: the human personification of the middle finger. The placid exterior was a disguise, though, one so transparent that Mason could practically see the rage boiling underneath it. When Ramses found the man responsible for destroying his sanctum and uprooting him from his life, he was going to tear him apart with his bare hands. "They know where to find me."

"Which, fortunately, is no longer at my place," Mason said.

"No offense, but if I'd been forced to spend another night in that dump of yours I'd have put a gun in my mouth."

From Mason's experience, any statement qualified by a phrase like "no offense" was meant to have the exact opposite effect, but he didn't take the insult personally. The building he called home— which at various times in its existence had been a tire shop, a used-car dealership, and a gallery for graffiti artists ambitious enough to scale the twelve-foot chain-link fence—stuck out like a sore thumb, even from the abandoned industrial wasteland surrounding it. Ramses had largely had his run of the place for the past six months while his penthouse was being rebuilt and Mason was splitting time between the Denver and Manhattan field offices of the FBI, sifting through the fallout of the Times Square Massacre on New Year's Eve, during which the Scarecrow—a woman formerly known as Kameko

Nakamura—had dispersed Novichok gas from handheld vaporizer units at the stroke of midnight. She'd killed 107 innocent people and overwhelmed emergency rooms with thousands more, but she'd failed to assassinate her primary target, Slate Langbroek, whose family had been responsible for the twisted experimentation to which she and her cherished brother, Kaemon, had been subjected as children. The chairman of the executive board of directors for Royal Nautilus Petroleum might have escaped her wrath and slipped through the Bureau's net, but he'd eventually have to come up for air, and when he did, Mason and his team would be waiting.

Assuming, of course, the Thirteen didn't find him first.

Mason leaned against one of the elaborate terrariums, inside of which was a waterfall surrounded by tropical trees and blooming plants. The sound of running water and the scent of damp soil were strangely calming. When he didn't immediately see anything slithering or crawling around inside, he tapped on the glass.

"Do that again and you'll be wearing a cast," Ramses said. In another life, he would have made an amazing zoologist, albeit one who might not have made the best tour guide for small children.

A tortoise emerged from the foliage at the edge of the water. The right half of its shell appeared to have been burned.

"It survived the explosion?" Mason said.

"Nearly every animal in my collection did. Reptiles are resilient creatures. See the green tree python in that enclosure over there? He escaped the fire and was living in the ductwork until about two weeks ago. You should have seen the look on the contractor's face when he told me what he'd found."

"That snake's what, six feet long?" Layne said. "How did no one know it was there?"

"It happens more often than you'd think," Ramses said. "Just last year, a western diamondback broke out of its cage in Arizona and somehow got into the plumbing. It came right up through the toilet of a restaurant down the street four months later and bit a guy squarely on the ass. Some dude in Wisconsin had an eight-foot red-tailed boa that he thought had escaped his apartment complex; ten months later it fell out of the ceiling onto his neighbor while she was sleeping. Hell, the Bronx Zoo lost an Egyptian cobra, which keepers eventually found, and a venomous mangrove snake that's still on the loose. After the kind of beating the entire staff took in the papers and on social media, it's no wonder nobody stepped forward to claim the mamushi that turned up in Brooklyn a few months back."

"What in God's name is a mamushi?"

"A species of pit viper," Ramses said. "It's the deadliest snake in—"

"Japan," Mason said, finishing his old friend's sentence for him. He caught the tail end of a thought and tried to hang on before it slipped through his grasp. "Show me where they found it."

Ramses nodded and led them to a broad spiral staircase, which ascended into a marble anteroom with water trickling down three of the walls. The fourth was secured by a digital keypad and receded like the door of an elevator, admitting them into the private lair of a man who was probably even an enigma to himself.

Unlike the level below them, the residential suite had been completely remodeled. The living room looked roughly the same, with a monster flat-screen TV surrounded by furniture that appeared soft enough to swallow a man whole, only it was maybe half the size and there was no longer a swimming pool in the roof overhead. The computer setup off of the stainless-steel kitchen was gone, replaced by a security system displaying live footage of the building from every conceivable angle, inside and out.

Mason and Layne followed Ramses into the hallway, immediately forked to the left, and entered a room that hadn't been there before. A networked workstation with six monitors, modeled after the secure website the Thirteen had used to covertly communicate and influence global events, dominated the far wall, while the remainder had been plastered with photographic displays of everyone and everything even peripherally related to the secretive cabal. There were pictures of four generations of Langbroeks, whose involvement with the Nazi Party and the U.S. Army's chemical arsenal had laid the foundation for the Novichok threat; the Nakamura family, whose human experimentation for the Japanese army's nefarious Unit 731 had continued stateside after World War II and given rise to the Scarecrow; and members of the Richter and Thornton bloodlines, who'd conspired to engineer and release numerous historical pandemics using their pet monster, the Hoyl.

Somewhere, hidden among them, were the threads that would unravel the mystery of the Thirteen.

"What do you think of the new command center?" Gunnar Backstrom asked, swiveling around in the captain's chair at the terminal. He wore his bangs long to conceal the better part of the vertical scar that bisected his right eyebrow and cheek, and a Brioni dress shirt with a royal blue tie loosened at the collar, which was about as close as he came to going casual. "I'm just putting on the finishing touches."

"Impressive," Mason said.

Ramses slipped past Gunnar and opened a search window on the main monitor. He breezed through a series of links and brought up a map of Brooklyn. Four red dots, each labeled with a number corresponding to the legend at the bottom, were clustered just inland from the waterfront district.

"A man was bitten by a venomous snake in Mother Cabrini Park on May sixteenth," Ramses said. "Animal control subsequently trapped and euthanized a seventeen-inch, reddish brown serpent identified as *Gloydius blomhoffii,* also known as the Japanese moccasin or mamushi, suspected to have been illegally imported and kept as a pet. Subsequent sightings of snakes matching the same description have been reported in Carroll Park, near St. Paul's Episcopal Church, and in the parking lot of the Seventy-sixth Precinct, although no other specimens have been captured."

"What are you thinking?" Layne asked.

"If I'm right," Mason said, "we might have finally caught a break in the hunt for Dr. Tatsuo Yamaguchi."

The Japanese neurologist had risen to international acclaim as one of the world's foremost experts on the treatment of nerve gas exposure following the Tokyo subway sarin attack in 1995 by a cult known as Aum Shinrikyo. He'd vanished from the public eye shortly thereafter, only to reappear decades later as the personal physician of the Nakamura twins. As the lone link who could potentially connect the Scarecrow to Slate Langbroek—and, by extension, the Thirteen—Mason's team had spent the last six months scouring the globe in search of him, but so far hadn't turned up a single trace.

"Walk us through it," Gunnar said.

"Using the mamushi to kill the doctor she blamed for failing to save her brother's life fits the Scarecrow's MO. While she maintained a professional distance from the potential victims of the plot to release the Novichok, she took her time with the people she believed had wronged her on a personal level, using the stinger of a box jelly-fish, the neurotoxin of a puffer fish, and the venom of a swarm of giant hornets—all endemic to Japan—to make them suffer as she had."

"So you think that's why we haven't been able to find Yamagu-chi?" Layne asked. "Because he's already dead?"

"Either his body's waiting for us in an apartment within range of those four sightings or he got the hell out of there when he discovered the snakes," Mason said.

"Which means that everything inside that apartment should still be exactly how he left it and, one way or another, we'll find him, whether rotting inside or through whatever evidence he didn't have time to destroy."

"Someone would have noticed by now," Ramses said. "The first month he missed his rent payment, the landlord would have been banging on his door—"

"Unless he owned the place and had all of his bills set up to be paid automatically from an account that could comfortably cover all of his expenses for the foreseeable future," Gunnar said. He booted Ramses from the computer and scooted up to the console. His fingers blurred across the keyboard. "If that's the case, then I should be able to rule out a full ninety percent of the population in that area, focus on the remaining ten, and—"

A dialogue box appeared in the middle of the screen, eclipsing the lines of code scrolling past.

"Anomaly," Ramses said.

"He exploited the crack in the firewall," Gunnar said. They'd collectively decided to leave the vulnerability so that the hacker could communicate with them, and not just because he'd saved their lives. By doing so, he'd revealed that he wasn't merely inside their investigation into the Thirteen; he was inside the organization itself. Whatever his endgame, he needed them alive and they needed to fig-ure out why. "The system's attempting to trace his location before he slips back out."

Gunnar opened the tracking program on the adjacent screen, which displayed the green outline of the world map on a black back-drop. A beacon surrounded by pulsating colored rings formed on their location. An orange line shot straight from it to a white dot on the East Coast, from which another line streaked across the Atlantic to a green ring in Central Europe.

Three words appeared in the box: *¡El Nuevo Alarma!*

"It's an online Mexican shock rag featuring graphic coverage of cartel violence," Ramses said.

The orange line sliced diagonally across the Middle East to the tip of Somalia, then east toward China, where it faded before reaching a yellow dot that had only started to form.

"We lost him," Gunnar said. He minimized the tracking program, opened the *¡El Nuevo Alarma!* website, and scrolled past pictures of a silver sedan riddled with bullet holes, headless corpses displayed beneath a banner with words painted in Spanish, and body parts washed up on a beach. He stopped when he reached a photograph of a partially burned yacht with bodies littering its deck. It had been taken yesterday evening, if the date stamp in the corner and the angle of the shadows were to be believed. He cleaned up the resolution, zoomed in on the ship, and laced his fingers behind his head. "Well, what do you know?"

There was no mistaking Slate Langbroek's yacht. Or the reality that he was undoubtedly already dead.

"Do you think Anomaly figured out that we had a lead on Yamaguchi and fed us the yacht to buy the Thirteen enough time to beat us to him?" Layne asked.

"If he was in our system while we were researching the mamushi sightings, he could have easily pieced it together," Gunnar said.

"We have to find Yamaguchi first," Mason said. "And we need to get someone we trust on that yacht before whatever evidence it might hold disappears. Where's Alejandra right now?"

"Hunting the Jalisco New Generation Cartel," Ramses said, "which means she could be just about anywhere in the eastern half of Mexico."

"She's still closer than we are. Find out where that yacht is and see how fast she can get there."

Mason abruptly turned and headed for the door.

"Where are you going?" Gunnar asked.

"Brooklyn," Mason said. "Layne and I have some snakes of our own to hunt."

3

Mason had called Gabriel Christensen on his way to the airport and
relayed his theory about Yamaguchi and the mamushi. Chris was one
of the few people he even partially trusted inside the Bureau, which had
been infiltrated by the Thirteen to depths they were still struggling to
fathom. The former special agent in charge of the Denver Division had
been promoted to deputy director for the National Security Branch, a
role in which he liaised directly with the Department of Homeland
Security and the National Joint Terrorism Task Force. He'd been hesitant to act on Mason's intel, especially this close to Independence Day.
At least initially. After the massacre on New Year's Eve, every New
Yorker was already on edge in anticipation of the next major national
holiday and flooding the streets with law-enforcement officers risked
causing a panic, but he'd ultimately relented and arranged for additional units to patrol a single eight-block zone in Brooklyn. At that
very moment, FPS and NYPD officers were fanning out through the
Columbia Street Waterfront District and the Carroll Gardens, Cobble
Hill, and Red Hook neighborhoods to buy Mason time to find the location where the good doctor had been holed up and hamper the
movements of anyone trying to beat him to it.

Of course, Mason hadn't told Chris about Gunnar's involvement
for the same reason he refused to allow the deputy director to bring
in the FBI's digital forensics specialists to expedite the search; until he
knew the extent to which the organization had been compromised, he
needed to control the flow of information, even if it meant potentially
alienating one of his few allies on the inside. Chris had launched into
one of his trademarked rants about trust and giving Mason enough
rope to hang them both, but he'd ultimately acceded when Mason
promised to tell him everything he knew once Yamaguchi's apartment
was secured.

A Cessna Citation from the FBI's fleet had been waiting for Mason and Layne on the tarmac at Denver International Airport and
had started taxiing the moment they closed the door behind them.
They'd assumed forward-facing seats across the narrow aisle from
each other, opened their laptops on the tables in front of them, and
immediately set to work. They wore wireless earpieces that allowed

them to network multiple cellular devices and toggle between calls with the tap of a finger, although they were currently connected to only Gunnar, who tore through the financial records of the residents of the neighborhoods in question while Ramses coordinated the race to reach Langbroek's yacht with Alejandra Vigil, their friend within Cuerpo de Fuerzas Especiales, the special forces unit of the Mexican army.

She'd initially deserted her unit and crossed the border into the United States in search of her missing sister, a quest that had drawn her into the orbit of the Hoyl. After helping to prevent the release of his deadly flu virus, she and Ramses had gotten a lot closer than he generally allowed anyone to get, but in the end, whatever connection they'd shared hadn't been enough to keep her from returning to Mexico and rejoining the war against the drug trafficking organizations destroying her country from within, one bloody state at a time. Her battalion was currently stationed in Quintana Roo, where Cártel de Jalisco Nueva Generación—CJNG—was laying siege to residual elements of Cártel del Golfo and Los Zetas and fending off its chief rival, Cártel de Sinaloa, in an attempt to lay exclusive claim to the Gulf and Caribbean coastlines, so it was assumed that a luxury vessel found floating off the shore of Cancún, its decks covered with dead bodies, was the handiwork of Nemesio Oseguera Cervantes, aka El Mencho, or one of his lieutenants. Alejandra had arranged to join the unit dispatched to investigate and was already on her way to the Port of Playa del Carmen, where the yacht had been towed to a secure dry-dock facility.

"How long until she gets there?" Layne asked.

"Ramses says any second now," Gunnar said. "She's going to stream a live feed so we can be there, too. Virtually, anyway."

The clouds closed rank below them, forming a veritable carpet of white so dense it appeared as though they could walk right out onto it.

"Tell me you're close to finding Yamaguchi," Mason said.

"There are more than nineteen thousand residential units in our prescribed area of Brooklyn, nearly three hundred of which match our search criteria. Half are owned by corporations and foreign nationals, so following the money takes time."

"Which is something we simply don't have," Layne said.

"Trust me," Gunnar said. "You'll have an address before you touch down. I just need to work a little magic—Hang on. Ramses says

Allie's in position. I'm looping the two of them into the conversation and routing the video to your IP addresses as we speak."

The sound of background noise in Mason's earpiece changed as Ramses and Alejandra joined the conference call. His video player automatically opened and the footage appeared on the screen of his laptop. The picture was dark and grainy, the scant illumination provided by fluorescent tubes and what little natural light passed through the vents in the aluminum walls. Birds clapped their wings as they took flight from the shadowed rafters of an aging warehouse erected over the water. Two enormous gates in the far wall granted access from the ocean to bays that could be flooded to admit seafaring vessels and then drained so that workers could repair their hulls. One was currently in use by a sleek, futuristic-looking yacht that was well over a hundred feet long and had to have cost somewhere in the neighborhood of ten million dollars.

The camera traversed the concrete platform beside the vessel, taking in its bulk on the other side of a chipped metal railing. The radar mast was conspicuously absent and the skydeck appeared to have been blown right off the boat, leaving behind a ragged rim reminiscent of the surface of a decayed tooth. Fire had consumed the paint on the upper decks and taken bites out of the carbon-fiber hull. Water sluiced through cracks in the bow, spattering the murky surface surrounding it loud enough to drown out the voices of the men walking with Alejandra.

"Can you verify that it's Langbroek's boat?" Layne asked.

"An agent from Agencia de Investigación Criminal said the automatic identification system has been disabled, but a yacht like this is custom-built for every buyer," Alejandra said. She spoke with a thick accent, her voice rich and sonorous. "He contacted the builder and was able to confirm that Langbroek commissioned certain *unique* upgrades."

"What kind of upgrades?" Mason asked.

Alejandra climbed the ramp, passed through the midship boarding door, and cautiously stepped onto the main deck. The parallel planks were charred and warped, yet held her weight as she approached the mirrored window running the length of the main cabin, which had somehow survived the fire and explosion intact. Her reflection appeared on the glass, little more than her eyes and the scarring on her brow visible through the slit of her balaclava. She wore a tactical helmet, solid black fatigues, a bulletproof vest, and an FX-05 Xiuhcoatl assault rifle slung over her shoulder. Her face grew larger and larger as she leaned closer to the glass, but the tinting prevented the camera from picking up any details beyond the faintest impression of the curtains hanging inside.

"The main cabin was designed to function as a survival pod," she said. "It is completely enclosed by fire- and bulletproof glass, impervious to water, and contains its own dedicated forty-eight-hour oxygen supply."

"Can the survival pod be sealed from the outside?" Ramses asked.

Alejandra spoke in Spanish to someone off camera. His reply needed no translation, but she repeated it for the sake of clarity.

"No."

Mason immediately recognized the implications.

"Then whoever activated the pod is still inside," he said. His pulse raced at the prospect. "Slate Langbroek could be in there at this very mom—"

"I found Yamaguchi," Gunnar said, interrupting. "He's been living under a false identity. Two years ago, a man named Kenneth Nguyen paid four point one million dollars in cash for the corner penthouse of the building at One Forty-five President Street. Prior to that, he worked for the nationalized Vietnamese telecommunications company, VNPT, and maintained his primary residence in Hanoi, where he died a decade ago. All of the recurring bills belonging to the impostor using his identity are paid from a local account at the HSBC Bank in Midtown, which receives a monthly influx of funds from a trust established at Fidelity Bank in the Cayman Islands."

"That's our guy," Layne said.

"Alejandra," Mason said. "I need you to stall for me. Don't let anyone open that survival pod until I can arrange to have an American official on hand to make sure everything is done by the book. If Langbroek's still in there, we need him taken alive."

"Keeping him that way will be a whole lot harder," Ramses said.

"Don't I know it." Mason tapped his earpiece and connected to an open line. He speed-dialed Chris's number and started talking the moment the deputy director answered. "I need two favors and I don't have time to explain. First, I need you to discreetly lock down

One Forty-five President Street in Brooklyn. Get eyes on the corner penthouse apartment, make sure no one leaves that building, and have a tactical team waiting when I arrive. Second, who do you have near Playa del Carmen right now that you can trust to bring in Slate Langbroek?"

4

BROOKLYN, NEW YORK

The NYPD's elite Apprehension Tactical Team—the A-Team—had been waiting at St. Paul's Episcopal Church when Mason and Layne arrived. They'd changed into black tactical CBRN suits, driven three blocks to the complex on President Street in an armored vehicle, and stormed the lobby, where they'd split into two teams. Mason followed the first up the stairwell, the soft tapping of their footsteps and the whispering of their exhalations through the filters of their gas masks echoing from the confines. One of the officers scanned the hinges and seams surrounding the door to the seventh floor for trip wires before slowly opening it upon a paneled corridor granting access to matching penthouse suites. The second team blew past behind them and continued upward to secure the roof. They'd already disabled the elevator of the upscale apartment building, evacuated the lower levels, and barricaded the surrounding streets.

The men advanced into the corridor, their weapons trained on the door straight ahead, which granted access to the apartment owned by the long-deceased Kenneth Nguyen. Mason squared himself and sighted his Glock at the peephole, watching for a shadow to darken it, while the other officers cleared the frame of booby traps and used a handheld through-wall radar unit to confirm there wasn't an ambush waiting for them on the other side.

"Is everyone ready?" he whispered into his comlink, breaking radio silence.

A moment passed before Layne replied in a whisper.

"Roof team in position."

Mason glanced at the officers on either side of the door. One held an M4 carbine across his chest, the other a battering ram that had obviously seen its share of use. Their faces were invisible behind the reflection of the overhead chandelier on their polycarbonate face masks.

"We go on a silent three count," Mason whispered. "Three."

He stepped closer to the door. Readjusted his grip on his semiautomatic pistol.

Two.

Tried not to think about the venomous snake sightings that had led them here and the prospect of more mamushis waiting inside.

One.

The officer with the battering ram pivoted away from the wall, swung the heavy cylinder, and hammered the door, right beside the knob. The trim splintered and the door flew open.

Mason went in fast enough to absorb the rebound of the door against his shoulder. He took in everything around him as quickly as he could.

A foyer. Blond hardwood floors, bare ivory walls, crown moldings. A half bath, clearly empty. A closet door, closed. Ahead, the great room opened before him. The entire back wall was made of glass and afforded a panoramic view of the private balcony and, beyond it, the Manhattan skyline across the East River. The white leather furniture in the sunken living room had been arranged to face the dark screen of the TV mounted on the interior wall to the right.

"No sign of movement from up here," Layne whispered. "We're lowering ourselves to the balcony now."

The appliances hummed softly from the kitchen to Mason's left. A granite island with overhead cabinets separated it from the dining room. One of the officers passed behind the copper pots and pans hanging from them in a shooter's stance, his M4 at his shoulder. There was a stack of unopened mail on the table, its polished surface reflecting the bulbs of the lighting fixture overhead.

"Kitchen clear," the man's voice whispered through the speaker beside Mason's ear.

"Down here," the second officer said from the living room, where he crouched on the other side of the couch.

Mason gestured for the third officer to clear the hallway branching from the dining room before descending the single stair and rounding the love seat. He leaned over the second officer's shoulder and saw the black-and-white gobs crusted to the hardwood. The muscles in his lower back instinctively tightened.

"Reptilian fecal matter," the officer whispered.

The external infiltration team popped the lock and entered through the terrace door behind them.

"Guest bedroom's clear," the third officer said. "You need to check it out, though. Moving on to the master."

Mason rose and headed down the hallway. He stopped at the threshold of the guest bedroom, his back to an empty bathroom. The floor-to-ceiling windows were covered with blackout drapes to better view three computer monitors set up, side by side, on a desk nearly as wide as the room itself.

"It looks like a nurses' station," Layne said, squeezing in beside him.

The monitor on the left was divided into four quadrants, all of which were black. It was a video surveillance system, although the feed had been disrupted at the source. The central screen displayed flatlined vital signs—heart rate, blood pressure, pulse oxygenation, and respirations per minute—from a remote location. A warning beacon flashed, but the alarm had been disabled. The third monitor remained blank. The desktop tower that had once been connected to it had been broken open on the floor, its components disgorged and shattered as though beneath a heel.

The entire room had been devoted to monitoring Kaemon Nakamura, the Scarecrow's brother, who'd been disconnected from the corresponding medical equipment in the basement apartment his sister had used to access the subway tunnels and transported to New York–Presbyterian, where he'd died less than twenty-four hours later.

"Check this out," the third officer said from down the hall. He stood silhouetted in the doorway at the end of the corridor, limned by the glow of the tactical light on his helmet. "Looks like he was going to make a run for it."

Mason stepped past him and took in the master bedroom at a glance. There was a dresser to his left, the drawers closed and the top uncluttered. The door of the walk-in closet stood open, revealing a conspicuous gap where a row of suit jackets had been shoved aside to expose a hole in the false wall roughly the same size and shape as the suitcase lying open on the bed. The interior fabric was smeared with blackish streaks. The scabbard of a sword rested beside it.

The picture suddenly came into focus.

Yamaguchi had known that Kaemon wasn't going to get better

and, whether or not he explicitly knew of the Scarecrow's plans to release the Novichok on the other side of the East River, recognized that he was in big trouble. He'd had an emergency bag packed with clothes, a new identity, and enough cash to start over someplace else squirreled away for when Kaemon eventually died, but the Scarecrow had anticipated his hurried exit strategy and replaced the contents of the suitcase.

Mason caught movement from the corner of his eye, near the dresser. More from the opposite side of the room, within the shadows of the closet.

Yamaguchi would have grabbed the suitcase from its secret hiding spot, thrown it onto the bed, and opened it just long enough to confirm that everything was in order, only instead he'd found a short sword protruding from a mass of writhing—

Motion at the foot of the bed, mere feet away. A short, reddish brown snake slithered out from beneath the dust ruffle, the venom glands of its triangular head bulging.

"Screw this," the officer said. "I'm out of here."

"Mason," Layne said, her voice coming from both behind him and inside his helmet, with a slight delay. "Check this out."

He turned around and found her standing in the bathroom off the master suite, her light shining toward the back wall. She stepped aside as he approached and offered a better view of the shower stall. The glass door was closed tight, the marble walls smeared with brownish handprints. He was suddenly thankful for the gas mask and not just because of the snake crap spotting the tiles around him.

Yamaguchi's body lay on the floor inside the stall, legs folded underneath him, bare torso toppled to the side. He'd used his long-sleeved shirt to tie the handle to the inner towel rack. A short sword rested near his right hand, congealed in the crusted mess of blood and viscera that had spilled from the horizontal laceration across his lower abdomen. He'd been dead for so long that he'd become partially mummified, the sealed shower preserving his remains like an earthen tomb. His gray hair was dry and brittle, and his skin had shrunken to the bony framework, stretching the paired puncture wounds on his arms and chest. The edges of the fang marks were ragged and black with necrosis.

"He escaped the snakes by sealing himself inside, where they couldn't reach him," Mason said. "And then he waited as long as possible for someone to come to his rescue before committing hara-kiri to spare himself a slow, painful death when he realized that he was going to die."

"Why didn't he at least try to get out of there?" Layne asked.

Mason imagined himself doubled over in pain and trapped behind a single sheet of glass with deadly snakes repeatedly striking at him from the other side, facing the grim reality that his only hope of survival was to throw open the door, step out into their midst, and try to reach the front door before the venom overcame him.

"Would you have done so?" he asked.

Layne shrugged and shone her light onto a patch of skin that at first looked like a dark, oddly circular bruise on Yamaguchi's left pectoral region.

"What's that discoloration?" she asked.

Mason leaned closer to get a better view. Despite the combined ravages of desiccation and decomposition, he could still tell what it was, largely because he'd seen it before.

"It's a tattoo," he said.

The dragon had been designed in the East Asian style, with stubby legs, an almost serpentine body, and a head from which whisker-like scales flared. It faced the viewer, as though captured striking straight upward from a coiled position.

Layne nodded and glanced up at him, her eyes locking onto his. She recognized the significance.

The Scarecrow and her brother both had the exact same tattoo.

5

NEW YORK CITY

"The venom of the mamushi contains aggressive hemolytic and neu-rotoxic components," Todd Locker said. The crime-scene specialist wore his tiny glasses perched on the tip of his slender nose, his long dark hair bound in a ponytail, and spoke in an impossibly deep voice. A tattooed biomechanical design protruded from underneath the collar of his lab coat. The laptop on the desk in front of him projected an image of the viper onto the wall behind him. "Without immediate medical intervention, a single bite can prove fatal. And as you can see from the next slide"—he clicked the remote and a generic image of a man in the anatomical position appeared, his chest, neck, and face covered with hand-drawn Xs—"the victim was bitten sixty-three times."

Mason shifted in his seat and glanced at Layne, who sat across the table from him in the conference room on the twenty-third floor of the Jacob K. Javits Federal Building, home of the New York Field Office of the FBI. While they'd only seen a handful of snakes, animal control had collected thirteen of them from the dead doctor's apartment. Locker had already arranged to donate them to various zoos and launched a search of the surrounding neighborhoods for however many specimens had escaped.

The deputy director of the Rocky Mountain Regional Forensic Laboratory was one of the few people who knew the true nature of the threat posed by the Thirteen. Mason had fought to have Locker assigned to the FBI's Hazardous Evidence Response Team, or HERT, which had spent the last six months combing through the mountains of evidence left in the wake of the Times Square Massacre in an attempt to understand how the Scarecrow had manufactured four thousand gallons of the deadliest chemical weapon known to man and nearly dispersed it from subway trains beneath the busiest city in the country without anyone having the slightest idea what she was doing. It was only logical that he take charge of the forensic investigation into Yamaguchi's death.

Locker clicked the button again and a picture of the sword Yamaguchi had used to end what must have been incredible pain filled the screen.

"The *wakizashi* is a traditional weapon used to perform a ritualistic form of suicide-by-disembowelment known as seppuku," he said. "It was originally practiced by samurai to avoid being captured by their enemies and was later adopted by individuals looking to restore honor to themselves and their families. Behavioral believes that the mercy shown by the presentation of the weapon reflects an internal conflict within the Scarecrow. Yamaguchi might have failed to save her brother, but he'd been their personal physician for nearly half their lives. He was likely the closest thing to family they had. While she believed he needed to suffer, he also deserved to die with honor."

Locker switched to a detailed image of Yamaguchi's bare thorax, from his pelvis to his chin.

"The incision across his lower abdomen is approximately five inches deep, as you can tell by the scoring on the inside of his hip bone. He nicked his abdominal aorta, which caused him to bleed out in under two minutes. Considering the advanced levels of organic decomposition, a virtual autopsy will be performed by CT scan, with the ME on hand should further physical evaluation be required."

"Can we be certain that Yamaguchi didn't have any help?" Special Agent Diana Algren asked. She wore a skintight skirt suit and a cream blouse that did little to hide her black bra. Her chestnut hair was longer in the front than in the back and framed a face that seemingly aged before their eyes.

"Based on the trajectory of the abdominal laceration and the fact that his were the only prints on the hilt of the blade—or anywhere else in the apartment—I'm leaning toward that conclusion."

Algren nodded and returned her attention to the slide. The former head of the Dodge-Hill Strike Force had been assigned to the HERT in a supervisory role to maintain investigational continuity. While her actions during the hunt for the Scarecrow hadn't been treasonous on their face, she'd allowed her ambition to get the better of her and cut a deal with Rand Marchment to advance her career, one that allowed the deputy secretary of the Department of Homeland Security to manipulate the strike force, control its personnel, and protect Slate Langbroek. He was still in a coma at New York–Presbyterian, but his condition had been upgraded to stable. The moment he woke up, assuming he ever did, there would be a line of people waiting to talk to him, with Mason right at the front.

Locker clicked the remote and a photograph of the makeshift nurses' station in the smaller of the two bedrooms appeared.

"The monitor on the left received the video feeds from the four cameras we found pointed at Kaemon Nakamura's bed in the basement apartment on Forty-ninth Street," he said. "The setup in the middle was devoted exclusively to monitoring and documenting his deteriorating physical condition."

"Were you able to pull anything off the third computer?" Chris asked. He sat at the head of the table, his unreadable expression never wavering. While he might have been the oldest among them, he was easily the most intimidating. He had the physique of a man half his age and radiated a palpable aura of command. "There has to be something good on there for Yamaguchi to have taken the time to destroy it before he grabbed his suitcase and ran for his life."

"Not as of yet. We had it couriered to the regional forensics laboratory in Trenton. If they can't salvage the data, no one can." Locker tapped the remote and brought up an image of the passport with the doctor's face and the fake name under which he'd been living. "The Nguyen alias appears to be a dead end and we can't find any trace of Yamaguchi over the last quarter of a century. Like the Scarecrow and her brother, he seems to have dropped off the face of the planet sometime in early '96."

Locker switched to the next image and enlarged a picture of the three dragon tattoos side by side. The only apparent distinction between them was the color and condition of the surrounding skin.

"Which brings us to the tattoo," he continued. "Our computer specialists scanned all three examples into the system and generated a comparison of relative size, dimension, age, and ink density, in addition to more than two hundred points of reference within the artwork. They found a ninety-seven percent match between the three, well within the margin of error when taking into account the abilities of the individual tattooists, which implies they were created from the same template, presumably at some common location."

"What about its theoretical meaning?" Mason asked.

"Ryūjin, the dragon god, is the tutelary deity of the sea in Japanese mythology. There are hundreds of Buddhist and Shinto shrines devoted to him, all of which feature different artistic representations. Dragons are mentioned frequently in *Kojiki*, the oldest book in the Japanese language, the same tome from which the Scarecrow borrowed her identity. There are as many different incarnations of dragons as there are myths, most of which involve someone turning into one in order to kill someone else, which is probably the reason the motif is so prevalent in the tattoos of the yakuza, so we can't afford to prematurely rule out a connection to organized crime."

The back door of the conference room burst inward and Derek Archer, the secretary of the Department of Homeland Security, entered without knocking. He struck an imposing presence with his square jaw, thick neck, and shoulders that tested the limits of his suit jacket.

"Pardon the interruption," he said.

"I was just about to wrap things up," Locker said.

"Then you won't mind if I steal Special Agents Christensen, Layne, and Mason."

Adrenaline surged through Mason's veins. He knew exactly what that meant.

They followed Archer down the corridor and into a small conference room. The recessed lighting cast pyramidal shadows on walls paneled with acoustic-damping material and illuminated the seal of the Bureau at the front of the room. There was a signal jammer in the center of the gray laminate table. The black box was spiked with a dozen antennas that disrupted both the transmission and reception of a wide range of radio and cellular waves, disabled the GPS beacons on their phones, and prevented digital recording devices from working.

"Sit," Archer said, assuming the head of the table. He'd risen through the ranks of first ICE and then the DHS before assuming command of the busiest and most violent sector on the southern border. The president had appointed him to his cabinet not for his politics, but because there was no one on the planet more qualified to lead the defense of the homeland. He took the fact that his organization had been compromised on his watch as a personal affront and made sure that until he knew whom he could trust, no information even peripherally related to this investigation went beyond this circle.

He removed a briefcase from underneath the table, pressed his index finger to the biometric scanner to unlock it, and opened it on the tabletop. The black foam insert held a computer tablet. He removed it, plugged a flash drive into the USB port, and propped it in the case so they could all see.

"The guy who runs the DEA shop in Mexico City is an old friend of mine and someone I trust completely," he said. "This footage was recorded by his special response team less than an hour ago."

A crackle of static rippled across the screen, followed by a blinding blue glow. The camera struggled to rationalize the glare, which finally came into focus as an acetylene torch surrounded by a corona of sparks. An agent wearing camouflaged tactical gear and a welder's helmet carved a molten line through the sealed glass door of Langbroek's survival pod. He stood, raised the shield from his sweaty face, and ducked out of the way. A second agent stepped into view, a semiautomatic rifle clutched in one hand and the handle of the door in the other. A third agent took up position at the threshold. They entered silently and fanned out, leaving the cameraman to record from the entryway.

It looked like a tornado had torn through the cabin. Paintings had fallen from the walls, cabinets had disgorged their contents, and everything that wasn't physically bolted down was either smashed or scattered across the floor.

"We believe the state of the cabin resulted from the explosion on the skydeck," Archer said.

The camera panned across the bedroom once more, lingering on the open door of the bathroom, before lowering to the mess on the floor. It passed over clothing and blankets and a jumble of shoes and settled upon what almost looked like a burned log from a campfire. It was charcoal black and coarse, with the scaled texture of an alligator's back. It disappeared beneath a scorched comforter before reappearing again several feet away—

"Christ," Layne whispered.

The crescents of the ribs showed through the cooked torso. A neck shrunken to the cervical spine protruded from prominent clavicles. The skull was black and skeletal, its jaws frozen in the scream that had died on the dead man's lips.

"He immolated himself?" Layne said.

"The cabin's equipped with a fire-suppression system," Archer said. "Any flame larger than that of a candle would have triggered the release of the foam retardant."

"Then there has to be someone else inside there with him," Mason said.

"Keep watching," Archer said.

The DEA agents cleared the cabin and the adjoining bathroom in a matter of seconds and converged at the foot of the bed, where they commenced sorting through the mess. Kicking aside mounds of blankets and clothing in an effort to force anyone hiding underneath them to reveal himself. By the time they'd removed the clutter from on top of the victim, it was obvious there was no one else in there with him.

"How'd the killer get past them?" Layne asked.

"You watched the same footage we did," Archer said. "No one got past them."

"Someone must have figured out how to seal the pod from the outside."

"The manufacturer swears the only way to engage the security features is from inside that room."

The cameraman zoomed in on the dead man, who appeared to be stuck to the tile by a crust of his own blackened flesh, right in the center of a pattern of smoke discoloration. His body was contorted in a way that left no doubt as to the agony he'd endured.

"So how did he die?" Layne asked. "Spontaneous combustion?"

Mason didn't care how the victim had died. At least not right now. All that mattered at that moment was confirming his identity.

"Are we sure it's Slate Langbroek?" he asked.

"We're still awaiting formal DNA analysis," Archer said, "but the teeth are a superficial match to his dental records."

Mason felt numb. He'd desperately hoped to bring in Langbroek alive and extract every ounce of knowledge he possessed about the Thirteen, but there was a part of him that was content in the knowledge that Langbroek was dead. And that he had suffered.

The video ended and Archer removed the flash drive.

"We theorize he was attacked through the glass by a directed-energy weapon," Archer said. He made eye contact with each of them in turn to convey the gravity of his statement.

"When do we leave?" Mason asked.

"There's a plane waiting for you at LaGuardia, but you're not going to Mexico."

"Then where the hell are we going?" Layne asked.

"Texas," Archer said, sliding a flash drive across the table.

6

A twin-engine turboprop King Air C90 had been waiting when they arrived and in the air within fifteen minutes. Mason had expected to board either a military transport or an overcrowded commercial flight, not a tiny privately chartered plane with a pilot who'd mumbled a rushed introduction and drawn the curtain to seal off the cockpit. Archer obviously wasn't taking any chances. He didn't want anyone at either the DHS or the FBI, which had been compromised at multiple levels, to know where they were going, at least not until it was too late to do anything about it.

Mason occasionally heard the pilot's voice, although not well enough to make out his words over the roar of the propellers. In fact, he and Layne could barely hear each other and they were sitting scant feet apart in brown leather seats to either side of the aisle, his laptop open on the foldout table in front of them.

"We're off the reservation on this one, aren't we?" Layne said.

"I guess that remains to be seen," he said. "Let's just try not to find ourselves in a position where we have to find out."

He plugged the flash drive Archer had given them into the USB port and appraised the contents on the monitor. There was a single file folder, inside of which was a collection of photographs and a handful of documents with names that offered no hint as to their contents.

"Start with the pictures," Layne said.

Mason opened the first of twenty-six pictures and found himself looking at a house that had been burned nearly to the ground. The roof had collapsed upon the main level, leaving charcoaled joists standing from the rubble. Dust and ash still seeped from the broken windows of the few intact walls, fueling the haze that clung to the surrounding shrubland. The puddles on the rutted dirt driveway and the hardpan that passed for a yard suggested the fire department had made a valiant, if futile, effort.

The next few pictures showed the house from various angles, including the rear elevation, where the deck had fallen from the sliding glass door that opened off of what appeared to be the living room. The wood around it was black and burned nearly all the way through where the flames had climbed the siding to reach the eaves. They could barely make out the shapes of the criminalists in their white jumpsuits picking their way through the interior.

"What are we looking at here?" Layne asked.

Mason could only shake his head in response.

The next dozen or so images featured partial footprints marked with numbered placards on the soot and exposed dirt, a field that had burned for as far as the eye could see, detailed images of a handful of creosotes and paloverde trees that had managed to hang on to a few withered leaves, and remains that appeared to belong to a dog. Or at least that's what they kind of looked like from the right angle. The fire had burned so hot and fast that the animal's hindquarters and tail had been rendered unrecognizable chunks of bone and ash.

"When were these taken?" Layne asked.

Mason hovered the cursor over the file name and revealed the date embedded in the title.

"December seventeenth of last year."

"Does the date mean anything to you?"

"Not yet."

The remainder of the photographs had been taken inside what was left of the structure, where furniture had burned to the wooden framework and springs, appliances had been smashed by timber beams, the paint on the bathtub had blistered, the foot of a bed protruded from beneath a section of the tiled roof, a rifle lay partially buried at the base of a scorched wall, and a body that hardly looked human anymore rested on the floor, its condition seemingly identical to that of the corpse on the yacht.

"He does bear a striking resemblance to Slate Langbroek," Layne said.

"I believe that's the whole point," Mason said. He backed out of the photos and opened the first document, which turned out to be the incident report filed by the Rio Grande City Fire Department. He scanned through it and summarized the details for Layne. "A fire truck responded to reports of smoke just before dawn, but by the time it arrived there wasn't anything the firefighters could do for the house. They found the dog—a German shepherd—after corralling the wildfire. Shortly thereafter, they discovered the body inside the house and called in the criminal investigations unit and the arson squad out of McAllen, who determined there were no traces of chemical accelerants or shrapnel to suggest the use of an explosive device."

"So if they ruled out arson, what do they think caused the fire?"

"There are two distinct flashpoints. The first fire started inside the house, either in the bedroom or in the hallway immediately outside of it, presumably as a result of faulty wiring or outright negligence. The second started near where they found the dog, which they speculate was actively burning when it escaped the house and ignited the bushes where it fell."

"That poor thing," Layne whispered, turning to face the window where a seamless mat of lumpy clouds stretched out below the wing.

"You're fine with the dead guy, but not the dog?"

"It's different," she said, but she didn't elaborate. She didn't have to.

Mason closed the file and opened the next one in the series. He immediately recognized the crime-scene response team's administrative worksheet, followed by the narrative description, a series of sketches, and the evidence recovery log.

"Forensics was able to isolate a handful of partial footprints belonging to two distinct individuals from those of the firefighters, although the lack of recent rainfall made it impossible to determine their age. They found two .243 Winchester brass casings inside the house—one in the living room and the other in the hallway—and a Browning rifle near the victim. While they were able to confirm that the rounds were the same caliber as the rifle, there's no way to determine when or where they were fired, let alone if it was the victim who pulled the trigger."

"Gunshot wounds?"

"No skeletal trauma whatsoever," Mason said. "The ME stated that based on the physical presentation of the remains, he believes the fire was the cause of death."

"The dead guy didn't asphyxiate first?"

"No, he was still alive when he started to burn."

Mason studied Layne's expressionless face in the reflection on the circular window, beyond which the blue sky abruptly vanished as they entered the clouds. She felt the weight of his stare and turned to face him.

"People die in fires all the time," she said. "Just because the victim's physical condition resembles that of Slate Langbroek doesn't mean the two are in any way related. There's obviously something wrong with this scene, though. I mean, a guy doesn't go shooting up his house for no reason, at least not unless he's drunk, which I guess could explain how he started the fire in the first place, but if the fire inspector ruled out arson, there's nothing criminal to investigate. And even if there were, it's a problem for the locals, so what does this have to do with us?"

Mason minimized the forensics report and opened the third file—a photocopy of the dead man's picture and the biographical data from his personnel file—and suddenly he understood exactly what it had to do with them.

"His name was Ryan Austin and he was the agent in charge of the Rio Grande City Border Patrol Station."

Layne chewed on her lower lip and drew her left foot up onto her seat.

"That opens up a whole new can of worms, doesn't it?" she said.

"Especially when you consider he's responsible for the smuggling lines across the border from Tamaulipas, which is under the control of the Jalisco New Generation Cartel."

"You think they had him killed?"

"Attempting to make his death look like an accident isn't El Mencho's style. His men would have decapitated Austin and left his head in the center of town to send a message to his replacement."

"The cartel definitely would have benefitted from his death, though."

"Without a doubt, but murdering a federal agent on American soil would be treated as an outright declaration of war." Mason closed the personnel file and opened the final folder. Inside were copies of letters on official CBP letterhead, all of them signed by Ryan Austin and addressed to various senior-level officials within the DHS, including Deputy Secretary Rand Marchment. While Marchment was nowhere near the top of the power structure of the Thirteen, he'd obviously been high enough on the ladder to recognize the threat that Austin posed to their operations, which included smuggling illegal immigrants infected with the Hoyl's lethal flu virus across the border. "When it comes to operations, CJNG is like any other billion-dollar corporation. It's not going to risk bringing down the wrath of the United States military when it already has established pipelines the border patrol can't . . . plug . . ."

His words trailed off as he skimmed the letters, which detailed reports of inexplicable crop damage and deceased livestock.

"What?" Layne asked.

Mason glanced out his window as the plane started its descent. A vast expanse of brown land stretched away from them to the south, toward where the Rio Grande river snaked across the horizon, its banks fringed with green.

"I hope you brought your passport."

7

STARR COUNTY, TEXAS

The plane landed at Starr County Airport, which was little more than a single runway with a hangar and a couple of outbuildings, but at least the Wi-Fi was strong enough to alert Mason that Gunnar had left a message on his phone while he was in the air. He found a rental Ford Explorer waiting for him, programmed Austin's address into the in-dash GPS, and headed north, away from Rio Grande City and into the brushland.

He wanted to see Austin's house for himself. He'd become something of a self-educated expert on arson during the year he'd spent hunting the Hoyl, or at least the incarnation known as F4. The monster had been the fourth generation in a lineage of men who'd all taken up the mantle, devoted their lives to creating deadly pandemics, and used fire to incinerate the evidence of their crimes. While he might have been dead, his father—F3—was still among the living and undoubtedly as eager to meet Mason as he was to meet him. If he was going to poke a stick into a burrow that could very well have been dug by the Thirteen, he needed to be prepared for anything that might slither out.

Mason tossed the stealth phone he used to communicate outside of formal federal channels to Layne and asked her to call Gunnar on speaker. His old friend answered on the first ring.

"Is it Langbroek?" Gunnar asked. Alejandra had obviously informed him about the remains they'd found inside the survival pod. "Are you sure he's dead?"

"The teeth matched," Layne said.

"Dental records can be switched or counterfeited in any number of ways."

"We're waiting on DNA confirmation."

"Which can be easily manipulated—"

"It's him," Mason said. "His body was set on fire inside a sealed room that couldn't be accessed from the outside."

Gunnar fell silent. Snarls of creosotes and sage blurred past through the dusty windows.

"You said, 'His body *was set* on fire,' not 'He set himself on fire,'" he finally said. "That's a semantic distinction of no small consequence."

"They didn't find any traces of chemical accelerants inside the cabin and flames large enough to immolate him would have set off the sprinklers."

"You think he was killed by a directed-energy weapon?"

"Man, did you ever make that leap in a hurry," Layne said.

"It's the future of warfare," Gunnar said. "The Chinese already have DEWs in production with enough power and accuracy to carve an armored vehicle like a Thanksgiving turkey at half a mile."

"Tell me you haven't been holding out on me," Mason said.

"Of course not. I just have my finger on the pulse of the defense industry. While this technology was undoubtedly designed to be used against us, that doesn't mean investors in this country aren't lining up to make themselves rich in the interim." Gunnar paused. "And you're one to talk, Mace. You should have told me the moment you learned Langbroek was dead."

"You're going to have to forgive me. Things are moving kind of quickly here."

"I should say so. What on earth are you doing in Texas?"

Mason chuckled. His old friend was just about the only person in the world who could simultaneously triangulate the GPS beacon in his phone and carry on a conversation without missing a beat.

"I'm still in the process of figuring that out," he said. "We've got a border patrol agent whose death seven months ago might be related to Langbroek's."

A rapid-fire clamor of keystrokes buzzed from the cell phone.

"I assume you're referring to Ryan Austin, Patrol Agent in Charge of the Rio Grande City Station. From everything I see here, it looks like he suffered an unfortunate accident."

"And maybe that's the case, but my gut is telling me otherwise," Mason said. The computerized voice from the dashboard announced their destination was five miles away. "What can you tell me about him?"

"He was born in Starr County in 1981. Eldest of two, high school football player, upper middle of his graduating class. Joined ICE on his eighteenth birthday, worked as a field agent while he earned a degree in criminal justice, and transferred to the DHS at its inception. He's been in charge of the Rio Grande City Station for five years and looks like he's being groomed for bigger and better things."

"That's all on the Internet?" Layne said.

"Everything's on the Net if you know where to look."

"What about this area of the border?" Mason asked.

"The Rio Grande City Station is second only to Ajo Station in Arizona in terms of quantity of drugs seized, at nearly a million pounds annually, although that number has dropped consistently since 2011 as the trafficking focus has shifted from cocaine and marijuana to meth and fentanyl, both of which are worth considerably more by weight and are easier to smuggle by volume. With an average seizure of twenty-eight pounds, you have to figure most of it is crossing the border in backpacks or in the trunks of cars passing through the points of entry."

"The cartels can't be losing much sleep over the prospect of the border patrol ruining their business."

"Certainly not enough to kill a federal officer and go to the trouble of making his death look like an accident. Besides, we're talking about the kinds of animals who cut up their competition with chain saws and hang the leftovers from highway overpasses with signs nailed to their chests so the media can deliver their message to the entire country. I wouldn't say the word *subtle* is in their vernacular."

"That's my impression, too."

"So you're thinking something else might be crossing the border and Austin caught on to it?"

"We've seen it before," Mason said. It was through the open desert on the Tohono O'odham Reservation—near Ajo Station—that the Hoyl had trafficked the immigrants he'd infected with his deadly flu virus. "Why fix it if it isn't broken?"

"We're only beginning to look into it," Layne said, "but Austin was concerned enough to go all the way up the chain when his sector chief and the commissioner of the CBP didn't handle things to his satisfaction."

"How high up the chain?" Gunnar asked.

"We have copies of letters written directly to his superiors, including the deputy secretary of the Department of Homeland Security. All of them dated within the last year."

"He popped up on Marchment's radar."

"And now he's dead," Mason said.

The computerized voice announced Austin's ranch was coming up on the right. A narrow dirt road appeared from the trees so suddenly that Mason nearly missed it. The tires grumbled over a cattle guard and rocked on the rutted trail as they passed through an open gate that had been dragged back into the paloverdes. Like the rest of the fence, it was eight vertical feet of chain link crowned with coils of concertina wire. The padlock that had once held it in place protruded from the dirt beside a metal post with three optical sensors nearly concealed by a sage bush.

"What were his complaints?" Gunnar asked.

"Dead livestock and damaged crops on both sides of the border," Layne said.

"What does that have to do with national security?"

"We'll look into that on our end," Mason said. "I need you to work some magic on yours."

"You want me to see if there's any point of intersection between Austin and Langbroek."

"Exactly, although I'm inclined to think that if there is one, it's circumstantial at best. I'd be surprised if their paths ever crossed, but they both definitely crossed the same person. It can't be coincidence that Anomaly led us to Langbroek and now we're looking at a second murder theoretically committed by the same killer."

"You're working under the assumption that the Thirteen are responsible for both?"

A thick layer of grit had accumulated on the windshield, through which the rotting black carcass of the house materialized.

"Yeah, and if I'm right, once they figure out that we're here, things are going to get dicey in a hurry." The trench of shrubbery abruptly gave way to an amoeboid expanse of windswept earth. The Explorer coasted right up to the hole where the front door had once been and idled for several seconds before Mason killed the engine. "And see if you can figure out what Dr. Yamaguchi was doing between 1996 and the time he appeared in Brooklyn under the Nguyen alias."

"Do you think that's somehow related to what's going on here?"

"If there's one thing I've learned, Gunnar, it's that everything's related."

Mason nodded to Layne, who ended the call. They waited for the rooster tail of dust trailing in their wake to overtake the car and settle around them before opening their doors.

8

The wind rippled through the shrubland with a sound that reminded Mason of placing a seashell to his ear. An old windmill turned in the distance, barely visible through the paloverdes, every minute shift in direction causing the tail to swivel with a metallic screech. Cows lowed from somewhere far away and a lone hawk rode the thermals high against the cloudless sky. It was a location seemingly isolated from modern man, one that smelled faintly of dust, manure, and vegetation in bloom, a perfect time capsule stolen from the days of pioneers and prospectors, sheriffs and outlaws, or at least it would have been, were it not for the burned house that would likely rot in this dead swatch of dirt until long after the trees had claimed the fences and rust stilled the windmill's vanes.

Nature had erased whatever footprints might have lingered, as though purging this place of the taint of man. The charcoaled wood had the unmistakable scent of a doused campfire, yet the concrete foundation and the few walls left standing looked solid enough. There was no crime-scene tape fluttering on the breeze or cut flowers left to die on the porch in memorial. It was as though the whole place were as dead as its owner.

Mason and Layne circled the house in silence, studying the exterior and the surrounding countryside. The photographs from the forensics report had done an excellent job of capturing the physical condition of the site, if not its isolation or the magnitude of the empty brush country. Clumps of grass had begun to grow from the black earth. Saplings reached for the sun from the sparse gaps between the scorched branches of their forebears. Sporadic clusters of green leaves grew from shrubs that appeared otherwise dead. It wouldn't be long before this entire area grew dense and lush again.

"Did you notice the infrared motion detectors along the sides of the house?" Layne asked.

"There were some just inside the gate on the way in, too." Mason stared at the rubble that had once formed the rear deck and, five feet above it, the sliding glass door off the living room. "Austin doesn't seem like the kind of guy who'd leave his back door open for any length of time, does he?"

He turned in the opposite direction and struck off through a maze of dead shrubs reminiscent of sea urchins. The soot came away on the tread of his boots, leaving behind patterns of rich, dark soil. It didn't take long to find where the dog had died, its shape partially preserved among jagged bits of bone in the lone swatch of earth spared from the blaze.

"Which direction were the footprints heading again?" Mason asked.

"Roughly east and west."

"So from the house toward this spot, and from this spot back toward the house."

Assuming the tracks belonged to Austin, why would he walk out here only to turn back around again? Had he seen something from inside the house he wanted to investigate? Had he heard something out here, crashing through the brush, and decided to check it out or . . . ?

Mason looked from the soil where the dog had died back toward the house, which would have been concealed from view by the bushes, had they still been flush with leaves. Austin's dog would have heard something out here long before he did. The moment he opened the door, his German shepherd would have barreled straight toward it, barking the entire way.

"The dog died first," Mason said, striking off toward the house.

After a moment's hesitation, Layne fell into stride behind him.

"What makes you think that?" she asked.

"A rifle is practically useless at close range, even in the hands of a trained marksman. If Austin suspected there was something out here, he would have stayed on the deck, where he had an elevated view of the acreage and the benefit of his scope's magnification. He might even have had night vision. He wouldn't have risked giving up his advantage and heading out into this forest unless—"

"Something happened to his dog," Layne finished for him.

Mason nodded and looked up at the open back door.

"But the fire inspector's report said the dog was the source . . ." Layne started to say, before falling silent while she worked through her thoughts. "Whoever was out here set the dog on fire?"

"And Austin came running when he heard his dog cry out and saw the smoke rising from the same place."

"How do you set a German shepherd charging at you at twenty miles an hour on fire before it can attack you?"

"The same way you set a man on fire inside a sealed survival chamber."

Mason picked his way through the broken planks, brushed off the ledge, and boosted himself up through the open door. He turned around and stared off into the distance toward the small clearing where they'd found the dog's remains. Even with the bushes skeletal and black, he could barely see it, but it was definitely well within the range of a rifle. Austin could have easily fended off just about any attack from the deck. No one would have been able to approach his house without forcing his way through the branches of shrubs that would have given away his location, which meant that the only way to mount a successful attack was to draw Austin out.

"The dog was a distraction," Mason said. "By the time Austin realized it, his killer had already gotten past him."

He turned his back on the yard and surveyed the living room. It was impossible to imagine how it had once been. There was little left of the furniture, most of it buried underneath sections of the fallen roof, from beneath which emanated the scent of mildew, where water-breeding insect larvae stagnated beneath the rotting wood. The crime-scene response team had found the first casing right about where he was standing now. If Austin had indeed fired his rifle from this spot on the night he died, he'd chosen a terrible angle from which to defend his back door.

Layne entered the house through the gap where the front door had once been, directly ahead of him and on the other side of a partially burned interior wall. From where he stood, he could almost envision lining up a shot at her around the corner of the wall, one that likely would have caused her to duck to her left and into the kitchen.

"His killer was already in the house," Mason said.

"Why risk going inside at all when he could have easily done to Austin what he did to the dog?"

"Because there was something in here that he wanted."

"It would have been even easier to take once Austin was dead."

Suddenly, everything fell into place for Mason.

"He needed something that was inside the house, something investigators would have noticed was missing if they weren't otherwise overwhelmed by finding one of their colleagues lying dead on the floor. And he needed to make the whole thing look like an accident so that no one had any reason to search for something that wasn't here."

He veered away from Layne and toward the hallway where the second casing had been found. The pass-through kitchen to his left would have connected to the foyer, had the ceiling not collapsed. There was a bathroom to his right, and straight ahead, a shattered window at the end of the hallway, beside which was the master bedroom. Austin's first shot had driven his intruder from inside the front door, through the kitchen, and into the hallway, where he'd managed to get off one more round before being consumed by the same weapon that had been used on his dog.

Mason recognized the spot where Austin's body had been discovered. The medical examiner had been forced to take the entire section of flooring as the victim had been practically melted to it. His rifle had been resting against the base of the wall to the right, impractical at such close range.

"The killer had to know there'd be an investigation, regardless of whether or not it appeared accidental," Layne said from behind him. "Austin was the head of a border patrol station. There have to be established protocols in place for every contingency. Besides, he would have kept anything of a potentially incriminating nature at work."

"Unless he couldn't work on it at the station because his superiors didn't believe him, because they thought he was wasting their time and resources investigating something that had no bearing on his job, something with which he ultimately became so obsessed that he took it up on his own time and worked on it while he was at home."

Mason turned around, squeezed past Layne, and hurried out the front door. His thoughts were firing at a million miles an hour and he needed to act quickly before he lost his momentum.

He opened the car door, grabbed his laptop, and awakened it right there on the driver's seat. Found the file with the forensics report. Scanned through the contents until he found the evidence recovery log. He was looking for two things specifically. The first item was halfway down the list: a Browning BAR ShortTrac rifle, with an X-Sight II HD optical scope. The second, as he'd expected, wasn't there.

Layne emerged from the front door just in time for him to blow past her on his way back into the house. She said something from behind him, but he couldn't focus on her words. He weaved through the rubble in the living room, skirted the hole in the hallway, and entered the lone bedroom.

The warped springs of the mattress protruded at odd angles from the frame, which had broken and flattened to the floor under the weight of the roof. A wall-mounted TV had become a melted snarl of plastic and glass on the floor. All that remained in the closet was a collection of wire hangers standing from the ashes. The bureau and dresser had burned to such an extent that they were hardly recognizable, while the desk in the corner had been incinerated to the metal framework of the drawers, legs, and the rim of the writing surface. A warped power strip rested underneath it.

"The killer collected his personal computer," Mason said.

"You can't be certain he had one," Layne said.

"True, but tell me you know anyone in his age group who doesn't."

"You're grasping."

"Something that required a surge protector and more than two outlets was plugged into that power strip."

"Say you're right," Layne said. "What does that prove?"

"That he was onto something about the dead animals and crops. And the Thirteen had him killed to cover it up."

9

The drive from Austin's homestead to McAllen, Texas, took just under forty minutes. Layne used the time to comb through the online editions of just about every newspaper in South Texas, but couldn't find any articles related to lost livestock or unusual crop damage. There were plenty of stories about violence on both sides of the border, the ingenious ways the cartels circumvented the border patrol's best defensive measures, and the kinds of human-interest stories that served as the backbone of life the world over. That didn't mean the information wasn't out there, only that they were going to have to work a whole lot harder to track it down. It was possible that entire herds and fields of crops died with such regularity that such events weren't newsworthy or maybe even that the editors had quashed the stories. Regardless, they'd reached a point where they were going to have to risk revealing themselves if they were going to get the answers they needed, and there was only one place to start.

The McAllen Public Safety Building was right in the center of a greenbelt at the heart of town. The two-story structure more closely resembled a shopping mall than the combined home of the police department, municipal court, and city jail. Not to mention the Forensic Evidence Acquisition and Recovery Unit, which had been tasked with going through what was left of Austin's house and collecting the items listed on the recovery log.

Mason waited until they pulled into the parking lot before calling ahead to arrange a meeting with whoever was in charge. If anyone on the inside was involved in a potential cover-up, he didn't want to give them enough time to destroy the evidence.

A man wearing khakis, a yellow collared shirt, and a lanyard with his ID badge approached them the moment they entered the lobby, his hand extended.

"Edmund McWhinney," he said, giving each of their hands a firm shake. He appeared to be in his sixties, with a fringe of gray hair combed over his bald pate and jowls that jiggled when he spoke. "Director of the Crime Scene Investigation Unit. I'm pleased to be able to help you in any way that I possibly can. It's not often we're called upon to assist the FBI in an investigation."

The older man turned without another word and strode across the tiled lobby toward twin steel doors. He tapped his badge against the sensor on the wall and the electromagnetic lock disengaged with a thud that echoed ahead of them down the sterile corridor.

"We didn't expect to be greeted by such a high-ranking official," Layne said.

The director glanced over his shoulder and offered a coy smile.

"Don't let the title fool you, Special Agent. A town the size of McAllen is subject to even more aggressive budgetary constraints than our big-city counterparts, which means that everyone wears multiple hats, including the director, especially when all of his employees decide to take a long holiday weekend. While my days in the field might be largely behind me, I run this crime lab and most every piece of equipment in it."

"So you're familiar with the Austin case."

McWhinney's stride faltered. Mason caught a cloud settle over the man's expression in his reflection on the tinted window of the office to their left. He appeared to have aged a decade by the time they reached the end of the corridor and he once more turned to face them.

"Ryan Austin was well liked around here. You don't get too many law-enforcement officers of any stripe that are willing to take the time to learn what we do and the importance of our work."

"How so?" Mason asked.

The director's expression softened and the ghost of a smile played upon his lips.

"He showed up with a sack of sandwiches one day while he was still a rank-and-file patrol agent and asked me to explain how the gas chromatograph–mass spectrometer worked and how we used it in the examination of trace evidence. Another day he brought coffee and we taught him how to compare foot- and fingerprints to subjects that aren't already in the system. He once took a full week off and volunteered in our ballistics program. That's the kind of guy he was. He had a curious mind and a generous soul. None of us had any doubt he'd go on to achieve great things."

McWhinney buzzed them through the last entrance on the right and into a small anteroom with a mirrored reception window and a single door. His slender fingers typed a four-digit code into a numeric keypad mounted above the knob. He stepped back, held the door, and ushered them into a lab with so much equipment crammed into such a small workspace that it made Locker's mobile crime lab look spacious by comparison.

The organic instrumentation room contained equipment that analyzed everything from drug and blood-alcohol levels to trace and DNA evidence. The adjacent room resembled a high-school science lab, with cabinets mounted over plain black countertops with microscopes and Bunsen burners. At the end of the corridor was a workspace with a pair of detective stations, complete with lighted armatures and magnifying lenses. A desk piled high with resource tomes and file folders concealed the back wall. There were so many sticky notes on the frame of the monitor that it was a miracle anyone could see the screen at all.

McWhinney closed the door behind them and gestured for them to take whatever seats they could find, while he assumed the swiveling chair at the administrative desk, leaned back, and laced his fingers on his belly. He studied their faces with a combination of curiosity and suspicion.

"You want to know if I agree with the fire inspector's report," he finally said.

Mason shrugged and raised his eyebrows.

"Well . . . ?"

"Yes and no." The director of the crime lab sighed and seemed to deflate. "I find myself in a unique position with which I am exceedingly uncomfortable. I've devoted my life to the dispassionate analysis of physical evidence, which, during the course of my forty-plus years trying to keep up with the rapid advances in the field of forensic science, has never once lied. And yet I find myself wondering why a man I considered to be of higher intellect found himself mere feet from a window and unable to escape a fire in his own home."

"The medical examiner seems to think he started to burn before he was overcome by the smoke."

McWhinney shook his head as though to dispel the mental image.

"I have no reason to doubt him. He sees that kind of thing on a surprisingly regular basis."

"What about the rifle casings?" Layne asked.

"All I can say with any authority is that they were the same caliber as the weapon we found near the body."

"Did you confirm that the strike mark of the firing pin on the cartridge matched the weapon?"

"We had no reason to do so," McWhinney said. "There was no sign of a struggle and the victim had no skeletal or penetrating trauma. Besides, the nature of the fire makes it impossible to even speculate as to when the bullets were fired, if they were fired inside the house, or in which direction the shooter was facing."

"You didn't recover any slugs?"

"I assume you stopped by the house first." McWhinney leaned forward and studied his hands in his lap. He spoke without looking up at them. "There are aspects of this investigation I find troubling, but I can't be certain I don't feel that way because I need there to be a reason that a man I liked and respected died in such a terrible way."

"Did everything you collected from his home make it into the evidence recovery log?" Mason asked.

"Of course," McWhinney snapped. It took a moment for him to catch on to what Mason was really asking. "I can't speak to the time before my team arrived on the scene, but I can say with complete confidence that if it was there, they collected it."

"No sign of a personal computer?"

"Not that I'm aware of."

"How about a personal cell phone?"

"That's the kind of thing that would have definitely been logged."

"Doesn't that strike you as odd?"

"Not out in the country where he lived," McWhinney said. "He wouldn't have been able to get more than a single bar on the best of days."

"He had one for work, though," Layne said.

"Yes, but it was a satellite phone, not your standard cellular model. The kind his agents carry in the field. We recovered it from his nightstand."

"And checked the call log, I assume."

"Nothing either incoming or outgoing on the evening preceding the fire."

Mason leaned closer in an effort to see the director's face. He wanted to gauge the man's reaction to the questions he'd been building up to asking.

"What about the rifle?" he asked.

"The Browning? We have it in lockup."

"How about the scope?"

McWhinney furrowed his brow momentarily before looking up at Mason.

"It was severely damaged in the fire."

"But if I'm correct, that particular model has a recoil-activated video recording feature."

"If the operator manually engages it."

"Did you access the internal processor or attempt to ascertain if any footage was potentially being captured via Bluetooth?"

"Like I said, there was no indication of foul play. We had no reason to do so."

"What if we asked really nicely?" Layne said.

McWhinney finally caught up with the conversation. His expression metamorphosed from confusion to comprehension and he offered a firm nod.

"That'd be just about all the reason I'd need."

10

The digital riflescope was shorter and heavier than the standard glass optical scope Mason was accustomed to using and had a rubber eyepiece fitting that resembled that of a camcorder. While the outer casing had survived relatively unscathed, the buttons that controlled the internal functions had melted and allowed the fire to reach the Obsidian II Core processor, which looked like someone had poured acid on it. The microSD card had seen better days, but McWhinney seemed optimistic that he'd be able to access some amount of data, assuming the footage had been set to record in the first place.

Of course, it was possible the director of the forensics department would be able to pull off a miracle and all they'd have to show for it was a startled coyote about to take a bullet between the eyes. Then again, they could get lucky and find a recording of a man capable of setting fire to a German shepherd and its owner, a border patrol agent whom Mason believed had stumbled upon something that got him killed.

McWhinney had promised to call them the moment he retrieved viable imagery, although he'd been reluctant to commit to a timeframe, which left Mason and Layne with time to kill. Fortunately, there was a restaurant around the corner where they could grab some barbecue and peruse the messages that had come in while they'd been in the forensics lab. Mason waited in the car for Layne to return with a couple paper baskets of brisket and fries before opening the first message, which was from Archer and confirmed what they'd expected: The DNA from the victim inside the survival pod on the yacht matched the sample obtained from Slate Langbroek's home on Shelter Island.

"I'd been holding out hope that it wasn't him," Mason said.

"I would have liked to take another whack at him, too," Layne said, wiping a dribble of sauce from her chin. "We should probably just be happy that he's off the board, though."

"Maybe, but it's only a matter of time before someone else takes his place among the Thirteen."

"You know Gunnar's keeping a close eye on the line of succession within Royal Nautilus."

"He's wasting his time. The next threat will come from somewhere else entirely."

Layne stuffed the last of the meat into her mouth and appraised Mason from the corner of her eye while she chewed.

"I think you just wanted to be the one to put him in the ground," she finally said.

On some unconscious level, he knew she was right, but they could have really used the information Langbroek had taken with him to the grave.

The second message was from Locker, who'd attached the results of Yamaguchi's lab tests and virtual autopsy, which showed just about what they'd suspected. The toxicology screening had come back negative and there'd been no physical trauma beyond the snakebites and the laceration he'd inflicted upon himself. The only incidental findings were a marked reduction in white matter and enlarged lateral ventricles in his brain, although both were considered to be of unknown etiology and questionable significance. There were no updates from the digital forensics team in New Jersey, which was still attempting to access whatever data had been stored on the smashed computer from the doctor's monitoring station.

"Which amounts to a whole lot of nothing," Layne said. "These guys know how to cover their tracks."

"They've had plenty of practice."

"Then we're approaching this all wrong." She slurped sauce from her fingertips, rolled down the window, and tossed the empty basket into the trash barrel beside the car. "We need to go on the offensive. Put the pressure on these guys and force them to make a mistake."

"What do you propose?"

"Say we're right and Austin was killed to shut him up about the dead crops and animals. What does that tell us?"

"There's something about whatever afflicted them that someone doesn't want anyone to take a closer look at."

"Why?"

"Because it creates problems for whoever's responsible," Mason said, finishing off his sandwich.

"And how would we know who that is?"

"There's something readily identifiable about them."

"Exactly, so rather than working backward and trying to prove that Austin was murdered—"

"We should be trying to prove the theory that got him killed."

Mason wiped his hands on a napkin, balled it in the empty basket, and passed it to Layne, who tossed it into the barrel. He leaned back over the seat, grabbed his laptop, and opened the file containing the letters Austin had sent to his superiors. He tilted the screen for Layne, who scooted closer so she could read the text.

There were four letters in total, each written approximately one week apart and over the course of twenty days spanning the timeframe between November 26 and December 14, just three days prior to the fire that had taken his life. The composition was crisp and professional and concisely detailed the facts without any form of interpretation, so as not to lead the recipient to a predetermined epiphany, but rather to allow him to reach his own conclusion. The first two were addressed to Maurice Padilla, chief patrol agent of the Rio Grande Valley Sector and Austin's direct superior, the third and fourth to Keith Dandridge, commissioner of U.S. Customs and Border Protection, his boss's boss, and presumably the one whose declination to take action had led Austin to go over his head to Rand Marchment. In bureaucratic circles, this constituted the establishment of a paper trail, a form of documentation designed to force a formal written reply one way or the other when verbal communications had failed to achieve the desired effect.

Austin had detailed a total of six incidents: three in the first letter and one more in each of the subsequent versions. There was no hint of frustration or desperation, only the restatement of facts and the introduction of new material, and each time he'd simply requested that the recipients contact him at their earliest convenience. Perhaps had he been more forceful he'd still be alive. Then again, he'd signed his own death warrant the moment he recognized the implications of the first incident.

"What the hell is a javelina?" Layne asked.

"Some sort of wild boar, I think."

Whatever they were, seven of them had been found by an agent on horseback within a remote, well-circumscribed wooded area approximately twenty meters in diameter. There'd been no indication of poaching or predation, although with the physical ravages of both decomposition and scavenger activity, the agent likely wouldn't have been able to determine cause of death anyway. He'd merely noted it in his daily log and left the bodies for nature to run its course.

The second incident involved a field of sorghum that had withered and died within a forty-eight-hour time span. The farmer had filed a

report with the Starr County Sheriff's Department as part of a routine insurance claim, but he'd insisted the damage had looked like
sabotage, perhaps by a competing farm, although according to the
adjuster's findings, the concentrations of herbicides and pesticides in
both the soil and the plants were within normal tolerances.

Austin had written the first letter three days after the third incident and referred to specific phone conversations with his sector chief
on each of the previous two days. Five cows had been found dead
on an open-range ranch just west of Rio Grande City. They'd been
described by the veterinarian who responded to the rancher's call
as having "burnlike dermal lesions of unknown origin and localized
sections of missing or discolored fur" and being surrounded by "am-
ple evidence of gastrointestinal distress." The doctor had collected
blood and tissue samples before gathering the remains for immediate
cremation in an effort to prevent transmission of the unknown ailment
to the rest of the herd. Subsequent lab analysis had demonstrated a
dramatic decrease in white blood cells and platelets, which theoretically accounted for the resultant skin erosions and internal bleeding.

"That doesn't sound like the same kind of weapon used on Austin and Langbroek," Layne said.

"Maybe they were field-testing it and hadn't gotten it working
properly yet."

The remaining letters featured additional incidents that had all
occurred on the Mexican side of the border prior to the discovery of
the dead javelinas. There were reports of the loss of a field of corn, an
entire coop of dead chickens, and an abandoned building strewn with
cat and rat carcasses. While details of the respective incidents were
sparse, all of them had occurred in Ciudad Camargo, the Tamaulipan
municipality directly across the border from Rio Grande City.

"You mind?" Layne asked, gesturing to his computer.

Mason shook his head and allowed her to commandeer his laptop.
He closed his eyes and tried to wrap his head around the implications
of Austin's findings, especially as they pertained to national security.
If someone had perfected a directed-energy weapon, it would be of
unlimited value to Cártel de Jalisco Nueva Generación, which would
suddenly find itself in possession of a weapon the likes of which neither its rivals nor the U.S. military had, tipping the balance of power
inexorably in its favor. He could see how eliminating the man responsible for preventing the flow of money, drugs, and firearms across the

border would help open a temporary window of operational invulnerability, but what could that possibly have to do with Slate Langbroek and the Thirteen? Was it possible the two factions had formed some kind of unholy alliance? Had the Thirteen tapped into the cartel's existing infrastructure to smuggle something a lot deadlier than drugs across the border? And, if so, what was in it for the cartel?

To find the truth, they were going to have to bring in someone who knew both CJNG and the Thirteen intimately, and there was only one person who fit that mold. He opened his eyes and fired off a text to Alejandra. With any luck, she'd be able to provide the insight they needed.

"Check this out," Layne said.

Mason glanced at his laptop and found himself staring at a photograph on his computer screen. The man in the foreground had dark skin and wore coveralls and a dirty baseball cap that sat high on his head. His expressionless face was deeply lined by time and the elements. Behind him was a chicken coop the size of a mobile home, the dirt inside covered with so many feathers and avian carcasses that it almost looked like it had snowed.

"The caption's in Spanish," she said, "but I'm pretty sure it says something to the effect of 'hundreds of chickens die overnight.'"

Mason couldn't focus on her words. In his mind, he was back in Arizona, where the discovery of a dry riverbed littered with the bodies of dead carrion birds had led them to the Hoyl's plot to smuggle a mutated bird flu virus across the border through the open desert. If they were facing a similar threat here, only with the added element of a veritable army of bloodthirsty *sicarios* standing in their way, then they were about to find out how good they really were.

Mason watched the shrubland streak past on either side of the highway in his peripheral vision, the asphalt a black blur before him as the Explorer hurtled toward Rio Grande City at ninety miles an hour. The address of the closest of the three incidents on the Texas side of the border was programmed into the in-dash GPS. The land where Austin's patrol agent had found the cluster of dead javelinas fell under the auspices of the Texas Parks and Wildlife Department and served as something of a forested buffer between the city limits and the Rio Grande river, an overgrowth of deciduous trees that concealed the traffickers crossing the border, day and night.

The computerized voice guided them away from the highway and onto a gravel road that led south between fields of crops. A couple miles later it instructed them to turn left at the T-intersection and immediately announced their destination was on the right, where a dirt side road appeared from a dense thicket of paloverde, catclaw, and hackberry trees.

"I guess this must be our turn," he said.

Twin tire tracks wended away from the road and into the forest. The stripe of weeds between them raked the undercarriage. An aluminum gate had been dragged back into the shrubs; the chain that had once secured it lay broken on the ground. A rusted sign pocked with bullet holes read:

CAUTION

SMUGGLING AND/OR ILLEGAL IMMIGRATION ARE COMMON IN THIS AREA DUE TO THE PROXIMITY TO THE INTERNATIONAL BORDER.

PLEASE BE AWARE OF YOUR SURROUNDINGS AT ALL TIMES AND DO NOT TRAVEL ALONE IN REMOTE AREAS.

DIAL 911 TO REPORT SUSPICIOUS ACTIVITY.

"That's one way to keep out the tourists," Layne said.

Mason rolled down his window and watched the gaps between the trees for a spot to pull off. It had been a mounted agent who'd discovered the dead javelinas and this place was too far from town for him to have ridden his horse, which meant that the animal had to have been transported out here in a trailer, likely to the same spot every time. Any patrol pattern was essentially the repetition of a well-established routine, one designed to cover the most ground with the least effort and in the shortest amount of time. All they had to do was find where that pattern started and follow the beaten trail.

He found the pull-off near a bend in the road, which gradually disappeared into the weeds. The limbs of the adjacent trees were broken where new growth was constantly trimmed by the horse trailer. He rocked the Explorer over rounded stones exposed by years of erosion, parked in the shade, and killed the engine. The rumble of the distant Rio Grande announced itself over the ticking of the engine.

Layne gave him a put-out look, shoved open her door into the trees, and squeezed out through the gap. He waited until she'd scooted all the way around the side of the SUV before climbing out and stretching his arms over his head.

"So which way are we supposed to go?" she asked, opening the GPS map on her cell phone.

"That way," Mason said. He nodded toward a pile of horse dung that couldn't have been more than a few hours old, if the preponderance of flies was any indication. A dozen feet later he found a passage between the trees. "Right through here."

The trail opened into a meadow fringed with hackberry trees. The knee-high grass swished against their jeans as they headed southsoutheast toward an escarpment crowned with trees, from which they were afforded a decent view of the valley below them. The forest grew all the way to the edge of the river, its bank bristled with cattails, its surface dimpled by the rocks lurking just underneath. It couldn't have been more than four or five feet deep in the middle. The far side looked just like the near, and prevented them from seeing anything beyond the tightly knit vegetation all the way to the far rise.

Mason heard a faint thrumming sound in the distance that reminded him of an oil derrick.

A riot of hoofprints followed the topography to the east. To the right, a stone outcropping reached across the river and within fifteen feet of the opposite bank, where a path led into the forest. To the left, cedar elms and willows transitioned to mesquites and catclaws before giving way to shrubland.

"Somewhere over there," Layne said, picking her way downhill through the cacti.

Mason slid down behind her, kicking up a cloud of dust in the process.

The marker corresponding to the GPS position the horseback agent had noted in his report was on the far side of a maze of creosotes and sagebrush to the northeast. Layne pushed through the branches ahead of them until they were right on top of the beacon and stepped out into a small clearing. There was hardly enough room to contain the skeletons of animals far larger and infinitely more ferocious looking than Mason had expected. The interlacing teeth to either side of their slender snouts were long and sharp. Patches of dried tissue and hair clung to bones dark with putrefaction.

"They weren't killed by the same weapon as Austin and Langbroek," Layne said.

Mason furrowed his brow. She was right. The remaining fur wasn't even singed. As far as he could tell, there was nothing unusual about any of the carcasses. The ground beneath them, however, was another thing entirely. The wild grasses had withered and died, leaving behind bare soil and brown blades as brittle as straw. One of the larger javelinas had died at the base of a creosote, the leaves of which had fallen from the thorny branches.

Mason used his cell phone camera to document the site, starting with the remains and moving eastward through the clearing until he reached the mouth of a burrow excavated from the roots of a dead shrub. The earth around it was littered with dead leaves and bits of broken straw.

"I need something to collect a soil sample," he said.

Layne produced a piece of gum from her pocket, folded the strip into her mouth, and offered him the foil wrapper. It wasn't perfect, but it would have to do. He filled it with as much dirt as it could hold, pinched the edges closed, and wedged it into the coin pocket of his jeans.

"I think Austin might have been onto something," Layne said.

"Yeah," Mason said. He stood and looked to the west, where the setting sun bled the forest crimson. "And we'd better hurry up and figure out what it is."

By the time they made it back to the car, only a few slanted columns of moonlight passed through the canopy. Mason was still lost in thought when he climbed behind the wheel and started the engine. The headlights fired into the weeds, casting shadows that appeared to writhe on the gentle breeze.

"You know as well as I do that whatever killed those boars leached into the ground and killed the vegetation, too," Layne said.

"Which rules out a biological agent," Mason said.

"So do you think we're dealing with more Novichok? That would explain how so many animals were killed in such close proximity to one another and why the surrounding vegetation died."

"I'm sure the cartels would pay through the nose for a chemical weapon, but why would they go to the trouble and expense of getting one just to waste any amount on a bunch of pigs?"

"Do you have a better idea?"

Mason shook his head. He didn't, and that was what worried him.

"We need to see the other sites Austin was investigating," he said.

The Explorer juddered across the uneven ground as Mason guided it away from the river. He propped his phone in the cupholder so he'd be able to see when it was within range of a cellular tower while Layne programmed the address of the farm with the dead crops into the GPS, which directed them out of the refuge, onto the gravel road, and back to the highway. The tires had barely hit the asphalt when Mason's phone chimed to alert him to an incoming message.

He pulled off onto the shoulder and checked his notifications. He had a total of ten missed calls from three different phone numbers, each of which had left a single voice message. He dialed his voice mail, entered his password, and put the phone on speaker so Layne could hold it while he drove.

"First new message, received today at 5:54 P.M.," the computerized female voice said.

"Mason," Locker said in his unmistakable voice. "Something caught my eye while I was comparing the medical examiner's notes to the results of the virtual autopsy. I was hoping you wouldn't mind taking a peek and letting me know what you think. It's probably nothing, but I want to get your opinion all the same. Give me a call when you've had a chance to look at the files."

"Second new message, received today at 6:03 P.M."

"Mace," Gunnar said. A hollow humming sound suggested he was calling from a plane, presumably his own private jet. "Sorry to call your work phone, but I really need to get ahold of you and you aren't answering your personal line. Check your email and call me back."

"Third new message, received today at 6:39 P.M."

"Special Agent Mason? This is Ed McWhinney down here at the crime lab in McAllen. I was able to salvage some static imagery from the microSD card in the scope, although I doubt it'll be of much use.

I've seen clearer pictures of bigfoot, if you know what I mean. Call me back, okay? Here . . . let me give you my cell phone number in case I've already left by the time you get this message."

Layne plugged the digits into her phone as he rattled them off. She ended the messages and looked expectantly at Mason, who slowed the SUV in anticipation of the oncoming turn. He again veered south onto a gravel road and headed toward the river. He'd expected the drive to take longer.

"It's like everyone waited to call until we were out of range," she said. "Where should we start?"

"Let's circle back to the messages," he said, tossing her his stealth phone. "The directed-energy weapon is the key. Go to my presets and hit the scarab avatar. If anyone's heard about DEWs hitting the open market, it's Ramses."

The phone rang straight through to voice mail. Layne left a message after the beep. She'd just terminated the call when the phone pinged in her hand to announce an incoming video call. She rolled her eyes and swiped to answer. The screen momentarily darkened before Ramses appeared, wearing an open-collar shirt, a suit jacket, and a smirk.

"Why couldn't you just answer your phone like a normal person?" Layne asked.

"For one thing, I needed to make sure the connection was properly encrypted," he said. "For another, I prefer dealing with people face-to-face. It strips away the nuance. Besides, if you were looking this good, tell me you wouldn't want to share it with the world."

She sighed and shook her head.

"This isn't a social call," Mason said.

"You know, I was just thinking to myself how no one had gone out of their way to try to ruin my day yet. Tell me that's not why you're calling."

"I'm guessing by now you've heard about Langbroek," Mason said.

"Couldn't have happened to a more deserving guy."

"So then you know how he was killed."

Ramses made it his business to know everything about everyone, which served him well in his chosen profession as a middleman of sorts between people of questionable taste and the purveyors of their vices.

"Yeah, but I'm kind of sketchy on the details," he said. "Gunnar seems to think we were dealing with something a whole lot more exotic than you'd find in your standard arsenal."

"You know anything about it?"

"Please. I'm a pillar of the community. How would I know about such things?"

Layne groaned, eliciting a chuckle from Ramses.

"In one thousand feet, turn left on County Road One," the GPS announced.

"Where the hell are you?" Ramses asked.

"South Texas," Mason said. "Just this side of the border."

"You must have done something seriously wrong to piss off your boss that badly."

"Can we get back to the reason we called?" Layne said.

"I've already reached out to a few business associates, but they've only heard rumors."

"About DEWs?"

"Not specifically," Ramses said. "There's supposedly a weapon out there called 'the dragon,' or something like that. They say it can spit fire."

"That sounds promising," Mason said. "Find out everything you can for us."

"What do you think I'm doing? The guys who know about what you're looking for aren't the chatty kind, and they don't do business over the phone. Give me some time. You'll know when I do."

Ramses ended the call without another word. Mason knew better than to read anything into it. He glanced to the south and could barely discern the canopy of the trees lining the Rio Grande river from the night sky. They'd driven three sides of a giant rectangle. If he was right, they couldn't have been more than half a mile as the crow flies from where they'd documented the javelina bones.

The Explorer turned down an arrow-straight dirt road toward a small farmhouse with an enormous outbuilding. One of the garage doors stood open, the interior light revealing a man wearing bib overalls covered with grease and a dusty ball cap. He turned at the sound of their approach and shielded his eyes from their headlights. His shoulders slumped. He closed the hood of the tractor he'd been working on, wiped his hands on a rag, and stepped off to the side as though to set something down on his tool cart. When he faced them again, there was a shotgun in his hands.

12

The man leveled the shotgun at Mason through the front windshield.

"The hell?" Layne said, reaching for the holster under her left arm.

"Not yet," Mason said.

He eased the car into park, rolled down his window, and raised his hands so the man could see them.

"You got no business here!" the man shouted, an unnerving note of panic creeping into his voice. "Back right out of here the same way you came in!"

"Federal agents!" Mason yelled.

"Don't no one come out here after dark unless they're looking for trouble."

"I have identification. I'm going to reach slowly—"

The moment he started to lower his hand, the man fired directly over their heads. He ejected the spent shell, chambered another, and aligned it with Mason's face once more.

"What you're going to do is get the hell off my property," the man shouted. "You got to the count of three to back out of here before the next shot goes right through the glass!"

"How about now?" Layne asked.

Mason ignored her.

"Listen to me very carefully," he said. "We're special agents with the Federal Bureau of—"

"One!"

"—Investigation. We've come out here because of a report you filed with the Starr County Sheriff's Depart—"

"Two!"

"Damn it!" Mason said. "We're looking into the death of a border patrol agent who seemed to think there was something really wrong with your field!"

The man said nothing for several seconds, indecision written all over his face.

"Which patrol agent?" he finally asked.

"Ryan Austin, Patrol Agent in Charge of the Rio Grande City Station."

"Let me see your badges. Toss them out here on the pavement so I can get a good look."

"He's aiming a deadly weapon at two law-enforcement officers," Layne said.

"Remember where we are and how it must look pulling up to his house after dark in a black SUV."

"He thinks we're with one of the cartels?"

"Wouldn't you?"

Mason slowly lowered his hand, pried his badge jacket out of the back pocket of his jeans, and tossed it out the window. It slid across the oil-stained tarmac and came to rest in front of the man, who waited for Layne to throw hers before kneeling and flipping both of them open. His aim never faltered as he alternately examined their identification and sighted Mason down the long barrel. He nodded to himself, stood, and lowered his weapon to his side.

The two agents opened their doors and stepped out onto the driveway, their hands still raised.

"Mind putting away that shotgun?" Layne said.

"Wouldn't be the first time some narco showed up making demands. I have people I'm supposed to pretend not to see sneaking through here twenty-four hours a day and can't sleep some nights for all of the gunfire down by the river. Hell, a border patrol agent was shot in that field right over there. I've had three break-ins this year alone and would have to take off my shoes to count all of the bodies I've found on my own goddamn land, so you'll have to forgive me for being a little jumpy."

The man took a deep breath to compose himself, opened the slide, and set the shotgun back down on the tool cabinet where he'd found it. He turned around and proffered his dirty hand as though nothing had happened.

"Tom Thompson."

Mason and Layne eyed him warily as they retreived their badges.

Up close, he looked considerably older. He had vertically lined cheeks, hooded eyes, and the handshake of a man no cow wanted tugging on its udders. Layne met his stare from beneath the brim of her FBI ball cap and held it, like two bulls locking horns, her right hand very clearly resting on the grip of her sidearm.

Thompson removed his hat and held it over his heart.

"Sorry I scared you, miss."

"You've obviously mistaken my expression for one of fear, when it's actually one of dread at the amount of paperwork I'd have to file for shooting you in the kneecap."

The man cracked a crooked grin.

"You remind me of my Agnes. God rest her soul. That woman was as beautiful as a sunrise, but she had more venom than a diamondback."

"You point that shotgun at her, too?"

"Wouldn't be here today if I had."

Layne allowed herself the hint of a smile.

"What can you tell us about the nature of the damage to your field, Mr. Thompson?" Mason asked.

"Nothing that wouldn't be better served by showing you." He grabbed a flashlight from the top drawer of the tool cabinet. "I hope you didn't wear your good shoes."

Thompson switched on a blinding beam that turned night into day in its direct vicinity and struck off toward the field to the east of the outbuilding. He entered a slender gap between rows of crops taller than he was, their cornlike leaves brushing against his shoulders.

"This here is sorghum," he said. "Although you probably know it as millet."

"Those little pellets in birdseed?" Layne said.

Mason fell in stride behind them. Walking into a field that restricted visibility to such a great extent put him on edge; it reminded him of the cornfield back in Colorado where they'd found the Scarecrow's victims bound to crosses.

"It's a whole lot more than that," Thompson said. "It's an ancient grain. High in protein, low in fat, and contains calcium and vitamin B. Plus, it's gluten-free for all those California types. It can be ground into flour for bread, refined into dextrose to sweeten stuff, and used instead of wheat in beer. Hell, you can even make it into ethanol for biofuel. It's also one of the hardiest grains on the entire planet. It can grow where nothing else can and withstand heat, drought, and even this rotten soil."

"Which is why you reported it to the sheriff when your field died," Mason said.

"Something like that. All these years I been paying insurance premiums, it's about time I was able to get some of that money back."

He led them out of the field and onto a dirt road that didn't look like it had ever been graded. The sorghum was considerably shorter on the other side, which made it easy to see the pattern of bare soil right in the middle.

"I rotate planting and harvesting these fields so that I have mature plants every season. The Chinese buy sorghum in bulk and use it instead of domestic corn in their animal fodder, you see, so I might make a little less in the long haul, but it's guaranteed income. This field here was maybe as tall as my knees when I noticed the die-off."

He walked down a row framed by stalks that nearly reached his armpits.

"The report said it happened in under twenty-four hours," Layne said.

"Maybe a little longer. By the time I noticed the plants starting to wither, there was nothing I could do to stop it."

"The insurance adjuster took soil samples, correct?" Mason said.

"He checked for all kinds of pesticides, herbicides, microbes, pH, and soil crusting, but didn't come up with anything. He even checked to make sure I hadn't salted my own field, for all the good that would have done me."

The height of the crops steadily diminished until they reached the area that had looked dead from a distance. There were actually small plants about four inches tall growing from the mounded dirt, although they were wiry and malformed. Mason removed his cell phone from his pocket and crouched to take pictures of them.

"Sorghum grows in three stages," Thompson said. "Each one lasts about thirty-five days. This field here should be right about the end of the second stage—what we call the heading stage—when you start to see all of those seed clusters budding and preparing to flower."

"The plants through here are obviously starting to regrow," Layne said. "Did you treat the soil with anything first?"

"Like I said, the tests showed there was nothing wrong with the soil. I only replanted once I got my check—which, I might add, took just shy of forever—to prove them wrong."

"And?"

"Look at these sprouts. See how thin they are? And they should easily be in the six-leaf phase by now, but as you can see they haven't even developed their third leaf sheath."

"What causes something like that?"

"Beats the heck out of me. I've never seen anything like it in all my years."

"Could the plants have been sprayed by chemicals that aren't ordinarily part of routine testing?" Mason asked. "Something that might linger in the soil?"

"I suppose it's always possible. Don't ask me how anyone could get any nonagricultural chemicals in that kind of volume all the way out here without me knowing, though."

"Do you mind if we collect a sample?" Layne asked.

"Knock yourselves out," Thompson said. "Just make sure you tell me if you find out anything."

Layne used the foil from another stick of gum to collect a small amount of dirt.

Thompson made small talk while he guided them back to the outbuilding where they'd left the Explorer, but Mason tuned him out. He realized that if they were able to rule out the presence of chemical agents, there were very few options left as to what could have killed both the animals and the crops so quickly, all of which scared the living hell out of him.

13

Thompson gave them his business card and offered to brew a pot of coffee. Now that he'd started talking, he didn't appear to be in a hurry to stop. He probably didn't get a lot of visitors, let alone of the variety he didn't want to shoot. They thanked him for the offer and again promised to follow up if they learned anything about his soil. Layne programmed the address for the ranch where the cattle had mysteriously died into the GPS while Mason navigated the gravel roads back to the highway.

"Why don't you see if you can get ahold of McWhinney," Mason said. "I'm curious about the images he was able to recover from the scope of Austin's rifle."

Layne dialed the number from her contacts and put the call on speaker.

"Director?" she said. "This is Special Agent Layne returning your call."

"I'm sorry I didn't have better news for you," he said. "You're welcome to look at the digital files for yourselves. I can be back to the lab in about half an hour, if you want to meet me there."

"We're actually over near Rio Grande City and have one more stop to make, so it'll probably take us closer to an hour."

"That's perfectly all right. I hadn't yet turned in for the night as I was hoping you might call first."

"Can we ask another favor of you, Director?" Mason said. "I'd like to send you some pictures and get your thoughts about what we're looking at."

"What kind of pictures?"

"The kind I'd rather not discuss over the phone."

"You've piqued my curiosity."

"We'd also be grateful if you'd be able to run a couple of soil samples for us."

"That might be tricky," McWhinney said. "I hesitate to conduct any tests on taxpayer-funded equipment without proper authorization."

"We can discuss that when we get there," Layne said. "In the meantime, let me get your email address."

She grabbed Mason's cell phone, opened a blank email, typed the director's address above the header, and terminated the call so she could focus on sending the pictures of the javelina carcasses and the stunted sorghum. Mason already had a pretty good idea what the director was going to say, but he wasn't entirely sure of the implications.

They'd barely reached the speed limit when the computerized voice from the dashboard announced their turn was coming up on the right. Once again, they turned south and headed down a gravel road toward the Rio Grande. The shrubland picked up once more where the seemingly infinite rows of sorghum left off. The spectral shapes of cattle materialized from the darkness and the sporadic gaps between bushes before falling away into the cloud of dust trailing the vehicle. They passed a homestead off in the distance to the left, little more than a cluster of aging buildings against the horizon. The long driveway was barred by a rusted gate, although the chain on it sparkled in their headlights and the tire ruts saw enough use to keep them from growing over with weeds. Their destination was ahead and on the right.

Mason immediately recognized that the acreage aligned geographically with both of their previous stops.

"Do me a favor," he said. "See if you can plot the locations of all of Austin's discoveries on a single map."

Layne sent the last in the series of emails to McWhinney and set Mason's phone back in the cupholder.

"We both know what it's going to show."

"Maybe, but there's something we're missing."

"You mean like the addresses of the incidents on the Mexican side of the border?"

"If I'm right, the map will show us exactly where they are," Mason said. "Figuring out the reason why all of the sites fall along the same straight line is the key to understanding why Austin was killed. He had to have been on the verge of exposing a threat far more dangerous than some dead animals and withered crops might suggest for the Thirteen to have risked stepping from the shadows to assassinate the head of a border patrol station. There's a lot more going on down here than meets the eye and we need to find out what it is before people start dying."

The fence on the right side of the road transitioned from barbed wire to ten-foot-tall wrought-iron bars crowned with razor wire and security cameras, an abrupt demarcation that separated where the cows grazed from where the humans lived.

Mason turned into the mouth of the driveway and coasted up to the gate blocking the road. The columns were made of mortared fieldstones, the bars adorned with the outlines of longhorns to either side of the meeting stiles. The arch above them was engraved with the name ROBINSON RANCH, on one side of which was a brand that looked like a lightning bolt inside a circle, and on the other, the Lone Star of Texas. There was obviously more money to be made from cattle than there was from sorghum.

He climbed out and stood with the Explorer's headlights at his back, casting his shadow through the gate. It was an automatic model with an electromagnetic lock, the kind that could be disengaged by typing the combination into a keypad. There was also a call button that would alert the people inside the house so they could unlock it remotely. Mason pressed it and waited several seconds before inspecting the gate itself. The left half swung inward with a gentle push.

Mason heard the lowing of cattle in the distance as he glanced up at the security cameras, then at the keypad. The dark house was little more than a silhouette flanked by barns and outbuildings off to the southwest. He held down the call button and watched for lights to appear inside.

Something was wrong.

Layne rolled down her window.

"They aren't answering their phone," she said.

Mason dragged both halves of the gate open, got back into the Explorer, and drove toward the house. The driveway veered to the left, presumably in an effort to use the vegetation to obscure the view of the house from the main road, before straightening out once more.

"What do you hope to accomplish if no one's home?" Layne asked. "There have to be several hundred acres out here. We don't have a prayer of stumbling upon the spot where the cows died in the dark."

"You're right."

"So what's the plan?"

"I figure the first thing we should probably do is knock on the door."

"You think they're in there and just not answering their phone or the buzzer on the gate?"

"No," Mason said. "I think they're dead."

The driveway terminated in a roundabout. At the center was a knoll bristling with cacti and succulents. The state and national flags hung listless from twin flagpoles, upon which motion sensors had been mounted. One of the garage doors stood open, its interior conspicuously empty.

"What makes you say that?" Layne asked.

Mason parked and stared at the dark house for several seconds.

"Just a gut feeling," he said.

He climbed out of the car and waited for Layne before approaching the porch. The scuffing sounds of their footsteps echoed from beneath the overhang. Mason pressed the doorbell and listened for the sound of footsteps inside. Layne looked through the front window and leaned from side to side in an effort to see through the gap in the curtains.

"No sign of movement."

Mason banged on the door with his fist, causing it to shiver in its frame maybe just a little too hard. He tried the knob, which turned easily in his hand. He drew his Glock, raised it in a two-handed grip, and pressed his back to the wall.

"After you," he said.

"So now that there could be someone waiting inside with a shot-gun aimed at whoever walks through the door first, you're all about chivalry."

"Then you cover me."

"Forget that."

She stepped back, kicked in the door, and went inside, low and fast. The knob hammered the strike plate on the wall with a loud cracking sound that reverberated throughout the house.

Mason switched on his mini Maglite and followed her into the tiled foyer. The control panel for the security system was mounted on the wall to his left, but it wasn't activated. There were coats on the coat-rack and dirty boots on the entry mat. The industrial-size kitchen was dark and smelled of spoiled food and rotted garbage. There was a fine patina of dust on the dining-room table.

"Call the sheriff's department," Mason said. "See if they can tell you why the people who lived here contacted them in the first place."

He passed through a doorway that locked from the inside and headed down the hallway off the main room. The walls were adorned with black-and-white photographs of a lineage defined by bushy brows and strong chins. He flipped the light switch several times with his el-bow, but nothing happened. The room to his left must have served as a bunkhouse, if the half-dozen or so beds crammed inside were any indication. The bathroom across the hall looked more like something he'd expect to find at a gym. There were no personal accouterments of any kind in either of them.

"Lyle Robinson called the sheriff's department at least half a dozen times since reporting his dead cattle, the most recent of which was about three weeks ago," Layne said from the other room.

Mason found her in the opposite hallway outside of what appeared to be the master bedroom. The bed was made, but the comforter was rumpled. A lamp lay overturned beside the nightstand, upon which a dark digital clock sat.

"Did they say why he called?" Mason asked.

"He complained that there was a lot of extra traffic on the road outside his gate, which isn't a crime by any stretch of the imagina-tion, but it does imply increased smuggling activity in the area. The sheriff's department followed up with the border patrol every time, although nothing ever came of it."

They entered the bedroom to find the closet door standing open. Clothes littered the floor beneath half-empty racks. A wall safe was barely visible behind button-down Western shirts on hangers.

"Looks like the Robinsons left in a big hurry," Layne said.

"That's what we're supposed to think," Mason said. He walked into the bathroom. The toilet and shower appeared clean. He opened the medicine cabinet and appraised shelves brimming with lotions, ointments, prescription bottles, and vials of clear liquid. "If they were in such a rush to leave that they couldn't be troubled to lock their front door or close their gate, they probably wouldn't have bothered relocking the safe in the closet. And one of them is diabetic. There's no way they would have left without their insulin."

"So where are they?"

There was nothing Mason could say. Eventually their bodies would turn up, likely in the car missing from the garage, but he and Layne had their work cut out for them in the meantime and they couldn't afford to waste any more time. They needed to get McWhinney started on the soil samples and cross the border before they attracted too much attention.

Mason had no doubt that the secret the Thirteen had killed Austin to protect was hidden at one of the three remaining incident sites in Mexico. He and Layne needed to get there before anyone so much as suspected they were coming, which meant they were going to need help.

Fortunately, he'd prepared for this contingency.

He awakened his stealth phone and hit Alejandra's preset. She answered on the third ring.

"Where are you?" he asked.

"I just got off the plane," she said. "Your text was not very informative. Are you going to tell me why I risked a court-martial to come to Reynosa?"

"Don't worry, I'll have Archer square the whole thing away with your CO. Just meet me on the Mexican side of the McAllen-Hidalgo International Bridge in two hours, okay? I need someone who understands the cartels and how they function. If the Thirteen are working with CJNG, like I suspect, then I have a feeling our inquiries might be met with some . . . resistance."

14

ELSEWHERE

The man in the hospital bed knew he was going to die, and not in the metaphysical sense. He had his death planned, right down to the date and time. And he had made his peace with it. In fact, a part of him was even looking forward to it. His had been a long life of ignominy, and soon it would end in the very same manner it should have nearly four decades ago.

"*Kakaya ruka segodnya?*" the woman asked.

The man held out his right arm in response, exposing the scar tissue on the inside of his elbow.

With a nod, the woman drew the technetium-99 into the lead-lined syringe and set it on the counter beside her. She removed her heavy gloves, draped them over the shielded L-block window, and took her customary seat beside him. He closed his eyes and nodded for her to proceed.

"*Ya izvinyayus', moya lyubov',*" she whispered.

The man brought her hand to his lips and kissed it. He wished he could have loved her as she loved him, but his heart had always belonged to another.

She tied off the tourniquet and smacked the vein. A sharp pinch and she slid the needle into the vessel. She released the strap from his upper arm, pushed the plunger, and flooded his body with the radioactive isotope. He tasted metal in his mouth, felt the—

—*sensation of pins and needles assaulting his face. They are out of time. The chain reaction has already begun.*

The ground shudders, driving him to his knees. He pushes himself up from the floor and hurries to catch up with Nikolai Mikhailovich Tarasov, whose white smock and cap appear red under the emergency lights illuminating the corridor.

Something has gone terribly, terribly wrong. They have run routine tests like this one numerous times at the V. I. Lenin Nuclear Power Plant, but never has anything like this happened.

Their goal had been simply to confirm that the water coolant system would be able to maintain the temperature of the reactor in the event of a blackout. They had decreased the power output of reactor no. 4 to 700 megawatts, just as planned, which had triggered the burn-off of xenon-135 and started a negative-feedback reaction that lowered the output of the core to a mere 200 megawatts. As an extra precaution, they had activated additional water pumps. The backup generators must not have been able to keep up with the electrical demands ordinarily satisfied by the turbines, which they had been forced to shut down for the test. The flow rate had decreased and the temperature had risen, causing steam voids to form in the coolant lines. Without the necessary volume of water to absorb the excess energy in the form of neutrons, the reactor had entered a positive-feedback loop, whereby the power levels continued to rise on their own.

The control rods should have counteracted the chain reaction, though. There is no way the power should have continued to ramp up with the neutron-absorbing rods in place to prevent further fission events. He had even pressed the EPS-5 button, which should have completely shut down the reactor.

A thunderous boom shakes the earth and sends him sprawling. His head hits the wall and he feels a trickle of warmth roll into his eyebrow.

The reactor must have exploded. All of those neutrons that should have been absorbed by the control rods and the water were at that very moment hurtling outward from the core at one tenth of the speed of light, passing invisibly through walls and windows, concrete and brick, without so much as slowing. Tearing through people as if they were not even there, including Nikolai and him. If they did not cool down the core right now, the entire population of Pripyat would be dead within a matter of hours.

He lunges to his feet and stumbles down the corridor. His stomach lurches and acid rises into the back of his throat. He spits it onto the floor and shoves aside the knowledge of what it means.

The reactor can be manually flooded using the handwheels on the pipes at the end of the hallway. While it might already be too late for the two of them, he prays it is not too late for the others.

He grips the wheel. Groans with the strain. Forces it to turn with a metallic shriek. He hears the rush of water funneling into the pipes

even over the alarms blaring from the control center and the contin-
uous rumble of the accelerating meltdown.

"Ty dolzhen uyti!" *he shouts.*

Nikolai has a wife and two grown children. He needs to get out
before he suffers irreparable physical damage, assuming he has not
already, yet the older man stays and dials open the second valve.

Two more to go.

A hiss and scalding steam envelopes them.

He fights through it until he finds the next handwheel in the se-
ries and starts cranking. Behind him, he hears the squeaking sound of
Nikolai opening the other valve.

Another eruption of stomach acid, only this time he cannot con-
tain it. It runs down his chest beneath his smock as he staggers away
from the pipes and into the smoke-filled corridor, losing sight of his
fellow engineer. He leans his shoulder against the wall to keep himself
upright and wills his trembling legs to run.

"Nikolai Mikhailovich!" *he shouts.*

Concrete corridors pass in his peripheral vision. Silhouettes race
past him, desperately trying to find a way out. He shoves into the mass
exodus of humanity and allows it to carry him through the emergency
exit. He falls to his knees beneath the stars, vomits, and struggles to
stand.

"Nikolai Mikhailovich!"

He fights upstream through the men trying to reach safety until
he finds the older man lying across the threshold, being trampled
by his friends and coworkers in their hurry to escape. He grabs Ni-
kolai by the collar. Drags him across the dirt lot. Falls repeatedly,
and yet somehow he finds the strength to rise again.

He glances over his shoulder and sees the craterous ruin where
the no. 4 reactor had been. A cloud of steam billows into the night
sky, spreading deadly radiation the likes of which the world has never
known. A light flickers from its depths. Flames, he realizes. But there
is only one thing that can possibly be burning with all of the water
flooding the reactor.

The core itself is on fire.

They are all going to die. Every single one of them. They are all
going to—

The man leaned over the side of the bed and vomited into the waiting basin, purging himself of the memory and what little food he had been able to stomach. Nothing that had happened had been his fault, yet the world had held him accountable. The time had finally come to turn the tables and hold it accountable for what it had done to *him*.

Soon, millions would know his suffering.

And pray for the mercy of death.

PART 2

We shall have world government, whether or not we like it. The question is only whether world government will be achieved by consent or by conquest.

—James Warburg, financial adviser to Franklin D. Roosevelt, testimony before the Senate Committee on Foreign Relations (February 17, 1950)

15

JULY 3

It was midnight by the time they hit the highway heading east toward McAllen once more. The debate as to whether or not to alert the Starr County Sheriff's Department to the situation at the Robinson Ranch had gotten heated, but Layne had ultimately relented. While Mason had agreed that he would have wanted people looking for him if he and his family had gone missing, they couldn't risk derailing what little investigative momentum they had. There would have been questions they weren't prepared to answer, chief among them why they'd been inside the Robinsons' house in the first place, and if anyone in the department was compromised, the entire operation could be blown right there. They'd already taken a big enough gamble by approaching McWhinney.

Layne had breezed through the convenience store at a truck stop and loaded up on coffee and energy bars while Mason filled the tank. They needed to be prepared to spend some serious time in the Explorer. The map of the incidents on American soil formed a line that crossed the Mexican border on its way to Ciudad Camargo; somewhere along that line lay the remaining three sites Austin had documented in his letters: the ruined cornfield, the farm with the dead chickens, and the building filled with cat and rat carcasses.

They couldn't afford to waste the drive time, so Layne volunteered to use Mason's laptop to follow up on the messages from Locker and Gunnar in the hope that the images might be large enough for him to view at a glance from the corner of his eye. The highway was ruler-straight, but rocketing through the unlit countryside at nearly a hundred miles an hour left little room for error.

"Where do you want to start?" she asked.

"How about chronologically?"

Layne nodded, logged into the task force's secure server, and opened the files Locker had wanted them to view. While she scanned the medical examiner's notes and compared them against the results of the virtual autopsy, Mason caught glimpses of close-up photographs and hand-drawn illustrations on the screen in front of her. He was about to ask what was taking her so long when she finally spoke.

"The only difference between the two files is something that the ME visually appreciated that wasn't picked up on the CT scan, undoubtedly because it's a superficial detail."

"What is it?"

"He said that upon magnified examination of the tattoo on Yamaguchi's chest, he was able to distinguish subtle differences between shades of the same colors of ink, which he attributed to variations in concentration or a significant gap in time between the completion of different parts of the design, allowing for a degree of fading. And while it wouldn't be outside the realm of possibility for the artist to switch ink supplies during the process of creating an elaborate design like that dragon, the symmetry of the discolorations made it worth noting."

Mason slowed and pulled to the side of the road so he could look for himself. It took him a moment to understand what the ME was implying.

"There's a second tattoo underneath the dragon," he said.

"More like the dragon was designed to incorporate an older, pre-existing design, if you're willing to read between the lines a little."

"He had the exact same tattoo in the exact same place as the Scarecrow and her brother."

"So either they decided to get matching dragon tattoos after Yamaguchi got his or all three of them have the same design hidden underneath it."

"Can you bring up the photographic comparison of their tattoos?" Mason asked.

"Give me a second."

A semi roared past, kicking up sand from the shoulder and

rocking the SUV on its suspension. Mason watched its taillights shrink to red pinpricks against the flat horizon.

There were any number of reasons to cover up a bad tattoo, most of them completely benign. Locker was probably right that there wasn't anything there, but the placement couldn't be coincidental. It was almost like a cattle brand, a readily identifiable symbol that helped distinguish one herd from another, a telltale marking that a cattle thief would want to immediately burn over in order to dodge questions about the animal's provenance.

Layne opened the image and zoomed in first on the coiled dragon on the Scarecrow's chest, then on the identical design on her brother's.

"Maybe . . ." she said. "I can kind of see it."

Mason nodded his agreement. If the ME was right about there being an older design concealed beneath the dragon, the artist had done such a phenomenal job of covering it up that they'd likely never know what it was, at least not without—

"An advanced form of imaging," he said, finishing his thought out loud. A glance at the side mirror confirmed there were no headlights behind them. He hit the gas and accelerated onto the highway. "Send Locker a message. Tell him that was a great catch and let him know we're looking into it. And see if you can get Gunnar on the phone."

Layne messaged Locker through the secure cloud and grabbed Mason's stealth phone from the cupholder. She scrolled through his speed-dial settings until she found an avatar that looked like a revolver, tapped it, and left a message when the call went straight to voice mail.

"Why don't you open his email while we wait for him to call us back?" Mason said.

"Why don't you let me drive and you can play secretary?"

"You know it's not like that."

She sighed theatrically, but she did as he asked. Of course, whatever it said, she was going to make him work to get it out of her.

"What is it?" he asked.

"He tracked down Yamaguchi." The excitement in her voice was palpable. "He's right here in this picture."

Mason pulled over so hard and fast that the SUV slewed on the shoulder.

"When was it taken?" he asked.

"February third, 2007."

"Where?"

"Omsk."

"What was he doing in Russia?"

She turned the monitor so he could see a black-and-white photograph from a newspaper. It showed a pair of men wearing dark winter parkas and ski caps emblazoned with their agency insignia, collecting samples of snow from a drift. Another man in a matching winter uniform appeared to be conducting interviews beneath the awning of an official-looking building and in front of a small crowd of onlookers, one of whom stood apart from the others, intently watching the scene before him, a cloud of breath captured pluming from his lips. There was no doubt in Mason's mind that he was looking at Dr. Tatsuo Yamaguchi. The caption was written in Cyrillic, but Gunnar had typed the translation below it: AUTHORITIES FROM THE MINISTRY OF EMERGENCY SITUATIONS, MCHS, EXAMINE THE ORANGE SNOW THAT FELL OVERNIGHT IN OMSK.

"*Orange* snow?" Mason stared at the image for several seconds before pulling back onto the highway. "What's the significance?"

Layne opened her browser and searched for the answer.

"I'll read it to you," she said. "'The Siberian Orange Snow Incident was an anomalous phenomenon that occurred in early February 2007. The snow itself was oily, malodorous, and reportedly contained high levels of trace minerals, fueling speculation that it was caused by industrial pollution, a rocket launch, or even a nuclear accident. Further testing, however, revealed significant amounts of clay and sand dust, suggesting a more innocent explanation. A heavy sandstorm in neighboring Kazakhstan had likely thrown particles into the stratosphere, from which they descended with the snow.'"

"So then why was Yamaguchi there?" Mason asked.

His phone rang in Layne's hand and she answered it on speaker.

"I take it you finally opened my email?" Gunnar said.

"How'd you find Yamaguchi's picture?" Layne asked.

"I wrote a program that utilizes facial recognition and a host of proprietary algorithms to comb the Internet. If the subject of the search has been captured on camera and the picture uploaded to the Web, my program will find it, even if he's just walking past in the background of someone else's snapshot."

"That's frightening."

"Why do you think the government invests so heavily in social media? It's like having its own constantly evolving pictorial database where people essentially spy on themselves and beam the evidence straight to the NSA."

"That's kind of why we called," Mason said.

"To talk about the surveillance state?"

"No, to see if we could tap into that computer expertise of yours."

"How so?"

"The medical examiner noticed that the dragon on Yamaguchi's chest appears to have been tattooed over another design."

"What makes him say that?"

"Subtle differences in the shades of the same colors of ink, which might or might not be the result of natural fading over time."

"So the dragon incorporates parts of the underlying design to create a single tattoo meant to conceal its predecessor."

"That's the theory."

Gunnar was silent for a long moment. Mason heard a voice in the background, but it was too faint and distorted to make out the words.

"Okay," he said. "I could probably write an algorithm that assigns a different color scale to heighten the contrast and apply a Fourier transform to clearly delineate the two designs as functions of time, but I'm going to need a physical variable that allows me to separate them."

"Like what?"

"Like the molecular density of the different inks or the relative depths of dermal impregnation. Think in three dimensions. Something that would allow me to virtually lift one design from on top of the other like a transparency."

"What about a CT scan?"

"While a CT image is really nothing more than the visual expression of a mathematical equation that demonstrates the differences in the linear coefficients of soft-tissue structures of similar composition, this would be a lot more complicated than simply delineating the liver from the kidneys and the spine. We're talking about microscopic differences in the depth and penetration of the ink, layers of scar tissue invisible to the naked eye. I'd need access to the raw data. Not the reformatted images, mind you. I mean the original analog data—the ones and zeroes—the smallest subset of data acquired by the radiation receptors in real time. The yes-or-no proposition corresponding to single photons of light that are either attenuated by the body or miraculously pass through it."

"Where can we get something like that?"

"You can't. It's stored directly on the computer that runs the scanner. If you can tell me where the study was performed, I can probably access it myself, as long as it's networked to the mainframe."

Mason glanced at Layne.

"New York–Presbyterian," she said.

"I'll get back to you," Gunnar said, terminating the call.

A faint aura of light spread across the horizon to let them know they were nearing McAllen.

"Even if he can somehow pull the old tattoo out from underneath the dragon," Layne said, "what can it possibly tell us?"

"What Yamaguchi and the Nakamura twins were doing during the years we can't account for," Mason said. "Which just might help us pick up the trail of the Thirteen."

16

McWhinney was waiting in the lobby when they arrived. He offered a compulsory handshake and, without a word, led them straight to the forensics lab. There was obviously something he was dying to show them, although the expression on his face wasn't one of triumph. The moment he closed the office door behind them, he slipped on an elbow-length lead glove and held out his hand.

"The soil samples?"

Layne placed the folded foil packets on his palm. He recoiled and looked at her in dismay, but shook his head as though to clear it of doubt and carried them to a station with a scale, pipettes, and various solvents and preparation trays.

"Are you sure you're okay with running those samples for us?" Mason asked.

"I believe doing so is definitely in the best interests of this community."

The way he said it suggested he knew something they didn't, perhaps even what the results would show. Layne caught it, too. She glanced at Mason and raised the question with her eyebrows.

"Alex?" McWhinney said. A freckled kid wearing a lab coat and goggles on top of his head appeared from the doorway to the break room. He didn't look like he'd slept, or even been outside, in recent memory. Mason pegged him for a grad student paying his own way through med school. "Can you please prepare these samples and run them through the XRF spectrometer?"

"What's that?" Layne asked.

"An X-ray fluorescence spectrometer provides chemical analyses of geological samples. We use it to match soil collected from a footprint at a crime scene to its point of origin by mapping its unique elemental composition, including heavy and reactive metals, and comparing it against our database."

The director removed the glove and offered it to the lab tech, who donned it, along with its opposite number. He switched on a machine that looked like a cross between a microwave and an Easy-Bake Oven, lowered his goggles, and took a seat at the stool in front of the samples.

"Please, Special Agents," McWhinney said. "If you'll follow me . . ."

He led them down the hall to the administrative office/detective station. The mess had been cleared from the desk and the sticky notes removed from the frame of the monitor. He assumed the main chair, awakened the screen, and revealed a blurry picture.

"What did you find?" Layne asked.

"Pull up a chair," he said. "We have much to discuss and, I'm afraid, time is of the essence."

Layne looked uneasily at Mason before dragging over a chair from the nearest workstation, where several of the photographs he'd taken in the sorghum field were pinned under magnifying lenses. He rolled over a chair of his own and the two of them flanked McWhinney.

"I was able to extract four viable images from the microSD card in the digital rifle scope, although, like I said, none are especially useful." He zoomed out of the picture on the screen, which resolved into an image captured in the traditional gray-and-green scale of a night-vision apparatus. "With the possible exception of this one."

A rectangular light washed out the upper right quadrant. It almost looked like a window, if one were willing to use a little creativity. A hazy, ill-defined shape of human proportions eclipsed the majority of the left side of the picture.

"Unfortunately, the damage to the data is extensive," McWhinney said. "This is about as well as I can clean it up, but if you continue zooming out and allow the edges to smooth on their own . . ."

He shrunk the picture until it was about a quarter of its original size. While the increased contrast and detail weren't extraordinary, they enhanced the contours of the target just enough to reveal the outline of a man's head and left shoulder where they blocked the light coming through the window.

"That's inside the hallway where Austin's body was found," Layne said.

"I agree," McWhinney said. "And this, I believe, is the man responsible for his death."

Mason tried to glean any identifiable details from the image, but he couldn't even see the man's face, which, he suddenly realized, was because it was concealed.

"He's wearing a mask," he said.

"Not just any mask. If we zoom in until it fills the screen, we can see the reflection of another shape on it."

While it wasn't clear by any stretch of the imagination, it looked a whole lot like a man—with his head lowered, his right elbow raised, and the barrel of a rifle projecting from the left side of his neck—silhouetted by the fire burning behind him.

"It looks like a motorcycle helmet," Layne said.

"Oh, it's much more elaborate than that," McWhinney said. "If you lean closer, you can see a prismatic effect on its surface, the slightest variation in coloration one would expect to find on the gold Kapton-coated polycarbonate visor of an astronaut's helmet, or a firefighter's, which meshes with what appears to be a respirator over the lower half of his face, and the seal around his neck where it connects to his suit."

Mason could just barely make out the coupling and the hose attached to the left side of the respirator.

"He intended to set the house on fire while he was still inside," he said.

"Suits of the kind we're talking about aren't readily available to the public, nor are they even remotely affordable. They're generally reserved for CBRN and firefighting units, the military, and radiation workers."

The way he said the last words made the hairs rise on the back of

Mason's arms. They practically confirmed his suspicions about what had happened to the animals and the crops.

"The plants," he said.

"Exactly." McWhinney abruptly stood and nearly knocked over Layne on his way to the workstation behind her. "Look at these seedlings you photographed. The developmental retardation shown by this sorghum resembles that of the rice plants studied in Minamisoma, Japan, less than ten miles from the Fukushima Daiichi Nuclear Power Plant, where the levels of plutonium in the soil were just under four picocuries per gram, or one hundred times the natural background level."

He returned to his computer and opened a new tab displaying a slideshow of images that scrolled past on their own. They depicted disaster workers wearing white suits, gloves, and helmets with face shields and gas masks standing in a flooded rice paddy, followed by close-ups of the plants themselves. The seedlings were similarly stunted, but the older plants looked normal, like the full-grown sorghum they'd seen earlier in the night.

"As you can see, the mature plants aren't as readily impacted as the juveniles," McWhinney said. "The radiation damages the DNA directly, which causes the chromosomes to mutate in random ways during the growth cycle. In the case of the rice in Minamisoma, it triggered the genes responsible for self-defense, which caused everything from uncontrollable replication to cellular death."

"What about the animals?" Mason asked.

"Entire populations of pale grass blue butterflies demonstrated high mortality rates, an overall reduction in size, and shrunken forewings. Tens of thousands of seals and sea lions lost their fur or died. Cattle as far as fifty miles away exhibited localized sections of white or missing fur and superficial lesions, while nearly all of those within the exclusion zone died. Starfish and anemones liquefied. Dead seabirds and fish littered the shores as far away as Alaska."

"That was a nuclear meltdown," Layne said. "We would have noticed if something like that happened here."

"Had you not watched the tsunami on TV, you might never have known. Outside of the fire and water damage, the immediate physical changes to the vegetation were minimal. Animals died, but there would have been no reason to suspect radiation, especially when plutonium produces alpha radiation, rather than the gamma radiation emitted by uranium reactors like the one in Chernobyl, which was supposed to make Fukushima safer in the event of an accident. Alpha rays aren't like gamma rays, or even X-rays. They have no penetrating power whatsoever. They can't pass through your clothing, let alone your skin. The damage comes from either inhaling or ingesting them, which is what happened to all of those animals. Once those within the hot zone drank the water, the radiation tore right through their lungs and digestive systems."

"And then leached into the soil as their bodies decomposed," Mason said. He thought about the veterinarian's description of the dead cows on the Robinson Ranch and the infertile earth surrounding the javelina bones. "But where could the animals around here have come into contact with—?"

The lab tech burst into the room behind them. He was somehow even paler than before and looked like he might throw up.

"Plutonium-238?" McWhinney said.

"Plus 239 and 240," the kid said. "No isotopic iodine, cesium, or strontium."

McWhinney blanched before their eyes. He took a deep breath and composed himself. When he spoke, it was in a tone of resignation.

"Please forward the results to the EPA and DHS and let them know that I am at their disposal."

"You can't let them know we were here," Mason said. "At least not yet."

"Are you asking me to lie to representatives of the federal government in an investigation with national security implications?"

"We can't afford to have our freedom of movement restricted."

The director turned and looked him squarely in the eyes, visibly taking his measure.

"I can buy you a little time," he said, "but under no circumstances will I attempt to deceive them."

"That's all we need," Layne said.

"You should go before I change my mind," McWhinney said.

Mason nodded his gratitude and he and Layne sprinted for the door.

17

Mason slammed the gearshift into reverse and stomped the gas. Layne barely had time to buckle her seat belt before the tires caught and he jammed the transmission into drive, sending them rocketing toward the main road. The Department of Homeland Security wouldn't take any chances with a potential nuclear device in play. There would be agents on site within minutes of McWhinney's call. Once they confirmed the veracity of his intel, the news would travel straight up the chain. And the first thing the powers that be would do is close the border, which meant that if he and Layne intended to cross it first, they didn't have a second to lose.

Layne programmed the Hidalgo Port of Entry into the GPS and the map appeared on the screen.

While Archer had said he'd be willing to run interference for them, the mere mention of the word *nuclear* changed the dynamics of the situation. He'd be forced to convene the cabinet and the Joint Chiefs of Staff to brief the president on a threat the likes of which none of them had ever faced and one for which there was no precedent. They needed to talk to him before he became unreachable, but first they needed to understand exactly what they were up against.

"See if you can get Locker on the phone," Mason said.

"Turn right on Pecan Boulevard," the computerized voice said. They were already nearly upon the intersection. Mason stomped the brake, turned hard, and swung across the twin yellow lines into the oncoming lanes. "In one thousand feet, turn left on North Twenty-third Street."

A residential neighborhood blurred past on the left, a Salvation Army depot to the right. He turned south and accelerated past block after block of chain restaurants and auto parts stores.

Layne hit the speaker button on her phone and the sound of ringing filled the interior.

"Looks like you'll stay on this road the rest of the way," she said. "It'll turn into International Boulevard in about ten miles and take us straight to the—"

"This had better be good," Locker said, his voice erupting from the speaker and cutting her off.

"Mason and I need your help," Layne said. "What do you know about plutonium?"

"In what context?"

"We collected soil samples that demonstrated the presence of plutonium-238, 239, and 240."

Locker fell silent for several long seconds.

"What about iodine-131, strontium-90, and cesium-137?" he finally asked.

"Negative."

"Where are you?"

"South Texas," Mason said. "Right on the border."

"I guess that makes sense, given the context," Locker said, "but definitely not where I'd set up a PUREX processing lab, if you know what I'm saying."

The problem with talking to Locker was that he tended to start a conversation at a random point only he knew and jump around in ways that might have made sense inside his mind, but tended to make those around him dizzy.

"Not even close."

"Weaponized plutonium is really quite stable and doesn't cause significant environmental exposure outside of its immediate vicinity, especially if it's properly housed and stored, and it's not like just anyone can get their hands on it. Any kind of measurable soil contamination likely means you're dealing with the waste products of a reclamation project that somehow got into the groundwater, which means you have a serious problem. More to the point, *we all* have a serious problem."

"That's why we're calling," Layne said. "We need to know what we're up against."

"You can't just dig up plutonium and make it into a bomb," Locker said. "You need massive quantities of uranium and a nuclear reactor to produce it, so if you wanted to get your hands on enough to build a weapon, the easiest way to do so would be by isolating it from nuclear waste."

"Walk me through it," Mason said.

"Most commercial reactors use low-enriched uranium-235, which is compressed into pellets, stacked inside fuel rods, and loaded into a reactor that bombards them with neutrons to split the atomic nuclei and release massive amounts of heat. That's fission in a nutshell. Once that fuel rod's exhausted, what's left is roughly ninety-eight percent U-238 and other stable by-products, plus residual amounts of U-235 and plutonium-239. That plutonium is considered highly enriched, but not quite weapons-grade. And while there's not very much of it, it can be collected and reprocessed into pellets or cakes using the PUREX process."

The urban landscape gave way to crops and shrubland, followed by several blocks lined with run-down strip malls, behind which residential housing stretched off into the night.

"What makes you so certain we're dealing with spent fuel rods?" Layne asked.

"The presence of plutonium-240, first of all. It's a by-product of reclaiming plutonium-239 from reactor-bred plutonium, not of its direct enrichment. Plus, the nuclear industry is so tightly regulated that every single atom produced by a breeder reactor is accounted for. Not to mention the fact that it's a hugely expensive and volatile process, as the army learned out at Rocky Flats in Colorado. The concentrations of isotopic iodine, cesium, and plutonium in the soil where the plants once stood are so high to this day, thirty years later, that you can't get within half a mile of it. And most importantly, any reasonably competent chemist with the ability to follow a recipe and access to chemicals you can find at just about any hardware store could do it in his garage if he were able to get ahold of some spent fuel rods, which is basically the whole premise of the North Korean nuclear program."

"Aren't the spent fuel rods as closely regulated as the new ones?"

"At that point they're classified as 'high-level waste,' not nuclear fuel, and there are literally tens of thousands of them stored in water baths and dry casks at every nuclear plant in the world, with no actual plan as to how to house them beyond the immediate future. And they're breeding plutonium as fast as they're using it, so there's no incentive to recycle the rods, which take a decade to cool off anyway."

"That doesn't explain how someone could acquire them," Mason said.

"Think about the countries that continually produce nuclear waste but aren't subjected to the same regulation and oversight as we are, countries like Pakistan and the United Arab Emirates or even China and India. Russia is a case study in disaster all by itself, with the Soviet Union falling apart right in the middle of the evolution of nuclear energy and the government losing control of nearly every aspect of its arsenal, including guns and Lord only knows what else. Not to mention its commercial waste products. Heck, anyone ambitious enough to brave the fallout at Fukushima Daiichi could have plucked the rods right out of the cooling tanks and no one would have ever known with as many as were found washed out to sea."

"So what about this PUREX process?"

A sign announced they were entering the town of Hidalgo about the same time the GPS stated that in one mile they'd use any lane to continue onto International Boulevard.

"All you really have to do is collect the pellets from the fuel rods, dissolve them in nitric acid to separate the uranium-235 and plutonium-239, and then mix them with kerosene and tributyl phosphate to trap them. From there, it's a simple chemical process of reduction, extraction, and vitrification to create a solid, glasslike chunk that's about ninety-three percent plutonium-239, a fissile isotope with a half-life of twenty-four thousand years, the ability to produce an absurd amount of kinetic energy and heat, and the smallest critical mass of any material capable of sustaining a nuclear chain reaction, which means you could literally produce a nuclear device the size of the Fat Man bomb we dropped on Nagasaki with as little as twelve pounds. And trust me when I say you have to be producing at least that much to contaminate the groundwater, let alone soil any distance away from the lab."

"So why aren't we faced with this kind of threat on a daily basis?" Mason asked. "There are plenty of rogue regimes out there who hate us. Most of them even have their own reactors."

"The biggest problem is that the process is inherently hazardous. It produces a small amount of plutonium-240, which, in an attempt to return to a stable isotopic state, releases excess energy in the form of neutron radiation."

"Which should make it easier to detect once we're within range."

"True, but you're missing the big picture," Locker said. "Even the emission of a single neutron can destabilize the fissile material, causing it to detonate prematurely. Wherever that plutonium is now, it's a ticking time bomb that could go off at any second."

18

"We have a serious problem," Mason said as soon as Archer answered the phone.

Traffic on International Boulevard slowed to a crawl as they neared the green awning signifying the entrance to McAllen-Hidalgo International Bridge, on the other side of which was the Mexican town of Reynosa.

"That's about the last thing in the world I wanted to hear," the secretary of the Department of Homeland Security said.

"Which doesn't change the fact at all."

"Spit it out already."

"Your suspicions were spot-on: Austin was murdered. We were able to access a picture of his killer from the memory card on the scope of his rifle, but it doesn't show any identifiable details. I'll have Layne send it to you directly."

"Way ahead of you," she said.

Mason glanced over at the screen of his laptop, which rested on his partner's thighs. She'd already attached the image and was in the process of composing the header.

"Austin was definitely onto something. You read his reports, right? We took samples of the soil from the various locations where the crops had withered and the animals had died and had them tested—"

"I thought the insurance company already did that," Archer said.

"It tested for chemical agents, not radiological."

Archer was silent for so long that Mason had to check to make sure he hadn't dropped the call.

"Mr. Secretary?" Layne said.

"I need details," Archer said.

"The director of the crime lab in McAllen made the connection," Mason said. "Had he not, we probably would have just run the soil samples through the GC-MS again, and not the XRF spectrometer, which confirmed the presence of plutonium-238, 239, and 240, the combination of which suggests we're dealing with an unknown quantity of fissile material reclaimed from spent fuel rods."

"You're certain?" he said. "My team in Playa del Carmen picked up traces of radiation on Langbroek's boat, but nothing along those lines."

"Unfortunately, that's about the only thing we *are* certain of," Layne said. "We can't even begin to guess how much plutonium is out there, let alone where it is. Whoever's responsible has at least a seven-month head start on us, so it could easily be anywhere in the world by now."

"So what's your plan from here?" Archer asked.

"Austin noted three more sites in Mexico," Mason said. "The source of the environmental contamination has to be somewhere nearby. Once we find the lab where they're processing the fuel rods, we'll hopefully be able to figure out who's reclaiming the plutonium and where they've taken it."

"Most of the cops down there are owned by the cartels. The moment you start asking questions, you'll be putting bull's-eyes right in the center of your chests."

"Understood."

"And you're going to have a hell of a time getting back across the border."

"We don't have much of a choice in the matter, do we?" Layne said.

"Keep me posted," Archer said. "I want to know everything you know the moment you know it."

He terminated the call as the Explorer passed through the CBP checkpoint and crossed over the Rio Grande. They entered Mexico several seconds later and approached the customs and security gate, where agents in black uniforms checked their identification, examined their undercarriage with a mirrored pole, and paced circles around their car with a canine unit. Mason and Layne showed their passports instead of their badges and sold the story that they'd rented the SUV with the intention of taking a road trip along the Gulf. The last thing they wanted was a corrupt agent tipping off the cartels to the presence of federal agents in their midst. Besides, both of them hoped to be long gone by the time anyone even knew they were here.

Alejandra was waiting in the greenbelt where the traffic from the American side let out. She tossed her backpack onto the rear seat and climbed in behind it. Mason caught a glimpse of her scarred face in the rearview mirror. It had been months since he'd seen her last. Gone was the spark of life he'd grown accustomed to seeing in her eyes. She looked older, harder, much like she had when he'd first met her. And it made him sad.

The computerized voice of the GPS guided them south through the city to Federal Highway 2, which would take them all the way to Ciudad Camargo, across the border from Rio Grande City.

"Tell me why I am here," Alejandra said.

"The border patrol agent in charge of the Rio Grande City Station reported a series of incidents involving dead crops and livestock," Mason said. "When he didn't get the response he wanted from his immediate superiors, he ran his concerns all the way up the chain to Rand Marchment. Three days later, he died in a fire inside his home. It was ruled an accident, but we learned that he was killed by the same directed-energy weapon as Slate Langbroek."

"What does that have to do with Cártel de Jalisco Nueva Generación?"

"We discovered traces of isotopic plutonium that we suspect are the result of someone attempting to reclaim fissile material from spent fuel rods," Layne said. "And we believe the lab responsible is just this side of the border."

"Nothing happens this side of the border without the approval of the cártel," Alejandra said.

"Exactly, which is why we think the Thirteen cut a deal to use CJNG's existing infrastructure."

"I can see Ismael Zambada or the sons of El Chapo negotiating with the Thirteen on behalf of Cártel de Sinaloa," Alejandra said. "They are practical businessmen who know how to play the long game, which is the reason they have been able to survive for four decades, while so many rivals have come and gone. El Mencho does not cut deals, though. The leader of CJNG is as ruthless as he is brutal. He controls half of the drug plazas on the border, nearly all of the Gulf shipping ports, and slaughters anyone who tries to move in on his business. He is not threatened by any single border patrol agent and even the Thirteen have nothing to offer that he cannot simply take for himself, unless . . ."

Her voice trailed off. Mason glanced at her reflection in the rearview mirror. Her brow furrowed and her lips moved, as though silently working through a complex equation. He waited her out.

"CJNG is essentially one of the largest private corporations in

Mexico," she said. "As one of the most powerful cartels, it fixes drug prices and sets its own profit margins, doing for narcotics what OPEC did for oil in the seventies. It has more than fifty billion dollars in assets, not including the hidden labs it uses to cook methamphetamines, but what it does not have is legitimacy. Unlike other successful corporations, it cannot spend its money without washing it first. That is what El Cuini, the brother-in-law of El Mencho, did for CJNG before we took him down. We have since frozen thousands of bank accounts and closed many front companies in an effort to cripple the organization. If there is one thing the Thirteen could offer El Mencho that he desperately needed, it would be to launder his money."

"And in exchange, he could offer the Thirteen a lab to process the spent fuel rods and the means of smuggling the resultant fissile material across the border," Mason said.

"Not to mention a sizable cut of CJNG's profits," Layne said.

"So we're dealing with a member of the Thirteen who has ready access to the banking industry and the ability to circumvent regulations," Mason said.

"And an unknown amount of weapons-grade plutonium."

"We need to find that lab if we hope to have any chance of figuring out what they intend to do with it."

"The lab will be heavily guarded," Alejandra said. "We should be prepared to be met with, as you said, resistance."

Layne brought up the satellite map of the area that fell along Austin's line and zoomed in as far as she could go. Based upon the topography, the dead cornfield was likely one of six irregularly shaped plots of land covering the mile-long stretch heading southwest from the U.S. border. The chicken farm was probably on one of the narrow properties separating them. There was just one possible location for the building reportedly filled with cat and rat carcasses, however. The only suitable locations that fell along that line for fifteen miles were in a residential development consisting of seven parallel streets, each one block in length and packed with houses, side-to-side and back-to-back, the majority of which appeared on satellite and aerial imagery to have been abandoned. Most had collapsed roofs, fallen walls, and graffiti on every visible surface. The few remaining residents, if there were any, could be counted on not to see or hear anything, let alone report it to the authorities, who probably wouldn't even come if they were called.

It was a solid staging ground from which to smuggle a radiological weapon of mass destruction across the border.

Telephone lines paralleled the highway, the drainage ditches separating them from the asphalt wild with weeds and willow saplings. Snarls of vegetation planted as windbreaks concealed the fields to the right, while rows of mounded dirt raced past to the left, shimmering like the sea beneath the moonlight. The GPS instructed them to turn left and head north for three miles, into the brushland. Small towns defined by run-down warehouses and smoke-shrouded factories blew past. A slight right and they were heading northeast through the countryside once more.

"There have to be a couple hundred houses crammed into an area the size of a single city block," Layne said. "I don't even know where to begin."

Mason watched the right side of the road for their destination, which the computer voice promised was only a thousand feet ahead. The deciduous trees lining the Rio Grande river materialized from the horizon. The spot where they'd found the javelinas was roughly a mile to the northeast, the Robinson Ranch another mile past that. He slowed as he approached the turn without seeing a single light. The houses themselves were barely visible through the trees separating them from the highway.

"I don't like this," he said.

"Neither do I," Layne replied.

There was no sign of life. Mason rolled down his window, and even then heard little more than the buzz of the Explorer's tires on the road and the rustle of the wind through the trees. They passed a gravel road that wended off into fields left to grow feral with tumbleweeds and thornbushes. The entrance to the development was just past a sign covered with overlapping graffiti. A concrete building that must have once served as the office squatted lifelessly on the other side, its front doors and windows missing, its facade tagged with illegible words, its parking lot overgrown with thistles.

"This is the place," Alejandra said, assembling the stripped Colt M1911 from her bag. "I can feel it. Be ready for anything."

Mason turned onto the narrow street and followed the headlights into a development that looked to have been completely deserted. There wasn't a single car parked along the street all the way to where it ended against a wall of trees.

"Keep your eyes open," he said.

Layne drew her Glock and chambered a round. She sensed it, too. Something wasn't right.

The Explorer coasted toward the intersecting street, from which six parallel roads branched, three to the north and three to the south. He was suddenly acutely aware of the fact that there was only one way into and out of the project, and once he turned, he would no longer be able to see it.

19

The roads were more gravel than asphalt and riddled with potholes. There were no sidewalks, only slender strips of waist-high weeds growing right up against dwellings that resembled adjoined mobile homes, their boxlike facades staggered and painted different colors to make them appear separate. There wasn't a single window or door left. The glow of the Explorer's high beams did little to illuminate the interiors of the single-room structures, the majority of which were decorated with spray-painted graffiti and contained shadows deep enough to conceal any number of people.

"It doesn't look like anyone's lived here in a decade," Layne said.

"This is the only development along Austin's line," Mason said. "The building where he documented the dead rats has to be out here somewhere."

The central east-west street ended at another perpendicular branch, on the other side of which was a seemingly impenetrable forest of creosotes and mesquites. Mason turned left and stared down the gap between the backs of the houses, which was barely wide enough to contain the salt cedars and knapweed that had claimed the rear porches and overcome the concrete-block dividers. He turned left again and headed down a road nearly identical to the last.

"The rules of engagement are different here," Alejandra said. "*Sicarios* do not hesitate; you must shoot first and ask questions later. If you become separated or injured, you cannot allow yourself to be taken alive. They will rape you, set you on fire, flay your skin—"

"Worse things will happen to a lot more people if we don't find that lab," Mason said. "We need to figure out how much plutonium they were able to reclaim and where it is now."

He turned right at the end of the road, passed another sliver of tiny backyards, and veered right down the next row. There was one more street north of them, beyond which satellite imagery showed only a few isolated farms hidden among the irrigated fields and undeveloped acreages.

Alejandra tugged on a black balaclava that revealed only her eyes, the same one she had been wearing in the video from Playa del Carmen. She caught Mason's stare in the rearview mirror.

"You know the war is already lost when the good guys are the ones wearing masks," she said.

The roofs of several of the houses on their left had collapsed, the rubble accumulated in the doorways and interiors, the sparse moonlight illuminating—

A shadow passed over a ragged section of plaster.

"Did you see that?" Mason whispered. He resisted the urge to hit the brake so as not to betray that he'd sensed something was amiss. "Over there, on the left. I saw movement through the front door."

He craned his neck in an effort to look upward through the empty doorways and windows, toward the roofline of the houses behind them. A silhouette appeared against the sky, only to disappear again.

"There's someone on the roof of the house in the next row," he whispered.

"If we turn left at the end of the street, our only option will be to turn left again," Layne whispered. "We'll be driving right through his sights, but if we turn right and break the pattern, he'll know we're onto him."

Mason's federal cell phone vibrated to alert him to an incoming message. His laptop chimed a split second later. Whatever was going on, he wasn't in a position to deal with it now.

"We have to force him to make his move on our terms, not his," he whispered.

He released the steering wheel, unbuckled his seat belt, and hit the button to kill the interior light.

"What the hell are you—"

Mason opened his door and stepped out. Rolled to absorb the impact. Used the momentum to spring to his feet and sprint through the front door of the nearest house.

Layne's silhouette passed across the rear windshield as she climbed over the console and assumed the driver's seat. She closed the door with a faint click and braked as she neared the end of the street.

Mason waited just long enough to make sure she recognized what he intended to do. The moment she turned left, he ran through the small house and out the hole where the rear door had once been, propelled himself up the back wall of the house behind it, and scurried onto the roof.

As he'd expected, the shadow he'd seen from below had run to the last house in the row, perched like a gargoyle at the front corner, and seated a Kalashnikov against his shoulder. The man would have been invisible in his black hooded sweatshirt and jeans had he not been silhouetted by the headlights of the Explorer as it rounded the corner.

Mason lowered his shoulder and raced toward him from behind. He needed to take the man out of the equation before he could get off a shot and alert the entire compound, if he hadn't already.

Movement from the corner of his eye.

Too late, he realized his mistake. The man in front of him could have easily fired straight down and turned the Explorer into Swiss cheese while it was still on the side street. The only reason to wait and allow it to turn the corner was if he was trying to lead it into the cross fire of a second—

Discharge flashed from the muzzle of a rifle directly across the street. Bullets struck the front of the house and ricocheted from the rooftop, right behind Mason's heels.

The man in the hoodie rounded on him, his eyes wide and white through the holes in his ski mask. Mason hit him squarely in the chest and drove him to the ground, slamming the side of his head against the raised ledge. The man tried to raise his rifle, but Mason pinned his arm to his side and rolled away—

A strobe of discharge from across the street.

Mason felt the impact of the bullets pounding the man's back.

Staccato bursts from a semiautomatic pistol interrupted the mechanized thrum of the second man's Kalashnikov.

Mason shoved the body from on top of him and over the edge of the roof. He raised his head just in time to see the man across the street lifted into the air, his rifle spitting bullets up at the stars. Below him, Layne had contorted her torso out of the driver's-side window and continued firing even as the car bounced up into the weeds, where the bumper came to rest against the front of a house.

There was no time to waste. If there were any other sentries, they were undoubtedly already on their way.

Again, his phone vibrated inside his jacket.

He swung his legs over the side and gripped the edge of the roof. He was just about to let go when he saw a gravel road through a gap in the trees to the east, one that had been invisible beneath the canopy on the satellite map.

"Hurry up!" Layne shouted.

Mason dropped, landed in a crouch, and sprung back to his feet. He hurried to catch up with his partner, who was already backing the SUV onto the road and swinging around to face him. The headlights swept across the body of the man in the hoodie, reflecting from the pool of blood beneath him. Mason tore off the man's mask and looked upon a face made inhuman by the sheer quantity of tattoos, despite which he could tell the gunman couldn't have been much older than fifteen or sixteen.

The Explorer screeched to a halt beside him.

"What are you waiting for?" Layne said. The passenger window had been shattered, the side panel pocked with bullet holes. She leaned across the console and opened the door. "Get in!"

Mason climbed up onto the seat and closed the door. His laptop chimed from the floorboards and his phone vibrated again. He pulled it out of his pocket and glanced at the screen. He'd received multiple messages from an anonymous number, each of which consisted of the same three words: GET OUT NOW!

"Anomaly," he said. "The Thirteen know we're here."

"They are not the only ones," Alejandra said.

A glow appeared from the dirt road through the trees. It grew brighter and brighter as it streaked toward them and resolved into the headlights of a pickup truck with an array of spotlights on its roof.

"Everyone buckle up," Layne said.

She bared her teeth and pinned the gas pedal to the floor. The Explorer rocketed forward, heading straight toward the vehicle bearing down on them.

"What the hell are you doing?" Mason asked.

"They'll move."

"You're out of your mind!"

The pickup accelerated toward them. A flicker of discharge erupted from above its roofline, where Mason saw the outline of a man standing in the bed, clinging to one of the spotlights. A fusillade of bullets sparked from the hood and impacted the windshield, spiderwebbing the glass right in front of his face.

"They'll move," Layne said again.

Two shapes took form inside the front seat of the truck, little more than shadows behind the onrushing headlights.

Mason raised his pistol, braced himself, and fired straight through the windshield, which disintegrated into balled glass that struck his face and chest. He shielded his eyes with his left hand and continued firing with his right until his clip ran dry.

The truck's headlights vanished below the level of the Explorer's grille. The driver clasped his neck and jerked the wheel to the side.

Layne adjusted ever so slightly to her right, tearing through branches that slashed at Mason through the frame where the windshield had been, filling his lap with twigs and leaves.

There wasn't enough room for the truck to pass on their left. The driver's-side mirror of the Explorer snapped off and tumbled across the roof. Sparks filled the air as the sidewalls of the two vehicles met, going fifty miles an hour in opposite directions. The pickup's bumper clipped the trunk of a tree and the tailgate flipped up into the air. The entire vehicle cartwheeled down the road behind them, its headlights and taillights alternately flashing in the rearview mirror.

Layne jammed the brakes and skidded to a halt.

Mason jacked his spent clip and slammed home another. He threw open the door and climbed out into a haze of dust, stained red by their taillights.

The pickup rested upside down on its roof, facing away from them, its tires spinning impotently on bent axles. The gunman who'd been standing in the bed had been ejected. A trail of blood led down the road toward where his legs protruded from the underbrush. His upper half was another twenty feet away, spotlighted by the solitary functional headlight. The two men inside the cab were in little better shape. The driver had taken a bullet to the throat, just below his chin, and an airbag to the face with enough force to tear the wound wide open. The passenger was still in his seat, pinned by the airbag and immobilized by the seat belt, which might have saved his life had the impact with the tree not driven the engine block into his lap.

They wouldn't be getting any information out of these guys.

"How did Anomaly know we were here?" Layne asked. "And why would he try to warn us?"

"Worry about that later," Alejandra said. "More men will be coming—"

Wood splintered from the trunk of the tree beside her before they even heard the crack of gunfire.

Mason hit the deck and scrambled into the undergrowth, bullets chewing up the earth behind him. He caught a flash of discharge from across the road and came up firing. His first shot elicited a shout of pain; his second ended it. He scurried deeper into the forest as automatic gunfire shredded the shrubbery behind him.

Alejandra moved through his peripheral vision, stealthily taking up position behind the inverted pickup. A shadow emerged from the woods. She put a bullet through its head and ducked back down before return fire pounded the vehicle, popping the tires and shattering the remaining glass.

Mason used the discharge to zero in on their locations. Three men with Kalashnikovs: two walking straight up the road, one cutting through the trees to his right, maybe twenty feet away. He ran straight toward the man attempting to outflank them, firing as he went. Hit him squarely in the chest and ducked behind a trunk before the remaining hostiles could draw a bead on him. Bullets tore through the branches all around him. He dove onto his side and sighted down the nearest enemy—

Layne fired a tight cluster into the man's center mass before Mason could pull the trigger.

The final *sicario* squeezed off a barrage of steel to cover his retreat and ran away from them. Alejandra stepped out from behind the pickup and shot him squarely in the back. He landed on his chest and skidded through the gravel. His feet scraped uselessly at the dirt.

She strode to his side and rolled him over with her boot.

"*¿Quántos más de ustedes hay?*" she shouted, planting her foot on his chest and aiming straight down at his face. "How many more of you are there?"

He sputtered a mouthful of blood and offered a single shake of his head.

Alejandra raised her left hand to shield her face from the blowback and pulled the trigger. The report echoed away into nothingness.

Mason could only stare at the back of a woman he no longer knew as she returned to the Explorer.

"Like I said," she whispered, "the rules of engagement are different down here."

20

The dirt road traced the contours of the topography until it reached an opening in the forest, through which they caught a glimpse of a homestead, barely visible downhill. There appeared to be five buildings concealed beneath the dense canopy of deciduous trees, which had hidden them from satellite imagery. It was obvious from their condition and the untended growth in the distant fields that the place had been abandoned for some time. There was no sign of movement or a trap waiting to be sprung, yet Mason's gut told him that something wasn't right.

"If these guys have a DEW, they could hit us through the walls of any one of those buildings without being able to see us," he said. "We'd be dead before we even felt our skin start to heat up."

"If they had such a weapon, they would have used it already," Alejandra said. "The cártels are not known for their restraint. They would have hit us the moment we turned from the highway."

"We'll take a stealthy approach," Layne said. "They might not need to be able to see us to hit us, but they still need to know where we are."

She released the brake and the Explorer coasted to the edge of a windswept clearing enclosed by a horseshoe of man-made structures. To their right was a run-down farmhouse, its porch and roof sagging with water damage. Beside it was a small stable that was little more than a covered patch of bare dirt. A barn sat off in the trees at the end of the cul-de-sac, its doors standing wide open upon the empty bay where the men had presumably parked their truck to prevent it from being seen from the air. The corrugated aluminum outbuilding next to it was streaked with rust and weakened by the elements, unlike the adjacent prefabricated structure, which couldn't have been more than a few years old.

Layne turned around and parked facing the road in case they needed to get out of there in a hurry. They drew their weapons and climbed out into the cool night. The first hint of the coming dawn bloomed from the horizon, where a faint blue stain spread through the treetops.

"We clear the buildings one at a time," she whispered. "Starting with the house and working our way around. I'll go through the front. Mason, you take the back. Allie: Watch the rooftops and the tree line and make sure they aren't using a spotter for someone with a DEW inside one of the structures."

Mason nodded and scampered off into the woods, around the side of the house, and to the back porch. The door was broken and stood slightly ajar. He nudged it open with the toe of his boot and followed his Glock into the mudroom, which gave way to a kitchen that reeked of cigarette smoke. The sink was spotted with orange-rimmed burns and the beer bottles on the table were overflowing with butts. The tile in the hallway had been ripped up and the bedroom stripped to the bare floorboards. Layne had just secured the main room and the front hallway when he caught up with her. They exited through the same doors by which they'd entered and cleared the stable without more than a cursory glance into the decrepit wooden structure, which couldn't have housed more than a few goats or sheep.

With the barn doors open, they could clearly see there was no one hiding in the loft. The ground inside was discolored by oil stains and what appeared to be enough dried blood to convince Mason that he didn't want to know what had happened to the poor souls who'd visited this place against their will.

There was only one entrance into the aluminum building, a flimsy door held in place by a padlock that Mason lacked the skill set to pick, but a few solid kicks were enough to wrench the hasp from the rusted metal. The door slid open on its runners, revealing twin layers of plastic sheeting that had been stretched across the opening from the inside.

His breath caught in his chest. He'd encountered a similar setup at the rock quarry in Arizona where they'd first discovered the victims of the Hoyl's virus hanging in wooden stalls, left to rot.

He turned on his mini Maglite and aligned it with his pistol, parted the sheeting, and ducked into a massive space illuminated by the open vents and the cracks between the warped ceiling panels. The astringent scent of chemicals made his eyes water and burned inside his chest. Elbow-length rubber gloves and full-body CBRN suits hung from the wall to his left.

"Document everything," he whispered.

Hundreds, if not thousands, of metallic tubes, roughly thirteen feet long and as wide as his pinkie, had been bundled and stacked against the wall beside a particleboard workbench. The caps, springs, and aluminum pellets that had once sealed them and maintained the proper pressure on the contents had been sorted into buckets. The racks against the side wall were stuffed with industrial-size containers of kerosene and brown glass bottles of tributyl phosphate. Piled beside them were fifty-five-gallon drums of nitric acid, several of which had been emptied, repurposed, and dragged into the center of the room beside a decklike platform made of two-by-fours. The slurry of chemicals in the bottom looked like it could dissolve steel.

Layne's cell phone camera flashed behind him, casting his shadow onto the massive ovens aligned at the back of the building, their horizontal doors resting open to reveal the ceramic blocks inside.

"This is where they've been harvesting the plutonium from the spent fuel rods," Mason said.

"How did they get so many?"

Mason could only shake his head. This was way beyond his limited understanding of the process, which was theoretical at best. He'd never seen a functional nuclear laboratory, let alone a jury-rigged version capable of performing the PUREX process under conditions that made a meth lab look like a model of safety and sanitation. The entire place had to be radioactive, its waste undoubtedly the source of the contamination that had caused the deaths of the animals and crops. Worse, it was also responsible for the production of an unknown amount of weapons-grade plutonium-239.

DOE 3013 containers designed to ship radioisotopes were stacked on pallets to his right. The outermost of the nested sleeves were labeled with lines resembling bar codes. A quick glance confirmed they were all empty.

"If the plutonium's not here, then where is it?" Layne asked.

"I hope to God it's in the building next door," Mason said. "If not, there's no telling where it might be by now."

He hurried out of the lab, rounded the corner, and converged on the lone entrance to the prefabricated unit at the same time as Alejandra. She took up position beside the door, gripped the handle, and nodded her readiness. He pressed his back to the wall on the opposite side of the doorway and waited for Layne to do the same before starting a silent countdown with his fingers.

Three.

Two.

One.

Alejandra threw open the door and automatic gunfire erupted from inside, kicking up the dirt between them and whanging from the interior walls.

Panic fire. Untrained. Undisciplined.

Mason rolled out from behind the wall and started firing. His first shot took the black-clad man in the gut, his second the chest, his third the forehead. He stepped over the corpse and sighted down the warehouse, listening for any sound that might betray the presence of someone lying in wait.

A forklift was parked between pallets of marijuana, bound in cellophane packages the size of pillows and stacked nearly to the ceiling. There were thousands of bricks of cocaine as thick as bibles, sacks of pills and the powders they used to cut and repackage them. There were even bundles of greenbacks and pesos, all sorted and shrink-wrapped and waiting to be shipped in crates large enough to haul watermelons. It reminded Mason of the CBP's evidence warehouse at Ajo Station in the Sonoran Desert, where the border patrol catalogued and stored the drugs they'd confiscated on their way into the country. There had to be tens of millions of dollars' worth of products and cash in this one building alone.

Unfortunately, there were no DOE 3013 containers in sight and there was no telling when any amount of plutonium had last been here. For all they knew, the lab could have been abandoned seven months ago when Austin first started putting the pieces together and the nuclear arsenal the Thirteen had been building was long gone, but if that were the case, then why would Anomaly attempt to warn them off? Surely it couldn't have been to save their skins, unless he was using them as pawns in the civil war waging within his organization, in which case they could neither trust nor anticipate his motivations.

"We're missing something," Layne whispered as they advanced between the narrow aisles.

Mason sensed it, too. Nothing about this setup made sense from a trafficking perspective.

"I can't think of a worse place from which to run a distribution center," he whispered. "There's only one road leading into or out of the housing project. Trucks coming and going at all hours of the day and night would be noticed right away. And you saw the condition of the road coming back here. It wouldn't stand up to regular use. They must be using some other means of moving their product."

Mason reevaluated his surroundings with that new understanding in mind. All of the drugs—even the marijuana—were bound in small enough packages that a single man could easily transport them, unlike the bales he remembered seeing in Arizona.

"They're smuggling this stuff on foot," he said.

"There are agents all over the other side of the border," Layne said. "I can see them stuffing backpacks with fentanyl, but crossing the Rio Grande with a container full of plutonium is another thing entirely. The moment the DHS found a single gram of weaponized nuclear material on the American side of the border, it would descend upon this area with every agent at its disposal. It would be an invasion the likes of which this country has never seen before, one that would strangle the distribution lines of the cartels, which might have some of the most ferocious foot soldiers on the planet, but even they wouldn't be anything close to a match for the U.S. military."

"You're right," Mason said. He furrowed his brow as he tried to chase an elusive thought. He felt as though he were on the brink of a revelation.

"Why'd you say it like that?" Layne asked, but he didn't respond; he was already searching for something he suddenly knew had to be around here somewhere.

"What are you looking for?" Alejandra asked.

Mason found the gouges on the dirt floor near the back of the building, where one of the pallets had been repeatedly dragged aside. He knocked over the tower of cannabis on top of it and lifted it to reveal the hole in the floor.

"Well, what do you know?" Layne said.

21

Mason shone his flashlight down into a chute that reached well beyond the range of his beam. Between the tunnel leading to the slaughterhouse where the Hoyl had tested his virus on undocumented aliens and the subway lines through which he'd tracked the Scarecrow, he'd seen enough of such suffocating confines to last a lifetime.

"You must realize there are narcos down there right now," Alejandra said. "Good cártel soldiers trying to smuggle everything they can carry to the other side before we seal the tunnel."

Mason nodded. He didn't need her to remind him what awaited them down there in the darkness. He'd spent a full year of his life tracking the trafficking lanes of the various cartels in search of the Hoyl and learned all about tunnels like this one. And considering the relationship between this investigation and the manhunt for the Scarecrow, it was possible that any number of traps had been rigged along the way.

"We need to find the plutonium," he said.

"It's possible they've been stockpiling it down there," Layne said.

"I hope you are right," Alejandra said. "If not, it is long gone."

"Keep your weapons trained on that tunnel," Mason said. "I'll be right back."

He turned and ran back to the car. There was no way he was leaving his computer behind. If he was right about where the tunnel let out, they wouldn't be seeing the Explorer again, not that he'd miss it. The bumper was crushed, the left headlight smashed, and the side panels riddled with bullet holes. There was hardly any paint left and it didn't look like the back door would open without the jaws of life.

Mason hurried around to the passenger side, opened the door, and stuffed his laptop into its hardshell case. He slung the strap over his head and shoulder and checked to make sure there wasn't anything else he needed before running back into the warehouse, where Alejandra and Layne waited, their guns sighted on the darkness below them.

"You really think this goes all the way across the border?" Layne asked.

"Surely it will at least take us as far as the river," Alejandra said.

Mason stepped between them and shone his light down between

his feet. The hole was perfectly square and paneled with sheets of plywood supported by a framework of pipes. An extension ladder led down into the pitch-black depths. He bit the end of his flashlight to hold it in place and started his descent, one hand on the rungs, the other aiming his pistol past his heels and into the darkness. The ladder shook with every step and felt like it could collapse at any second, especially once Layne and Alejandra mounted it above him. Their footsteps echoed as though from a well.

He had to be thirty feet down by the time he reached the bottom. The light from the surface was a memory, the air colder, heavier, and considerably more humid. It smelled of damp earth and mildew. The wood paneling was soggy and misshapen and looked like it had been down here for years. He couldn't even begin to fathom the sheer quantity of drugs that had been pumped through this pipeline during that time.

Mason's beam limned the mouth of a tunnel heading away from him and to the northeast, the same direction as the line that connected the incidents Austin had reported. He ducked inside and traced the contours of a rectangular space about the width of his shoulders and just tall enough for him to be able to walk in a crouch. The earthen walls were rocky, damp with condensation, and gouged by the sharp end of a pickaxe. Crumbling sections had been reinforced with wooden cribbing, like a mineshaft, but for the most part it appeared structurally sound, or at least that was what he told himself.

Time passed slowly as they walked, their heavy breathing echoing around them, potentially masking the subtle sounds of a *sicario* lurking just beyond the range of their flashlights or a man in a fireproof suit preparing to release a deadly beam of radiation from a directed-energy weapon. Mason kept his eyes peeled for motion detectors, photocells, and trip wires, anything that could be used to trigger whatever traps might have been laid for anyone who didn't know exactly how to circumvent them.

"We've got to be getting close to the river by now," Layne whispered. Her voice had a quality of finality, as though she were speaking from inside her grave. "The walls are getting damper by the minute."

Mason nodded his agreement. He suspected that the tunnel would let out before it reached the Rio Grande, somewhere near the outcropping he'd noticed yesterday, where the river narrowed to such an extent that they'd be able to wade across and disappear into the trees on the American side within a matter of seconds. Surely tunneling underneath it would be overly ambitious, even for the Jalisco New Generation Cartel; not only would the logistics be daunting, they'd be lucky to find earth that was solid enough to hold its form, unless they attempted to drill through the bedrock, in which case surely someone on the other side would have noticed.

They settled into a rhythm, their footsteps striking first in time, then in opposition, before aligning once more. Mason's shoulders burned from simultaneously ducking his head and holding his pistol and flashlight raised in front of him. He glanced back sparingly at Layne and Alejandra, who alternated walking forward and backward to make sure that no one was trying to sneak up behind them.

The ceiling lowered so subtly that at first he didn't notice, at least not until he hit the crown of his head for the third time. Puddles started to accumulate in the recesses on the ground. He felt as much as heard a faint humming sound.

"Is that the river?" Layne whispered.

"I don't think so," Mason whispered. "The sound's too rhythmic, too mechanical."

"What else could it be?"

He hesitated to speculate. The way he saw it, anything that caused vibrations was just about the last thing in the world they wanted with thirty feet of earth above their heads and not another soul on the planet who knew where they were.

Rivulets of water trickled down the walls, reflecting their beams. Droplets rained from the ceiling. The thrumming sound grew louder, the vibrations more intense. He smelled the faintest hint of smoke and burning oil, a motor of some kind. He was reminded of standing on the opposite bank of the river and listening to what he'd thought at the time was an oil derrick somewhere beyond the trees lining the far bank.

"Careful," he whispered.

The ground grew muddy and slick and the standing water rose above the tops of his boots. A black rubber pipe crested the surface like a sea serpent's back. The reflection of his flashlight beam shimmered from the ripples radiating from it. He finally understood what was creating the sound.

"It's a water pump," he whispered.

There was only one good reason they'd need one down here. He was about to share his observation when the answer became obvious. The tunnel terminated at the mouth of a massive pipe protruding from earth braced with chicken wire and aluminum posts. It was the same kind of PVC pipe that construction companies used for oil and natural gas lines, black and maybe three-and-a-half feet in diameter. Water dribbled from the lip and accumulated in the knee-deep pool below it.

"Jesus," Layne whispered.

Mason knew exactly what she meant.

It was the perfect place for an ambush.

The prospect of slithering through there on his belly for any length of time made his stomach clench. They'd be fish in a barrel inside that tube. He crouched to the side, careful not to make himself an easy target, and shone his light inside, but the beam diffused before reaching the far end. He pried a rock from the wall, stepped back, and threw it side-armed into the tunnel. It skipped a half-dozen times before the sound faded to nothingness.

"It has to be at least fifty feet long," he whispered.

"What's that over there?" Layne whispered.

He followed her line of sight to the wall on the opposite side of the pipe. At first, it looked like someone had tried to brace the chicken wire with a bunch of weathered planks. And then he saw the wheels bolted to the bottom of them. He darted across the opening and lifted the closest one out of the water. Mud drained from the rear coupling. He glanced up at Alejandra and Layne, who nodded their understanding. The narcos transported drugs through the pipe on these makeshift skateboards. If they used them in a similar manner, the added speed would at least minimize their exposure.

"If there's anyone waiting to ambush us on the other side—" Layne whispered, but Mason cut her off.

"Then they've already seen our lights and know we're here. They could have shot me the moment I directed my beam through that pipe. Fifty feet is nothing, even to a marginally skilled marksman."

"Are you willing to gamble our lives on that assumption?"

"What's the alternative? We turn around and go all the way back? Take our chances with the Mexican authorities?"

"Whoever else was in this tunnel must be long gone by now," Alejandra said. "Why would they risk a direct confrontation when they could just crawl out of the tunnel and vanish into Texas?"

Layne looked each of them in the eyes for several seconds.

"You realize that getting shot isn't the worst thing that can happen to us down here, right?" she whispered.

Mason passed one of the wooden contraptions to Alejandra and lifted another out of the water for himself. He knew precisely what Layne meant; he didn't relish the idea of being buried alive and he wouldn't soon forget what the directed-energy weapon had done to Austin and Langbroek. Worse, he had to believe that men willing to risk their lives to reclaim radioactive nuclear material were undoubtedly the kind who wouldn't hesitate to use it.

22

Surely whatever foot soldiers might have been down here had seized the opportunity to escape. Why else wouldn't they have simply fired their weapons straight through the pipe the moment he and the others were within range? The problem was he couldn't shake the feeling that they weren't alone. It was a primitive instinct honed by his hindbrain through countless generations of evolution, a warning he'd learned better than to ignore.

"Take my flashlight," he whispered to Layne. "Alejandra's, too. Walk about a hundred feet away and turn them off. One at a time. And then get back here as quickly and quietly as possible."

"If anyone's there, you want them to think we turned around and went back to the warehouse."

"It ought to buy us at least a few seconds. Besides, I don't want them to see what I'm doing."

She nodded and did as he'd asked. The light immediately dimmed when she turned around and faded with every step she took. Mason stayed out of sight, off to the side of the pipe. He slipped off his jacket, stuffed it with armfuls of mud, and set it on the dolly.

The intonation of Layne's footsteps changed as she emerged from the shallow water and scuffed onto dry ground. She hesitated only briefly before switching off the first beam.

Alejandra hugged a dolly to her chest, readjusted her grip on her pistol, and faded into the shadows when Layne snuffed the second beam.

Mason used what little light remained to fix his position in relation to the mouth of the pipe and the second dolly he'd set aside. When Layne killed the lone remaining light, and the darkness smothered him.

He set the first dolly inside the tube and weighed it down with the few stones he'd been able to feel beneath the mud. Slid it cautiously forward, conscious of the sound of its wheels on the hard plastic. He couldn't hear a thing from the other end, not so much as a whisper, although he could have easily failed to detect it beneath the hum of the pump and the gentle shushing sounds of Layne walking slowly toward him, keeping her feet immersed so as not to produce a single splash.

Mason found the second dolly in the darkness and silently rolled it in behind the first. He hoped these precautions were unnecessary and they were simply wasting their time, but the consequences of being wrong would be disastrous. He felt the movement of water against his legs, sensed as much as heard Layne closing the gap between them.

A cracking sound emanated from the depths and the amount of water draining from the pipe audibly increased, raising the level of the pool nearly to the lip. The pump chugged and sputtered.

Layne's hand brushed against his lower back. He took it and guided it to the dolly he'd leaned beside the pipe for her to use.

"Stay right behind me," he whispered directly into her ear. "Tell Alejandra to do the same. If there's anyone waiting for us, we don't want to give them time to reload."

He stuffed his torso inside the tube, maneuvered his computer bag over his shoulder, and lowered his chest to the board, but he quickly realized that the tube limited his range of motion to such an extent that he wouldn't be able to move his arms to propel himself. Although it took some doing, he managed to balance his laptop on his chest and flip onto his back on the dolly. He planted his palms against the rounded top and pulled himself back and forth, slowly, testing out the contraption, surprised by how easily the wheels rolled through the water.

Mason reached out for the first dolly with his left hand, gripped the edge, and rolled far enough into the pipe that Layne could slide in behind him. He hoped Alejandra was ready to follow, because once he started moving, things had the potential to go south in a hurry.

A solid push with his right hand and he was moving, gaining

momentum with every push. The wheels hit the seams with a *clack-clack, clack-clack* that could undoubtedly be heard throughout the tunnel. He prayed their trick with the flashlights had bought them a few seconds of confusion or they were in big trouble.

Cracks in the PVC admitted curtains of freezing water, forcing him to hold his breath to keep from inhaling the fluid. The dolly accelerated until he could no longer keep up with pushing. He reached under his waistband, wrapped his fist around the grip of his pistol, and shoved the board ahead of him to create just enough distance between them—

Discharge strobed, followed in rapid succession by the deafening reports of a pair of semiautomatic pistols. He caught a glimpse of the top of the pipe—wet with condensation, discolored by mold, and riddled with cracks—and suddenly understood why the men hadn't fired through it.

Mason drew his weapon and leaned his head back. More flashes and bullets tore through his stuffed jacket on the board ahead of him, filling the air with mud and splinters. The dolly splashed down into the water mere feet away.

Two shooters emerged, one from either side of the pipe. Their pistols trained on the dolly. Their barrels flickering with discharge.

Mason raised his weapon and aimed at the man on the left, who must have seen through their ruse. He was already turning, his gold-plated semiautomatic scything through the air, when Mason pulled the trigger. His first shot caught the man high in the chest; the second hit him in the jaw and lifted him from his feet, his blood spattering the wall.

Darkness fell once more.

Mason tried to hold the dolly steady, but his sudden movement had destabilized it. He was in the process of rolling when he erupted from the pipe.

A burst of light, a concussive clap, and he felt the heat of a bullet pass within inches of his face. It impacted somewhere inside the tube with a sound like a ceramic bowl shattering.

Surprise registered on the face of a man with thick black hair and a goatee. Mason raised his Glock toward the center of the man's stained T-shirt and—

He splashed down into the cold water without warning. Went

straight to the bottom. Slid through the mud on his shoulder and the side of his face. Tried to maneuver the skateboard between his body and the shooter.

A burst of discharge from the barrel. Right above him. He planted his left hand against the slick earth, propelled himself upward. Breached the surface, his mouth filling with the filthy water. Raised his pistol as the man lowered his.

Mason fired first.

The bullet punched a hole through the man's chest, which appeared to collapse in on itself. His eyes widened and he bared his teeth. And then it was dark once more.

Layne launched from the tube behind him with a gasp and a splash. Mason slogged back toward her, thrust his hand into the water, and grabbed her by the arm. He barely dragged her out of the way before Alejandra burst from the pipe. She breached the surface a split second later, retched up a mouthful of fluid, and fell silent.

A rumbling sensation passed through the earth.

Layne struggled to her knees, switched on one of the flashlights, and aligned it with her pistol. She aimed them deeper into the tunnel, then back into the pipe. Mason could hardly see the dead narcos in the dim glow. The first appeared to have rebounded from the wall and fallen forward into the water near the second, whose body was submerged, blood diffusing around him.

"Are you guys all—" Mason started to ask, but he was cut off by a thunderous cracking sound, followed by a rush of frigid water. Plastic shards and rocks tumbled from the mouth of the pipe. The ground shuddered as the broken pipe collapsed beneath the weight of the river. "Go!"

He lunged to his feet, lifted Layne from the mud by her armpits, and propelled her ahead of him. Jerked Alejandra from the water and spurred her to motion. Ran for his life. Stones tumbled past his ankles. The flooding threatened to sweep him from his feet.

The flashlight swung wildly in Layne's grasp, making the entire tunnel appear to lurch from side to side as though on an invisible fulcrum. The murky water outpaced her beam, rose to her thighs, swept her feet out from underneath her. Her back went under, followed by her head. Her lower legs broke the surface near the submerged light.

Mason dove forward and let the water carry him. He felt her shoulder. Got a grip on her upper arm. Pulled her to the surface, driving himself under in the process. His back impacted the hard ground, nearly knocking the wind out of him. He was momentarily inverted until the water swept past him into the darkness and left him sputtering where he lay.

Layne shone her light into his face. He shielded his eyes and struggled to keep his head above the surface, which receded past him with a sensation that reminded him of sinking into the sand on a beach as the tide rolled out.

"Did you see any more of them?" she whispered.

"No." He coughed until he cleared the aspirated fluid. "Just the two."

"What the hell were they still doing down here? They could have made a break for it and we'd have never known."

"Maybe they thought there was still a way to salvage their operation."

"More likely they were terrified of what the cártel would do to them when it found out what happened here," Alejandra said.

Layne slowly turned in a circle, her light probing every crack and crevice within its range. There was no sign that anyone else had been down here, let alone that they were still nearby.

"We need to keep moving," she said.

Mason extended his arm. She clasped his hand and helped pull him out of the water. He accepted his flashlight, lit it up, and swept it across the cracked ceiling overhead. While this side of the tunnel might have been far better constructed, it was considerably older and hardly looked able to withstand any kind of seismic event. The walls were made of concrete and striated with high-water marks, some kind of sewer built years ago to either divert fresh water from the river or flood it with waste.

They'd crossed underneath the Rio Grande, which meant they were once more on American soil. Or beneath it, anyway. He suddenly realized that he knew exactly where the tunnel let out. It had been staring him in the face the moment he turned down the gravel road toward the Robinson Ranch, where the dead cattle had been reported.

"Pick up the pace," he said, striking off down the tunnel once more. "We still have a long way to go."

23

Mason's internal compass told him they were nearing a mile from the Rio Grande and had yet to diverge from their northeasterly course. They'd passed rusted irrigation pipes as thick as his thighs and surface-access chutes that had been sealed from the outside, where he imagined them opening near water pumps and central pivot sprinklers overgrown with weeds. While the tunnel continued on indefinitely, presumably all the way to some central waterworks in Rio Grande City that had been modernized half a century ago, they found their exit without any difficulty.

An extension ladder ascended into another chute paneled with plywood sheeting and bracketed with plumbing pipes, just like the one through which they'd first entered, two miles away on the Mexican side of the border. The rungs were crusted with dirt and the entire works shook as he climbed, but thirty feet later he reached the top and found it blocked by a rusted iron hatch. He shone his light around the seams to make sure no one had welded it closed or rigged it with trip wires.

With a final glance down past his feet at Layne and Alejandra, he pressed his shoulders against the hatch and propped his gun hand on the forearm holding the flashlight. Took several rapid breaths. Drove with his legs. Emerged into darkness. Swung his light and pistol in an arc from left to right.

The hatch slammed flush against the floor behind him. The thunderous crash was still reverberating through the building when he scurried from the hole and knelt on the hard-packed earth. He turned slowly in a circle, his heart thudding in his ears. Smelled fuel and motor oil, dust and hay, and a biological scent he would have recognized anywhere. It was old and faded, but there was no doubt in his mind that something had died here and been left to rot.

Layne crawled from the earth behind him. Her light swept his shadow across the floor in front of him, like the minute hand on a clock. Alejandra emerged and shone her light up into the rafters.

Mason took in his surroundings as quickly as he could. They were in a barn, its vaulted roof supported by a framework of rough-hewn timber. The section of the plank floor that ordinarily concealed the shaft leaned against the half-wall behind him, above which was a loft brimming with desiccated straw. A doorway stood open upon the shadows housed underneath it. Layne aimed her flashlight inside and revealed a jumble of wheelbarrows and shovels and rakes and pickaxes alongside bags of seeds and grains, their contents spilling out onto the bare earth through the torn burlap. Tarps covered what he suspected were bundles of marijuana like they'd seen on the other end.

A row of horse stalls ran the length of the barn to his right, enclosed by horizontal slats with hinged gates. Broken lengths of weathered wood and all kinds of rusted junk had been piled against the wall to his left. On the far side of the mess was an old tractor, a thresher, and even an archaic horse-drawn plow. The area near the massive barn doors straight ahead had been cleared to make room for much more modern vehicles, including a Ford F-250 with rear wheel wells that had been expanded to accommodate two tires each. There was easily enough room beside it to load and unload a panel truck.

Mason rose and advanced with his flashlight shining backhanded from his left fist, its beam aligned with the sight line of his Glock. He made sure no one was hiding behind the junk before turning his attention on the stables, where he'd half expected to discover dead men and women hanging from meat hooks, like he'd found in Arizona. He breathed an audible sigh of relief when the first one revealed nothing more traumatizing than soiled hay.

He wasn't as lucky with the second.

"Over here," he whispered.

Alejandra and Layne caught up with him and added their beam to his.

"Are they even human?" Layne whispered.

The skeletal trauma was so extensive that it was impossible to tell for sure. At least not until they saw the teeth scattered on the floor. Based on the discoloration of the bones, the victims had to have been killed years ago, perhaps even around the same time this barn was being repurposed to house the smuggling tunnel.

The remains in the adjacent stall were more recent, although not by very much. The two victims had been brutally beaten and dismembered, their severed heads propped against the rear wall, their faces barely recognizable as human. Their chests had been burned black and their appendages had the color and texture of leather. The residua of high-velocity blood spatters clung to the walls in arches, the wood carved with a blade to read: AQUI ESTAN TUS 'FIELES' SEGUIDORES.

"'Here are your "faithful" followers,'" Alejandra whispered, translating. "It appears to be a message for a rival cártel. Or maybe for the men moving drugs through here, a reminder of the consequences of stealing."

There were more bodies in the next stall. They weren't fresh, but they hadn't been there too long, either. The thighs terminated above the knees, where the ends of the femurs exhibited the telltale markings of a chain saw. The same held true of the arms, which had been cast aside into opposite corners with the severed heads. Again, there were words carved into the wood: ESTO NO ES UN JUEGO.

"'This is not a game,'" Alejandra whispered, turning away from the morbid tableau.

Even after the previous stalls, Mason was unprepared for what they found in the final one. There was no message, no overt demonstration of physical brutality. The two corpses were wedged into the back corner, where it appeared as though one had attempted to shield the other with his body. The straw around them was scorched, their flesh cooked to their bones. They'd died like frightened animals, cowering before the same monster that had murdered Austin and Langbroek, a blast from a high-powered DEW simultaneously lighting their skin and hair on fire and liquefying their insides. It must have been a spectacularly painful way to die, one he wouldn't have wished upon anyone.

"How long ago?" Layne whispered.

"Hard to tell," Mason whispered. "If I had to wager a guess, I'd say maybe a month ago."

"Do you think the cartel has a DEW of its own?"

"If it did, there would be no mistaking it," Alejandra whispered. "These bodies would not be hidden in a barn; they would be displayed for all to see."

"Then why would they need to bring in an outside contractor to take care of these two?" Mason asked. "The guy with the DEW has to be a professional to be able to track someone as elusive as Langbroek and make the execution of a border patrol agent look like an accident. It's overkill for a couple of nobodies."

"Maybe they were not nobodies," Alejandra said. "Or perhaps they were not the problem of the cártel."

The way she said it caused the entire picture to suddenly come into focus for Mason. It wasn't CJNG's mess that the man with the DEW had been dispatched to clean up; it was the Thirteen's.

Mason turned around and found himself staring at his reflection in the dusty passenger window of the truck. He didn't need to check the registration in the glove compartment to know whose vehicle it was any more than he had to wait for forensics to run the DNA of the remains to identify the victims.

"Meet the Robinsons," he said. "They made targets of themselves the moment they reported the nature of the physical injuries to their cattle. Maybe they would have been fine if they'd left well enough alone, but they had to be eliminated when they kept calling the sheriff's office to complain about the traffic on their road. They were abducted and taken from their house, which was staged to make it look like they'd left in a hurry, a fact easily corroborated by their missing truck." He patted the roof of the pickup. "They died within a quarter of a mile of their home."

"Time to call it in," Layne said.

"Yeah," Mason said. He swung open the barn doors upon a vast, empty expanse of brushland. "This is where the trail ends."

He walked out into the night and stared up at the stars. A chill rippled through his body that had nothing to do with the breeze tousling the tall weeds in the fields. Just when he thought he'd seen the true depths of mankind's capacity for evil, he found a place like this that convinced him he'd only begun to scratch the surface.

Behind him, Layne called Chris on her cell phone. She spoke in little more than a whisper, as though out of respect for the dead.

"I must return to Mexico while I still can," Alejandra said. "Someone needs to secure the warehouse on the other end of the tunnel. If the police get there first, there will be nothing left when I arrive."

Mason nodded. He understood how such things worked.

"I can arrange a ride," he said, but his words rang hollow. He wouldn't be able to explain her presence at the crime scene, let alone on American soil, and they both knew it. Besides, she'd already crossed the border several times before on her own and knew how to fend for herself.

"If anyone can find the plutonium, it is you, James." She hugged him and gave him a kiss on the cheek. "Tell Ramses he knows where to find me."

And with that she struck off across the field, her silhouette fading into the darkness.

Mason unslung his computer and sat down right there on the ground, amid the gravel and the thistles. He felt a marrow-deep exhaustion the likes of which he'd never experienced before. He was so tired of death, so tired of the suffering inflicted by cruel men for no other reason than they could. If the monsters ultimately behind this nightmare, the Thirteen, had their way, cruelty would be all that was left. Everything that was good and decent would be stripped from the world, and for what? Profit? Power? Was any amount of either worth the damnation of their species?

He pulled his cell phone from the front pocket of his jeans. The screen was damp, but, surprisingly, it still managed to power on. His notifications let him know that he had a handful of messages, which he had no desire to listen to. All he wanted to do was close his eyes and welcome the merciful respite of sleep. And yet somehow he found the strength to call his voice mail and type in his password.

"You have three new messages . . ."

He tuned out the computerized voice and watched Layne pace the width of the barn in the open garage. They'd taken an unnecessary risk with the pipe and nearly paid the price for it. Hurling himself into oblivion was one thing, but he had no right to take her with him. And what did they have to show for it? They were still no closer to finding the plutonium than they'd been before and they didn't have the slightest idea who had it or how it related to the man with the DEW and the Thirteen.

"Mace," Gunnar said. The excitement in his voice caused Mason to jump to his feet. "Call me the second you get this message. You are not—I repeat, *not*—going to believe what I just found."

24

Mason and Layne watched the forensics team from outside the cordon surrounding the barn, where men and women in white jumpsuits photographed the remains in the stalls and collected bone and tissue samples. A group of border patrol agents wearing waterproof suits, body

armor, and helmets with spotlights waited impatiently for them to finish their work so they could descend into the tunnel. Another unit
piloted the drones surveilling the warehouses on the other end of the
tunnel, with the blessings of the Mexican government, which just happened to have a special forces operative on hand to coordinate the
federal response with local law-enforcement agencies.

Archer had done what he could to keep Layne and him from getting caught up in the situation, but no one was buying their story
about the coincidental discovery of both the plutonium reclamation
lab and the drug tunnel, despite assurances from high-ranking officials within the DHS and FBI. Both agencies had dispatched their
best counterterrorism and criminal exploitation units to join the investigation, alongside the DEA, ATF, Rio Grande City Police, and
Starr County Sheriff's Department, not that they were likely to find
anything more than Mason and Layne had. The plutonium was long
gone, as was the man with the DEW, and the upper echelon of the
cartel was a dozen layers removed from the narcos working the trafficking operation, the majority of whom were lying dead near the
housing project or inside the tunnel.

Mason walked away from the barn and stared out across the
brushland. He and Layne were wasting their time here, but he didn't
have the slightest clue as to where to go next.

McWhinney had confirmed that the F-250 belonged to Lyle Robinson. The serial number on his hip replacement had matched that of
the larger of the two bodies. They could only assume that the female
he'd been incinerated trying to protect was his wife, Sally. The director was currently in his mobile forensics lab running various samples through the GC-MS as quickly as he could, while the handheld
XRF spectrometer had already confirmed the presence of plutonium
isotopes in similar concentrations to the samples they'd collected
from the other two sites. The results corroborated Locker's theory
that the waste products from the PUREX process had seeped into
the groundwater—specifically a minor aquifer called Yegua-Jackson,
which the locals used for both irrigation and watering their livestock,
unknowingly exposing their animals to the alpha radiation that tore
them apart from the inside out—in small enough amounts that the
land could be fairly easily remediated without drawing the attention
of the national media, but in high enough concentrations to suggest

that production had been going on for some unknown number of years before they'd detected it. Worse, the plutonium would be nearly impossible to find unless they got lucky and stumbled upon its trail.

Gunnar had yet to return Mason's call regarding the revelation he'd made. The other messages had been from Locker, who said the computer forensics specialists had been able to recover a handful of files from the smashed hard drive in Yamaguchi's apartment and would forward them as soon as they were in his possession, and Chris, who stated that he was now running point since Archer had been summoned to D.C. by the president and would be indisposed for the foreseeable future. With the annual Salute to America event planned for the following evening, when nearly a million people would descend upon the National Mall to watch the military parade and a fireworks show, they weren't taking any chances.

"We're being summoned," Layne said, wrenching him from his thoughts.

Mason followed her line of sight to where McWhinney leaned out the rear door of his mobile forensics lab, gesturing for them to follow him inside. Layne beat him across the driveway and preceded him into a vehicle that looked like a cross between an ambulance and a panel truck. One side featured a countertop covered with so much humming equipment that Mason could barely tell where one unit stopped and the next started, while the other was dominated by a wall of cabinets that could also be accessed through the external hatches beneath the raised awning.

The director hurried down the narrow aisle ahead of them and slid into the driver's seat. The lab tech they'd met earlier, Alex, sat beside him in the passenger seat with the computer screen mounted to the dashboard swiveled to face him and the keyboard extended on its armature. Mason and Layne squeezed into the space between them.

"Show them what you just showed me," McWhinney said.

Alex glanced back and acknowledged them with an inclination of his chin.

"The physical presentation of the crime scenes inside the stalls made them appear to have been staged, right?" he said. "So I figured whoever was responsible had to be sending someone a message."

"We'd already assumed that was the case," Layne said.

"Of course, but setting up such visceral tableaus inside a barn few people are ever going to enter is the surest way to reach the smallest audience possible, so I got to thinking . . . how do these guys showcase their work to the world? After all, that's their whole shtick, right?"

Mason saw exactly where he was going.

"You found them online," he said.

"On the website of a Mexican crime tabloid called *La Prensa*," Alex said, opening the window where he'd bookmarked the page. "While we have rags like the *National Enquirer* to keep us up to date on celebrity affairs, alien abductions, and three-headed babies, they have newspapers like this one to report on all of the ghastly deeds of the cartels, who figured out that they could use the paper to send messages to one another. Wage their wars on the media front and in the court of public opinion."

"So they took the pictures here and sent them to this paper," Layne said.

"This newspaper alone has a quarter of a million subscribers to its print edition and its website gets fifteen million unique visitors every month. Pictures like this one go up every day."

The horse stall in the photograph was readily identifiable, as was the message mocking the intended recipient's "faithful" followers. A man wearing a balaclava with a skull design stood front and center, staring at the camera, his exposed skin crimson with blood, his eyes flat and dead. He clutched fistfuls of the victims' hair and displayed their mangled heads for the camera. The beating had been so savage that it had altered the bone structure of their faces. Their dismembered bodies were naked and covered with lacerations so deep that the edges had peeled back from the adipose layer underneath.

"No one claimed credit," Alex said, "but this was two years ago, at the height of the war between the Gulf Cartel and CJNG, so it had to be one of them. They wanted whichever group had sent these presumed assassins to know what had happened to them. More important, they wanted the people reading the magazine to see them as the victims in all of this. 'We're just innocent businessmen trying to do our jobs while our rivals send thugs to kill us.' A 'see what they made us do?' kind of thing."

"That's insane," Layne said.

"Be that as it may, it's noteworthy that no one took credit for the murders in this picture, either."

Alex minimized the first image and brought up another. A group of narcos wearing ordinary street clothes posed behind the freshly butchered remains of two men. While the killers were only visible from the waist down, it was obvious which of them had inflicted the most damage. His bare stomach and slacks were drenched with blood, unlike the jeans of the others. The words carved into the wall—ESTO NO ES UN JUEGO—were barely visible beside his right hip.

"When was this published?" Mason asked.

"Just about a year ago, which meshes with our preliminary estimates of TOD."

"Even if we managed to identify these men and somehow tracked them down, I can't imagine they'd know anything about the production of the plutonium," Layne said. "They kept that PUREX lab padlocked and separated from the rest of the operation."

"It's not *their* identities that are of interest here," Alex said. "They're probably low-level hit men, not lieutenants. *Sicarios,* not *tenientes.* Disposable. Look at the faces of the victims."

Their heads were displayed on either side of their bodies and balanced so that they stared up at the camera through heavy-lidded eyes. The blood had been hurriedly wiped from their faces, leaving a ring around their jaws and hairlines.

"They're Caucasian," Layne said.

"That's not all," McWhinney said. "Show them, Alex."

He switched to a screen Mason recognized as the results of a facial recognition search using the FBI's Next Generation Identification system, which housed the largest dedicated repository of biometric data in the world. The faces of the men smiling back at him from the monitor were obviously the same men, although Mason couldn't help but question the results.

"Kostov Mironov and Patrushev Panarin?" he said, reading from the screen.

"Definitely not your standard narcos," Alex said.

Mironov had an unmistakable strawberry birthmark on his cheek, while Panarin had a sharp widow's peak that made him look almost like Dracula. They'd appeared so genuinely happy in life that it was hard to imagine either of them choosing a path that led to such a horrific end in a barn half a world away from their homeland.

"So who are they?" Layne asked.

"That's the question," McWhinney said. "These pictures appear on the website of the Russian embassy in Mexico, on a page listing missing nationals."

"They entered Mexico legally, but they never left?"

"Or at least they didn't get very far," Alex said.

"What were they doing in Mexico in the first place?" Mason asked.

"Your guess is as good as mine," McWhinney said. "Outside of these pictures, these men might as well have been ghosts. There's no record of them in any of our databases. We've already filed a request for law-enforcement assistance with INTERPOL, but Lord only knows how long that could take."

"Unfortunately, time's something we just don't have."

Mason's phone rang. He glanced at the number of the incoming call, then at Layne.

"I need to take this," he said to McWhinney. "Can you send all of this to my email?"

He shook the director's hand, clapped Alex on the shoulder, and answered on his way down the narrow aisle toward the back door.

"What took you so long?"

"In case you've forgotten," Gunnar said, "you have me working on about a million different things at once. And I have to handle business for which people are actually paying me, I might add."

"You know how much I appreciate everything you do, so why don't you just skip ahead and tell me what you found."

"It would be better if I showed you."

"Just upload whatever it is to the cloud and I'll take a look—"

"No," Gunnar said. "I mean in person."

"That's not going to happen anytime soon."

"I'm sending an address to your phone. Be there in an hour. We have an appointment to keep."

25

It had taken Mason and Layne more than forty minutes to extricate themselves from the bedlam at the barn. The local police and sheriff's departments had asked questions they weren't prepared to answer and grown increasingly frustrated with their evasiveness. As had the FBI agents, for which Mason felt a pang of guilt. The ATF contingent, however, had been ready to rip out their throats, and probably would have had the agents from the DHS's Federal Protective Service not interceded. Apparently, a cabinet secretary unilaterally instigating the investigation into the death of a single border patrol agent bought a lot of goodwill, enough to secure them a ride to a motel within blocks of the address Gunnar had given them, with mere minutes to spare. They'd waited just long enough for the agent's vehicle to disappear over the horizon before heading around the side of the building and into the alley behind it.

Gunnar's instructions had been to make sure they weren't being followed, go to the address he'd provided, which turned out to be another motel, and enter the attached diner through the office. In a booth near the back, they'd find a man and a woman—Flaco and Bonita—who would give them instructions as to what they were supposed to do next.

Mason's old friend wasn't one to play cloak-and-dagger for no reason. If he insisted upon such extreme precautions, there had to be a damn good reason for it.

They followed the course Layne had plotted on her cell phone: down the alley, up the intersecting street, and through a residential neighborhood that let out across the street from the restaurant. The Best Western looked like every other Mason had seen. There were two levels of rooms accessible by external walkways and concrete stairs with iron railings. The sign below the glowing blue-and-yellow logo read: NO VACANCY. A glance around the side at the dirt lot revealed a surprising number of vehicles, nearly all of them interstate long haulers and commercial vehicles.

He and Layne entered through the office, nodded to the clerk staring down at his phone, and entered the restaurant through its inner door. A freestanding sign instructing them to seat themselves stood in front of the hostess stand. There were several truckers on stools at the bar, their heads lowered to their plates and a muted rerun of SportsCenter on the TV above them. The cook appeared in the pass-through window and set a pair of plates underneath the heat lamp for the waitress, who carried them to the booth in the back corner, where a Hispanic man and woman sat across from each other. She set the steak and eggs in front of the man and a short stack of pancakes before the woman.

"I'll be with you in just a sec," she said on her way back to the kitchen. "Menus are on the tables."

"Don't worry about us," Layne said. "We won't be here very long."

At the sound of her voice, the couple in the booth turned to face them. The man had to be easily 350 pounds. His tiny head sat on a neck so bulbous and fleshy it made his earlobes bow outward. His wifebeater showcased the stretch marks near his armpits, and his suspenders hardly appeared strong enough to support his chinos. He had a face made for scowling and green tears tattooed near the corner of his eye. The woman was his opposite in every way. She was petite and emaciated, her cheeks hollow and her eyes sunken. She was the living embodiment of a corpse, presumably as a result of the drugs that caused her to restlessly scratch at the scabs on her forearms.

"The hell?" Layne whispered.

Mason walked right up to their table.

"Flaco?" he said to the man, and then to the woman: "Bonita?"

The woman recoiled and looked across the table at the man, who scooted his girth out from the booth, locked eyes with Mason, and punched him squarely in the gut. His breath burst from his lips and he dropped to one knee. Layne reached for her pistol, but he caught her wrist first.

"*¿Que mierde te pasa?*" the man said in a booming voice.

"He wants to know what's wrong with you," Layne said.

Mason bared his teeth and struggled to his feet. Air flooded into his chest with a sensation like popping a sealed container.

The man produced a folded piece of paper from his front pocket, held it up between his index and middle fingers, and tossed it to the ground at Mason's feet.

"*Vete a la mierde de aqui.*"

Mason stared down the man while Layne retrieved the paper, unfolded it, and read what it said.

"We have what we need," she said. "Let's get out of here."

Mason clenched and unclenched his fists at his sides. He didn't know who this guy thought he was, but a part of him really wanted to find out.

"Now's not the time," Layne said, stepping between the two of them. Her voice was surprisingly calm. She slipped off her jacket and cap and set them on the booth beside the woman, who stared at them with open revulsion before putting them on. "Give him your shirt."

"Why would I—?"

"Because you don't have your jacket anymore. Now do as I say and give him your shirt."

"It's not like it will fit him," Mason said.

His lips writhed over his teeth. No matter how big or strong this guy might be, an overhand right to the bridge of his nose would drop him like a sack of grain.

"Mason," Layne snapped.

He felt the weight of eyes upon him and turned to find the men at the bar staring at him. Even the cook had stopped what he was doing to watch through the pass-through window. The waitress picked up the phone and started dialing.

"No need," Mason said. He slipped off his T-shirt and tossed it onto the table. "We're leaving."

The waitress studied him for several seconds before replacing the receiver on the cradle.

"This way," Layne said, guiding him toward the kitchen. She burst through the swinging door, navigated a maze of equipment, and exited by the rear door. A run-down pickup truck was parked outside. She opened the driver's-side door and climbed in. "You coming or what?"

Mason cautiously opened the passenger door and eased into the seat. There were bags of fast-food trash on the floorboard and holes in the dashboard where the vinyl had been peeled away from the foam. It smelled like a cross between hot sauce, exhaust, and cigarette smoke. He unslung his computer, set it on his lap, and tried to fasten his nonfunctional seat belt.

Layne started the truck on the second try and pulled out into the alley. Something under the hood clanked and it sounded like there were loose cans in the bed.

"Why'd we have to give them our clothes?" Mason asked.

Without looking, Layne tossed the paper on his computer case and turned left onto the main road, which took serious effort without the benefit of power steering. He recognized Gunnar's handwriting.

"'Take off any identifiable clothing and give it to Flaco and Bonita,'" Mason said, reading out loud. "'Exit through the kitchen. There's a truck waiting in the alley with the keys in the ignition. Head east. Turn left at the first cross street. In four blocks you'll find a gas station. Park on the side of the convenience store, beneath the tree.

You'll see a Ford Taurus. The keys are underneath the trash barrel beside it. Further instructions are in the glove compartment.'"

Mason tucked the paper into his pocket and watched Rio Grande City crawl past. Kids played in dirt yards and dogs barked from behind fences. Men and women pushed strollers along sidewalks and fixed cars in their garages and worked in their gardens, completely oblivious to the nuclear threat in their midst.

The Taurus was waiting where Gunnar had said it would be. Layne parked beside it, left the keys to the truck on the seat, and climbed out into the shade of an elm tree.

"I'll grab some drinks and something to eat," she said. "You get the car keys."

They were under the trash barrel, as promised. He started the car and removed the note from the glove box. There were no instructions, only an address: 5918 Fairgrounds Road. He backed out of the parking spot and pulled around in front of the convenience store at the same time Layne emerged from the front door with a white plastic bag in one hand and a Dallas Cowboys T-shirt in the other. She opened the door and tossed the shirt into his lap. He put it on while she cracked a bottle of Mountain Dew for herself and a Monster Energy drink for him.

"What are we supposed to do from here?" she asked.

Mason handed her the note and took a drink from the mercifully cold can. The carbonation burned his parched throat, but he wouldn't have traded the sensation for anything in the world. By the time he set the drink in the cupholder, she'd already programmed the address into the GPS on her cell phone.

"Turn right and head west," she said. "In about two miles you'll merge onto Fairgrounds Road."

He followed her directions and drove back through town. The city eventually gave way to industrial lots and a stretch of bare dirt lorded over by a water tower.

"What the hell was that back there at the diner anyway?" he asked.

"No clue. I don't think I've ever seen a guy that big move so fast. How's your stomach?"

"Hungry."

She grabbed a protein bar from the bag, opened the wrapper, and held it out for him. They entered another residential district with up-scale homes on one side of the street and trailer homes on the other.

"In five hundred feet, take a slight right onto Fairgrounds Road," Layne's phone said.

The street before them led diagonally to the northwest. Mason recognized it as the route they'd initially taken to get to the city from the airport. The runway materialized from the plains to their right, leading toward the lone hangar and the prefabricated buildings be-hind it. They turned right at the sign and drove around the side of a warehouse with twin garage doors and another with a faded sign above the door. There were only a couple other cars in the lot, from which they could see Gunnar's sleek Cessna Citation XLS ready and waiting to taxi onto the runway.

"It would have saved us all a lot of trouble if he'd just told us to meet him at the airport," Layne said.

Mason parked the sedan in the lot and left the keys in the ignition. He grabbed his laptop and struck off toward the private jet, its stairs lowered and its turbines humming. They'd just walked around the cor-ner of the hangar when a man dressed in all black emerged from the interior, right behind them, and spoke in a thick Austrian accent.

"Come with me if you want to live."

26

ELSEWHERE

The man enjoyed his daily visits to the park in his wheelchair. He closed his eyes, basking in the warmth of the sun on his face and listening to the laughter of children. The wonder and awe in the voices of the tour-ists streaming past reminded him of just how special this place truly was, especially now, with red-white-and-blue fan buntings hanging from every railing and flags flying everywhere he looked. In another life, this existence would have been more than enough for him. He and his family could have been happy here, but that had simply never been in the cards. The world was a cruel, unforgiving place, as so many would soon learn.

"How're you holding up, Professor?"

The man opened his eyes and glanced up into the face of the young policeman, whose expression betrayed the fact that he already knew the answer.

"There is nothing ailing me that the fresh air cannot at least temporarily cure, Officer Harris," he said.

The policeman gave the man a gentle squeeze on the shoulder and resumed his post, once more hiding his eyes behind the reflection on his sunglasses. The man fought the urge to cast aside his sweater and scratch off his skin at the point of physical contact. He settled for imagining the officer's uniform catching fire and his flesh melting from his bones as a churning cloud of destruction washed over him, carrying before it the screams of the dying.

"*Dolzhny li my poyti posmotret' fontan?*" the woman whispered into his ear.

The man nodded in response. He did so love the fountain, as she well knew. He could sit there all day, reveling in the rumble of the central geyser and the patter of the ring of arched flumes striking the surface. On such a beautiful day, he would be surrounded by families, the joy radiating from them a palpable sensation he allowed to resonate in his chest, if only momentarily, before envisioning their bodies burning where they fell.

He tucked his bony arms underneath the knitted blanket covering his frail legs. Regardless of how slowly the woman pushed him, even the gentle air currents chilled him to the marrow. He watched a group of children picking teams for a game of football, a spandex-clad mother strapping her child into a stroller for their morning jog, an elderly couple strolling arm in arm—

Frenzied barking.

He turned and saw a pit bull mix bearing down on him, trailing its leash and its teenaged owner, who sprinted in an effort to catch up. The mongrel stopped mere feet away from the man, bared its teeth, and barked at him with such ferocity that he instinctively recalled the—

—*animals stalking the ruins of Pripyat, house pets abandoned in the rush to evacuate, left for dead. They had grown feral during the five grueling years he had spent in a Siberian labor camp, expelled from the Communist Party and the life he had lived within this very city, once a beacon of hope, now a memorial to his failure.*

This is the last place in the world he would have expected to find himself, seventy-two hours removed from walking through the prison gates, a free, if entirely diminished man. There was simply nowhere else he could think to go. The world he had known upon starting his sentence had become unrecognizable in his absence, the structure imposed by the party replaced by fear and uncertainty, the once-monolithic buildings falling into disrepair, claimed by trees and bushes growing wild from their foundations and the asphalt aprons where residents once parked. He recognizes the windows of the apartments where his friends and loved ones had lived, men and women who had welcomed him into their homes, but who now would not even acknowledge his existence, even Lizabeta Tarasov, whose husband he had nearly died trying to save.

The silence is so potent that he can almost hear the radiation washing over him, like invisible waves breaking against a forgiving shore.

They had all been so happy, once upon a time, naïve professionals and new families starting their lives together in the shadow of the V. I. Lenin Nuclear Power Plant, a technological marvel that would make the Soviet Union the envy of the modern world and its workers heroes to their comrades. Everything had been so perfect before the disaster, which had destroyed all they had worked so hard to achieve. No matter how often he relived that night, no matter how many times he scrutinized every minute detail and decision, he could not see anything he would have done differently. Something outside of his control had gone wrong and this is the result, a city as dead as many of its former inhabitants and as forgotten as the rest.

The man walks as though in a trance, through buildings that have aged even more poorly than he has, their windows broken and their facades crumbling, their walls streaked with water damage and their basements flooded. He tours apartments carpeted with ash and appointed with moldering furniture. Gas masks protrude from the rubble, cast aside like the stuffed animals and dolls slowly vanishing beneath the dust. He visits the long-stilled Ferris wheel and the concrete sarcophagus housing the living reactor, a great bellows he feels beneath his feet, like the lungs of a dragon drawing fiery breath. His vision blurred by tears, he wanders until he finds himself in the control room, as he has always known he would.

The metal panels and consoles have begun to rust, bleeding the slate-tiled floor a reddish orange color. He finds the station where *he worked with pride for so many years, clear up until that fateful night, and climbs on top of it. The ceiling has collapsed, exposing the iron girder overhead. He tosses the rope he brought with him over the top and secures it in a knot. The other end he loops around his neck and cinches it tight. With one final glance at the carcass of the life he once knew, he steps from the edge.*

His head jerks back, his throat clamps shut, and his legs twitch. He feels his tongue pushing past his teeth, his eyes bulging from beneath his lids. Despite himself, he claws at the rope, willing his fingers to create a gap large enough for a single breath to pass, for the pressure to abate—

The rope snaps and drops him to the floor. Gasping, he rolls onto his side and finds himself staring at a litter of mixed-breed puppies underneath his old workstation, suckling from the teats of a skeletal springer spaniel. She lacks the strength to rise and merely bares her teeth, issues a low-pitched growl, and barks—

"Sorry about that," the teenager said. "I don't know what got into him. Come on, Max."

The man forced a smiled and watched the boy and his dog trot away, content in the knowledge that neither was long for this world, as he reminisced about how he had felt seeing that new life struggling to emerge from the dead land. He had come back to feed that spaniel every day until she whelped her litter, and then he had fed her offspring, too. And he had realized that life went on, even in the face of such brutal odds.

For the first time, he had imagined leaving behind the nightmare and starting over, perhaps even finding a wife and starting a family. He had allowed himself to dream of traveling the world and experiencing its beauty, right up until the moment he read the leaked report detailing the inherent flaw in the control rods, which had been responsible for their failure to stop the chain reaction that caused the explosion. The party had known for years and covered up the truth. It had left him to rot in a prison camp rather than accept responsibility. The state had stolen years of his life, destroyed his name, and made him a pariah. And for what? A government undone by its own corruption and a country that had become a fractured reflection of its former self?

That singular revelation had untethered him from his past, present, and future. From his very life. He had been unable to see a way forward and incapable of distinguishing the truth from the lie of his experience.

The man had become lost.

At least until he had found salvation among a group of like-minded individuals, discarded by an unsympathetic society, men and women who had wanted nothing more than to remake the world.

Or, failing at that, destroy it.

And here he was now, on the cusp of achieving that dream.

It saddened him that the woman he loved had not lived long enough to see it.

And that neither would he.

PART 3

A great industrial nation is controlled by its system of credit. Our system of credit is privately concentrated. The growth of the nation, therefore, and all our activities are in the hands of a few men. . . . [W]e have come to be one of the worst ruled, one of the most completely controlled and dominated, governments in the civilized world—no longer a government by free opinion, no longer a government by conviction and the vote of the majority, but a government by the opinion and the duress of small groups of dominant men.

—Woodrow Wilson, twenty-eighth president of the United States,
The New Freedom (1913)

PART 3

27

"You really need to work on your Schwarzenegger impression," Layne said.

"I didn't think it was that bad," Mason said.

"Hasta la vista, baby," Ramses said. A mechanic working on a single-prop plane and the guy refilling the fuel truck both looked up as though he were talking to them. He made guns from his index fingers and thumbs and pointed one at each of them. "I'll be back."

"I revise my opinion."

"Why do you have to say such hurtful things? I just flew halfway around the world to help you."

"Weren't you in Denver?" Layne said. "That's, like, a two-hour flight."

"Two hours of my life I'll never get back," Ramses said, striking off toward the runway. He wore a black leather jacket with a form-fitting T-shirt underneath, jeans, and scuffed leather biker boots. A silver Teutonic cross hung from his neck by a chain. He was one of very few people who could pull off the look without appearing pretentious. "Now, this is the plan: Get your ass to Mars."

"No, really. Where are we going?"

"*Total Recall*. It's one of the all-time classics."

"Maybe before I was born."

Gunnar leaned out the side door behind the cockpit and hollered down at them.

"Would you guys hurry up?"

He vanished back into the interior as Ramses mounted the steps. Mason spoke to his back.

"Alejandra said to tell you that you know where to find her."

Ramses froze. His grip tightened on the rails, but he didn't look back.

"You saw her?" he said, his voice uncharacteristically soft. "How did she look?"

Mason contemplated the answer for several seconds before answering.

"Sad," he finally said.

Ramses nodded to himself and hurried up the ramp onto the plane. Mason was glad he couldn't see the expression on his old friend's face.

The turbines ramped up with a whine as soon as they were on board. The cockpit door was closed, the pilot's voice muffled. The stairs rose behind them the moment they turned down the aisle.

There were four seats, two on either side, facing each other across the polished tables between them. Farther back was another partition, which separated Gunnar's sleeping quarters from the main cabin. He owned apartments in half a dozen cities around the world, but considering how much he traveled through the course of his work as a corporate espionage gun-for-hire, he needed not just his home base, but his literal home, to be mobile.

Gunnar had taken the forward-facing seat on the right side, his laptop on the table in front of him, his suit jacket hanging over the back of his chair. He'd loosened his tie and undone the top button of his shirt. He was obviously laboring under an extreme amount of stress, which scared Mason almost as much as the prospect of the plutonium being in the hands of someone who intended to use it.

"Sit down already." Gunnar looked up from beneath his bangs, the scar he'd received from the Hoyl slashing straight down his cheek. "We have a lot to go through and not a lot of time to get through it."

Ramses settled into the seat beside him, leaving Mason and Layne to ride backward. She took the seat opposite Gunnar and dialed up the airflow overhead.

"What was with the cloak-and-dagger bit?" she asked.

"There's been a satellite overhead since before you arrived, but it didn't appear to have a bead on you specifically," Gunnar said. "I figured that would change now that everyone knew you were here, so it's in all of our best interests for them to keep thinking you're in that motel for as long as possible. They'll have a devil of a time tracking you after that and by then we'll be impossible to find."

"Clever," Mason said, "but what was with the guy in the restaurant?"

"Did you walk right up to them and call them by their names?" Ramses asked.

"Of course."

Ramses burst out laughing. His face reddened and his eyes started to water. He could barely speak.

"What did . . . what did they do?" he asked.

"The guy punched me in the gut."

As if it were possible, Ramses laughed even harder, so hard he nearly fell out of his seat.

"Christ," Layne said. "Flaco and Bonita. You called them 'skinny' and 'pretty.' They thought you were insulting them."

Mason groaned.

"You knew that and you let me do it anyway?" he said.

"I thought those were their names. How was I supposed to know?"

Ramses had tears on his cheeks. He couldn't seem to catch his breath.

"Really funny," Mason said. "I'll remember that."

"Good," Ramses said, "because it'll give me all kinds of pleasure to remind you every chance I get. I just wish I could have been there to see it."

"You didn't even know them, did you?"

"Are you kidding? I paid them each a grand for their time and the use of their cars and told them where they could pick them up when you were done. Best money I ever spent."

The plane rolled slowly toward the runway before making an abrupt, ninety-degree turn. A hiss of air and the cabin pressurized, forcing Mason to work his jaw to relieve the uncomfortable sensation in his ears.

"Can we please get back to the task at hand?" Layne said. "Starting with where we're going."

"Colorado," Gunnar said. "I have a business associate who just might be able to shed some light on where the plutonium's headed."

The plane accelerated and the turbines screamed. A lurching sensation and they were airborne, the shrubland falling away below them, a marbled pattern of green and brown stretching as far as the eye could see.

"Is that why you called?" Mason asked.

"No," Gunnar said. He turned his computer so they could all see the screen, which featured a digitized image of the dragon tattoo Yamaguchi had shared with the Scarecrow and her brother. "This is why I called."

"You figured out what was underneath it," Mason said.

"With deductive skill like that it's a wonder you aren't in charge of the whole FBI by now," Ramses said.

"Can you focus for two seconds?" Layne said.

Ramses raised his hands in surrender and winked at Mason from across the table.

The plane passed through clouds that looked like cotton and rose into a sky so pristine and blue that it appeared almost magical. There wasn't so much as a hint of turbulence.

"First off," Gunnar said, "the dragon tattoo itself is significant, but I'll get to that in a minute. You need to see what's underneath it first to appreciate what we're dealing with."

He swiped his fingertips across his mouse pad and the dragon vanished, leaving behind an image with such poor definition that Mason could tell little more than that the overall design was circular, with indecipherable characters in the middle that vaguely resembled a stylized woman dancing.

"A few passes of some of my more aggressive filters and the application of an intuitive AI algorithm to help fill in the blanks and voilà . . . you have your tattoo."

The outside of the circle was fringed with the tips of twelve lotus petals, while two concentric rings surrounded the main design, which looked vaguely familiar to Mason, although he couldn't quite seem to place it. His initial impression of a dancing woman wasn't so far off. There was a filled circle near the top, above a wavy line reminiscent of a torso with its arms flared to either side. Below them was a third segment that resembled the number three with an extraordinarily long tail smashed together with a capital N in such a way as to replace its first vertical line and form a single character.

"I've seen this design before, but not quite like this," Layne said. "It usually looks more like the number thirty in cursive with the dot and the crescent above the zero."

"Precisely," Gunnar said. "It's the universal symbol for aum, the most sacred symbol in all of Hinduism. It signifies the essence of reality and consciousness. Vocalized, it's a primordial sound, one you've probably heard monks chanting while meditating. You know, aauuuuuummmmmm." He drew out the word for several seconds. "It's a spiritual incantation made while reciting sacred texts, during rituals and prayers and rites of passage, although in the Western world, we associate it more with yoga than with its use as a mantra."

"It sounds totally benign," Mason said.

"On the surface, maybe, but this particular bastardization of it is the symbol of the Japanese doomsday cult known as Aum Shinrikyo."

Mason knew all about the cult, which had released homemade sarin on the Tokyo subway in 1995, an attack meant to cripple the Japanese parliament and usher its David Koresh–like leader into power. While the death toll had been mercifully small due to the poor quality of the sarin, thousands of victims had been treated in overflowing hospitals throughout the city. It was during the aftermath that Dr. Tatsuo Yamaguchi earned his reputation as an expert on the treatment of exposure to chemical weapons, the notoriety from which had brought him into the orbit of the Scarecrow, who, along with her brother, had been experiencing the latent effects of the experimentation she'd endured at the Edgewood Arsenal as a child.

Or, at least, that was how Mason assumed they'd met.

This new information painted an entirely different picture, one that led him to a revelation that changed the way he looked at everything.

"Yamaguchi didn't just treat the injured that day," he said. "He released the sarin."

28

"Aum Shinrikyo, roughly translated, means 'teaching of the universal truth,'" Gunnar said. "Its belief system was a unique amalgamation of Indian and Tibetan Buddhism, Hinduism, and Christianity. Its followers worshipped Shoko Asahara—a charismatic blind man who somehow convinced them that he had supernatural powers—as the second coming of Christ. He saw dark conspiracies everywhere he looked and became obsessed with end-of-the-world prophecies, but it wasn't until he prophesied his own nuclear Armageddon at the hands of the Americans that things started to spin out of control."

"Sounds like things were just stellar right up until then," Ramses said.

"You have to look at this in a historical context. This was the early nineties. The bombings of Hiroshima and Nagasaki were still fresh wounds on the nation's psyche. They were Japan's version of nine/ eleven, only on a much grander scale. The fall of the Soviet Union left the U.S. as the sole nuclear superpower and we'd already demonstrated our eagerness to use our arsenal, so it wasn't unreasonable to believe we'd be willing to do so again. It was a message to which people responded in unpredictable ways, because when you believe that the world's about to end, you're absolved of accountability."

Mason studied the image on the screen. Cults attracted the disenfranchised by offering a sense of belonging. Tattooing them was a form of social contract, offering irrevocable membership in exchange for a lifelong commitment. He could see how such a relationship would appeal to marginalized people, but not to those who had already achieved a degree of success in life.

"How does an apocalyptic cult recruit someone like Yamaguchi?" he asked. "He was a trained physician whose entire career had been devoted to saving lives."

"Aum Shinrikyo wasn't a repository for the dregs of society," Gunnar said. "It attracted people from all walks of life, most of them impressionable twentysomethings facing an unknown future. Recruiters specifically sought out professionals and experts in their fields, among them scientists and doctors, architects and engineers, scholars and lawyers. These individuals were the next generation of society's elite and they knew it. They believed in their superiority to such an extent that the cult was able to use Isaac Asimov's Foundation Trilogy as one of its primary tools of seduction."

"Asimov wrote science fiction," Layne said.

"So did L. Ron Hubbard," Ramses said. "And you know what kind of couch-jumping crazy he unleashed."

"Foundation doesn't espouse a religious doctrine so much as a societal one," Gunnar said. "It's about a group of artisans and engineers who determine by scientific means that their galactic empire is going to fall, ushering in thirty thousand years of darkness, but if they somehow preserve and expand upon mankind's collective knowledge, they can mitigate the coming cataclysm and accelerate the rise of a new order. It's a classic example of 'The Chosen' literary trope, wherein the best humanity has to offer are assembled to save the human race, only rather than the most physically gifted specimens, Asimov gathered a team of enlightened intellectuals who went underground during an age of barbarism, biding their time until they could emerge and rebuild civilization."

"Sounds like a serious case of god complex to me," Ramses said. He reached up and pressed the button that turned on his overhead light. "How do I get the stewardess's attention?"

"Flight attendant," Layne said.

"There isn't one," Gunnar said.

"You should really get one."

"I assume that's your less-than-subtle way of asking for a drink."

"I wouldn't turn one down if you're getting up."

Gunnar sighed and headed toward the cockpit, behind which was a mini refrigerator. He grabbed three bottled waters and a beer for Ramses and returned to his seat.

"You make, what, ten million dollars a year?" Ramses said. "And you stock Heineken on your private jet?"

Gunnar ignored him, took a sip of his water, and picked up where he'd left off.

"The idea of being foremost among the survivors of the apocalypse, destined to rebuild the world in their image, attracted more than nine thousand followers, several hundred of whom believed with such fervor that they abandoned their families and friends, transferred all of their savings to Asahara, and moved into the cult's Kamikuishiki complex at the foot of Mount Fuji. Those whom the cult considered to be among the most valuable, however, led dual lives. They maintained their positions and status in the outside world, while simultaneously pursuing the ultimate goal of the cult, which, when Asahara's prediction failed to come to pass on the prophesied date, became all about making his prophecy a self-fulfilling one so he didn't lose his power over his flock."

"So people like Yamaguchi treated patients during the day and then plotted how to kill them all at night," Mason said.

"Exactly. The cult had entire warehouses devoted to the manufacture of assault rifles and chemical weapons, produced by men and women with no practical experience with either. They refined many of their own precursor chemicals in homemade labs and weaponized them in vats near where they slept. When the police finally arrived, they found the ground so saturated with chemicals that pools had formed. Imagine how many people Yamaguchi must have treated for exposure during the steepest portion of their learning curve. It's no wonder he knew exactly what to do in the wake of the attack."

"But that wasn't what brought him to the Scarecrow's attention, was it?" Layne asked. "The Nakamuras were members, too. Kaemon and Kameko were also prominent physicians and had more reason than anyone else to believe the U.S. was capable of using its nuclear arsenal. It was because of this relationship that they all disappeared in 1996, the year after the sarin attack—"

"And two years after they were photographed at the Twentieth Assembly of the Society for Lasting International Peace in Copenhagen, the same conference attended by Nitzan Chenhav and Yossi Mosche, the men who helped the Scarecrow create four thousand gallons of Novichok A-234, and Andreas Mikkelson, managing director of Royal Nautilus Petroleum. It was undoubtedly here where the Thirteen recruited them to its genocidal cause. Both parties believed they were better than the rest of humanity and had the intellectual and moral authority to save the world from itself, which, in an apocalyptic sense, relieved them of their culpability in its destruction."

"The end justifies the means," Layne said.

"So then where did they go for the next twenty years?" Mason asked.

"The answer lies in the second tattoo," Gunnar said, reverting to the dragon design. "And in the picture I sent you earlier."

"The one taken in Russia?" Layne said. "I thought the cult was Japanese."

"It is. Or, rather, it was. Aum saw the chance to expand into the former Soviet Union and, like the rest of the world, recognized the opportunity to purchase technology and weaponry at clearinghouse prices. So in 1992, Asahara dispatched his minister of construction, a guy named Kiyohide Hayakawa, to pave the way for Aum's recognition as a legitimate religious enterprise and negotiate deals with state-sponsored radio and TV stations to disseminate propaganda. And while the cult was fostering a reputable public image, its members were simultaneously training with the Russian armed forces and shipping all kinds of weapons back to Japan. They even obtained the blueprints for the AK-47 so they could build their own. And all of this without the direction of their figurehead, Asahara, who was holed up in the Mount Fuji complex, trying to keep the wheels from coming off his operation there."

"It sounds like two different organizations," Mason said.

"In a sense it was. After seventy years of Communist rule, most Russians had been successfully indoctrinated into a system of atheism and had no real understanding of spirituality or religion, especially the younger generations, which approached their recruitment in a practical manner. They were promised education in the fields of agriculture, medicine, and science and Hayakawa honored his commitments. He rapidly grew the Russian sect to an estimated thirty-six thousand converts, far more than Asahara ever had in Japan. More important, he gathered a flock that had seen the consequences of worshipping out in the open and convinced his devotees to take their sect underground. And not a moment too soon, it turned out. The sarin attack on the Tokyo subway changed everything. President Yeltsin ordered a thorough investigation of Aum's activities in Russia and the ministry of justice subsequently annulled its registration, closed all seven of its centers of worship, and commenced a rash of arrests."

Mason felt a subtle sinking sensation in his abdomen as the plane started its descent into Colorado, which always promised to be a rocky ride.

"Obviously the cult didn't go anywhere or you wouldn't be telling this story," Ramses said. "So why don't you cut to the chase. And get me another beer while you're at it."

"You know where I keep them," Gunnar said.

Ramses groaned as though the inconvenience were simply too great, but he stood up and headed for the refrigerator anyway.

"Just for that I'm taking two," he said.

"So what did they do?" Layne asked.

"They divided into different geographical branches," Gunnar said. "Each utilized its own largely autonomous leadership, simultaneously minimizing the cult's exposure and creating the close-knit communal relationships the converts craved. As these branches became increasingly isolated from one another, however, their beliefs began to diverge, especially after their founder, Hayakawa, was arrested in Japan and sentenced to death alongside Asahara and the other members responsible for the subway attack. By 2000, the groups had broken into factions. The majority denounced their former beliefs and changed the cult's name to Aleph in an attempt to regain legitimacy, while the remainder divided into smaller cells and went even deeper underground. As highly educated individuals, it's believed they infiltrated the diplomatic and scientific communities. The only known member who was ever caught has been in prison for years and hasn't said a word. At the time of his arrest, he was working at the Yakovlev Design Bureau, where they manufacture Pchela unmanned aerial vehicles, which are essentially knockoff versions of Predator drones used by the Russian air force."

"They sound like terrorists," Ramses said, draining half of his beer on the way back to his seat.

"They utilize the same basic modus operandi by hiding in plain sight," Gunnar said. "While they haven't taken credit for any attacks, they've been indirectly linked to the sarin and Novichok used in Syria and England, respectively."

"Then why don't we hear about these guys like we do al-Qaeda?" Layne asked. "They weren't even on my radar."

"Nor mine, and that's what makes this whole thing so disconcerting. They undoubtedly learned from the botched attack on the Tokyo subway and don't crave the limelight like other terrorist groups do. We can only assume they're still devoted to the apocalyptic teachings of Hayakawa, who, at the time of his arrest, had in his possession the schematics for a directed-energy weapon, technical drawings of a fission device small enough to fit in a suitcase, and blueprints for a nuclear-powered HALE UAV—a high-altitude, long-endurance unmanned aerial vehicle. He also had a map with detailed directions to what he called an 'arms market' in a city in Siberia."

"Let me guess," Mason said. "Omsk?"

"Close. Just to the east in Novosibirsk."

Mason sensed the convergence of events. He'd already encountered the Russian city once during his hunt for the Scarecrow. Novosibirsk had to be important, because if there was one thing he'd learned, when it came to the Thirteen, there was no such thing as a coincidence.

29

Mason had been confident he knew where they were going, but it wasn't until they passed over Denver and continued to the northeast that he had his proof. He elected to keep the revelation to himself, primarily because he wasn't sure how to explain it to Layne, or if he even wanted to try. At least not until the last possible moment. And maybe not even then.

They'd landed at Greeley–Weld County Airport to find a rental car waiting at the terminal, as arranged. They'd barely loaded into the black Chevy Tahoe, cranked up the air conditioner, and started driving away—with Ramses at the wheel, Gunnar in the passenger seat with his laptop open on his thighs, and Layne in the backseat beside Mason—when his phone rang. He sighed when he saw the number on the caller ID. He wasn't surprised that his father was calling, but rather that it had taken so long. He answered on the third ring.

"Tell me you aren't still in Manhattan," his father said.

Mason stared out the window at a field of winter wheat, and beyond it, the cottonwoods and willows lining the Cache la Poudre River. Signs promising a scrapyard and a truck washout materialized in the distance. The smell of the feedlots grew stronger by the second.

"I'm in just about the furthest place from it," he said.

"Good."

The sound of relief in his father's voice surprised him. The second-term senator wasn't prone to overt displays of emotion of any kind, especially not one that implied weakness. The third James Richmond Mason went by J.R., which was his way of distancing himself from his grandfather and father, who'd both insisted upon being called James. It wasn't that he'd disliked them by any stretch of the imagination, only that they'd set the bar so high that the last thing in the world he wanted was to have his accomplishments judged against theirs.

Mason hadn't known his great-grandfather, the first of his name, who'd died while he was still in the womb. As one of the most respected lawyers of his time, he'd represented the richest and most powerful men in the world, helped found multiple organizations dedicated to fostering international peace, and ended his career as chief justice of the Supreme Court of the United States. His son and

Mason's grandfather, James Richmond Mason II, had chaired the boards of any number of charitable foundations, raised millions of dollars for the overseas relief efforts following World War II, and served his country as the second of his bloodline to wear the robe of the chief justice, which was why it was so surprising that J.R. had gone to law school in the first place. How was he supposed to live up to the standards of his forebears when serving as anything less than the highest judge in the land would be considered failure?

It turned out Mason's father had an even grander destiny in mind, so he'd left the DA's office and entered politics. As a prominent senator, he chaired several subcommittees and sat on just about every other. He was so wired into the system that there were only a handful of people in the country who knew more than he did at any given time. And it had to drive him crazy.

"What's going on?" Mason asked.

"I was hoping you might be able to tell me. All I've heard here in the District is that there's a credible national security risk, one high enough to raise the terrorism threat level to red and close the southern border. Any one of America's myriad enemies would love to bloody her nose, especially on Independence Day, but the White House has thus far been less than forthcoming with information."

"How should I know? I'm just a rank-and-file federal agent—"

"Don't feed me that line. Every time I turn around, you're neck-deep in something Lord only knows you shouldn't be involved in. I'm half-convinced you're trying to give me a heart attack."

"If there's a point equidistant from every border, it has to be pretty close to where I am now."

"That's all I wanted to hear," the senator said. "You will tell me if you hear anything I should know."

It was a statement, not a question, or even a request.

Ramses rolled down his window and buffeted Mason with super-heated air. Just to be a dick. He glanced up and could tell from his old friend's eyes in the rearview mirror that he was getting a kick out of it.

"Look, Dad—"

"I know, I know," his father said. "You're a very busy man and you've already wasted as much time as you can afford on your old man."

"Old man, my ass." Mason laughed. "You'll outlive us all."

"I pray that's not the case, son." The way he said it gave Mason pause. He suddenly understood that his father wasn't fishing for information; he was seeking confirmation of something he'd already heard. "Just try to stay out of whatever's going on, James. For me. Please."

"Sure, Dad."

"You're a terrible liar."

Mason terminated the call and watched the city of Greeley blow past. He'd always associated this town with his wife, who'd been raised here by the same man who'd ultimately given the order for her murder. To the north were the corporate buildings belonging to the company formerly known as AgrAmerica, which had fallen into financial ruin after his father-in-law, Paul Thornton, had been exposed as a conspirator in the plot to release a deadly flu virus. As a reward for helping Mason rid himself of his toxic inheritance, his father had been saddled with a controlling stake in the company at a time when it had been impossible to unload his shares, but the senator hadn't complained. He'd simply changed the name to AgrInitiative, hired a fleet of MBAs to right the ship, and laid the foundation for a dawning business empire.

"What did your old man have to say?" Gunnar asked.

"Sounds like he has a pretty good idea of what's going on, but he doesn't know for sure."

"Which means the president's decided to take a wait-and-see approach to avoid causing a panic. Scary as it sounds, I'm sure this isn't the first time he's been forced to deal with this kind of threat."

"You're undoubtedly right," Mason said, "but with actionable intel—"

"Actionable implies a course of action, which is precisely what we currently lack."

"While we're on the subject, is anybody going to tell me where we're going?" Layne asked.

"We're going to the home of a business associate of mine—"

"And just what does this business associate of yours do?"

"His family made a fortune refining sugar beets," Mason said. He glanced out the window just as the sign announcing the city limits of Windsor flashed past. "And now he hunts Nazis."

Layne was silent for several moments. She tucked her feet up on the seat and stared off into space.

"Fine. Don't tell me. I thought we were past all of this bullshit."

"Layne—"

"Whatever you're going to say, you know exactly where you can shove it."

They drove through a downtown district filled with old Victorian homes and storefronts straight out of Mayberry on their way into neighborhoods that became increasingly modern with every passing block, as though they were traveling forward in time. The houses grew larger and farther apart until they left the town behind and entered rolling hills marked by gated estates set way back from the road.

Gunnar closed his laptop and used it to balance a contact lens case. He opened the caps and placed the lenses in his eyes, one at a time. Mason hadn't even known his old friend needed them. It was just another sign that the years were passing them by.

"How did this meeting come about?" Mason asked.

He'd expected Gunnar to reply, but it was Ramses who spoke.

"Remember how you asked me to look into that DEW for you? That's not the kind of thing you can even discreetly ask about without pricking a few ears, if you know what I'm saying."

"These are some pretty big ears."

"Not compared to some I deal with," Ramses said, but he didn't elaborate. "Like I said, nobody had heard anything more than rumors about this thing they're calling the dragon. Once I started asking about it specifically, I received a surprise visit from a guy dressed like Mr. Belvedere who claimed to 'represent the interests of his benefactor—'"

"Who simultaneously called me and suggested we arrange a meeting," Gunnar said.

"We could have set up a virtual conference in a secure online chat room," Mason said. "The only reason to invite us back here is because we have information he desperately needs and he's willing to trade something from his archives to get it."

"And based on the value of what's down there, whatever he's after has to be hugely important."

"Speaking of huge . . ." Layne said.

Ramses slowed as they rounded a sloping bend, to the right of which was a massive knoll spotted with sculpted shrubbery. A house perched on top of it like a crown, a sprawling mansion composed of several distinct additions of different architectural styles, which somehow only added to its grandeur. The main gate was already opening when he turned from the road onto the asphalt driveway.

Mason watched Layne from the corner of his eye as she studied the fence surrounding the estate, her eyes lingering on the nearly invisible surveillance system, and then on the property itself, where subtle paths had been worn into the lawn behind the bushes and along the perimeter. She furrowed her brow and looked him directly in the eyes.

"There are cameras every fifteen feet and signs of security patrols everywhere," she said. "You were telling the truth?"

The driveway leveled off at the top of the hill, where it encircled a fountain that glimmered under the late-afternoon sun. The Tahoe passed a carriage house and pulled up at the foot of the stairs of the magnificent home.

"Sometimes I wish I weren't."

30

An elderly gentleman with a rosy face and a bushy white beard flung open the front doors and extended his arms as though preparing to embrace them all at once. He wore a red-and-black-checkered robe over lavender pajamas and fuzzy socks inside Dearfoams slippers. He looked like Santa Claus in the off-season, a jolly soul who drank cocoa and played board games and bounced small children on his knee, but this persona was merely one half of the old man's split personality, an identity so likeable that it was impossible to believe that the other half even existed.

"My friends!" he bellowed. "Welcome once more to my home. It is my pleasure to receive you again. I only wish we could have met under more opportune circumstances."

"You are so full of shit, Mason," Layne whispered under her breath.

A younger man wearing a sweater vest over a shirt and tie appeared at the old man's side. He had thick black hair, a preponderance of moles, and a bulge underneath his armpit that left little doubt as to what he was trying to conceal. He offered an arm to his benefactor, who playfully swatted it away and descended the steps on his own.

Gunnar met him halfway with his hand proffered, only to find himself engulfed in a hug. He smiled despite himself and gracefully accepted several pats on the back before disengaging.

Mason followed suit and was greeted with a firm handshake and a clap on the shoulder.

"Young master James, it is wonderful you were able to make this trip in person," the old man said. "I do so dislike talking to people through a computer screen. It is disheartening the way the youth of today communicate. I often wonder if they will be able to disengage from their devices long enough to produce the next generation." He winked and turned to Layne. "And who might this angelic being be?"

Mason couldn't remember ever having seen his partner smile, let alone blush.

"Special Agent Jessica Layne," he said by way of introduction. "This is Johan Mahler."

"The pleasure is all mine, my dear." He took her hand as he would that of a princess and guided her up the stairs into his home. "Do come in, won't you?"

Ramses followed Mason onto the porch, where he acknowledged the man in the sweater vest with an inclination of his chin. "Asher."

"Oh, my," Johan said. "Where are my manners? Miss Jessica, if I may be so presumptuous as to use your first name, please allow me to introduce my companion and constant thorn in my side, Asher Ben-Menachem."

The man in the sweater vest shook her hand and offered an explanation in a thick Arabic accent filtered through a formal British education.

"I am Mr. Mahler's chief caretaker."

Mason also knew he was a former battalion commander in the Golani Brigade of the Israeli Defense Forces and Mahler's pet assassin, who, under the alias Seraph, had executed the war criminals his employer had used his vast resources to track to the ends of the earth.

"Do not worry," Johan said, draping his arm over Ramses's shoulder. "I did not forget about you. I am grateful you reached out to me, albeit in a most roundabout manner. I have been looking forward to making your acquaintance for quite some time. I shall call you Ramses and commend your parents on their originality."

Ramses smirked.

"I'll be sure to pass that along when I see them."

Johan stood at the foot of a grand staircase that branched in opposite directions at the landing, above which hung a painting of his land from a time when bison roamed the plains. The dirty trowel his grandfather had used to carve a fortune from the ground was encased in Lucite beneath it. He clapped his hands, beamed, and, with a flourish, gestured for them to precede him into the living room.

"May I offer refreshments while we prepare to get down to business?" he asked. "I have acquired what I am told is some excellent coffee since last you were here. Single-origin, direct-trade, or some such. Unfortunately, I am having difficulty controlling my diabetes, which means I have been forced to trade my customary cocoa for cacao, the difference being in the arrangement of the vowels and the fact that the latter tastes as though it is made largely of the dirt in which the former is grown."

"It is a small sacrifice to make for one intent upon keeping his toes," Ben-Menachem said.

"That is why the Lord, in all His infinite wisdom, gave us ten," Johan said. "Asher, will you please brew some coffee for all, as is the custom, and bring it down to the archives?"

"As you wish," Ben-Menachem said, turning to face them. "Now, if you don't mind, I must insist upon retaining your cellular devices while you are inside the archives. An inadvertent flash could cause the rapid deterioration of some of the more sensitive documents."

While that might have been true, it wasn't the real reason and they all knew it. Mason had hoped to be able to capture at least some small portion of the information housed below, but Johan was not in the business of giving away anything for free.

"Don't you trust us?" Mason asked.

"Your hesitation suggests I am justified in erring on the side of caution," Johan said. "Now, if you would be so kind . . ."

They surrendered their phones to Ben-Menachem, who disappeared without a word, leaving them to follow Johan through a living room with an enormous fireplace straight out of Valhalla and into a hallway adorned with framed photographs of Mahlers through the generations, from black-and-white pictures of severe men and women capable of clawing a living from the hard earth to children whose sparkling eyes didn't appear to have seen a solitary moment of suffering.

Mason immediately noticed that the security cameras had been upgraded and laser sensors had been installed. The combination pad
hidden behind the photo of Johan's grinning granddaughter had been
replaced with a palmprint scanner that mapped the unique config-
uration of blood vessels concealed beneath the skin, which, unlike a
retinal scanner, would fail to work if those vessels constricted due to
lack of blood flow, a feature designed to ensure that the operator was
both still living and in one piece.

Johan placed his hand over the laser and a section of the wall
opened, revealing a hidden staircase. He offered his arm to Layne
and together they descended into a narrow hallway, at the end of
which was a stainless-steel door. Like the outer entrance, it had been
retrofitted with a palmprint scanner. He again worked his magic and
the door popped open with a hiss of escaping air.

"The documents archived down here are irreplaceable, my dear,"
Johan said. "We must maintain constant temperature, pressure, and
humidity if we are to preserve them. The world, it seems, labors to
erase its own history. One must never forget the lessons our predeces-
sors learned on our behalf."

There was a third door with yet another scanner at the end of the
corridor. It couldn't be opened at the same time as the second door,
which meant that Johan had to wait for Ramses and Gunnar to come
all the way inside and close the door behind them before resting his
palm on the reader.

Mason's heart beat faster in anticipation.

The final seal opened and a rush of sterile air flooded past them.
Ahead lay artifacts that no one who saw them would ever forget, memorials to atrocities that not even the most violent of animals were
capable of inflicting upon one another. Mason was convinced that hidden among them were the identities of the remaining members of the
Thirteen.

"Lights," Johan said. The overhead fixtures snapped on, one after
another, leading away from them into the depths of the bunker with a
thoom-thoom-thoom that diminished with each recurrence. He made
a sweeping gesture with his free arm. "Welcome to my sanctum sanc-
torum."

Mason willed himself to retain everything he saw and commit
it to memory. The walls of the massive space were plastered with
maps from seemingly every city and country around the globe, with

handwritten notes, photographs, newspaper articles, and computer printouts tacked to them with color-coded pushpins. Cabinets full of servers, climate-control units, dehumidifiers, and electrical components of all kinds hummed in the pale bluish white light. Computer stations lined parallel tables in a manner reminiscent of the launch floor of NASA or a war room deep inside NORAD.

"You must be asking yourselves why I could not simply forward the information I have brought you here to see and spare us all this elaborate song and dance," Johan said.

"I'd be lying if I said the thought hadn't crossed my mind," Mason said.

"The answer, I am afraid, is that through the course of my many years on this planet, I have learned two universal truths." The intonation of Johan's voice changed as he spoke. So did his word choice and mannerisms, his posture and bearing, until the grandfatherly man had somehow vanished before their eyes, leaving in his place a being whose quality of otherness was simultaneously alien and all too human. "First, you must never underestimate your friends or your enemies, for they are both capable of extraordinary compassion and cruelty, and of changing roles due to events outside of your control. And second, you must always believe the powers that be when they tell you they are doing something of questionable morality and never believe them when they say they are not. A government that spies upon every conversation between its own citizens, through the airwaves and the Internet, and yet wants us to believe that there are hidden, encrypted spaces that it cannot monitor must be viewed with the same skepticism as the spider that entices the fly into its web with the smell of dead meat."

Johan guided them into the adjacent room, which resembled an old British hunting lodge, had the walls been adorned with placards instead of severed heads, undoubtedly to Johan's chagrin.

"This is the Trophy Room," he said. "My father, may God rest his soul, started this collection while I was but a child. It has been my life's work to see it to completion, only now I must admit that it will never truly be finished."

On the left half of each placard was an old photograph of a man or a woman, a black-and-white still life of an individual who'd been either swept away by a movement or taken advantage of it to inflict pain and misery upon others. Men and women in uniform or civilian clothing, with weapons or without, captured on film during a time when the world at large was oblivious to the plight of Johan's people, who'd been rounded up, corralled, and exterminated. On the right were close-ups of the faces of the men and women they would later become. The signs of aging were obvious, from the laugh lines around their mouths to the crow's-feet beside their eyes, the loosening of the skin along their jaws to the folds in their eyelids, and the relative enlargement of their noses and earlobes to the presence of scars where there had been none before. Only their eyes remained unchanged. They stared blankly into the room from beneath the Litzmannstadt coin that had been placed over the small-caliber entrance wounds in the center of their foreheads, but did little to conceal the patterns of blood spatter and the speckled tattoos of discharge. Photographs taken by men like the one making them coffee at that very moment, who took on the sins of the man for whom he killed and served as a surrogate for whatever punishment awaited him in the afterlife.

Layne had paled considerably, but her expression remained guarded. She obviously recognized the fact that they were walking into the lair of the most prolific and sadistic family of serial killers the world would never know and was still attempting to process the moral ambiguity of it all, the fact that she could see both the wrong and the right of the trophy hunting of murderers.

"You must understand that an enemy has infiltrated the highest levels of every aspect of society," Johan said. "It has committed itself to playing the long game with our lives, and now I fear that all of its patience and preparation have brought it to the moment of action, when nations will be cast aside in favor of a single global state, one ruled by a self-anointed master race that understands that any successful rule requires equal parts love and fear, respect and servitude. More importantly, it understands that the larger the kingdom, the more difficult it is to rule. As everyone from the Romans to the British have learned, in order to expand, an empire must simultaneously contract. It is far easier to control eight hundred million than eight billion, especially once they've been unencumbered by their own unproductive numbers. The sickly and the weak. The lazy and the mentally deficient. Those whose contributions to the greater good have been measured and found wanting. In the eyes of our enemy, the time has come to begin anew. Only this time, the world will be rebuilt in its image."

Johan abruptly stopped in the threshold of the adjacent room and turned to face them.

"The dragon is not a weapon. He is a man, and he is deadlier than any you have ever encountered."

31

"We know next to nothing about the Dragon and what little we do is anecdotal at best," Johan said, guiding them into a room that had changed considerably since Mason was last here.

Where before there had been whiteboards with handwritten notes beside pictures of men listed among Johan's personal most-wanted criminals, there were now touchscreen computer monitors larger than most televisions, turned on their sides so as to take advantage of their vertical dimensions, their contents hidden by screensavers featuring photographs of subjects captured at a distance, most of them poorly lit and out of focus, scrolling past one at a time in an almost taunting manner.

Mason recognized a man in his sixties with blond hair and piercing blue eyes. Here was the third incarnation of the Hoyl—Fischer F3—a mass murderer who favored hemorrhagic fevers as his weapon of choice. He was also the father of the monster who'd killed Mason's wife and whom he, in return, had put in the ground. Johan had made sure the display was impossible to miss so that Mason wouldn't be able to forget that his job wasn't finished.

"Until recently, we believed his very existence to be a myth, one implicating a single individual in the heinous crimes of many," Johan said. "His work reflects an overt element of sadism, one that suggests he simply enjoys inflicting pain and misery upon his victims."

He stopped in front of a screen displaying images of a man wearing a silver full-body CBRN suit with a reflective face shield. He was out of focus and pixilated, as though captured in the background of a photograph and enlarged to near life-size proportions. While it could have been anyone, or any number of different people, inside that suit, the proportions and posture remained unchanged from one instance to the next, suggesting it was the same individual in each.

Mason almost felt as though the Dragon were looking directly at him through time and space. Layne was already staring at him when he glanced in her direction. She must have felt it, too.

Johan caught their unspoken communication.

"You have seen this man, have you not?"

"We've seen a man wearing a suit just like this one," Layne said. "There's no way to be certain it was the same man underneath, though."

"You must tell me where you saw him," Johan said. He attempted to smile but only succeeded in showcasing bared teeth elongated by age. "The implications are of great consequence. This is no mere man. He is responsible for the deaths of tens, if not hundreds of thousands of innocent people."

"That's a big number for someone no one has ever heard of," Ramses said. "You have proof?"

Johan touched the screen. The images stopped scrolling and vanished altogether, leaving in their place the root directory of a local database containing files labeled: Affiliations, Aliases, Background, Imagery, Intelligence, Known Associates, and Methodology. He tapped the Imagery icon, which opened a subdirectory of dates arranged in chronological order, and touched the first one from 2004.

A photograph of an apocalyptic urban wasteland filled the central third of the screen. Smoke and ash hung heavily in the air. The buildings had been obliterated, leaving behind mountains of concrete and debris. Bodies had been dragged from the rubble and lined up for retrieval by men wearing desert camouflage fatigues and helmets, their faces painted black with soot. The Dragon hovered over them, together and yet apart from them, as he casually appraised the devastation.

"This picture was taken in Iraq during the Second Battle of Fallujah, during which thousands of insurgents and civilians alike were killed and two hundred thousand residents displaced."

He closed the 2004 file and breezed through the 2005 subdirectory, flipping from one image to the next. Each showed a similar scene in a slightly different location. Buildings converted to rubble. Bodies strewn in the streets or in dirt fields, among scorched and burning cars, heaped for collection or sealed in white plastic bags for mass burial. And in each one of them was the man in the silver CBRN suit, as though he were death himself, bearing witness to events of historical significance.

"Is he American?" Layne asked. "Part of the coalition forces?"

"He is a scavenger," Johan said. "Much like a carrion bird, he can always be found among the dead."

"What about the other dates?" Mason asked.

Johan opened the file marked 2011 and paged through images nearly identical to the others, photographs taken in different ruined cities, and with men in different uniforms, standing over different bodies. Only the man in the silver suit remained unchanged.

"These were taken during the First Libyan Civil War. The Arab Spring. When more than thirty thousand were killed, another fifty thousand gravely wounded, and the country left in shambles."

He closed the folder and opened another labeled 2014. The first picture was of a freshly excavated pit filled with bodies wrapped in plastic and aligned side by side in rows. A man driving a tractor had just begun to bury them. Several more wearing black fatigues and *she-magh* scarves that concealed their entire heads, crouched at the precipice, while the Dragon stood back and watched. There were dozens more pictures, all featuring ruined cityscapes and people with faces painted white by cement dust, the blood from their wounds standing apart like crimson beacons.

"This series was acquired in Syria," Johan said, "where more than five hundred thousand people have died since the start of the civil war. Do you not see the pattern of escalation?"

"He's just standing there in all of the pictures," Layne said. "How do you know he *did* anything?"

"We were able to locate many of the men in the photographs with him," Johan said. "And every single one of them was dead."

"That's well within the range of statistical probability," Gunnar said. He'd been unusually quiet, just staring at the various monitors, blinking as though he were awakening from a deep sleep. "Given the lives they'd chosen to lead, anyway."

"Perhaps you are right, but I am sure you would be interested to learn that a surprising number of them died from symptoms one might associate with acute radiation syndrome." Johan saw the spark of recognition in Mason's eyes before he could hide it. "That means something to you, does it not? Tell me where you saw him."

Mason weighed his words carefully. He couldn't afford to give away too much before he had what he needed in return.

"We were able to recover a picture of him from the memory card of a digital rifle scope."

"Did the owner of this rifle hit him?"

Mason didn't reply.

"Then he is dead already," Johan said. "I assume this must have been the reason you were led to him in the first place."

Footsteps echoed from the depths of the sublevel. Ben-Menachem materialized as if from nowhere with a collection of steaming novelty mugs on a fancy silver serving tray. He held it out to each of them in turn. Mason grabbed the closest one to him, which read: WORLD's GREATEST GRAMPA.

"This is why you were seeking information about a directed-energy weapon," Johan said to Ramses, and then to Mason: "This man who failed to hit the Dragon . . . are you certain it was a weapon of this nature that killed him and not something else? Think carefully."

"It was used to set him on fire," Mason said. "And his house right along with him, with the intention of making it look like an accident."

"How many others died alongside him?"

"Just his dog," Layne said.

"That is not the Dragon's way," Ben-Menachem said. "A single victim is beneath him, a waste of his time and talents."

"Asher is correct," Johan said. "Perhaps you did not fully appreciate the condition of the bodies in the photographs."

He returned to the monitor, where men with rifles stood over corpses draped with blankets. Appendages protruded from underneath them. Johan zoomed in on a lower leg that looked like it had been roasted over a bonfire. The skin was cracked and blackened, the exposed tissue suppurated.

"Looks like a third-degree burn," Layne said.

"It is worse than that," Johan said. He closed the file from 2014 and opened the one from 2011. "You will be able to better appreciate the distinction on the bodies of the Libyans."

He scrolled through the pictures until he found the one he wanted. It was a close-up of soldiers loading corpses into the bed of a pickup truck, while distraught men and women attempted to fight through them to reach the remains. The victims' clothes were burned or missing altogether, their exposed skin covered with full-thickness burns and wounds clotted with a paste of soot and blood. The Dragon leaned over the edge, reaching for the hand of a dead man in what almost looked like a cruel mockery of Michelangelo's *The Creation of Adam*. The victim's chest and shoulder were bloody and raw where the skin had once been. The edges of the wounds were fringed with black, the surrounding tissue red and livid, as though one enormous blister.

"Jesus," Ramses said. He turned and ran his fingers through his hair. "What the hell is wrong with people?"

Johan switched to a picture featuring a group of armed men standing on one side and the Dragon on the other. He zoomed in on the lower left corner, where a man was sprawled on his back, one arm crumpled to his chest, the other splayed at his side. His chin was tilted to the sky and his mouth hung open. The upper half of his nose and the entirety of his face where his eyes had once been—

Mason couldn't bear it another second longer. He had to look away.

"The victims have the same types of radiation burns as we saw in Hiroshima," Johan said. "These people died from their injuries. Slowly. And in the most painful manner imaginable. This kind of radiation exposure cannot be targeted. It is a massive expulsion of invisible fury that expands outward and burns straight through the flesh of everyone in its path. This is why they call him the Dragon . . . because the victims left in his wake appear to have been burned alive."

32

"I have photographic evidence that he targeted this single individual," Mason said. "It might not be the clearest image, but there's no doubt that's him in the picture and the results speak for themselves. Like you said, the victim was burned alive."

Johan's face went blank and he disappeared inside of himself for several seconds.

"You must tell me the identity of this victim," he finally said.

Mason studied the older man's expression for any sign of recognition when he answered.

"Ryan Austin." Johan blinked and shook his head. He glanced at Ben-Menachem, whose features remained unreadable. "He was the border patrol agent in charge of the Rio Grande City Station."

Understanding slowly dawned in Johan's eyes.

"You reacted to the mention of radiation exposure not because of the murder of the agent you were dispatched to investigate but for a different reason entirely. I insist you tell me what you found. I fear we are already on borrowed time."

"We obtained soil samples that tested positive for isotopic plutonium."

"What about iodine and cesium?"

Mason locked eyes with Johan and shook his head.

"Environmental exposure without the fission by-products of uranium-235?" Ben-Menachem said. "The Dragon did not detonate one of his weapons."

"What kind of weapons?" Ramses asked.

"The kind that are responsible for the deaths you see on this screen."

"If he'd detonated nuclear bombs in Libya and Syria, we'd have known about it the moment it happened. It would have been all over the news. Hell, we'd have practically been able to see the mushroom clouds from here."

"You are assuming that a full-blown nuclear detonation was his intention."

"Hold up," Mason said. "What are you saying?"

Ben-Menachem glanced at Johan, who hesitated only briefly before nodding for him to proceed.

"Are you familiar with the concept of nuclear fizzle?"

"You mean a dud," Ramses said.

"Perhaps in the sense of actual yield versus expected yield, but a fizzle is still a deadly nuclear event."

"You're saying the Dragon's MO is to detonate these nuclear weapons using only a fraction of their full potential?" Layne said.

"Perhaps I can clarify," Johan said. "One can only design a nuclear device to be so small. You must have a certain amount of fissionable material in order to create the necessary chain reaction. The smallest warhead ever manufactured was the W54, which was as close as we have ever come to designing a device that could fit inside a suitcase. And yet at twelve inches wide, fifteen inches long, and more than fifty pounds, it was by no means discreet, especially when you consider it yielded a six-kiloton explosion. Not the kind of thing you can detonate without calling attention to yourself."

"Isn't that the whole point?" Ramses said.

"Only if you are willing to start a full-fledged nuclear war, but what if you could instead use a low-yield device to irradiate farmland so that nothing can grow, so that livestock produce food that is dangerous to consume? The starvation of a population creates a condition of hopelessness, one unsuited to supporting a foreign war. Or what if you simply used that weapon to make a swatch of contested land uninhabitable, creating an invisible wall that could be used to hem in your adversaries? There are countless ways to use such weaponry without creating a mushroom cloud that extends twenty miles into the sky and guarantees our mutually assured destruction."

"You must consider not just the heat produced by the blast, but also the spread of radioactive material," Ben-Menachem said. "That is the whole theory behind the use of a dirty bomb, only rather than radioactive waste, the Dragon uses actual fissionable material."

Ben-Menachem tucked the serving tray under his arm and approached the monitor. He closed the pictures, backed out to the root directory, and selected the Intelligence folder, inside of which was a header labeled: Libya. The satellite image it contained showed a demolished city, the majority of which resembled the surface of the moon. The ground was pitted where houses and buildings had once stood, the roads little more than faint impressions beneath the concrete dust. In the middle was a crater roughly the size and shape of a small lake. It served as the center of a transparent bull's-eye overlay, with orange arrows drawn from a column of boxes on the right side of the screen to specific locations within each of the rings. Inside of those boxes were radiation readings for isotopes of uranium, plutonium, iodine, and cesium, measured in picocuries per gram—pCi/g—and in amounts that made the soil samples they'd collected in Texas seem insignificant.

"These radiation readings were collected in 2016, a full five years after we believe the Dragon created that crater with one of his devices," Ben-Menachem said. "He caused the most visceral damage imaginable to as many people as possible and left the land uninhabitable for thousands of years to come. That is his way. Kill the soldiers and break the spirits of the survivors. And all with a nuclear bomb designed to yield only one or two percent of its potential. A six-kiloton explosion reduced to a mere six thousand tons in an area already under siege."

"Now imagine all of that radioactive material racing outward at thousands of miles an hour," Johan said. "Irradiating everyone and everything within the blast radius. It is in theory a weapon of both intimate and devastating proportions, one that can be easily transported and detonated by a single individual without it being a suicide mission. A single individual in a custom-designed protective suit that spares him, while still dosing the fools who are so interested in witnessing the suffering of their enemies that they can't see the invisible cloud of death enveloping them. I doubt that even at the end they had any idea what had happened to them. After all, people die of cancer every day. And who's to say that these men were not simply on the receiving end of the justifiable wrath of God?"

"So your hypothesis is that the Dragon deliberately builds flaws into these nuclear devices in order to cause premature detonation?" Gunnar said. He continued to stroll almost leisurely through the room, seemingly lost in his own thoughts. "Wouldn't that inherently destabilize the entire works?"

"We theorize that he has learned from these various tests how to buffer the reaction between the atoms to slow the speed at which the material reaches its optimal supercritical state, thereby producing free neutrons that prematurely start the chain reaction. This pre-detonation blows the remainder of the material apart."

"By that logic, his intention would be to inflict biological damage rather than massive thermal destruction, a waste of nuclear material that could easily devastate an entire country or fetch eight figures on the black market."

"While such a weapon sounds far less dangerous," Johan said, "I assure you that a single device of this nature could wipe out several city blocks and irradiate everyone within a five-mile radius before they even suspected the explosion was caused by anything more catastrophic than a gas leak. Worse would be in the coming weeks when thousands more people flooded area hospitals, suffering from the incurable effects of acute radiation syndrome. So please—I beseech you—tell me about these soil samples you mentioned. How high were the readings of the plutonium isotopes?"

"High enough to kill some crops and livestock," Layne said. "Ryan Austin was the one who reported the incidents, and it brought the Dragon to his door."

Johan looked at Ben-Menachem from the corner of his eye.

"This is the reason the DHS raised the threat level and closed the border," he said, turning to Mason. "Homeland Security would not react with such decisiveness in response to a mere sample of tainted soil. You must have found the Dragon's lab. Tell me what you saw."

His voice was high and tight, his eyes wide and bloodshot. If ever there was a moment to negotiate, this was it.

"You answer my question first," Mason said. "Who does he work for?"

"Lives hang in the balance," Johan said. "Now is not the time to make demands."

Mason crossed his arms over his chest and concentrated so as not to let his own desperation show on his face.

Johan sighed and seemed to deflate. When he spoke, it was in a tone of resignation.

"I fear that in this case we do not know. And that is what frightens me. Whether he is acting alone or in the service of a master, I worry there is no way to stop whatever has already been set in motion. So you must tell me, James, for the sake of countless innocent people, what did you find in the lab?"

Mason might have been willing to gamble with his own life, but not the lives of those he'd sworn to protect.

"We discovered fuel rod casings and the equipment to perform the PUREX process."

"He was reclaiming waste?" Johan couldn't hide his surprise. "You are certain?"

"I've seen it with my own eyes."

Johan turned once more to Ben-Menachem and spoke as though no one else were in the room.

"You know what this means."

"We have reached the end of the experimentation phase."

"And entered the endgame."

Johan whirled without another word and struck off across the room, his open robe flaring behind him.

"I told you what I know," Mason said to his back. "The least you can do is the same."

Johan abruptly stopped in the entryway and turned to face him with an expression that could have passed for sympathy.

"You must ask yourselves who benefitted from the utter obliteration of Iraq, Libya, and Syria," he said, and then he was gone, the slapping sounds of his slippers trailing him deeper into the sublevel, beyond the farthest point Mason had ever gone.

33

Ben-Menachem had seen them out of the archives and turned them over to the guard waiting in the hallway, who'd escorted them to the front door, returned their cell phones, and watched them drive away. No one in the Tahoe had spoken since Johan's sudden departure. Mason, for one, needed time to process everything he'd seen and heard. Whatever revelation Johan had made continued to elude him. Even more frustrating was the fact that he'd been surrounded by information about the Thirteen, but he hadn't been able to take advantage of it. He couldn't fathom why Johan didn't simply share it with him so he could end the threat once and for all. And then he remembered their conversation in the secure chat room during the manhunt for the Scarecrow.

What do you know about the Thirteen? he'd asked Johan.

More than you are capable of understanding as of yet, I'm afraid, the old man had replied.

You'd be surprised what I'm capable of understanding.

And you would be more surprised by what you are not.

The memory called to mind a question for which he had no answer.

"Why did we have to meet in person?" he asked. "We could have done all of that online without the frustration of having everything we've ever wanted to know about the Thirteen within our reach."

"It was a mutual decision," Gunnar said. He removed his laptop from its case and balanced it on his thighs. "Plus, I'm sure he wanted to bug your cell phones. And copy their contents, of course."

"You knew this?" Layne said. "And you just let us hand them over?"

"I figured it was a small price to pay for what we got in return."

"What we got . . . ?" Ramses said. "You just stood there, blinking like a freaking moron."

"Yes," Gunnar said. He removed the contact lens case from his laptop bag, set it on top of his computer, and unscrewed the circular lids. "Like a freaking moron."

He pulled at the corner of his left eye and his contact lens popped out. He held it up on the tip of his middle finger so they could all see the faint tracery of circuits built into the polymer.

"It's a miniature camera," he said, removing the lens from his right eye. "Powered by a photocell and activated by a deliberate blink. It transmits digital HD images via a built-in antenna."

"So every time you blinked—" Layne started to say.

"I was taking a picture that was being downloaded to this laptop right here."

"You're brilliant."

"Tell me something I don't know."

"You mean like how to pleasure a woman?" Ramses said.

"Hilarious," Gunnar said. He returned his contact case to his bag and opened his laptop. "We know Johan doesn't do anything without premeditation, so undoubtedly the imagery he allowed us to view is of no small importance. I need time to download and study the pictures to figure out why."

They headed back toward the town of Windsor, the houses aging before their eyes.

"Why do you think Johan took off so suddenly like that?" Layne asked. "What did he say? Something about reaching the endgame?"

"We have to assume he was referring to the fact that the Dragon had a ready supply of weapons-grade plutonium," Gunnar said, "which, I theorize, initially surprised him because he'd expected the soil samples to reveal isotopes in concentrations consistent with the detonation of a uranium-235 device, much like the values listed on the satellite image of Libya in 2016 demonstrated."

"Why would he be so much more alarmed by a plutonium device?"

"It's capable of creating a much bigger bang, for one. It also produces alpha radiation, which isn't useful for a weapon designed to inflict the greatest physical damage to its victims since it can't actually penetrate their skin. You'd need gamma radiation for that. So if I were to wager a guess, I'd say the Dragon transitioned to plutonium because either he hopes to create a much bigger fizzle or—"

"He intends to use the bomb to its full potential," Mason said.

"Bomb? For all we know there could be dozens of them, hidden in major cities around the world."

"That would be one hell of an endgame," Ramses said.

"True, but when it comes to the Thirteen, there's always a financial motive," Layne said. "Johan said we needed to figure out who benefitted most from the ruination of Iraq, Libya, and Syria."

"The obvious answer would be anyone able to secure the oil exploration rights," Gunnar said, his fingers buzzing across his keyboard. "Various commercial interests were able to do so in Iraq, but while Libya might be sitting on one of the ten largest oil deposits in the world, its production has been nonexistent since Gaddafi's overthrow and infighting among the still-warring factions makes it appear as though it might not ever start up again. And no one's getting a foothold in Syria while Russia's propping up the Assad regime and there's a European gas line to be laid."

"We can't talk about oil without looking at Langbroek and Royal Nautilus," Mason said.

"Nautilus launched its Syrian subsidiary years before the first hint of war and has seen minimal interruptions in its operations. It had already negotiated a deal with Gaddafi before his ouster, but thanks to the civil war, it's been unable to even start drilling. The only one of the three where you could make a case for Nautilus benefitting is Iraq, where it holds a forty-five-percent share of an oil field and processing facility in Basrah. Langbroek already controlled some of the most lucrative deposits on the planet. If we're looking at oil as the defining motivation for the atrocities, then Nautilus has to be considered a minor player. In fact, it appears as though just about every oil company drilling in the Middle East and Northern Africa has suffered to some degree since the Arab Spring."

"What other natural resources do they have in common?"

"Iraq and Libya have gold, but not in quantities worth destroying the countries to obtain. And Syria's main natural resources outside of crude oil are iron ore, gypsum, and phosphate rock, the mining of which isn't going to make anyone rich on a global scale."

"So what you're saying is you've got nothing," Layne said.

Gunnar smiled and laced his fingers in his lap. It was an affectation of patience an adult might employ when preparing to lecture a child.

"Maybe not in regard to these three countries and the relationship between seemingly disparate wars that I only this moment started researching, but that doesn't mean I haven't learned anything. I've been monitoring some curious flurries of activity on the stock market. News of Slate Langbroek's death hasn't even officially hit the wire and already the vultures are circling. As of the close of trading yesterday, Nautilus's percentage of institutional ownership was just under fifty percent, which means that nearly half of the company's available stock was owned by investment firms, foundations, endowments, and any number of entities that manage funds for others. Pension funds, mutual funds, whatnot. As of closing today, that percentage had risen to sixty-two percent, which might not sound like much, but acquiring twelve percent of a multibillion-dollar company is a significant coup."

"So who's responsible?" Mason asked.

"A combination of its previous top five corporate investors, namely Global Bank, Atria Asset Management, GDR LLC, Steele Wealth Management, and the American Investment Partnership, all of which increased their holdings by somewhere between ten and thirty percent. Of them, AIP is the biggest player, but as the most successful investment bank in the world, there isn't a Fortune Five Hundred company in which it doesn't own a solid stake with designs on acquiring even more. Global Bank and Atria are second and third, respectively, and definitely among the hungriest suitors."

"Why would AIP be so interested?"

"It's an investment bank founded more than a century ago on the principle of 'slow and steady wins the race' and has remained largely in the hands of the Douglas family ever since. It buys interest in companies with the intention of making consistent profit for its investors. Acquiring a larger share of Royal Nautilus Petroleum adheres to its traditional business model of investing in low-risk markets like bonds and treasuries. I've never dealt with it in a professional capacity, which should probably tell you how cautiously it approaches its business dealings. Global Bank and Atria are far more aggressive and willing to take serious risks."

"So what's your thinking?"

"All of these guys are just testing the waters. At least for now. My gut tells me that one of them is preparing to make a move, but it won't be an overt acquisition of stock. When the time comes, one of their subsidiaries will attempt to acquire some of Nautilus's more profitable subsidiaries. There's no doubt that the Thirteen ordered Langbroek's execution, which means that the remaining twelve already know exactly how they intend to start pecking at his financial carcass. And I'm confident that one of them will be more active than the rest. That's just the nature of power. Langbroek's death presents an opportunity to tip the balance in his favor. When we find him—"

"We'll find the Dragon," Mason said.

"How about in the meantime we find something to eat?" Ramses said. "I'm starving over here."

He turned onto the main thoroughfare through town and slowed the vehicle. Chain restaurants and coffee shops, interspersed with struggling local eateries, passed on both sides.

"I'll reach out to my contact at the Russian Ministry of Foreign Affairs," Gunnar said. "Maybe she can offer some help regarding the men who went missing in Mexico before they turned up in that barn. And surely she knows something about Aum Shinrikyo and its splinter factions, specifically in relation to the tattoo. It can't be coincidence that we're also dealing with a man who identifies as the Dragon. Maybe the Russians have access to intelligence on him that we don't."

"And I'll follow up with Locker," Layne said. "If we don't get the files the computer forensics lab salvaged from Yamaguchi's hard drive soon, we could be stuck waiting through the holiday weekend."

"Sounds great, but none of that tells me where to stop," Ramses said. "I'm making an executive decision. We're hitting the first restaurant with a bar that serves—"

Mason's phone rang. He glanced at the screen, which displayed the NO CALLER ID message, meaning that the phone number and identification had been deliberately blocked. The only other time he'd seen that message was when his father had called from inside the Capitol Building to let him know that his grandmother had died. He wasn't in the mood to dance around the senator's questions while he fished for more information. Of course, under normal circumstances his father would have either called from his cell phone or his office, so either this was an emergency . . . or it wasn't his father.

The man on the other end was already talking when Mason answered. The noise through the speaker was so loud that he had to cover his free ear in an effort to separate the words from the ruckus.

"—are you by now, Mason?"

He recognized Archer's voice and realized that the chaos in the background was a very bad sign.

"Colorado," Mason said.

"What the hell are you—? Never mind. Just get your ass back to New York. I can have a plane waiting for you at Denver International in twenty minutes."

"I have a ride. You don't have to worry about—"

"Call Christensen and work out the details with him. He's running point on this one. And for the love of God, don't tell anyone what's happening."

"That'll be easy," Mason said. "I don't have the slightest idea."

"I just received a call from the doctor at New York–Presbyterian. You know what that means."

Archer terminated the call, leaving Mason to stare at the silent phone in his hand.

"What was that about?" Layne asked.

"Turn the car around," Mason said.

"We finally decide where we're going," Ramses said, "and suddenly you have an opinion—"

"We need to get back to the plane. Rand Marchment's coming out of his coma."

34

ELSEWHERE

The man collapsed onto the bed the woman had set up for him in the main room. His daily sojourns under the sun took more and more out of him every time, leaving him unable to make the climb up the single flight of stairs to his bedroom. He had only survived this long through sheer force of will. Knowing that he would have to face only one more day was a relief he felt deep in his bones, a feeling so pervasive that he had to fight with every fiber of his being not to succumb to it.

"*Ne zakryvayte glaza,*" the woman said, propping a stack of pillows under his head. "*Ty yeshche ne zakonchil.*"

The man nodded his contrition. She was right; he couldn't risk closing his eyes for fear they might not open again, least of all before he finished his final mission.

Without so much as a backward glance, the woman left him. He listened to her footsteps ascending the stairs and crossing the hallway to her room before releasing a cough that darkened his lips with blood. He wiped it away and rolled onto his side to ease the pain in his chest.

A gathering of mannequins stared back at him, their featureless faces filthy, their outdated clothes gray with dust. Most were missing their arms, others their legs or heads. Cobwebs clung to the racks of sweaters and blouses that had been shoved aside to make room for his bed, the ground beneath them spotted with the carcasses of dead rats, one of which, much like the man, apparently still had a little life left in it.

The fur of the creature was patchy, its exposed flesh nearly translucent, its neck goitrous. It scratched at the tile with a malformed hind leg, its tail—

—protrudes from the trap in the corner, partially concealed behind a stack of dusty boxes. His eye returns to it again and again while he waits for the woman who brought him here to return, trying not to see the rat's situation as a portent for the one in which he now finds himself.

The lone bulb casts a bronze glare over the cellar, the crumbling concrete walls stained with ribbons of rust, a veritable blockade of wooden crates barring his view of the solitary door, which opens with a squeal. Footsteps clop down the stairs and five silhouettes draw substance from the shadows, their faces awash in darkness.

"Sister says you are a nuclear engineer," a man says. His hair is thick and dark, his voice deep, and he speaks with an American accent. He stands ramrod straight, his wrists clasped behind his back. "Is that correct?"

The man nods and wonders why he allowed himself to be brought here in the first place.

The woman who lured him here steps into the dim glow, her veiled habit concealing everything but her eyes, nose, and mouth. She sets a piece of paper on the small table in front of him. He pulls it closer and finds himself staring at the schematics for a device that looks like some kind of medical imaging equipment, only the radiation output appears to be focused and directed outward through a cameralike aperture—

"Can you build it?" a faceless woman asks.

He nods in response and feels a pang of shame as she steps from the shadows, for she wears sunglasses and clings to the arm of the Asian man standing beside her, his nose skeletal and his forehead the texture of melted wax. She is similarly scarred, and yet the way her raven black hair falls across her cheek . . . the softness and color of her lips, like the flesh of a perfectly ripe plum. . . . She is the most beautiful woman he has ever seen. And he realizes in that moment that he will do anything for her.

He clears his throat and gives voice to his answer.

"Yes. I believe I can."

"How about these?" the Asian man asks. He sets several banded blueprints on the table and unrolls them, one at a time, allowing the man to peruse them, scrutinizing his expression the entire time. "Can you produce them?"

The man's heart rate accelerates as he proceeds from one schematic to the next. He understands on a primal level that this is the point of no return. And with one word, he crosses the line that damns him.

"Yes."

The Asian man beams and the woman clutching his arm offers a smile that melts the man's heart. A second Asian man emerges from the darkness, a stethoscope protruding from the pocket of his lab coat, his eyes harsh with judgment.

"Can he be trusted?" he asks.

"The fact that you don't know who he is or what he's done proves that he can hold his tongue," the American says.

"I told you," Sister says. "He is the one."

For the first time in as long as the man can remember, he feels the stirrings of pride. His instincts had served him well. He was right to have followed the woman here. As she had promised, these people were just like him. They believed as he did, that the era of small-minded bureaucrats had passed and the time had come to usher in a new age of enlightenment. The world needed to be remade in the image of men like himself and the others in this room, whom the nun had told him were the most highly respected professionals in their fields, prominent doctors and scientists, some of them brought to Russia to finish the work they had started in Japan.

The man rises from his seat and stares at the woman in the sunglasses, whose expression shows no sign of the revulsion he has seen in the faces of so many others, and he allows himself to dream again. He will make this woman his own and he will build whatever she wants him to build, especially if it means he will have the opportunity to revisit the suffering he has endured on those who inflicted it. He glances once more at the rat in the trap and recognizes that they are indeed the same; the trap has liberated the vermin from its miserable existence, freeing it to become something more, something greater.

With tears streaming down his cheeks, he offers himself up to his new family, pledging to them his life—

—faded from the rat's eyes and it lay still, the radiation having taken its toll, just as it had with all of the others. Such was their penance for chewing through the side of the crate hidden behind the sweaters and blouses and exposing themselves to the suitcase contained within. They had been consigned to a painful end, just like all of those in that room so many years ago, although none of them had known it at the time.

Tatsuo had died in his fancy apartment, his guts spilled on the floor; Kaemon in a hospital bed, rotted from the inside out; and Kameko, the love of his life, on television, for all the world to see.

The man and the woman would soon join them, rising into the heavens on a fiery cloud of devastation.

Fortunately, they would live long enough to know that the American, who had manipulated them for the nefarious ends of his master, had preceded them to the grave. He might have thought they had forgotten about him, or perhaps that they had failed to make the connection to who he truly was, clear up until the moment he found himself walking into Grand Central Station with a remote detonator in his hands.

It was only fitting that if he could not die by the Scarecrow's hand, he would die by the Dragon's. In fact, it was almost poetic in a way.

He hoped that wherever Kameko was now, she was looking down upon him and smiling.

And that she would take pleasure in watching Rand Marchment burn.

PART 4

We have a well-organized political-action group in this country, determined to destroy our Constitution and establish a one-party state. . . . It operates secretly, silently, continuously to transform our government. . . . This ruthless power-seeking elite is a disease of our century. . . . This group . . . is answerable neither to the president, the Congress, nor the courts.

—Senator William Jenner, Indiana,
speech delivered to the U. S. Senate (February 23, 1954)

35

Gunnar's pilot had been waiting to take off the moment they were on board, but a three-hour flight meant they wouldn't arrive in New York until nearly 10 P.M. EST. The DHS had stationed Federal Protective Service agents at every entrance to the hospital and locked down Marchment's entire floor. Chris had volunteered to personally stand guard outside of the former deputy secretary's room until he awakened. While the doctor had based his prediction on increased brain activity and fluctuations in respirations and blood pressure, which often preceded the return of consciousness, he'd been careful not to offer any guarantees. It was always possible that he was wrong and Marchment would never wake up again, but they had to take the chance. He was their only direct link to the Thirteen and Mason wasn't about to let him die without spilling his guts first.

The regional computer forensics lab in New Jersey had come through for Locker, who'd uploaded a total of five files recovered from Yamaguchi's broken desktop tower to the secure cloud. He hadn't personally known what to make of them, so he'd also forwarded them to the brain trust at Quantico to see if they could figure out the significance.

"Just start at the top," Layne said. She sat in the same seat as before, which afforded her a decent view of Mason's laptop on the table in front of him. "Maybe we can make some sense out of them."

Mason opened the first file and found a document labeled "CBC With Differential/Platelet" dated November of the previous year. It contained a list of test criteria with the subject's results, units, and the reference intervals of normal values. Several readings were flagged

with HIGH or LOW, while the values for WBCs, platelets, and neutrophils were bolded, underlined, and marked with ALERT. The order-
ing physician's name was listed, but the patient was identified only
by a series of numbers.

"I don't have the slightest idea what any of this means," Layne said.

"We'll come back to it," Mason said. He opened the second file,
which contained another CBC test that had been run a full year prior.
At a glance, the numbers appeared to be in line with the results they'd
just viewed.

The third file featured dozens of squiggly horizontal lines, one
above the other. They were obviously waveforms of some kind, although Mason had no idea what any of the abbreviations assigned to
them stood for.

"It's an EEG," Gunnar said from across the aisle. "It measures
brain-wave activity."

"Can you tell how this one looks?"

"You'd need to ask a physician. I only recognize it because I had
one as a kid."

"All of these tests were performed during the past two years while
Yamaguchi was living in the U.S. under the Nguyen alias," Layne said.
"He couldn't have ordered them, so whoever sent them to him had to
have known him prior to assuming that identity."

"But the Scarecrow's brother's labs were on one of the computers
that was left intact," Mason said.

"Then they must be the Scarecrow's."

"What would be the point of destroying the computer with the
Scarecrow's results if he thought she was going to die while releasing
the Novichok? Why keep them on separate computers when he could
simply keep them in different files?"

Something about this felt wrong. Yamaguchi was trying to hide
something, and Mason would be damned if he wasn't going to figure
out what. He opened the fourth file, which turned out to be a medical
imaging report. The dictating radiologist detailed the findings of an
MRI of the brain and cranial nerves, wherein he'd noted degenerative
neurological changes but hadn't given a formal diagnosis, or speculated as to the implications.

The final file appeared to be a physician's notes summarizing
the results of tests for liver function, serum creatinine, and bone

densitometry. It was incomplete and offered neither diagnosis nor prognosis. Not even a treatment plan. It was merely a single page plucked from a file that must have once contained many.

"That's it?" Layne said.

"Locker said we were lucky to even get that much," Mason said. His phone rang from where it was plugged into the charger. It took him a second to recognize the incoming number.

"McWhinney," he said.

"You handle him," Layne said. She swiveled his computer so that she could view the file with the lab results and grabbed her phone. "I'll see if I can figure out where these tests were performed."

Mason answered the call before it went to voice mail.

"Special Agent? This is Ed McWhinney from the McAllen forensics department. You said to call you if I found out anything useful?"

"Hit me."

"Well, I don't know how useful this information might be to your investigation, but we were able to identify the victims in the stable near the back of the barn."

"The oldest remains? The ones that were just broken bones?"

"Correct. We found a pacemaker buried in the straw underneath them. Its serial number was registered to Hank Peters, the owner of the property. Former owner, I should say. We're still waiting on confirmation that the second set of remains belongs to his wife, Patsy."

"They were beaten to death on their own ranch?" Mason said. Layne covered the mouthpiece on her phone and glared at him. He lowered his voice before asking the obvious question. "How is it they've been dead for years and no one noticed?"

"That's a question for the sheriff's department, I'm afraid. I can only speculate."

"Someone has to have been paying the mortgage or else the bank would have found them when it initiated foreclosure proceedings."

"That makes total sense to me, but, unfortunately, I don't have access to that kind of information. And in response to your next question? No, neither had criminal histories or ties to the cartel. As far as I can tell they were like everyone else around these parts: They kept to themselves and stayed out of other people's business."

"Thanks, Ed."

"Oh, and I heard from the forensics unit on the other side of the tunnel in Mexico. They suspect that based on the number of empty fuel rods, whoever was operating that lab couldn't have harvested more than eight to ten pounds of plutonium, and that's *if* they were really careful and didn't waste any, which the soil tests hardly support. The Department of Energy estimates it takes about nine pounds to make a single nuclear weapon, although there are scientists who claim it can be done with as little as two pounds, so take that update with a grain of salt and thank your lucky stars they weren't able to produce more."

It wasn't much as far as good news went, but Mason would take all he could get.

"I'll let you know if we find anything else," McWhinney said.

The director hung up just as Ramses emerged from Gunnar's bedroom at the back of the plane, where he'd been holed up making calls of a nature better not made in front of an audience, especially one consisting of federal law-enforcement officers.

"There's nothing like that directed-energy weapon of yours on the streets," he said, slouching into the seat opposite Mason. "I can easily find a handful of clients willing to pay seven figures for one, but even I can't track down anyone who has access to a supply. One of my contacts said he'd heard about someone attempting to broker a deal with a source inside the Chinese military. Turned out the guy was a straw buyer for the DOD and wound up dropping off the face of the earth, alongside his contact in the PLA."

"You're certain the Chinese are the only ones with access to this technology?"

"Rumor is they haven't quite perfected it, but even if they had, I guarantee you they wouldn't share it at any price."

"So how did the Dragon get one?"

"I'm not convinced that he did. This Chinese DEW technology is straight out of the movies. We're talking industrial lasers capable of cutting open a submarine like a tin can or knocking a satellite out of orbit. Or at least that's what the Chinese claim they can do. Burning people alive, though? That's a different animal altogether."

"How so?" Mason asked.

"The energy level, for starters," Ramses said. "Lasers are designed to penetrate their targets, not set them on fire. And there are microwave weapons, but they heat their targets from the inside out. The Dragon's weapon is different. Remember what it did to the border patrol agent and the dead guys in that stall? They were uniformly burned. It makes me wonder if we aren't dealing with something capable of producing targeted bursts of gamma radiation."

"Like a portable nuclear device?"

"Only on a much smaller scale."

"You saw the crater that fizzle weapon created in Libya. That's not the kind of power a man can wield at close range, at least not without vaporizing himself in the process."

"You're probably right," Ramses said. "But we're also talking about a guy who built his own lab to salvage plutonium from nuclear waste in order to create his own bombs. If anyone could pull it off, my money's on this guy."

"You don't need fissionable material to create radiation," Gunnar said. "A portable X-ray machine converts electrical energy to electrons and fires them at a tungsten target to produce X-rays. With the right combination of energy and target materials, you could undoubtedly produce radiation that causes considerably more damage without requiring a thermonuclear chain reaction."

Layne set down her phone and pumped her fist.

"What?" Mason asked.

"Guess where both the lab and the hospital where the MRI was performed are located?"

Mason gestured impatiently for her to proceed.

"Come on, aren't you even going to try?"

And then it hit him. Yamaguchi hadn't destroyed the computer because it housed the Scarecrow's medical records; he'd smashed it because it contained someone else's. And something about the lab results would help whoever discovered the files identify the patient.

"Texas," he said.

"Houston. All of the studies were performed at the Mayo Clinic in Houston, Texas. Just a short drive up the Gulf Coast from Rio Grande City."

"I don't follow," Ramses said.

Mason looked him in the eyes and smiled.

"They're the Dragon's medical records."

36

Ben-Menachem's coffee had been strong, but not nearly strong enough to prevent Mason from falling asleep. Layne either, apparently. She'd crashed with her knees drawn up to her chest, the side of her head resting against the window, and her mouth hanging open, softly snoring. Without her ball cap, she looked strikingly feminine with the way her bangs curled around her cheekbone and her lips—

"What?" she said, without opening her eyes.

"You were snoring," he said.

"You're so full of it."

She shifted position, but her eyes remained closed.

Mason felt reinvigorated after the power nap. He probably wouldn't have awakened until they'd landed had it not been for the sound of Gunnar's voice, which seemed strangely out of place considering he was speaking in Russian. His old friend ended the call, typed some rapid-fire commands on his keyboard, and studied the screen with an impassive expression on his face.

"Why don't you ask your boy up there to heat us up some pizza or something," Ramses said from the bedroom, where he'd sprawled on the bed, laced his fingers behind his head, and crossed his ankles, his boots on the comforter.

"Because he's the pilot," Gunnar said. "And I'd prefer he focus his energies on flying the plane."

"Then you really need to get yourself one of those—"

"Flight attendants," Layne said. "They're called flight attendants."

"Whatever. Someone who brings food and drinks. A guy could resort to cannibalism in here."

"There's Culatello di Zibello and Caciocavallo Podolico in the refrigerator," Gunnar said. When Ramses didn't reply, he clarified, "Fancy ham and cheese."

"Why didn't you just say that in the first place?"

Ramses rolled out of bed and squeezed past them down the aisle.

"I take it that was the phone call you were waiting on," Mason said.

"Yeah," Gunnar said. "I anticipated my contact at the Russian state department would be willing to help, but I wasn't prepared for a deluge of information. Apparently the Federation absolutely loathes

cults of all kinds, especially Aum Shinrikyo, which it declared a terrorist organization in 2016."

"That was twenty years after the subway attack," Layne said.
She opened her eyes, yawned, and leaned her elbow on the table. "I
thought they broke into cells and went into hiding. What changed?"

"In late 2015, a counterterrorism operation discovered a group
operating in Moscow. There's no mention of what they might have
had in their possession when they were caught, but whatever it was, it
was serious enough to get the case before the Supreme Court and a ruling handed down in a matter of months. They also gathered information about the full scope of Aum's activities inside the country, which
included some thirty thousand members above and beyond their best
estimates."

Ramses slid into his seat and set the food on the table. He whit-
tled off a hunk of cheese, crumpled it into a few slices of ham, and
crammed the wad into his mouth, forcing him to speak around it.

"You think they were preparing an assault?"

"The Russians don't allow themselves to present weakness on
the international stage. If they were dealing with anything shy of the
threat posed by a weapon of mass destruction, they would have made
a show of thwarting the potential attack. They'd only suppress the details if they were dealing with something beyond their defensive capabilities, especially if Aum had come close to pulling it off."

"Yamaguchi and the Nakamuras appeared in the U.S. not long
after that," Layne said.

"It makes sense," Gunnar said. "Two separate groups were arrested in Montenegro following the court ruling, more than fifty of
them from Russia, Belarus, and Ukraine. They had thousands of dollars in cash and items described only as 'electronic devices.'"

"What were they doing in Montenegro?" Ramses asked. "Isn't
that right across the Mediterranean from Libya?"

"It is," Gunnar said, "but it's also the closest warm-water port to
Moscow."

"They were making a run for it," Layne said.

"What about the Dragon?" Mason asked. "We've established that
Yamaguchi and the Nakamuras were members of Aum Shinrikyo and
one of its splinter sects. If we're right and it was his medical records
stored on the computer Yamaguchi tried to destroy, are we to assume
he was a member, too?"

"It would help if anyone had ever actually seen him," Gunnar said, turning around his computer so he could show them the mosaic of police-booking photographs on the screen. There were a handful of men with Asian features and skin tone, but the vast majority had the kind of prominent jaws and brows Mason associated with people of Eastern European origin. "Even a partial physical description would be hugely beneficial. He could be any of these men and we wouldn't have the slightest clue."

"Are all of these people still in custody?" Layne asked.

"I can't say for sure," Gunnar said. "These were the foreign nationals arrested in Montenegro and extradited to their countries of origin, which makes these photos readily available through INTERPOL. My contact wasn't quite as forthcoming with her own intelligence, although she did send several photographs that I assume were acquired during the counterterrorism operation by an agent who managed to infiltrate Aum's ranks."

He switched to an image of a crowded room. It was dark and grainy and difficult to tell how many people were gathered in what appeared to be a small warehouse. The picture had been snapped from the back of the room, behind most of those in attendance, their heads silhouetted, their faces either in partial profile or completely obscured. There was a makeshift stage at the front of the room with a stack of wooden pallets that served as a table for the four people gathered around it.

The second image was similar to the first, only the meeting had obviously commenced. A man stood front and center, his features washed out by the light directed at his face. He gestured toward the wall behind him, where the other three were in the process of tacking up large maps.

The third showed the crowd beginning to disperse. A handful of people approached the stage, while the remainder milled about, talking. Several of their shadowed faces had turned in the direction of the camera, although none of them appeared to know that it was there.

"Let me see if I can clean these up a little," Gunnar said. He swiveled the laptop once more and set to work. "This shouldn't take too long."

Mason glanced out the window and saw the seamless urban sprawl of the Eastern Seaboard. It was terrifying to think how many people would be killed instantly by a nuclear detonation anywhere through here. And, worse, how many would suffer slow, grueling deaths from the fallout.

"This is good ham," Ramses said through a mouthful. "You guys should really try it. The cheese is kind of funky, though."

"That's because it's been aged in a cave for six years," Gunnar said.

"Full of bats, by the taste of it."

Layne held out her palm and beckoned with her fingers for Ramses to pass her a slice.

"There," Gunnar said.

He again spun his computer so they could all see the screen. The first image was considerably clearer, although there wasn't much he could do about the lighting. The majority of the faces remained shadowed, the location indistinct.

"What about the next one?" Mason asked.

Gunnar brought up the second photograph, which offered a better sense of scale. The man standing center stage had to be right about six feet tall, the other two men hanging the maps were roughly the same height, while the woman, who'd just finished her task and turned to face the audience, was considerably shorter. Gunnar zoomed in on the central figure, who had dark hair and a broad build. His features were still largely washed out, his eyes recessed into pools of shadow, but the contours of his cheeks revealed a coarse texture, as though acne-pocked or scarred.

Mason couldn't help but wonder if he was staring at an image of the Dragon, live and in the flesh.

"That's about as good as I can do, I'm afraid," Gunnar said. "There aren't nearly enough details to run a facial-recognition scan."

"What about the map itself?"

Gunnar altered the centering and zoomed in on the map behind the woman. While it was by no means crystal clear, there was no mistaking the bull's-eye-shaped design of Moscow, with the Moskva River weaving in and out of it. At its heart was the Kremlin, marked with a pushpin connected by lengths of twine to several others radiating outward along the major converging thoroughfares.

"They were going to assassinate the president," Layne said.

"I fear they were planning on doing a whole lot worse than that," Gunnar said. "With one of the Dragon's nuclear devices, they very well could have torn the heart out of Moscow."

Mason was just about to ask Gunnar to zoom in on the other

maps when something caught his eye. The woman on the stage wore a heavy parka unzipped in the front and a blouse underneath it that was just sheer enough to reveal the outline of her bra and a dark shape on her upper breast.

"This is them," he said, tapping the monitor. "This is the sect we're looking for."

Gunnar zoomed all the way in on where he'd been pointing. A couple passes of different filters and there was no mistaking the outline of the dragon tattooed on her chest, if not the finer details.

"What do we know about these people?" Mason asked.

Again, Gunnar turned his laptop and started typing, his fingers a blur on the keyboard, the rectangular light from the screen reflected in his blue eyes.

"They believe this sect is called Konets Mira," Gunnar said. "It means 'the end of the world.' And their leader goes by the name of Zmei."

Mason commandeered the laptop and zoomed out so he could better see the man holding the audience enrapt.

"What does it mean?" Mason asked, but he already knew.

"Zmei is the Russian word for dragon."

37

A squadron of police cruisers had been waiting for Mason and Layne on the tarmac at LaGuardia and had escorted them into the city in a chaos of lights and sirens, parting the late-night congestion with a frenzy of honking horns and squealing tires. Mason sat silently in the backseat of the lone black Crown Victoria at the heart of the entourage, while Layne did the exact same thing in the front seat. The driver, an FBI agent named Redmond, had been kind enough to introduce himself and leave them to their thoughts. If he didn't know for sure what was going on, he had to have a pretty good idea based on the tension and urgency. And their destination, of course.

New York–Presbyterian was a sprawling megahospital complex on the west side of Manhattan, near the Hudson River, a massive H-shaped structure connected by glass sky bridges to the surrounding buildings, including specialty campuses, surgical centers, and the

Columbia Medical School. The motorcade pulled up to the service entrance around the side of the Milstein Hospital Building. Mason and Layne jumped out of the car before it even stopped moving and ran toward a solid steel door flanked by a pair of FPS agents carrying M4 carbines and wearing combat boots, navy blue fatigues, and bulletproof vests. One of them banged on the door when they neared. It promptly opened and a third agent admitted them into a dingy corridor that smelled of hospital food and garbage. He made no introduction as he guided them down the hallway toward the waiting elevator.

"The ICU is on the fourth floor," he said. He had a gray goatee, a shaved head, and the shoulders and neck of a bull. "There are two units in the south tower. A and B. We commandeered the latter exclusively for our guest of honor."

The elevator looked like it had been attacked with a sledgehammer and the metal walls were scored with grooves from linen and food carts. He pressed the button for the fourth floor and the doors rattled closed.

"Has he woken up yet?" Layne asked.

"I don't know, but I wouldn't shed a tear if he didn't wake up at all."

The floor shuddered and started to rise. Gears clanked overhead and the car wobbled with each floor it passed.

"No one can get in there with him, correct?" Mason said.

"Outside of medical personnel, no one can get within fifty feet of him, let alone within line of sight."

"You're sure?"

The agent glared a challenge at him.

"Insult my competence again. See what happens."

The elevator rumbled to a stop and the door slowly opened, revealing another agent dressed exactly like all of the others, her face partially concealed by the M4 seated against her shoulder.

"'Bout time you guys showed up," she said, lowering her weapon. She had dark skin and eyes and spoke in a tone of command. "Follow me."

She strode down the narrow hallway and used a badge with a smart chip to open a security door, on the other side of which was an officer stationed at a desk with views of a dozen different cameras on various monitors. He nodded as they passed, eliciting a grunt from their escort. She badged a set of double doors and hit the silver pressure plate that opened them automatically.

The ICU looked nearly identical to the one in which Mason's mother had died nearly two decades prior. It had the same off-white floor tiles, the same laminate countertops surrounding the nurses' station, and the same smell of sterility that served to mask the scents of urine and death. Where in his mind's eye there had been clipboards, there were now banks of monitors displaying all of the pertinent details of the occupants in each of the beds, only one of which was currently in use.

A pair of nurses looked up from their workstations; one drew the contents of a small vial into a syringe while the other made notations in a digital chart. They were both female, which was by no means unusual, but their almost Amazonian physiques and hard eyes marked them as military, most likely temporarily reassigned from Walter Reed National Military Medical Center for their security clearances as much as their skills. The doctor seated at the station below the assignment board had the bearing of a veteran as well, the cut of his dark hair as square as his jaw. The badge affixed to the lapel of his lab coat identified him as a vascular surgeon, presumably the same one who'd repaired Marchment's torn carotid arteries. He dipped his chin in acknowledgment but made no effort to rise. He seemed content to sit there studying whatever was on the computer screen in front of him.

"Back and to the left," the FPS agent said, taking up post beside the doctor.

There were two more agents near the end of the hallway, outside of a room that presumably belonged to their quarry. Considering Chris wasn't standing in the hallway with them as he'd promised, that could mean only one thing.

Marchment was awake.

"I don't like this," Mason said. "Too many people know he's here."

"This place is as secure as you can get," Layne said. "They're using hand-selected, outsourced personnel and they have the whole place locked down. What would you have them do, send him to Gitmo and try to treat him there? He's the closest thing to a witness we have. Keeping him alive is the only thing that matters."

She was right and he knew it.

They passed negative-airflow rooms with glass walls and pressurized doors. The curtains inside had been drawn wide open so as not to leave anywhere to hide inside. Each contained a single bed that abutted a modular wall with suction and oxygen hookups and outlets for the various pieces of equipment surrounding it. There was a monitor at the bedside for vitals and another on the adjacent counter for the physician to enter notes. The rooms on the right side of the hallway looked out upon the distant lights of Fort Lee across the river, while those on the left afforded a view of the Herbert Irving Pavilion, the Milstein Hospital Building's mirror image, on the other side of the rounded glass expansion of the Milstein Family Heart Center.

It was on the latter side that they housed Marchment, away from the surrounding streets and the river, a location concealed from nearly every angle. The only exposure they needed to worry about was from within the hospital itself and that remained under their direct control. It was impossible for an assassin to run the gamut of security and the only potential sight line for a sniper was from a handful of windows in the Irving Pavilion, which the FPS directly controlled.

The agents stepped away from the door as Mason and Layne approached the third room from the end. The curtains had been drawn tightly over the dim interior. It was impossible to tell if there was even anyone inside until they opened the door and heard the sound of voices and a monitor beeping in time with the patient's heart rate.

Mason's mouth grew dry and his pulse rushed in his ears.

There, on the bed in front of him, lay the emaciated form of the former deputy secretary of the Department of Homeland Security, Rand Marchment, who'd compromised first their investigation into the smuggling of the Hoyl's virus through the Arizona desert and then the manhunt for the Scarecrow, a decision he undoubtedly regretted after the monster drugged him, opened a flap of skin on his neck, and used the flow of blood in his arteries to power a hydroelectric remote device designed to trigger the release of Novichok from the subway trains departing Grand Central Station. Had Mason not disarmed it before the timer hit zero, millions of people would have died, and had Ramses not reacted so quickly and stanched the flow of blood, Marchment would have bled out within a matter of minutes.

The doctor glanced up at them from the bedside, removed her stethoscope from her ears, and draped it over her neck.

"He's still incredibly weak, so you're going to have to go easy on him," she said.

Mason wanted to reply, but he couldn't seem to find the voice. Every ounce of his strength was invested into restraining himself from tearing Marchment apart with his bare hands.

"He's been awake for maybe twenty minutes," Chris said. He sat in a chair at the foot of the bed, wearing the same suit for the second straight day. He'd obviously slept in it, if he'd slept at all. "He hasn't said a word yet, though."

A clear sheet of Plexiglas on wheels had been positioned in front of the lone outside window. It was the same kind of bulletproof shielding used to protect VIPs in public places. Even if a sniper somehow managed to line up a shot, there was no way it was getting through.

Marchment's left wrist was cuffed to the bed frame, although the precaution hardly seemed necessary. He appeared to have aged decades since Mason had last seen him in the main concourse of Grand Central Terminal, dressed like a scarecrow in a flannel shirt, overalls, and a conical straw hat, his pupils wide from the effects of the hallucinogens he'd been given and a detonator clutched to his chest. He'd lost a lot of weight in the interim. His face was gaunt, his cheeks stubbled. His hair had been cut short and was now entirely gray. The scars on his neck where the surgeon had replaced the flap were stark white.

"I can't look . . . that bad," Marchment rasped.

"Trust me," Layne said. "You do."

"The only fluids he's received for the last six months have been through his arm," the doctor said. "There's a cup of water on the tray. I suggest helping him drink some if you expect him to be able to talk."

"Can you give us a few minutes?" Mason asked.

"Not a chance. I'll give you as much latitude as you need, within reason, but until he's stable enough to be discharged, he's my responsibility."

Mason nodded. Right now, he didn't care what the doctor knew or didn't know. He didn't care about confidentiality and sure as hell didn't care about protocol. There was an unknown quantity of weapons-grade plutonium out there at this very moment and this man was their only link to the faction that possessed it.

Rand Marchment was their sole living connection to the Thirteen.

And Mason fully intended to find out everything he knew.

By any and all means necessary.

Damn the consequences.

38

Chris set up a digital camera and aimed it at Marchment. He started recording, stating the location, date, and the names of the subject, federal agents, and medical personnel in attendance for the record, and then returned to his chair. The doctor hovered near the back of the room, while Mason and Layne dragged a pair of chairs to the side of the bed, in what was essentially a reversal of fortunes. Mason clearly remembered when Marchment, then head of the Bradley Strike Force, had been waiting for him to awaken in a hospital room much like this one to debrief him on the operation at the rock quarry. An operation that had cost the lives of a dozen dedicated agents. An operation Marchment had personally sabotaged from the very start.

Chris nodded for Mason to proceed.

"Do you know where you are?"

"Hospital," Marchment croaked. His eyes seemed incapable of focusing together for any length of time. He nodded toward the plastic cup of water on the tray. "Please."

Mason flexed his jaw muscles in frustration. He reluctantly grabbed the cup and held the straw to Marchment's lips.

"Do you remember how you got here?" Chris asked.

Marchment took several slow swallows before releasing the straw from his lips. He furrowed his brow and traced the scar on his throat with his trembling fingertips. His eyes widened and he glanced out the window. The beeping sound of his heart rate accelerated.

"You don't have to worry," Layne said. "The Scarecrow's dead. She killed herself, along with more than a hundred innocent men, women, and children, in Times Square."

"No such thing . . . as innocent," he whispered.

"You know how this works," Mason said. "We're going to ask you some questions and you're going to answer—"

"I have nothing . . . to say."

"We can protect you," Layne said.

A rasping laugh.

Marchment leaned forward and once more Mason brought the straw to the former deputy secretary's lips.

"You don't understand . . . what you're up against," he said.

"I think we do," Mason said.

"If you did, you'd realize there's nothing . . . you can do to protect me. I'm already dead."

"We've kept you alive this far," Chris said.

The monitor continued beeping faster. Sweat bloomed from Marchment's brow.

"Good luck doing so now that I'm awake. They would have been content to just let me die."

Mason set down the cup and rose from the bedside. He was grateful he'd sacrificed his jacket; it had to be eighty degrees in this infernal hospital room. He paced the length of the room like a caged animal.

"Why'd you do it?" Chris asked. "People died because of you."

"Even more have to die so that others might live."

"I've heard this speech before," Mason said. "You think you're saving mankind when you're merely delivering it into the hands of monsters."

Another rasping laugh, only this time it degenerated into a cough.

"History is full of great men who were considered monsters in their time," Marchment said. "They were the only ones capable of doing what needed to be done. We're on a collision course with extinction. Wars rage on every continent. The global population is out of control. We're destroying the environment. The uneducated and impoverished slaughter one another over land where nothing can grow. Humanity is an infection, parasitizing itself and destroying the planet. Someone needs to save us from ourselves, and there's only one way to do it."

"If your employers are such noble people, why are you so worried about them trying to kill you?" Layne asked.

"Because they know that everyone cracks under the right amount of pressure. No one can hold out forever. They can't afford for me to tell you even what little I know."

"Or what? Someone will try to stop them? What does that tell you about what they're trying to do?"

"The Scarecrow and Slate Langbroek are both dead," Mason said. "Who do you have to fear?"

Marchment tried to laugh, but he went straight to coughing. Droplets of crimson speckled his chin and the front of his gown. His face suffused with blood and a blister swelled on his forehead. Warning lights flashed on his monitor, which started to alarm.

The doctor rushed to the bedside and dragged over the crash cart.

"Langbroek . . . knew he was . . . screwed." Marchment retched, but managed to swallow back down what little water he'd consumed. Blood leaked from the corner of his mouth. "He was . . . nothing."

Mason's damp T-shirt clung to his chest. He smelled something burning, felt his gorge rise.

"Who else is involved?" Layne said.

"You should ask . . . your partner."

Mason whirled to face Marchment, who smiled at him. His teeth were pink and his gums were lined with blood. Smaller blisters bubbled on his lips.

"Jesus," Mason whispered. He pulled Layne out of the chair and shoved her toward the door. "You need to get out of here."

"What are you talking about?"

"The Dragon's here."

The nurses were already snapping on gloves when they burst into the room. Layne glanced back as she brushed past them into the hallway.

"He's burning up," the doctor said. She tore off Marchment's gown. His chest was bright red and drenched with sweat. The uppermost layer of skin separated and filled with fluid as they watched. "Charge paddles!"

Marchment screamed. It was a horrible, animalian sound. A fine mist of blood burst from his lips. The skin on his face and scalp blackened, split, and started to burn.

Mason rushed to the window, slid the shield aside, and leaned against the glass. There was no one in any of the windows of the pavilion on the opposite side of the hospital. No one on the roof of the heart center or behind the glass walls of any of its floors. No one on the ground four stories down.

And then it hit him.

The Dragon didn't need to be able to see his target to kill him. Not with a weapon capable of firing radiation through any number of walls or even—

"The floor," he finished out loud.

Marchment's cries metamorphosed into strangling sounds as his chest filled with blood and his viscera started to cook. Mason caught one last glimpse of his nemesis's panicked eyes, staring out at him from a face burned to the texture of a pine tree's bark, and ran into the hall. The FPS agents guarding the doorway were on their transceivers, trying to coordinate their response from anywhere other than inside the room, from which a smell like roasted pork grew stronger by the second.

"Hold containment positions!" one of the agents shouted into his com.

Mason had to yell to be heard over the alarms from Marchment's room and the thunder of footsteps charging in their direction.

"Where's the nearest stairwell?"

The agent gestured down the corridor, toward a lighted green exit sign. Mason broke into a sprint and was nearly to the nurses' station when silver lights flashed and the fire alarm sounded.

"Code Blue!" the vascular surgeon yelled as he rounded the corner.

He nearly barreled into Mason, who dodged right, hurdled the counter, and ran straight for the stairwell door. Hammered the release bar. Shouldered the door into the concrete wall. Grabbed the railing and launched himself to the landing. Rounded the bend. Raised his hands when the agent guarding the door to the third floor aimed an M4 at his chest.

"FBI!" Mason shouted. "Has anyone gotten past you?"

The agent lowered his weapon and shook his head.

"Have your men lock down every way out of here. I don't want anyone leaving this building!"

"This is a hospital," he said. "The moment that fire alarm went off, they started funneling patients outside through the nearest exits."

"Damn it!" Mason shouted.

He shoved past the guard, darted into the third-floor hallway, and was nearly run down by a nurse pushing an unconscious patient's bed. Employees rushed from one station to the next, following training ingrained through countless drills, closing doors and turning off lights, their bewildered faces flashing in the magnesium glare from the alarm beacons. He fought his way through them and into a corridor lined with curtained enclosures. It was a PACU, where patients were brought after surgery to be monitored while they emerged from under anesthesia. The majority of the curtains were open and the beds empty.

Mason found the stall directly underneath Marchment's room. One of the acoustic tiles had been removed and a haze of smoke hung inside the drop ceiling. The ductwork and conduits were scorched, the insulation blown against the girders actively burning. The bed was still made, but the covers were mussed where someone had obviously stood on top of it.

He heard footsteps and grabbed a nurse on her way past.

"Who was in this room?"

"No one," she said, shrugging out of his grasp.

The hall dead-ended to his right, forcing him to head back toward the nurses' station, where a man wearing a blue jumpsuit with the hospital's logo and a badge identifying him as FACILITIES shut down the central flow of oxygen.

"Where's the nearest exit?" Mason shouted.

"The stairs are right over—"

"There's been a guard at that door all night. How many other ways are there to get off this floor?"

"The elevator's straight down that hallway," he said. "And there's a set of stairs right beside it."

Mason started to run in that direction—

"There are also sky bridges on both sides of the hospital. One leads to the psychiatry building across Riverside and the other to neurology on the other side of Fort Washington."

Mason stopped in his tracks. It was the perfect setup. The Dragon could have fled in any number of directions and exited through any of the interconnected buildings. He'd been able to assassinate Marchment without ever setting foot on the secured fourth floor.

"The nearest sky bridge?" he said.

"Down the hall and to your right."

Mason ran until he reached the intersecting hallway, rounded the corner, and slammed into a cleaning cart that had been abandoned in the middle of the corridor, toppling it onto its side and scattering cleaning supplies and trash across the tiled floor. He scrambled to his feet and propelled himself—

Something caught his eye. A plastic trash bag, open on the floor, a silver sleeve protruding from inside.

Mason crouched and pulled on it until the upper half of a silver CBRN suit slid out. He lunged to his feet, blew through the door, and raced out across the sky bridge. Through the glass walls he could see employees and ambulatory patients gathering on the street below, cars moving in and out of the parking lot and streaking past on Riverside Drive. Police cruisers, fire trucks, and ambulances converged from seemingly every direction at once.

Mason leaned back and bellowed in frustration.

39

JULY 4

They'd evacuated the entire Milstein Hospital Building, transporting emergent patients by ambulance to other critical-care facilities and cramming the remainder into every other nook and cranny throughout the hospital complex. The media seemed to be buying the story about a small fire on the third floor triggering the inadvertent release of radiation from the radiosurgery suite, which housed the Gamma Knife and radiation therapy unit, but it wouldn't hold up to any kind of real scrutiny.

Mason donned a black tactical CBRN suit and waded through the bedlam to the room where Rand Marchment had been murdered, mere feet away from him. He hated the former deputy secretary of the DHS with every fiber of his being. He'd aided and abetted the Hoyl in his plot to unleash a virus capable of triggering an extinction-level event and run interference for the Scarecrow in her quest to release enough Novichok to kill everyone in Manhattan. He was a monster the likes of which few in the history of mankind could compare, and yet still he hadn't deserved to die in such an awful manner.

The sheets were scorched and the body looked as though it had been cooked over a bonfire. The FBI's Evidence Response Team couldn't risk moving it until Locker had completed his documentation of the site, especially considering that even their most careful attempts to remove the blankets had resulted in layers of tissue peeling off with the fabric. A pair of special agents wielded RIIDs—radioisotope identification devices—that almost looked like bullhorns. The scintillation detectors used sodium iodide crystals to convert radiation into pulses of light, which were then transformed into electrical energy and processed to produce characteristic spectra that identified the invisible radionuclides lingering in the room.

"You should get out of here for a while," Locker said, placing his hand on Mason's shoulder and offering a reassuring squeeze. "This is going to take a while and you're no good to anyone like this."

"I was right here with him when he started to burn," Mason said.

"Consider yourself fortunate that you weren't any closer than you were."

Mason nodded. The doctor and nurses who'd attempted to stabilize Marchment were down the hall being treated for radiation burns to their arms, chests, and faces. He'd never forget the horrible sounds of their screams and hoped to God they survived their injuries. The prospect of any of them dying from wounds sustained while trying to save Marchment made him physically ill.

"What have you found so far?" he asked.

"We've detected significant amounts of cesium-137 and hafnium-178, both of which are capable of producing gamma radiation, although it's unclear how the killer was able to generate them at will and channel them into a coherent beam. I know DARPA looked into creating a gamma ray weapon by using X-rays to bombard hafnium in hopes of triggering transmutation, but as far as I know they weren't successful."

"Where does someone get these isotopes in the first place?" Mason asked.

"If this guy has access to uranium-235, he can create as much cesium-137 as he wants," Locker said. "But outside of the Los Alamos National Laboratory, which doesn't deal with just anybody, I don't have the slightest idea where to acquire hafnium-178. He would have had to fabricate it himself."

"So what you're saying is that this guy who manufactured nuclear weapons from spent fuel rods in a run-down Mexican warehouse also managed to design a gamma ray weapon that even our best and brightest military scientists couldn't, with unlimited resources at their disposal."

"While that might sound terrifying on the surface, it's hugely helpful from an investigative standpoint. Those aren't the kinds of skills just anyone can acquire. You're looking for someone with specific education and experience, and there can't be very many people who fit the bill."

Mason smiled for his benefit. It wasn't much, but it was still the best lead they had.

"Call me if you find anything else, okay?"

He glanced one last time at Marchment's body before heading out into the hall. The FPS agents wore similar suits with dosimeters clipped to their chests to monitor their exposure, although the levels of radiation outside of the room itself were surprisingly low. The Dragon had managed to confine the radiation into a tightly collimated, high-powered beam, much like a Gamma Knife, which could be used to remove tiny tumors from the brain and auditory nerves, only on a much larger scale.

Layne had commandeered an office down the hallway to meet with a radiation oncologist and a medical dosimetrist in hopes that they might be able to shed some light on the files that had been salvaged from Yamaguchi's smashed computer, while Chris had every digital forensics agent he could scrounge going through surveillance footage in an effort to figure out where the Dragon had gone. Considering he'd removed his protective mask and suit, one of those cameras had to have captured an image of his face. He'd taken a risk by stepping out of the shadows to assassinate Marchment and, with any luck, potentially compromised whatever plans he had for his homemade nuclear device.

Mason shed his protective suit in the repurposed break room and was preparing to head down the corridor to join his partner when his federal cell phone vibrated to alert him to an incoming message. All identifying information had been stripped. He read it once, and then again.

ANSWER ME.

The phone vibrated in his hand. His heart rate accelerated and his pulse pounded in his temples. Taking a deep breath, he waited for the number of the incoming call to appear, but the screen remained blank. He answered on the third ring.

"Anomaly, I presume."

"Special Agent James Mason," the hacker said in a voice composed of many. Mason detected at least five different speakers, all of their words seamlessly blending together. He heard a deep-voiced man, a young girl with a lisp, a formal British gentleman, a teenage boy with a Bronx accent, and an elderly woman. "I trust you did not shed a tear for Deputy Secretary Marchment."

"I was hoping to have a few minutes alone with him before he passed on."

"He would not have told you what you wanted to know."

"If you really believed that, you wouldn't have taken the risk of killing him," Mason said. "You know as well as I do that I would have made him talk."

"And what would you have forced him to tell you, Special Agent? What do you want to know?"

"I want to know who benefitted from the ruination of Iraq, Libya, and Syria. Who's responsible for unleashing the Dragon and what's his endgame?"

"Rand Marchment did not have that information."

"He undoubtedly had enough to point me in the right direction."

"Like your new friend Johan Mahler? Has he allowed you to study his archives or does he give you just enough information to wind you up like a tin soldier and send you into battle?"

Mason's breath staled in his chest. The only way anyone could have known about his meetings with Johan was if he was being surveilled. Anomaly was obviously watching him through passive cameras and digital devices, patiently stalking him, like a hungry predator. As if in confirmation, a black-and-white screen grab from the security camera inside Marchment's room appeared on his phone. The image had captured him in the process of turning to face the deputy secretary, who smirked at him after having just responded to Layne's question about who else was involved in the nuclear plot by telling her to ask her partner.

Was it possible Marchment had been right? Did Mason already know who was controlling the Dragon?

"Trust me," Anomaly said. "If we wanted you dead, you would never see us coming. And we most certainly would not have warned you of the impending helicopter crash or the ambush in Mexico."

Mason said nothing for several seconds as warring thoughts collided inside his head.

"What do you want from me?" he finally asked.

"Your help. There are those among us who have lost their way and need to be reminded."

"You mean eliminated," Mason said. "I refuse to be a pawn in your civil war. Try to manipulate me all you want, but I'll never help the Thirteen."

"You will," the voices said. "And when the time comes, you will do so of your own volition."

Anomaly terminated the call, leaving Mason staring at the darkened screen, his nerves thrumming like downed power lines. The Thirteen's resident hacker had been trying to find out if Marchment had spilled his guts and Mason had inadvertently told him exactly what he wanted to know, sacrificing any leverage he might have had. There was no time to deal with that now, though, not while the Dragon was still out there, and getting farther and farther away with every passing second.

He shoved his phone into his pocket and hurried to catch up with his partner, who already appeared to have wrapped up her interviews. She shook the hands of the two men and turned to face him as they walked away. Her expression told him she'd learned something good. She beckoned for him to hurry and ducked back into the office, where she'd taken notes on a lined pad.

"The Dragon's dying," she said the moment he entered the room.

"Start from the beginning."

She glanced at her notes as she spoke.

"The lab tests show dangerously low levels of neutrophils, white blood cells, and platelets, which are all signs of a compromised immune system. The presence of 'pathological hepatic isoenzymes of bone-specific alkaline phosphatase' and elevated levels of serum blood phosphorus and calcium suggest rapid bone degeneration. Increased levels of blood urea nitrogen and creatinine in his kidneys also indicate muscular deterioration. Throw in the results of the EEG and MRI, which show diminished blood flow to the brain, damage to the motor cortex and the acoustic and cranial nerves, and you have a recipe for an extreme case of chronic radiation syndrome."

"His body's cannibalizing itself," Mason said. He envisioned the photograph Gunnar had received from the Russian state department, of the man standing center stage, his face in shadow, the scarred texture of his skin clearly evident, and suddenly realized that the plutonium-240 wasn't the only thing that was a ticking time bomb. "How long does he have?"

"Without access to more lab data, the doctors can only guess," Layne said. "A chronic disease like this could take years, if not decades, to prove fatal, depending upon the nature of the radiation exposure and the individual's radiosensitivity, but they seem to think that he's reached the end stages."

"So this is a suicide mission."

"That's their assessment."

Mason took out his phone, snapped a picture of her notes, and sent it to the cloud. He was just about to return the device to his pocket when it buzzed in his hand. He answered on the first ring.

"The security office is on the main floor, near the entrance," Chris said. "You need to get down here right away."

"Tell me you found him."

"No," Chris said. "We found *her*."

40

"If I'm correct, that flash you see right there is from a plasma beam," the digital forensic tech said. He had a hipster beard, a waxed mustache, and glasses with thick black frames. The badge hanging from his lanyard identified him as P. BADGETT. "Let me show it to you again."

Mason leaned over the specialist's shoulder to better see the monitor. He recognized the PACU hallway from a vantage point above the nurses' station. Most of the curtains were drawn, blocking his view of anything inside. He picked out the enclosure underneath Marchment's room just as a greenish blue light spread across the ceiling from the narrow gap above the curtains.

"What's the significance?" Mason asked.

"Previous attempts to build a gamma ray gun were largely unsuccessful because they used a dental X-ray machine to fire a beam of electrons at a hafnium disc. That's like trying to knock the passengers out of a flying plane with a shotgun. A laser-driven, plasma-wave accelerator is actually capable of altering the physical structure of a gas by separating its free electrons to make plasma, which is kind of like a fourth state of matter. The ions left behind still want those jettisoned electrons, so they exert their own electrostatic force to pull them back, only to have the laser yank them away again. What this does is produce alternating positive and negative charges, like the AC electricity inside your walls, creating an oscillating waveform of pure energy that bombards the cesium and converts the hafnium into a solid beam of gamma rays. It's a truly ingenious concept."

"And you can tell all of this from a flash of light," Layne said.

Badgett mumbled something.

"I didn't catch that."

"I said it's the principle behind the gamma ray gun in *Fallout 4*," he said.

"The video game?"

"My buddies and I tried to build one in my garage, but we ended up burning it down."

"The security footage," Chris said.

Badgett offered an apologetic smile.

"Sorry," he said. "I tend to get overly excited about these things."

He rewound the footage until a diminutive figure wearing powder blue scrubs, a matching bouffant cap, and a surgical mask walked in reverse from behind the curtains, pushing a wheeled metal suitcase behind her. There was no doubt in Mason's mind that the subject was definitively female.

"We can track her all the way back to where she entered the hospital from the underground parking structure," Chris said. "We're still working on how she got in there."

Badgett rolled the video forward again. Nearly a full minute passed after the curtain closed. The light flashed and the woman wearing the silver CBRN suit emerged. A quick glance over her shoulder and she walked straight down the hallway, trailing the case and a faint slipstream of smoke behind her.

"She makes a beeline for the sky bridge," Badgett said, switching from one camera to the next as he spoke. The woman disappeared from the bottom of the first screen, only to reappear again at the top of the second. One moment she was crossing a distant hallway and the next she was rounding a corner and walking away from the camera. "When she gets there, she takes off the suit, stuffs it into a bag, and disposes of it in the cleaning cart right here."

The woman looked away as she passed the next camera, which revealed her to be wearing a pair of leggings, an oversize sweater, and her dark hair pulled up in a scrunchie. She looked like every other female medical student on campus.

"We found the scrubs underneath the bed in the PACU," Chris said. "Forensics is already examining them for skin and hair samples, but unless her DNA is in the system . . ."

Mason knew exactly how much good that evidence would do them without an existing sample against which to compare it.

The woman walked across the bridge, out of the range of one camera and into the view of another. She either turned her head or looked down so as not to reveal her face. They followed her all the way along the third-floor corridor of the New York State Psychiatric Institute and onto the elevator, which opened two floors later in the main lobby, without anyone inside.

"She climbed out through the ceiling hatch," Chris said. "A security officer found her clothes in a plastic bag at the bottom of the shaft. We have yet to determine where she exited the building or what she was wearing when she did. The hit was well planned and executed, and she obviously had help."

"You mean because she's a girl?" Layne said.

"No, Special Agent, because she knew exactly which room was Marchment's and how best to reach it without being detected. And someone had to have tipped her off that he was coming out of the coma. This plan must have been in place from the very beginning, but she and whoever else were content to just let him wither away and die if that's how it played out."

"What about prints from the elevator?" Mason asked.

"We pulled some good ones from the lip of the hatch, but they don't match any in AFIS."

"Where could she have gone that we can't find her on one of these cameras?"

"Let me show you something," Badgett said. He closed the internal security footage and opened the live feed from an external camera on a building overlooking the courtyard between the hospital and the surrounding clinics. There were people everywhere, hoping to get a look at whatever was causing the commotion. "There are fourteen hundred graduate students housed in the dormitories and towers right back here off Haven Ave. And it appears as though they're all out here on the streets, along with what has to be every available police officer in the city. She could have easily blended into the crowd, even with as many cameras as we have out there."

There was something they were missing, something above and beyond the fact that no matter how hard Mason tried, he simply couldn't think of this young woman as the Dragon.

"Have you been able to isolate a decent image of her?" he asked.

"Show them what you showed me," Chris said.

Badgett nodded and dragged over his laptop. It was a custom model, like Gunnar's, only the outside was plastered with stickers advertising various craft brews and IPAs.

"None of these pictures is perfect by any stretch of the imagination—she'd obviously cased the place and knew where all of the cameras were—but if we can somehow piece them all together? Who knows? Maybe we can build our own Frankenstein's monster and produce a single useful image."

He opened a page filled with thumbnail images and clicked

through them one at a time. They featured the woman from various angles and vantage points. Everything about her was hazy and pixilated as a result of motion and magnification. There was a shot of her left eye above the surgical mask and below the bouffant cap. An almost spectral image of the contours of her face behind the reflective shield of the helmet. Her right eye and cheekbone as she pulled the sweater over her head. A blurred profile of her face as she drew her shoulder-length, straight hair into a ponytail. The slope of her neck, her jawline, and her ear. Her head lowered, her eyes concealed by her bangs, and the ghost of a smile on her lips as the elevator doors closed in front of her.

None of the pictures by itself demonstrated enough detail to initiate a facial-recognition search, but there was enough for Mason to realize that he'd seen her before. He needed to be sure, though, and he didn't want to compromise his source; he wasn't prepared to divulge the fact that Gunnar and Ramses were in the city and actively working the investigation with him.

"Based on the shape of her eyes, the prominence of her brow and cheekbones, and her skin tone, we suspect she's of mixed Asian and Eastern European ancestry," Badgett said. "She's approximately five foot six, one hundred and twenty pounds, and between twenty-five and forty years old."

"Can you email those images to me?" Mason asked.

"Sure, what're you thinking?"

"I find it hard to believe that a woman that young and who moves that fluidly can be dealing with any kind of chronic medical condition, let alone one that supposedly has her at death's door."

"You don't think the lab results from Yamaguchi's computer are the Dragon's?" Layne said.

"No," Mason said. "I don't think she's the Dragon."

"Then who is she?"

"I don't know, but I think it's about time we found out," Mason said, gesturing for Layne to follow him and heading for the door.

"Where are you going?" Chris asked.

Mason stepped out into the hallway and waited for Chris to catch up.

"Do you trust me?" he asked.

"I should ask you the same," Chris said, his jaw muscles flexed as though he were grinding walnuts between his molars, shells and all.

"You know why I'm here, don't you? Why I was offered the promotion to deputy director for the National Security Branch?"

Mason searched his boss's face for the answer that had thus far eluded him.

"You're the only one the president trusts to find out how deeply the FBI has been compromised."

"I could have done that from Denver without tipping anyone off to my intentions."

The truth hit Mason squarely in the face.

"You're our handler," he said. "We're off the books on this one."

"There are factions that find your . . . *proximity* . . . to the cases involving the flu virus and the Novichok to be somewhat troubling."

"Are you one of them?"

"I'd be a fool not to harbor any suspicions."

"And yet here we are."

"It's a risk-reward proposition, Mason. I'm assuming all of the risk, so I'd sure as hell better be rewarded."

"I never saw you as the ladder-climbing kind."

Chris gritted his teeth and jabbed a finger into Mason's sternum.

"You know goddamn well I couldn't give a rat's ass about that kind of thing. Something bad is happening out there and I'll be damned if I'm going to let it happen on my watch."

"Then you have to trust me," Mason said.

"I need to know you're building a case and not flying a black flag."

"I'm trying to find an unstable homemade nuclear bomb that could go off at any second."

"That doesn't answer my question."

"Believe me, Chris. There's a part of me that wishes it didn't."

Mason turned and started down the corridor toward the stairwell.

"Call us as soon as you pick up her trail," Layne said, falling into stride behind him.

Several seconds passed before Chris returned to the office and closed the door softly behind him.

41

Mason had commandeered the Crown Victoria from the agent who'd picked them up at the airport and arranged to meet Gunnar and Ramses at a twenty-four-hour diner a couple of blocks outside the police cordon. They needed to be ready to move as soon as Chris picked up the assassin's trail and, if things started moving as quickly as they expected, there was no telling when they might have the chance to eat again. They'd arrived to find two breakfast specials and a carafe of coffee waiting for them and lit into both with equal exuberance.

"So you think that nuclear device is within a four-hour radius of here," Ramses said. He wiped his mouth with his napkin and deposited it on his plate. "And you base that reasoning on what? A hunch?"

"The moment the Thirteen learned that Marchment was coming out of his coma, they would have set into motion whatever contingency plan they had in place to keep him from talking," Mason said.

"So they dispatched this assassin—the real Dragon or otherwise—at approximately the same time we left Colorado," Gunnar said. "Your reasoning's sound, but unfortunately it doesn't help us very much. If she traveled by plane, she could have originated anywhere east of the Rocky Mountains, a vast swath of land that encompasses all of the major cities in the Midwest, southern Canada, and the entire Eastern Seaboard. We can significantly narrow our search parameters if she traveled by ground, but that's still an impossibly large area, including Boston, D.C., Philadelphia. . . . You get the picture."

"We also got this," Mason said. He brought up the file with the images Badgett had sent him and spun his phone diagonally across the table to Gunnar, who glanced down at it for a long moment before offering a crooked half smile. "I thought you might find that more to your liking."

"What is it?" Ramses asked. He snatched the phone away from Gunnar and swiped through the images. "You're telling me this little girl is responsible for this whole mess?"

"There's no doubt she killed Marchment," Layne said.

"You're missing the big picture," Mason said. "We've seen her before. In the pictures Gunnar's Russian contact sent us. That's the woman from Konets Mira, the splinter cell of Aum Shinrikyo. The one photographed just starting to turn toward the camera after pinning up the map of Moscow."

"You're certain?" Ramses said. "All I see is an eye here and an ear there. I'd need to see those pictures again. I only remember looking at her chest."

"There's a surprise," Layne said.

"I was talking about the tattoo. Why do you always have to bust my balls?"

"That's the same woman, all right," Gunnar said. He opened the picture in question and held up Mason's phone beside it. The two photos were almost mirror images of each other; the former offered a glimpse of her cheek, forehead, and chestnut hair, while the latter concealed them beneath the surgical attire, but the woman's eyes were identical. "I don't need a computer program to tell me that."

"But you don't think she's the Dragon, either," Layne said.

"I looked through the notes you took during your meeting with the oncologist and the dosimetrist. This woman is in better physical shape than whoever's medical files were on Yamaguchi's computer."

"We can't say with any certainty that those results belong to the Dragon. That's only our working assumption based upon Yamaguchi's perceived rationale for trying to destroy them."

"I'm not saying she's not *a* dragon, just not *the* Dragon."

"What on earth are you talking about?"

"Let me show you something." Gunnar turned his computer and brought up two images, side by side. The first showed the man in the CBRN suit in the picture McWhinney had recovered from the scope of Austin's rifle, the second an image of the woman captured rounding a blind corner during her escape from the hospital. "We can use the walls beside both figures to determine their relative heights. It doesn't take a genius to recognize that we're dealing with two different people. The guy in the first picture has to be nearly half a foot taller, just like the man in the images we saw in Johan's archives."

"He passed the torch?" Mason said.

"Or maybe franchised his likeness. Either way, one could make a case for the necessity of doing so based upon the fact that he's dying, which supports our theory as to why he's decided to upgrade the potential of his nuclear devices. For my money, he intends to go out with a bang, not a fizzle."

"Taking a lot of innocent people with him," Layne said, pouring herself another cup of coffee.

"Speaking of Johan's archives . . ." Mason said. "Anomaly knows we were there. He called me, using voice-altering software, while I was still inside the hospital. I think he was trying to find out how much Marchment might have told us, but he also made sure I knew that he was watching me."

"Is he becoming a threat?" Ramses asked. "Can we trust him or are we going to have to move against him? I don't like the idea of working with someone who's playing both sides."

"If he wanted us dead, he could have just sat back and let it happen. Besides, he basically confirmed that whoever's pulling his strings is using us to take members of the Thirteen off the board."

"I'm with Ramses," Gunnar said. "When it comes to Anomaly, there's always an ulterior motive. It's not like him to lay his cards on the table like that. I'm inclined to think he's more concerned about what Johan might have shown us than anything Marchment might have said."

"Have you had a chance to look at the pictures you took with the contact lenses?" Layne asked.

Gunnar spun his laptop so that it faced him, his fingers dancing across the keys. When he turned it around again, the image on the screen was of a video monitor displaying a man Mason immediately recognized. The third incarnation of the Hoyl, F3, stared back at him through inhumanly blue eyes. He was barely visible over the shoulder of an underling in a white isolation suit, who gripped a screaming primate by the scruff of its neck. Subsequent pictures had captured the father of the man who'd killed Mason's wife in dense jungles and primitive villages from which hemorrhagic viruses had later emerged.

"Johan wants me to remember that F-Three is still out there," Mason said. "And that eventually we're going to have to deal with him."

"So what does that mean?" Ramses asked. "We're his hit squad now, too?"

"Anomaly outright accused us of doing Johan's dirty work. I don't like the implication, either, but at least we know which side the old guy's on."

"Do we, though? I mean really?"

Gunnar breezed through the pictures of the Dragon and the destruction he'd wrought until another sideways television screen appeared on his monitor, this one featuring a woman they'd seen before.

She'd been photographed at a distance, little more than her blond hair and black attire visible. In each image, she was surrounded by men in camouflage fatigues, the patterns of which changed with their surroundings. Only the corpses scattered around them remained the same.

"Valkyrie," Gunnar said. "The woman associated with the rat-lines used to smuggle war criminals like Adolf Eichmann and Josef Mengele out of Germany in the aftermath of World War Two."

"Is she a player here?" Layne asked.

"I don't think so. She's connected to Colonia Dignidad in Chile, where we believe the surviving Nazis continued their experimentation with biological and chemical weapons for the Pinochet regime."

The following image was of a blank television display.

"I touched the monitor to see if I could access the hidden files, but it locked me out," Gunnar said. "It must have fingerprint-scanning capabilities. That was when Ben-Menachem arrived with coffee. I figured it was better to acquire some imagery than none, so I only photographed the home screens, and could only acquire so many more without attracting his attention."

The next series of pictures featured a man none of them had seen before. He wore his long hair braided and had dark skin made even darker by the tattoos covering seemingly every inch, including the sclera of his eyes, which made it impossible to tell where he was looking. Even his teeth had been inked to make them appear sharpened. He dragged a screaming woman by the hair in one picture and stood knee-deep in bodies in another, fresh blood shimmering on his face and bare chest.

"Who is he?" Layne asked.

Mason shook his head. There was something about the subject . . . an instinctive reaction that raised the hackles on his neck. He didn't know who this man was, and he hoped he would never have to find out.

Subsequent images showed an indistinct figure, little more than a silhouette clinging to the shadows in an alley, the adjacent street awash with police lights. Again, barely distinguishable from the darkness of a dense pine forest, the needled branches whipping on a violent wind, a helicopter's spotlight striking the flattened grasses in the field before it.

The final series of pictures were of a man who looked nothing like the others. He was young and handsome, with round glasses, an expensive suit, and a leather briefcase. In the first picture, he'd been caught looking over his shoulder on a busy sidewalk, and in the second, stepping from the revolving doors of an upscale building. The third picture was obviously a crime-scene photo. The man lay on his back, his suit disheveled, his lips parted. His right eye stared blankly into the camera, while his left was obscured by blood. The lens of his glasses had broken and embedded itself in his socket, protruding from the side of his nose, the soft tissue under his eyebrow, and the corner of his eye.

"Why would this guy be on Johan's wall if he's already dead?" Ramses asked.

"That's what we're supposed to think," Gunnar said.

He opened the final image, which featured a man wearing a baseball cap and a T-shirt. He'd been photographed at a distance, preparing to climb into a cab. A cloud of e-cigarette smoke rose from his lips, nearly concealing the damage to his left eye.

The ground fell out from beneath Mason.

"Zoom in on his face," he said, his pulse rushing in his ears. The magnification blurred the image, but there was no mistaking the inverted U-shaped scar around the socket. Anomaly spelled his name using the Greek letters alpha and omega—the beginning and the end. While the former looked like a normal A, the latter resembled a horseshoe. "Every hacker has a unique signature so there's no mistaking his work; Anomaly uses his defining physical characteristic as his."

"Holy shit," Ramses said.

Mason silently echoed the sentiment. They were looking at the face of the hacker who'd both saved their lives and hurled them headlong into danger, who'd used them to take Slate Langbroek off the board, and who was attempting to manipulate them, at that very moment, to further his master's deadly machinations. And now that they'd identified him, they finally had the chance to turn the tables and use him to lead them to the Thirteen.

"I'll run him through my facial-recognition program and see what else I can find," Gunnar said.

"We'll have to come back to him," Layne said. "Right now, our priority is finding the Dragon and we're running out of time."

Mason nodded his agreement. She was right. Anomaly would have to wait.

"I have to believe he would have personally handled Marchment's assassination if he were physically able to do so," Gunnar said. "I agree with Johan's assessment that he enjoys making his victims suffer, but he also shares the Thirteen's genocidal goals. No one joins a cult without buying into its tenets with every fiber of his being. This is his swan song, the realization of Shoko Asahara's apocalyptic vision and Kiyohide Hayakawa's quest to make it a reality."

"So this all goes back to Aum Shinrikyo's desire to bring about the end of the world and start over again with the best and brightest humanity has to offer," Mason said.

"At least for the Dragon. He's obviously an extremely intelligent individual with vast knowledge and practical experience in nuclear physics. Experts in any field are narcissists by nature. I can see how the idea of serving as foundation stock for a new, enlightened version of the species could be seductive."

Mason raised his eyebrows and looked at his old friend in a different light.

"Seductive enough to entice someone like you?"

Gunnar hesitated before answering.

"As an individual possessing what one might consider rather advantageous mental capabilities, I can admit that from a purely biological perspective, the idea holds a certain theoretical appeal. A society devoted to the pursuits of intellectual enlightenment could usher in an age of peace and prosperity never before experienced in the history of our species. The flaw with such utopian pursuits, however, is that human nature invariably intercedes. Not everyone believes we're all created equal, even in a world bereft of what the Thirteen considers the unproductive elements of society. In their minds, they're the chosen ones, which is where their ideology intersects with that of Aum Shinrikyo, and why the Dragon has devoted himself to their cause. This is the most critical step in the realization of his beliefs. If the world won't end on its own, someone needs to give it a push."

"Then we aren't dealing with indiscriminate nuclear destruction," Mason said. "He has a specific target, or targets, in mind."

"Which brings us to what Johan said about asking ourselves who benefitted from the ruination of Iraq, Libya, and Syria." He opened an image displaying a time line from 2000 to the present day. "I think we were right in assuming the Thirteen's motives are financial, but not in the sense we initially thought."

"How so?"

"It all comes down to the petrodollar."

42

The waiter cleared their plates and brought a fresh carafe of coffee. It tasted like it had been brewed from stale grounds and left on the burner too long, but the caffeine served its purpose.

"So this is about oil," Layne said.

"It's about the dollar itself," Gunnar said. "A petrodollar is an ordinary U.S. dollar that's been used to purchase oil. The name is an intentional misnomer. The system originated in the seventies when an oil crisis in the Middle East caused prices to skyrocket. Negotiating for all oil transactions to be conducted in a single currency—ours—not only stabilized the market, but inextricably bound it to the U.S. economy. Oil-producing countries benefitted because they controlled access to the product, while we controlled the supply of dollars, which every nation needed if they wanted to buy oil."

"What does that have to do with anything?" Ramses asked.

"Everything. The world uses nearly a hundred million barrels of oil a day, thirty-five billion barrels a year. At roughly a hundred dollars a barrel, that's three point five trillion dollars in U.S. currency that has to be in circulation at any given time for the express purpose of buying oil. And don't forget about the trillions we need to come up with every year to cover the federal government's operating budget and all of the pork our politicians stuff into every bill they pass. To meet the demand, we have to print more and more money, which we're happy to do because it makes it look like our economy is booming, but you can't flood the market with dollars without reducing their value in the process. That's the basic premise of inflation. The more bills we print, the less each one is worth, infecting the market with even greater instability than the initial agreement was designed to eliminate."

"So why not stop printing the money?" Layne asked.

"Because the global economy would collapse if we did," Gunnar said. "The whole thing is one big house of cards built upon the U.S. dollar, which is a fiat currency, meaning that its value isn't backed by a commodity like gold, but rather by the unwritten guarantee that it will hold its value as long as our government remains viable. Without that commodity sitting in a vault somewhere, every new bill we issue gets us deeper and deeper into the hole."

"So we're continually printing money and accruing debt just to keep the system afloat?"

"That's exactly what we're doing, but here's where the process gets tricky. There isn't enough gold in the world to back the sheer volume of greenbacks we've printed, so if there were ever a run on the banks, every single one of them would fail. And why is that? Because all of our liquidity is tied up in our national debt, which isn't money borrowed from other countries, like people have been conditioned to think; it's the sum of loans made to our government by our own banks, on top of which interest is continuously being paid. If we were to stop the presses, we wouldn't be able to pay the interest, so the principle would come due. All at once. That's roughly thirty trillion dollars. All of the banks in the world combined don't have a fraction of that money and the Treasury Department can't just call up the Mint and tell it to start printing hundred-dollar bills."

"Why not?" Ramses asked.

"You're kidding, right?" Gunnar looked around the table as though expecting one of the others to chime in. "Because the Federal Reserve controls the issuance of our currency. The Department of the Treasury is merely responsible for ensuring that anytime someone spends one of our bills, whoever's on the other side of the transaction receives compensation. Back when we were on the gold standard, it monitored stockpiles at facilities like Fort Knox to make sure that we only circulated as much paper money as we could back. It can't print a single dollar without being able to guarantee its value, which is where the Federal Reserve comes in, but don't let the name fool you. While the Fed might be America's central bank, it's neither part of the federal government nor does it retain the reserves to cover all of the dollars in circulation. It's a private bank, one that dictates the country's monetary policy and lends the government the collateral to print the money it needs."

"If it doesn't have the reserves, then what does it use as collateral?"

"The debt is the collateral, Mace. For the Fed, it's all about the debt."

Mason contemplated his old friend's words for several seconds. Everything he was saying was so counterintuitive that it almost felt like he'd missed the punch line of a joke.

"Debt's a liability, not an asset," he finally said.

"Oh, but it is an asset. It's created by a promissory note, a written pledge to repay a certain amount of money. Let me try to break it down so you can understand it." As if by magic, a hundred-dollar bill appeared in his hand. "If I gave you this money, what would it be?"

"An asset."

"It's a piece of paper," Gunnar said. "Without the full faith and credit of the United States government to back it up, it's worth less than the sum of the ink and paper it's printed on, a fancy piece of stationery we call a Federal Reserve note. It says so on every bill, along with the phrase 'The United States of America will pay to the bearer on demand,' meaning the government is responsible for the amount of debt on that paper. So to print a hundred-dollar bill like this one, the first thing you need is a hundred dollars' worth of collateral. Of course, if you had that to begin with, you wouldn't need to print the bill, but that doesn't change the fact that you need it to buy something you really, really want. Now, everyone knows you're good for the money, so you write an IOU that says you'll pay back that hundred bucks, with interest, and someone says, 'Sure, I'll buy that IOU,' and gives you the collateral. In that scenario, you're the government and your IOU is issued as what's known as a Treasury security, or simply a treasury. The lender is an investment bank called a primary dealer, which bids on that treasury at auction and then turns around and sells it to the Federal Reserve at a profit of around three percent. The Fed then hangs on to all of those treasuries until such time as it determines that it needs to reduce its reserves and sells them on the open market."

"Why does the government need the investment bank?" Layne asked. "Why not just sell the treasuries directly to the Federal Reserve and save the interest?"

"The Fed needs to maintain a degree of separation to avoid the appearance of impropriety. Think of it as the government's personal banker, who buys treasuries from primary dealers in transactions conducted entirely by electronic means—numbers added to one digital ledger and subtracted from another—and gives the government permission to go ahead and roll the presses, turning debt into currency and essentially producing money out of thin air. The investment bank gets an immediate return on its expenditure and the Fed hangs on to that government debt as an asset, stockpiling those IOUs in much the same way that we once stockpiled gold. And there's little financial risk for any of the banks involved because the American taxpayer is on the hook for every cent of that debt."

"A bank like that would make the perfect partner to wash the cartel's money," Mason said.

"I doubt even CJNG has big enough cojones to attempt to launder its money through the central bank of the United States, right underneath the noses of every federal agency in existence." Gunnar paused and cocked his head. "Although it might be possible using a primary dealer like Global Bank or AIP . . ."

"Both of which have already increased their institutional ownership of Royal Nautilus Petroleum."

"That's what investment banks do," Ramses said. "They invest the bank's money. So what if they buy Langbroek's holdings or a ton of treasuries and sell them at a profit? Isn't that the whole point?"

"The whole point is that every time a treasury is issued and more money is printed, the value of our currency diminishes. The dollar loses a little bit of its buying power and the prices of consumer goods rise in response, creating a spiral of inflation. So as our country outspends its budgetary constraints and runs up an out-of-control national debt, that unwritten guarantee of 'the full faith and credit of the United States' begins to sound hollow. Now ask yourself: What's an oil-producing country to do when it realizes it has tethered its entire economy to a sinking ship?"

"It attempts to untether itself," Mason said.

"Which is exactly what Iraq did," Gunnar said. "And why it had to be destroyed."

Mason's phone vibrated. He snatched it off the table and answered before the second ring.

"We picked up the girl on a security camera across the street from the psychiatric building," Chris said. "She'd changed clothes again and was wearing a hijab, but she couldn't hide that case. We located her again at a parking garage on the Columbia campus, where she'd stashed a black sedan. We're in the process of tracking her now."

"They found her," Mason said, sliding out of the booth. He covered the receiver and spoke back over his shoulder: "I'll call you guys as soon as I know anything. Be ready to move when I do."

Mason put Chris on speaker and rushed to catch up with Layne, who shouldered through the front door and ran down the sidewalk. He weaved through the crowd gathered to witness the commotion at the hospital and caught up with her as she climbed into the Crown Vic. She strapped herself into the seat beside him and accepted his cell phone.

"She's heading north on the Hudson Parkway," Chris said.

Mason gunned the engine and peeled out of the parking lot, slewing sideways onto West 165th. He accelerated past the hospital toward Riverside Drive, a chorus of police sirens wailing ahead of him. Layne braced her knees against the dashboard as he gained on the cruisers, their flashing lights staining the tunnel underneath the George Washington Bridge.

"She got off the highway on the other side of the bridge," Chris said.

Brake lights flared ahead of them. The first squad car streaked past the turnoff; the second struck the yellow barrels lining the ramp, throwing clouds of sand into the air. Mason followed the remaining cruisers around the tight turn, past the DO NOT ENTER and AUTHORIZED VEHICLES ONLY signs.

"I've lost her under the trees," Chris said. "Wait . . . there! Take a sharp left into the parking lot."

The police cars locked up their brakes and skidded past the entrance. Mason swerved in behind them, his headlights striking the side of a Hyundai Elantra. The driver's door stood open, the interior empty.

"Where'd she go?" Mason shouted.

"Over there!" Layne shouted, pointing through the thicket and toward the road. A silhouette appeared in the lights of the reversing police cars and vanished into the trees on the other side.

"She's heading into the Hudson River Greenway," Chris said. "Satellite's useless back there."

Mason jumped from the car and took off through the trees. He hit the road at a sprint and dodged the squad car parked across the entrance to the walking path. An officer charged downhill and around a blind bend ahead of him, the trees closing in from both sides, blocking out the night sky. It was so dark that Mason could barely tell that the path curved into the mouth of a tunnel. He heard the crunch of broken glass underfoot as he passed a darkened streetlamp and realized what was about to happen.

It was the perfect place for an ambush.

A flash of green light limned the concrete arch of the tunnel, followed by an echoing scream.

Darkness fell as Mason drew his weapon and entered the tunnel. The officer rolled from side to side on the ground, bellowing in agony and clutching at his face.

"Go!" Layne shouted. "I'll take care of him."

Mason raced from the tunnel and out across a footbridge. A shadow materialized from the darkness ahead of him. He caught a reflection from the boxlike contraption in the woman's hands as she whirled to face him. A green light bloomed from within it. He dove from the path and slid across the ground to the base of a rock formation. The scent of burning leaves filled the air. He took several sharp breaths and propelled himself back onto the path.

The woman was gone, the distant clapping sounds of her footsteps reverberating from beneath the George Washington Bridge. He pushed himself to run even faster. The moment he saw the construction parking lot at the base of the support tower, near the Little Red Lighthouse, he knew exactly what she intended to do.

Mason hurdled the railing and skidded down the slope as a pair of headlights rocketed out from beneath the bridge. He got off a single shot, shattering the rear windshield of the sedan speeding away from him along the greenway, the red glow of taillights fading into the distance.

He turned and rushed back to his car.

43

"I repeat, officers down!" The dispatcher's voice crackled from the radio. "All units respond."

Mason veered onto West 158th and sped north along the river, following the red-and-blue glow of the emergency lights radiating from underneath the Hudson Parkway, where he found a dirt lot enclosed by rusted girders and a highway on-ramp. It was as dark and con-cealed as any location on Manhattan.

Two police cruisers were parked diagonally in front of the assas-sin's Honda Accord. One of the officers lay in a smoldering heap on the ground; the other had crawled back into his vehicle and called for assistance, his grueling death broadcast over the airwaves.

Mason parked behind the Accord and climbed out. He and Layne switched on their flashlights as they approached the abandoned vehi-cle, the scent of burned hair hanging in the air. The driver's-side door stood open, the dirt underneath it scuffed by footprints, which disap-peared into the chaos of pedestrian and tire tracks mere feet away. Heat radiated from the interior, presumably from the directed-energy weapon. The woman had fired it through the front windshield at the officers who'd cornered her. They hadn't even realized they were being irradiated until it was too late to do anything about it.

An ambulance screamed down the road toward them, killing its siren as it pulled up to the police vehicles.

Mason hooked his Bluetooth over his ear and speed-dialed Gun-nar, who'd covertly hacked into the satellite feed and the city's network of traffic cameras.

"Anything?" he asked. "She can't have just disappeared."

"Negative," Gunnar responded through his earpiece. "You're in something of a blind spot. There are no cameras down there and you're invisible to satellite. This was a carefully orchestrated escape."

Mason watched the paramedics surveying the scene. They stood silhouetted against the lights of the incoming cop cars, as helpless as he felt. He heard a click as Layne joined the call on her earpiece.

"Something you said earlier has been eating at me, Gunnar," she said. A helicopter thundered overhead, its spotlight sweeping the river. "We all know that we invaded Iraq because of the events of nine/eleven and intelligence that Saddam Hussein was producing weapons of mass destruction. Are you trying to tell me that we've been fed a load of bullshit and the U.S. military was effectively sent to war to defend the petrodollar and enforce America's financial interests?"

While Mason understood his partner's skepticism, he'd never known his old friend to be wrong about monetary matters.

"Iraq has the second-largest oil deposit on the planet," Gunnar said. "In 2000, Saddam decided to start selling its oil in euros, so all of the U.S. dollars his country had accumulated needed to be converted, flooding the global market with greenbacks and raising the value of the euro, which further enriched Saddam and undercut the petrodollar. Worse, it diminished the international demand for the dollar and threatened its status as the reserve currency, the consequences of which would be catastrophic. We risked losing everything if we failed to overthrow Saddam and reinstate the petrodollar as the sole currency of exchange, so with the terrorist attack on the World Trade Center as a pretext, we launched a shock-and-awe campaign against a country from which not a single one of the hijackers originated."

"Where does the Dragon fit in?" Mason asked.

"Undoubtedly as part of that shock-and-awe campaign. The Thirteen sit atop of the financial pyramid. No one would be hit harder by the collapse of the dollar's value than they would."

Officers erected a barricade along 158th, while forensic investigators donned white jumpsuits, set up portable lights, and started documenting the crime scene. Sirens wailed in the distance. Mason tried not to think about the fact that the assassin could hit them with her DEW from just about anywhere and they wouldn't have the slightest idea what was happening until their skin started to burn.

"Why the sudden urge to transition away from the dollar anyway?" he asked.

"Our national debt had been slowly creeping upward through the nineties," Gunnar said. "Five trillion might seem insignificant now, but running up a tab greater than the GDP of most developed nations is a big deal. Without a commodity like gold to back it, the dollar risked becoming hyperinflationary. Iraq's finances were so inextricably tied to the dollar that if it collapsed, the country would go broke overnight."

"Why wouldn't they just use their own currency? Or better yet, join with the other OPEC countries to create a new one? They could use their existing gold stores and force their buyers to do the same."

Mason shone his light onto the floorboard of the Accord, where a hijab protruded from a duffel bag. The assassin had obviously changed on the fly.

"That's exactly what Gaddafi tried to do," Gunnar said. "So he had to be forcibly removed by any and all means necessary. He approached the African Union with the idea of converting the gold stores of its fifty-five-member countries into coins. Golden dinars. If all of the oil-producing countries in Africa suddenly demanded to be paid in this new currency, then buyers using U.S. dollars would be forced to pay the gold equivalent, which is many orders of magnitude larger."

"Then why not use the oil itself to back the currency? By doing so they'd control both the supply and the market value, creating an . . . energy-based . . . economy. . . ."

As he spoke the words, two pieces of the big picture snapped into place. He remembered the photograph taken at the Twentieth Assembly of the Society for Lasting International Peace in 1994, the same conference the Scarecrow and her brother had attended, a picture that had tipped them off to Royal Nautilus Petroleum's involvement in the plot to release Novichok from the subway and led them to the realization that Slate Langbroek was a member of the Thirteen. The caption had read: "Leading the charge for the global transition to a new energy-based economy and socialized health care model."

"Say you're right and the only reason we entered into any of these conflicts was to enforce the use of the petrodollar," Layne said. "Why would we not have simply taken the oil and used it to back our own currency?"

"Because we would have been viewed as the aggressors, not the liberators," Mason said.

"And we needed the petrodollar to remain unbound to any commodity so we could continue printing it at will," Gunnar said.

A string of police cruisers descended the off-ramp. They passed the turnoff without slowing and fanned out into the city, their sirens joining the chorus.

"So who benefitted from overthrowing Saddam and Gaddafi?" Mason asked.

"Every country that traded in petrodollars and, in doing so, tied its financial fortunes to the U.S. economy."

"Which is pretty much everybody, so what's the link to the Thirteen? Who's responsible for unleashing the Dragon and instigating the nuclear threat?"

Layne's federal phone vibrated in the pocket of her jacket. She glanced at the screen, tapped her earpiece to connect, and walked away from the chaos to better hear the call.

"Syria has to be the key," Gunnar said. "Its civil war marks a dramatic escalation and appears to be where everything comes to a head. It began accepting limited quantities of euros in 2008, well before the Arab Spring, which set the stage for civil unrest. The people demanded democracy, but Bashar al-Assad violently quashed their protests, earning international condemnation and charges of human rights abuses. The resultant isolation pushed Syria into an increasingly hostile alliance with China, Iran, and Russia, who vetoed a UN Security Council resolution imposing economic sanctions and seeking Assad's resignation, threats that only hastened the transition from the petrodollar."

"So we invaded," Mason said.

"Without the UN's support, we would have been seen as the instigators, so instead we chose to arm factions of, quote, unquote, 'moderate rebels' to overthrow Assad from within. While our efforts in Iraq and Libya had been met with little resistance from external forces, we found ourselves fighting a proxy war against Russia, using the rebels we'd trained and the government they'd propped up."

"If we were so concerned about Syria accepting 'limited quantities' of euros, why'd we wait so long to do something about it?"

"Because by then it wasn't just the euro. They'd entered into a deal for the direct sale of oil in a third currency that we simply couldn't abide."

"The Russian ruble," Mason said.

Layne terminated the call and ran back to the car. Police radios crackled and the helicopter hovering over the river abruptly shot across the sky.

"Chris's team picked her up on a traffic cam three blocks from here," Layne shouted. "They tracked her across the island in a silver CR-V, but they lost her near Harlem River Drive."

Mason jumped behind the wheel of the Crown Victoria and brought the engine to life with a roar.

"She's expanding her lead on us, buying herself time to get to her ultimate destination," he said.

"And where is that?"

"I don't know, but the last thing we want is for her to get there."

Mason stomped the gas and blew past the paramedics and forensic investigators. He took a sharp left and sped up the on-ramp, the Crown Vic drifting as he made a hard right onto 158th and rocketed underneath the Riverside Drive overpass, weaving through traffic, streaking eastward across the city.

"Look at the big picture," Gunnar said through his earpiece.

"When you think oil, you think Middle East, but Russia is the second-leading oil-exporting country in the world, behind only Saudi Arabia. It's already begun selling its own proprietary Russian Urals blend in rubles and fully intends to make a wholesale change when the time is right, which will not only strengthen the ruble, but utterly destroy the dollar, shifting the balance of power inexorably in the federation's favor."

Mason blew through a red light on Broadway and headed south. He swerved to avoid a cab, skidded sideways through traffic, and accelerated onto 155th Street.

Layne made a humming sound from deep in her chest. Her knuckles whitened on the handle of the door as the city roared past.

"So the Russians are literally poised to destroy the petrodollar and wipe out the economies of the entire Western world," Mason said.

"And we're fighting a war against them in Syria in hopes of preventing them from doing just that," Gunnar said. "Meanwhile, we've launched a global propaganda assault, demonizing them in the media, alleging collusion and meddling in our elections in what amounts to a trumped-up version of McCarthy's Red Scare. There's no doubt that Russia is our enemy, but if we were to reveal the full extent of its ambitions, we would expose our own in the process."

Towering redbrick housing complexes rose to the left; a greenbelt stretched away to the right. The white arches of the Macombs Dam Bridge materialized directly ahead, crossing the Harlem River.

"Take a hard right here," Layne said. "Then another quick right and drive around the block. She ditched the CR-V underneath the overpass."

Mason thought about the terrorist attack that had justified the invasion of Iraq and the allegations of human rights abuses that had brought the United States into the armed conflicts in Libya and Syria. And he thought about the map of Moscow hanging on the wall at the Konets Mira meeting and the nuclear bomb somewhere out there on American soil.

Everything suddenly made sense.

"The real question isn't who benefitted from the destruction of Iraq, Libya, and Syria," he said, "but who benefits from starting a war with Russia."

44

Mason pulled to the curb a block away from the police cars parked haphazardly across the road, their light bars flashing silently. He climbed out and turned in a circle, surveying the faces of the few on-lookers out on the street at this early hour. None of them appeared overly concerned by the mass of cruisers surrounding the silver CR-V parked against the curb or the armed officers swarming the block in search of clues as to where the driver might have gone. This was all a part of the assassin's plan. She probably had a dozen cars parked all around the city, and every time she switched vehicles they wasted valu-able time picking up her trail.

A blue, new-model Ford Mustang slowed as it approached and pulled up beside him. He recognized Gunnar in the passenger seat and removed his earpiece. His old friend hopped out and offered a sympa-thetic nod in greeting. Ramses's eyes were hooded, his face expres-sionless when he joined them on the sidewalk.

"What's the plan from here?" he asked.

"We need to anticipate her next move," Mason said. "Find a way to get out ahead of her."

"Easier said than done," Layne said. She walked around to the front of the Crown Victoria and sat on the hood, her face awash with the alternating red and blue glow. "What do we know?"

"Whether this woman is an acolyte or the new Dragon, she's in-credibly smart, well trained, and undoubtedly having a good laugh at our expense," Gunnar said.

"None of which helps us right now," Mason said. He watched the officers disperse into the surrounding neighborhood, their voices loud and angry. The woman had killed two of their brothers and sent a third to the hospital; they were out for blood. "We need to focus on what we know."

"We have a Russian cult, some dead Russians in a barn, and a Russian plot to destroy the dollar," Ramses said. "I might not be the smartest person in any room, but even I can sense a pattern forming here."

"Konets Mira is at the center of everything," Mason said. "Both the old and the new Dragons were at the core of the splinter cell. They were planning an attack on the Kremlin before the undercover agent derailed their plot, scattering their cult to the wind."

"The experience might have informed their selection of targets here," Gunnar said. "They were obviously looking to make a statement in Moscow, and I can think of no better way of making one here than by hitting the White House."

"There's no way anyone would get within half a mile of it with a nuclear device," Layne said.

"They wouldn't have to," Ramses said.

"Today would be the perfect day to try," Gunnar said. "An attack on Independence Day would be demoralizing, and if they successfully hit the Salute to America event, they could literally take out the president, half of the Congress, the Joint Chiefs of Staff, and the better part of the military. There'll be close to a million people on hand and tens of millions more watching on TV. It would be like the Times Square Massacre all over again, only on a much grander scale."

The red glare of the rising sun stained the sky to the east, slanted columns of light passing through the guardrails of the road above them and rousing the pigeons roosting in the exposed girders. All around them, the city began to slowly awaken to the new day, blissfully unaware of the events that had transpired while it slept. Or the nature of the threat posed by the woman who'd abandoned the CR-V.

"I thought their hatred was directed specifically at their own country," Layne said.

"Can you think of a surer way of guaranteeing Russia's utter obliteration than by making it look like the Russians were responsible for the destruction of Washington, D.C.?" Gunnar asked.

"You think the Dragon's running a false-flag operation? That he's playing both sides?"

"No, he's playing for a third side, one that stands to gain from a war between the United States and Russia, a Third World War fought for control of the world's finances by an entity independent of both superpowers."

"The Thirteen," Mason said.

"So they're just setting fires and stepping back to watch them burn?" Ramses said. "Or do you think they genuinely hope we destroy each other?"

"A nuclear war would further their population-reduction agenda and eliminate two potential adversaries in the process, but even the

Thirteen wouldn't be able to control it. Assuming they somehow survived, our mutually assured destruction would leave them ruling over an uninhabitable wasteland. We have to be missing something."

"Let me see if I can get anything out of my contact at the Russian state department," Gunnar said. "There's obviously plenty she's not telling me about Konets Mira and the men who were butchered in that stall in Texas, but maybe if I bring our theories to her she can either confirm or deny them."

"It's a start. In the meantime, we should—"

Mason's federal cell phone rang. He pulled it from his pocket and answered on speaker.

"We picked her up driving out from underneath that bridge half an hour ago in a gray Camry," Chris said. "The NYPD found it in a parking garage near the Met a few minutes ago. We're trying to figure out where she went and what she's driving now."

"We can be there in fifteen minutes—"

"Negative. You're useless to me here. I have digital forensic specialists combing through footage from security and traffic cameras all across the city. It's only a matter of time before we catch up with her and I want you and Layne there when we do."

Gunnar hopped into the passenger seat of the Mustang, opened his laptop, and set to work. The streetlights underneath the bridge flickered as the photosensors detected the first rays of the sunrise.

"She'll want to be out of the city before morning rush hour," Mason said.

"My thoughts exactly, which is why I need you and your partner off Manhattan, too," Chris said. "Every cop in uniform is chasing down a BOLO that changes every fifteen minutes and the entire city is on the brink of daily gridlock. I need you to be able to move on a moment's notice."

"I think I might know the Dragon's target, if not where the bomb is now."

Chris was silent for so long that Mason had to check to make sure he hadn't dropped the call.

"Listen to me very closely, Mason. Don't tell anyone where you're going. Just get your asses there right now. Let me know when you arrive, not a moment sooner. Are we clear?"

Mason understood exactly what Chris was saying. If their investigation was compromised, they couldn't afford to risk anyone tipping off the Dragon to the fact that they knew where he was. It was also a declaration of trust, one that caught Mason by surprise.

"Yes, sir," he said, but Chris had already terminated the call.

He'd just cut their leash.

"I've got her on one of the security cameras in the parking garage," Gunnar said. He climbed out of the car, balanced his computer on the roof, and swiveled the screen so they could all see a screen grab of the woman wearing a blond wig and a baseball cap. She'd been recorded looking over her shoulder as she emerged from the driver's-side door of a gray sedan, hauling a silver case across the seat behind her. She couldn't have been more than thirty years old, and yet her eyes appeared far older. "I can confirm, definitively, that this is the same woman from the Konets Mira meeting in Moscow."

"You should have shared your suspicions about the Dragon's target with Chris," Layne said.

"Archer's already in D.C. and you know damn well he's taking this threat seriously," Mason said. "He has a literal army of agents at his disposal and access to the heads of every law-enforcement agency, the Joint Chiefs of Staff, and the president himself. They've surely planned for this contingency and ran through every possible scenario a thousand times over."

"You know there's no way the president's canceling the event, regardless of the risk."

"And I also know that there's no more secure place on the planet right now. That event is locked down tight. They have uniformed and plainclothes officers and agents everywhere. Aerial and satellite surveillance. Bomb-sniffing dogs. Metal and radiation detectors at strategic locations all around the city and at every entrance to the National Mall."

"He could detonate a nuclear device a mile away and they'd still be within the blast radius."

"Then we have to make sure that doesn't happen."

Mason leveled his stare at each of them in turn to make sure they understood the gravity of the situation. They needed to understand that they could be embarking on a one-way trip.

"The hell if I'm missing this show," Ramses said. "I've always wondered what it would be like to watch hundreds of politicians get vaporized." He smirked. "No offense."

"My old man would be the first to admit that it might be a step in the right direction," Mason said.

"You're going to need help navigating the District and the additional security protocols," Gunnar said. "And I'm not about to let you guys take my plane without me being on it. I can't trust Ramses to let the pilot fly the plane."

"Layne?" Mason asked. He turned to his partner, who offered him a crooked half grin.

"This is why they pay us the big bucks," she said.

Mason smiled. There were worse people with whom to go up in a mushroom cloud.

He struck off toward the cop cars and tossed the Crown Victoria's keys to the first officer he found. The federal vehicle would be too easy to track using its GPS beacon. If they were going off the grid, then this was where its journey ended. By the time he returned, Layne had already slid into the backseat of the Mustang and Gunnar stood outside the door, waiting to assume the passenger seat.

"You expect me to squeeze back there?" Mason said.

"I'm going to need all the elbow room I can get if you want me to accomplish anything with Mr. Toad at the wheel," Gunnar said.

"Make sure your pilot knows not to land at either Dulles or Reagan. I don't want anyone to even sense we're coming."

"I'll call ahead and have him file a flight plan to Hyde Field."

Mason contorted his large frame into the tiny space and barely raised his knees before the seat slammed back into his shins.

Ramses closed the door, gunned the engine, and peeled away from the curb, nearly giving them all whiplash.

"Did you feel that kick?" he said. "The horses underneath that hood are just dying to be taken out for a run."

"There's no place for them to do so between here and the airport," Mason said.

He met Ramses's stare in the rearview mirror. His old friend's eyes narrowed as a smile formed on his face. Mason realized his mistake a split second before Ramses pinned the pedal to the floor.

"Just try to get us there in one piece," he said.

45

ELSEWHERE

Zmei's heart beat hard and fast, fit to burst. He had known this day would come since he first envisioned his grand plan, and he had been dreading it ever since. Accepting the inevitability of his death was one thing, even knowing the kind of pain that lay before him, but this was something else entirely. He knew what agony like this could do to a man; he had seen it in his eyes, heard the screaming of his very soul, and yet the reality of the moment was infinitely worse than he had ever imagined.

Sister rolled him onto his side so that he faced away from her. He focused on his breathing.

"*Ty gotov, lyubov' moya?*" she asked from behind him.

Zmei nodded his readiness and clutched handfuls of the bedsheet. He felt a pinch in his lower back, followed by the sensation of something cold sliding between his vertebrae. A sharp pain caused him to cry out. Sister retracted the needle a hair and the pain diminished. Pressure ensued as she forced the anesthetic into the subarachnoid space, absolving him of sensation. Numbness spread through his right leg, from his hip all the way down through his toes. He hardly felt her jab him again on the other side of the spine, only the blissful warmth rippling down his left leg.

He breathed a sigh of relief. The bupivacaine would block the pain receptors for roughly four hours; the additional epinephrine would buy him as much as two hours more. He'd debated using an opioid adjuvant, but he needed to keep his head clear, at least for a little while longer.

Sister bandaged his puncture wounds and rolled him onto his back. He stared at his bare legs, stretched out before him, for as long as he could stomach before raising his eyes to the ceiling, where a discolored water stain formed a map of some unknown continent.

"*Ty chuvstvuyesh' eto?*" she asked.

He glanced down and saw her poking his toes with the tip of a scalpel. When he didn't immediately reply, she thrust it through the nail of his big toe, eliciting a rush of blood. He shook his head so she would know that he did not feel it. She wrapped a belt around his right thigh and cinched it so tightly that the skin whitened and bulged around it. His foot was already turning purple by the time she finished doing the same thing to his left leg. He looked away before he lost his nerve, his stare fixating upon the bedside chair, on the cushion of which rested a chain saw. The woman hefted its weight, pulled the cord, and the engine—

—*roars to life, guttering rich black smoke. A sadistic grin slashes the face of the* sicario *who goes by the name El Carnicero. The Butcher. Every inch of his skin is tattooed, right down to the whites of his eyes and his teeth. His hair is braided and his sleeveless undershirt is already spattered with blood. He offers the weapon with a flourish, the chain blurring through the cloud in front of him.*

Zmei returns his attention to the men sprawled in the stall before him. Vadim Kozlov and Anatoly Lebedev had been faithful followers of Konets Mira since its inception. While they had never been welcomed into its inner circle, they had been like brothers to him, two of his closest friends in the world. When they had become separated in Montenegro, he had despaired at the thought of never seeing them again. He had imagined them spending their days behind bars, enduring countless hours of torture, or perhaps even shot to death in the streets like dogs, and had been overcome with joy when he learned of their escape and celebrated their arrival in Mexico, welcoming them back into the fold. Had it not been for the vigilance of the men from Cártel de Jalisco Nueva Generación, many of whom he had gotten to know quite well during the years he had spent in their midst, traveling from his home on the east coast every few months so he could harvest the residual plutonium from the fuel rods they acquired through their relationship with the man known as Tertius, he might never have learned of his comrades' betrayal.

Anatoly and Vadim had been photographed at the Russian embassy in Mexico City and meeting in a crowded public square with their handler, a counterintelligence agent Zmei remembered well from his time in Moscow. It was not enough that his family had been broken apart, separated for its own protection; now it was turning against itself.

Zmei stares down at the baseball bat dangling from his fist, blood dribbling from the spiked wood, and lets it fall from his hand. He has killed so many people during the last two decades that he has lost count and is unburdened by either sympathy or remorse. Never before has he looked his victims in the eyes while executing their sentence, however, nor has he taken the lives of anyone for whom he has felt anything other than contempt. Neither Anatoly nor Vadim is recognizable, their arms and legs broken and their faces rearranged by his rage. Blood bubbles from their lips, their chests rising and falling at irregular intervals. He wants nothing more than to carve the dragon tattoos from their chests and rip their still-beating hearts through the holes.

"You need to send a message," El Carnicero says. He speaks with a thick Spanish accent and without a hint of emotion in his voice. "They must know that however many spies they send, you will return them in even more pieces."

Zmei nods and accepts a balaclava with a skull design from El Cineasta, the Filmmaker, whose camera is one of the most effective weapons in the arsenal of the cartel. He tugs it over his head and looks at Sister, whose eyes are colder and darker than he has ever seen them before. She had taken the deception even harder than he had. Her entire life had been an exercise in devotion, first to her God and then to her family. The concept of abandoning her beliefs—even to save her own life—was as foreign and incomprehensible as the feelings she felt for the man who could not love her in return.

She catches him looking and gestures for him to proceed.

Zmei takes the chain saw from El Carnicero and stands over the bodies of his dying brothers, their eyes shivering with pain and fear. He raises the weapon, the deadly steel screaming, and—

Sister brought the whirring blade down upon his right leg.

Zmei shouted and averted his eyes. Warmth spattered his cheek and a pattern of blood ascended the wall behind the woman, like mud from the rear tire of a dirt bike. He bit down on his lip to stifle the cry and tried to focus on anything other than the acetylene torch propped against the chair.

Things would only get worse from here.

PART 5

A power has risen up in the government greater than the people themselves, consisting of many and various and powerful interests, combined into one mass, and held together by the cohesive power of the vast surplus in the banks.

—John C. Calhoun, *vice president of the United States (1825–1832), from a speech given on May 27, 1836*

46

By the time they reached the plane, Gunnar had already uploaded the picture of the assassin emerging from her car into the facial-recognition program he'd used to track the Hoyl through four historical incarnations and trace the Scarecrow to her formative years as a test subject at the Edgewood Arsenal. With any luck, he'd be able to find something they could use to lead them to the Dragon. Unfortunately, such miracles took time, and that was one thing they simply lacked.

Gunnar had also arranged for the delivery of a fresh pot of coffee, replacements for the beverages they'd consumed from the minifridge, and foodstuffs less offensive to Ramses's highly refined palate. He sat across from Mason, swilling Devils Backbone Vienna Lager and eating Cheetos from the bag.

"What about working backward from the weapon?" he said. "If I can't get one, that means it can't be gotten, so either the Dragon has a government source that deals with him exclusively or he made it himself."

"The forensics tech at the hospital seemed to think something like that could be made using a plasma laser and a combination of cesium and hafnium isotopes," Layne said. "Radiation detectors picked up traces of both on Langbroek's yacht and in Marchment's room."

"Anyone experienced with nuclear chemistry could easily acquire a ready supply of cesium-137 from the by-products of the radioactive decay of uranium-235," Gunnar said. "The hafnium is trickier, though. It's in high demand since it's used in filaments and electrodes and in the control rods of nuclear reactors due to its ability to absorb neutron radiation and prevent it from triggering a chain reaction, a trait that makes it the perfect choice for weaponization. It can hold a disproportionately large amount of gamma radiation while still remaining relatively stable in isotopic form. The problem is that demand greatly exceeds supply, with annual production worldwide of less than eighty tons, which is why it sells for nearly two grand a pound."

"Have there been any strange fluctuations in the market?" Mason asked. "Something that might hint at someone attempting to stockpile it for mass production of this weapon?"

"Nothing so overt, but you'd likely see such fluctuations in either the zircon or zirconium markets. Anyone looking to acquire mass amounts of hafnium would be better served producing it himself than fighting over such small existing quantities. You see, hafnium can be refined from zirconium, which is expensive, but not especially difficult to find since it has a wide range of applications in the industrial, biomedical, and nuclear industries. It's produced from the refinement of zircon, an orangish mineral found in high concentrations in granite and igneous rock, which is even cheaper and easier to acquire."

"So someone with ready access to a large amount of zircon in any form could produce it himself."

"If he had the right background and experience, I'd imagine it could be done," Gunnar said. He switched screens on his computer and scanned through a series of scientific articles as he spoke. "Refining zirconium from zircon sand is a fairly simple process requiring chlorine and heat, but producing weaponized hafnium from there is much more complex. It involves separating hafnium chloride from the zirconium, reducing it, purifying it, and bombarding it with protons in a particle accelerator to create the isomer hafnium-178, one gram of which contains the same amount of energy as six hundred pounds of TNT. More important, it has a half-life of thirty-one years, which means it's stable enough that you could practically hold it in your bare hands, even with it containing all of that gamma radiation, just waiting for some form of energy to come along and trigger its release."

"Do you think someone with the right skill set could convert it into a directed-energy weapon?"

"If he were able to harness a strong enough energy source to cause the hafnium to release its gamma rays, I can't see why not. He'd just have to be exceedingly careful, because hafnium's highly explosive in its powdered form."

"You said something about zircon coming from granite and igneous rock," Layne said. She looked up from her phone and chewed on her lower lip. "If someone didn't want people to know what he was doing, could he extract it himself?"

"If he were looking to produce just enough for his own purposes and was willing to put in the work, it wouldn't be all that difficult. Why?"

Layne held up her phone. On the screen stood a mountain of solid granite, riddled with erosion and framed by pine trees buried in snow.

"This is Taganay National Park in the southern Ural Mountains," she said. "It's just west of Omsk, where Yamaguchi was photographed with the orange snow, which just happens to be the same color as the zircon you'd need to produce hafnium. So I tracked down the report from the Ministry of Emergency Situations, which stated that the snow contained four times the normal levels of acids, nitrates, and iron and speculated that it was the result of an explosion at a nearby metallurgical plant the previous week."

Gunnar smirked. He appeared more than a little impressed.

"The process of refining zircon from igneous rock produces zirconium acetate and nitrate, and leaves behind plenty of iron. If they were still in the experimental stages and inadvertently created any amount of hafnium powder, which is so unstable that you could ignite it with static electricity, they could have easily created an explosion powerful enough to fill the sky with all kinds of by-products."

"Is there anything significant about Omsk itself?" Layne asked.

"Its proximity to Novosibirsk, a city with thirteen universities, any number of which offer access to particle accelerators or colliders," Gunnar said. "I'm guessing it also served as the home base of the Konets Mira, whose original founder, Kiyohide Hayakawa, if you remember, had in his possession at the time of his arrest schematics for a directed-energy weapon, technical drawings of a fission device small enough to fit in a suitcase, blueprints for a nuclear-powered high-altitude, long-endurance unmanned aerial vehicle, and a map to an arms market within the city."

"So that's where we should start," Mason said. "If you can get your Russian contact to confirm at least that much, then maybe we can—"

Mason's phone buzzed. The screen again displayed the NO CALLER ID message, just as it had when Archer called earlier. He walked down the aisle to Gunnar's bedroom before answering.

"Special Agent Mason," he said.

There was a long pause.

"James," his father finally said. "I don't have very long, but I wanted to take this opportunity to call you."

"Where are you?"

"It doesn't matter. I'm going to talk and I need you to listen. I mean, really listen. Can you do that for me?"

There was something about his father's voice, a faint tremor he'd never heard there before, one that might have passed for fear in anyone else's.

"What's happen—?"

"Damn it, James. Would you just listen to me for once in your life?"

Mason remained silent and waited for the senator to proceed.

"I haven't been the perfect father. Lord knows I didn't have one of those in my life, either. I'll never admit this to another soul, but your mother's death broke me. I don't know how else to explain it. She was the one great love of my life. Losing her—and especially in that manner—was more than I could bear. I know you blame me for driving her to drink. Nothing could be further from the truth, but I decided long ago that I'd rather you hate me than taint her memory in your eyes."

"Dad, I—"

"I failed her, son. Hell, I failed you, too. I sent you away to school at a time when you needed your family—needed me—the most. We all grieve in different ways, as you know better than most. You've experienced more loss than anyone should have to. Unfortunately, it's that loss that defines us."

Mason heard voices in the background, followed by the rustling sound of his father covering the receiver with his palm.

"Talk to me, Dad. What's going on?"

"You need to promise me something, James."

"If it's within my power—"

The senator cut him off with a laugh.

"You would have made a fantastic lawyer," his father said. "Just do this one thing for me, okay? It's important. Promise me you'll stay away from the District."

"Tell me what's going on."

"Promise me, James."

Mason didn't want to lie to his father, so he waited him out.

"Just one minute," the senator said. Again, there were muffled voices in the background. "I'm out of time, James. They're ready for me now. I just want you to know how proud I am of you. I should have told you that long before now. You're the best of both your mother and me. I love you, son."

His father terminated the call, leaving Mason staring at his phone in confusion and disbelief.

"What the hell was that?" Ramses asked.

He leaned against the frame of the door with his head cocked and a beer in his hand. Mason hadn't known he was there.

"I don't have the slightest idea. It almost sounded like my dad was saying good-bye."

"That's what people do when they end a call."

"No . . . I mean, he told me that he was proud of me and that he loved me."

"That's not a good sign."

"You're telling me."

Gunnar slipped past Ramses and sat on the edge of his bed, tracing his chin with his fingertips.

"What else did he say?"

"He asked me to stay away from the Capitol."

"And?"

"He told me he was out of time. That they were ready for him now."

Gunnar was silent for several seconds. Mason could almost see the gears turning behind his friend's eyes.

"We should turn around," he finally said.

"Why?" Mason asked.

"Because we're already too late."

47

The plane lurched as it struck a patch of turbulence. Wispy clouds drifted past the windows.

"We're not turning around," Mason said.

"You do understand what the senator was trying to tell you, don't you?" Gunnar said. "They're evacuating the Congress."

Mason recalled the fear in his father's voice. His old man had displayed more emotion during that one phone call than he had in all of the years Mason had known him. He had no doubt that Gunnar was right.

"They must know something that we don't," Layne said.

"It could always be precautionary," Gunnar said. "If the powers that be had credible intel that there was a nuclear device in D.C., you guys would have been among the first to know, and surely they would have enacted their civilian evacuation protocols. They wouldn't just sneak Congress out of the city and leave the people to fend for themselves."

"Like they did in New York City?" Ramses said. "Who do you think we're dealing with here? These are the same people starting wars in the Middle East to protect their overblown budgets and personal portfolios. These assholes don't care if the rest of us die."

"None of that matters right now," Layne said. "The fact remains that millions of lives hang in the balance and we don't even know where to start looking."

"I'll reach out to my Russian contact," Gunnar said. "She ought to be more forthcoming when I tell her where we believe the Dragon is now. Nobody wants a war that neither side can win."

"Be careful how much you tell her. Like Ramses said, too many lines of inquiry point at Russia."

"I have everything under control," Gunnar said. "Brokering information is what I do for a living."

He ushered them out of his bedroom and closed the door behind them.

"What now?" Layne asked.

"I don't know about you, but I could use another beer," Ramses said. "Anyone else while I'm up there?"

"It's not even nine in the morning."

"Excellent. I'm ahead of schedule."

"I'll try to get ahold of Archer," Mason said. "We need to know what kind of nightmare we're walking into."

"And I'll call McWhinney," Layne said, heading for her seat. She was already dialing when her butt hit the leather. "There's something bothering me about the barn where we found all of those bodies, but I can't quite put my finger on it. Maybe talking to him will help jar it loose."

Mason hit the preset for Archer's number and paced while it rang. If they were interpreting his father's call correctly, then the secretary of the DHS wasn't likely to be anywhere within range of a cellular signal. As he'd expected, the call went to voice mail, which, hopefully, was being checked on a regular basis.

"It's Mason," he said. "Call me back."

He'd just ended the call when his phone vibrated in his hand. He recognized the 212 area code, if not the actual number, and answered on the second ring.

"This is Special Agent Phil Badgett with the digital forensics unit," the caller said. "Deputy Director Christensen wanted me to provide you with a status update."

"Tell me you caught her."

"We picked her up on camera, heading west on I-Seventy-eight about an hour ago—"

"West?"

"As in inland, away from the ocean," Badgett said. "We were able to follow her all the way through Newark and the surrounding suburbs, but we lost her somewhere around Annandale."

"What do you mean you lost her?"

"While there are cameras at every intersection in the city, there aren't very many out there in the country. She must have had another vehicle stashed near Round Valley Reservoir and made the switch where we couldn't see her. The state troopers haven't even been able to locate the car she ditched yet."

"So we have no idea what she's driving or in which direction she's traveling."

"That doesn't sound very promising," Ramses said as he squeezed past Mason and made his way back to his seat.

"She doesn't have too many options," Badgett said. "She could double back, but she'd run right into our checkpoint on Two Eighty-seven. Outside of that, there's really nowhere to get off the highway until after she crosses the Pennsylvania state line. From Allentown she could head south toward Philly or go north and make a run for the Canadian border. I don't like her odds of making either, though. We have her picture circulating everywhere, choppers in the air over all of the major highways, and roadblocks being erected outside of Allentown and Harrisburg. Unless she's holed up in the wilderness or trying to navigate the rural roads, she's going to have to pass through one of them."

"What else is out there?"

"If she somehow made it through both checkpoints, she could continue due west toward Pittsburgh and Columbus or head south into Baltimore or D.C."

"How many highways enter Maryland from Pennsylvania?"

"Not so many that we couldn't have highway patrol sitting on all of them."

"Then make it happen."

"You have to admit it looks like she's trying to get as far away from Manhattan as she can, as quickly as possible."

"That's what she wants us to think," Mason said. "She's been following a carefully designed plan every step of the way. She must have anticipated that we'd set up roadblocks at all of the choke points and selected a route that not only passes through our net, but allows her to reach a specific location. We can't afford to let her get there."

"No one here has any intention of allowing that to happen," Badgett said.

Layne snapped her fingers to get Mason's attention and gestured for him to pass her a cocktail napkin from the counter beside him. The moment he handed it to her, she started writing.

"We're all counting on you, Badgett," Mason said. "Can you put Chris on the phone?"

"He ducked out a few minutes ago. I'll have him call you when he gets back?"

"Thanks, and do me a favor: Trace those back roads where you lost her and see where they go."

Mason terminated the call and found Layne staring expectantly at him.

"Who was that?" she asked.

"Badgett in New York. They lost the woman heading west out of Newark."

"West?"

"That was my reaction, too."

"We're taking a huge risk," she said. "If we're wrong about the Dragon being in the District . . ."

She didn't need to remind him of the consequences.

"What did McWhinney have to say?" he asked.

"He's still working on identifying the dismembered bodies from the second stall."

"The 'faithful followers,' right? The ones we're assuming were members of a rival cartel."

"Their remaining skin was practically mummified, so he injected their fingertips with a sodium carbonate solution to bring out the dermal ridges, but that's a slow process. He's hoping to have viable fingerprints by this afternoon and promised to call me directly if he's able to match them."

"And they're still holding the media at bay?"

"He said the DHS has that place sealed off so tightly you couldn't get a picture of the crime scene from space. Of course, they also fed the reporters a load of crap about hobbled livestock and bestiality that pretty much killed their curiosity. A remediation crew is ready to slip in the moment the last news van is gone."

"And the napkin?"

Layne smirked and handed it to him. She'd written three words and underlined each several times.

"McWhinney helped me figure out what was bothering me about that place. We assumed someone must have been making the mortgage payments to keep anyone from coming out to check on the owners, but that wasn't the case at all. The bank had actually been preparing to foreclose when it received an offer it couldn't refuse."

"Enter Lone Star Trust," Mason said, holding up the napkin.

"You know it. It's an investment company, not a bank at all. It bought the mortgage at a significant discount from the original lender and then turned around and initiated foreclosure proceedings itself. For all intents and purposes, it bought the loan and evicted the owners."

"It bought a defaulted loan?"

"On paper, it bought both a liability and an asset. A large debt and an even larger plot of land along the border. Entries on both sides of the ledger. I had to have McWhinney explain it twice."

"It bought the property without having to change the name on the title and list itself as the owner."

"That's how I interpreted it, too, but McWhinney explained that it's a fairly common practice. You're applying an ulterior motive to what's essentially a simple financial transaction. Lone Star could merely be holding on to the land until its value rises high enough to make it profitable to sell. You know, investing."

"What did he know about them?"

"Not a whole lot. They have branches in McAllen and Laredo and appear to specialize in commercial and industrial real estate."

"Have they purchased many other defaulted mortgages?"

"He didn't know."

"See what else you can find out about them."

She was on to something here. Mason could feel it. He glanced out the window at the urban sprawl below him and tried not to imagine the kind of devastation a single nuclear bomb could cause, assuming that was all they were up against. A second bomb completely changed the dynamics. For better or worse, they'd bet all of their money on a single horse.

Gunnar's laptop dinged from the table in front of her. They'd both barely looked in its direction when Gunnar burst from his bedroom with a smile on his face.

"What'd she say?" Mason asked.

"She arranged for us to meet with someone at the Russian embassy when we land."

"That's it?" Ramses said. "So what's with the shit-eating grin?"

"You heard that chime, right? It means my facial-recognition program made a match."

48

"Your forensics guy in Texas was right when he said the Russians you found in the barn had been scrubbed from the Internet," Gunnar said. "Outside of the official pictures posted on the website of the Russian embassy in Mexico City listing them as missing, my program was only able to make five matches."

Mason felt a sinking sensation he attributed to their descent into Washington, D.C., although it could have been because he recognized the location of the first picture.

"Why am I not surprised?" he said.

The picture had been taken in Copenhagen at the Twentieth Assembly of the Society for Lasting International Peace. The caption read: "Emissaries of the Russian Federation." Theirs were merely two faces among those of twenty-some men and women, lined up on bleachers as though posing for a class picture. They all appeared to be in their twenties or early thirties, junior executives well on their way to launching prominent careers. Kostov Mironov, with the strawberry birthmark on his cheek, stood at the left side of the top row, while Patrushev Panarin was in the row below him, his black hair combed back from his sharp widow's peak and his thin lips pursed as though in an attempt to conceal a smile.

"What exactly is an emissary?" Ramses asked.

"A low-level bureaucrat dispatched as a diplomatic representative," Gunnar said. "It's his job to make contacts, establish relationships, and lay the groundwork for future negotiations."

"Professional networkers," Layne said.

"In a political sense."

"So what were they doing at the SLIP conference?" Mason asked.

"One can only speculate," Gunnar said. "With all of the major players in attendance, they could have been sent on behalf of any number of industries. It's important to remember that many of what we consider private ventures here are nationalized to some degree in Russia. If the whole premise of that year's assembly was globalization, specifically in regard to transitioning to an energy-based economy and socialized health-care model, then they could have been dispatched to make contacts in any number of fields. Now, if you factor in Russia's traditionally staunch opposition to globalization efforts, I'm inclined to think that the majority of the emissaries represent the energy sector. Few stand to gain more from an energy-based economy than they do. Between oil and natural gas, they're sitting on a veritable gold mine of resources."

He minimized the first image and maximized the second. It was in black and white and obviously scanned from a newspaper article. Panarin was seated in the crowd gathered in an auditorium, as viewed from behind the man standing center stage at the podium. The caption was printed in German.

"It says something to the effect of 'Stephen Douglas, CEO of the American Investment Partnership, delivers the keynote address to a packed house,'" Gunnar said.

"That's the second time we've come across AIP in relation to this case," Mason said.

"Stephen Douglas was the poster child for globalization. His great-grandfather launched AIP in the nineteenth century with the sole intention of building an international entity that partnered with its host countries to invest in the futures of both. We're talking about things like funding orphanages for kids who lost their parents in World War One and rebuilding entire communities following World War Two. His family probably helped establish half of the charitable organizations devoted to reducing global poverty out there. I'd be more surprised if he weren't giving the keynote address."

"You said he *was* the poster child for globalization," Layne said.

"He died a decade or so ago."

"Who runs the company now?"

"His son, Avery, but he's largely CEO in name alone. He's more of your stereotypical spoiled-rich-kid type. He doesn't strike me as the kind who's ever seen the inside of a boardroom."

"Slate Langbroek used a similar cover to conceal his involvement with the Thirteen," Mason said.

"I never questioned Langbroek's intelligence," Gunnar said. "Douglas has always struck me as possessing more balls than brains, but we'd be foolish to underestimate a man with his resources."

He opened the third image, which featured men in business suits and hard hats walking through what appeared to be an oil refinery. Pipes of all shapes and sizes formed a veritable maze all around them. The caption read: "Russian energy minister tours Kurdistan operation with Iraqi delegation."

"Mironov is in the background over here," Gunnar said. He pointed at the screen where a man with a pinkish blotch on his cheek held the arm of a worker in coveralls and gestured toward a massive collection tank being fed by numerous pipes. "He appears to represent the operational faction rather than the diplomatic. This was taken in 2007, when Iraq was actively courting foreign investment in its drilling operations."

He switched to the fourth picture, which was focused on three men in business suits, all of whom held scissors in one hand and a section of long red tape in the other. A ribbon-cutting event of some kind. Behind them was a gray stone tenement that reflected the dreary Eastern European architectural style. Panarin stood on the sidewalk in front of it, his vampiric features standing apart from those of the newspaper reporters holding notepads and the boom operators trying to position their microphones to hear whatever the men were saying as they performed their ceremonial duties.

Gunnar minimized the picture and brought up its source data.

"This picture was taken in 2012 at the grand opening of GazNat's Project Operations Department in Saint Petersburg."

"I told you this was all about oil," Ramses said.

"Oil makes up a small percentage of GazNat's business, which is primarily built upon natural gas. In fact, its oil subsidiary, GazNat Neft, only exports thirteen percent of its domestic production, which accounts for somewhere in the neighborhood of four percent of the global market."

"What's GazNat?" Layne asked.

"It's the national energy company of Russia. Fifty percent of its shares are owned by the government, while eighty-five percent of the remainder is held by a few select oligarchs, who want nothing more than to be the sole suppliers of natural gas to Europe, which they see as the most lucrative market in the world, especially with the growing focus on clean-fuel usage."

Gunnar maximized the final image, which showed two men wearing suits and ties striding purposefully away from a crowd of people in a large venue. A woman in an expensive skirt suit walked between them, her briefcase cuffed to her wrist. Among those milling in the background were a man with a strawberry birthmark on his cheek and another just tall enough for his forehead and widow's peak to be visible over the head of a man facing away from the camera.

"This is from a Russian news aggregate feed," Gunnar said. "You can tell by the logo in the corner." He opened the source code and scrolled through it until he found the original caption, which was written in Cyrillic letters, and translated it out loud. "'GazNat officials, such as Alexey Fedorov, have been meeting with Ukraine and EU representatives in a bid to settle the gas crisis with Kiev.' This was posted in 2014, presumably right before the Euromaidan Revolution in Ukraine—a bloody coup orchestrated by the CIA to remove duly elected President Viktor Yanukovych and install the more favorable pro-EU and anti-Russian regime of Petro Poroshenko—resolved the natural gas impasse for them."

The flaps on the plane's wings rose with a mechanical whine. Below them, the city grew in both size and magnitude, spreading from one horizon to the other. Somewhere down there, quite possibly within their view at that very moment, was a man with a nuclear weapon and designs on killing everyone within its range.

"So what do you make of all this, Gunnar?" Mason asked.

"While our two dead guys obviously represented the energy sector, they appear to have been bit players. It would make sense to send executives like them to set the stage for exploration rights negotiations in Mexico, which would benefit from foreign investment in natural gas as a means of driving down its prohibitively expensive energy costs. The problem is that while the Mexican government might have the authority to enter into such negotiations, it isn't the sole body capable of doing so, and certainly not the most powerful. Or volatile. The cartels have already taken over a large percentage of the country's oil production through intimidation and outright theft, and they certainly aren't the ideal business partners in a venture of this magnitude. And the prospect of setting up shop right on the doorstep of the United States would be more than a strategic miscalculation; it would be an open declaration of war."

"Maybe these guys actually did try to negotiate with CJNG," Layne said. "That would explain how they ended up in that barn. It's possible they opened with a lowball offer and the staged scene in the stall was the cartel's way of reminding the Russians that they meant business."

"'This is not a game,'" Mason said, recalling the message carved into the wooden planks. "I'll reach out to Alejandra and see if she has any insight."

"No," Ramses said. The look in his eyes was one Mason couldn't interpret. He turned away and hit the preset on his cell phone. "I'll do it."

"Approaching the cartel would have been an unnecessarily aggressive tact," Gunnar said. "There are better potential energy partners in Central and South America, most of whom lack the extreme levels of violence, if not political stability. And while the U.S. would be enraged by the prospect of the Russians entering our hemisphere, it could be done in a manner that wouldn't serve to ignite hostilities."

"Which brings us right back around to where we started," Layne said. "Why were the Russians in Mexico and what was their relationship to the Dragon?"

The wheels touched down with a scream and the turbines roared to slow the plane's momentum.

"With any luck, the man waiting to meet with you will be able to answer those questions."

"You're not coming with us?" Mason said.

"I need to follow this line of inquiry and see where it takes me," Gunnar said. "I'm starting to think the petrodollar isn't the only commodity in play. There's something more at stake, but I can't see the full picture yet."

"That's great and all," Layne said, "but in case you've forgotten, we have more immediate problems. If the Dragon sets off his nuclear device, we're now well within its blast radius. And if we die, everything we know about the Thirteen dies with us."

Mason realized with a start just how right she was. They weren't just the only ones standing between the city and a horrific end, they were the only ones in a position to save the world from a nuclear catastrophe and the monsters poised to prey upon the survivors.

49

Ramses dropped off Mason and Layne at the front gate of the Russian embassy, a stark eight-story building flanked by residential, administrative, and ceremonial buildings. Against their better judgment, they surrendered their guns and cell phones to the security contingent in exchange for credentials that got them as far as the main lobby, a cavernous space tiled with black-and-white marble that reflected the light from the golden chandeliers. There were armed soldiers stationed throughout the chamber and manning the reception desk. A red carpet led between ornate marble columns to a broad staircase that branched in both directions from the landing.

A man wearing a black suit and a red tie descended to the main floor and approached them directly. He carried himself with the easy style of a diplomat, but possessed the broad shoulders and erect bearing of a military officer. His gray hair and lined face marked him as a man who'd experienced the fall of Communism in his prime, likely from the inside looking out. His smile didn't reach his eyes.

"Special Agents," he said in a blunt, halting Russian accent. He shook each of their hands in turn. "I am Dmitri Zadorov, first secretary of the Military Political Section. If you will please follow me."

Zadorov led them into a hallway lined with closed doors. He opened the third on the right, held it long enough for them to enter, and closed it behind them. They appeared to be in an informal sitting room with tapestries hanging from the walls, curios arranged on ornate bureaus, and a small table surrounded by plush armchairs, and yet to a trained eye like Mason's, the surveillance cameras were so poorly concealed they might as well have been set up on tripods.

He didn't like the idea of meeting inside the embassy, but he understood why Gunnar's contact had insisted. While on its grounds they were officially guests on Russian soil, which meant that their badges were useless to them here, which shielded Zadorov from the consequences of sharing information of a potentially incriminating nature. That Gunnar had been able to secure a meeting with such a high-ranking official on short notice was a testament to his standing in the international financial community, as well as his skill at acquiring whatever leverage he held over his contact.

Zadorov stood behind the chair at the head of the table and gestured for them to join him. He waited until they were both seated before settling in, removing a manila folder from underneath his jacket, and placing it on the table in front of them.

"You must explicitly agree that nothing we discuss will ever leave this room," he said. "I trust I do not need to explain the ramifications of disregarding that directive."

Mason brushed off the threat. He needed information and he was willing to do whatever it took to get it. Let the chips fall where they may.

"We understand your position and appreciate your taking the time to meet with us," Layne said.

"It is not, as you say, out of the goodness of my heart. I have a vested interest in the destruction of Konets Mira and do not care who delivers the killing strike, as long as it is done."

Mason reached for the folder, but Zadorov slapped his palm on it. He looked Mason dead in the eyes when he spoke.

"You are FBI. You will understand that we must do everything in our power to protect our country, things for which we will be judged not in this life but in the next."

Mason nodded and Zadorov slowly raised his hand. He opened the folder and revealed a small stack of photographs and reports. Once more, the Russian placed his hand on them. Apparently, whatever he'd done to acquire them was of no small significance and had come at a considerable personal cost.

"I served as a counterintelligence officer in the KGB until I was called upon to lead the counterterrorism agency for the Federal Security Service," he said. "I directed hundreds of successful operations and dismantled several domestic terrorist organizations. While your threats here come from foreign actors, we are forced to deal with internal hostilities from places like Chechnya and Ukraine."

"Ukraine's an independent country now," Layne said.

"Against the wishes of many of its people, but now is not the time for debate."

Zadorov passed the pictures to Mason, one at a time. He scrutinized each before sliding it across the table to Layne, who wore Gunnar's contact lenses and did a much better job of making her photographic blinking appear natural. The first few images were in the green scale of a night-vision apparatus, the subjects blurry and seemingly oblivious to their surveillance, while the remainder were much clearer. As Zadorov spoke, Mason started to piece together a general idea of the lengths to which the head of the Military Political Section had gone to acquire the information contained in the folder.

"My department utilized undercover intelligence operatives to detect such internal enemies and infiltrate their ranks," he said. "Through the sacrifices of these officers, we were able to avert attacks far worse than your nine/eleven, including the one for which I was rewarded with this posting."

"Konets Mira," Mason said.

He recognized the photographs Gunnar's contact at the state department had sent them, if not the handful from additional surveillance operations or the imagery captured in the wake of the resultant field operation.

"My operative had been with Aleph since the dissolution of Aum Shinrikyo and later splintered into Konets Mira with the followers devoted to Asahara's and Hayakawa's more violent ideological ends. He informed us that they intended to launch a multipronged attack on Moscow using a chemical agent to drive passengers on the metro lines aboveground and herd them toward the Kremlin, where a modified nuclear weapon would be detonated to achieve the most visceral damage possible."

"A fizzle device," Mason said.

"Then you are familiar with the concept," Zadorov said. "Imagine the most recognizable symbol of my country laying in ruins, bodies littering the streets, and countless people dying slow deaths from the effects of the chemicals and radiation over the next few years. The image conjures a far more intimate vision of suffering and defeat than a mushroom cloud rising from a distant horizon."

"You were obviously able to stop it."

"Yes, although it was, as you say, by the skin of our teeth."

"Then you must understand why we needed to meet with you in such a hurry."

"I was hoping that was not the case," Zadorov said, momentarily closing his eyes.

He slid another photo from the stack and placed it on the table in front of Mason. Eighteen men and women gathered for a group picture in a park, all of them smiling for the camera. The focus seemed to be on the five figures standing in the center. Three others knelt in front of them, while the remaining ten were either seated on the benches or on top of the picnic table behind them. The trees in the background were lush and green, the sky as blue as any Mason had ever seen.

"This is the only known photograph of Konets Mira," Zadorov said. "Do not let their appearance deceive you. Every single one of them would slit your throat just to watch you bleed."

It never failed to surprise Mason that the scariest monsters looked just like everyone else, allowing them to hide in plain sight.

"When was this taken?" he asked.

"2016."

"Well after they'd tested their fizzle devices on civilians throughout the Middle East."

"Not to mention their chemical weapons," Zadorov said. "This was a highly trained and extremely capable special forces unit the likes of which we had never seen before. Each of these people possessed a unique skill set that complemented those of the others. Among their number were counted scientists with expertise in nuclear and chemical engineering, military personnel with tactical and demolitions experience, doctors of various specialties, mechanical engineers, and even a lawyer."

Mason studied their faces. He'd seen nearly all of them before, especially the central five, who seemed somehow separate from the others, the nucleus around which they orbited. On one side were Dr. Tatsuo Yamaguchi and the woman who'd assassinated Rand Marchment; on the other, Kameko and Kaemon Nakamura—the Scarecrow, her mechanical eyes hiding behind sunglasses, and her brother, his skeletal nose a gaping maw. And in the middle stood a man whose face was scarred in a way that left the skin stranded in appearance, seemingly trapped in a state between liquid and solid. His left hand was a blur, as though captured in the process of reaching for Kameko's.

"Who is he?" Mason asked, but he already knew the answer. Or at least part of it.

"Zakar Borisovich Meier," Zadorov said.

"Z-Mei," Layne said. "Zmei, the Dragon."

"And the woman standing next to him?" Mason asked.

"That is his daughter, Valeria," Zadorov said. "She was born into the cult. Outside of that, we know very little about her."

Everything suddenly made sense. The Dragon had passed down the mantle to his child.

Mason handed the picture to Layne and accepted another from Zadorov. It was an identical photograph, only seven of the faces were circled, two were framed by squares, and four were crossed out, including the Scarecrow and her brother, which meant the other two were presumably deceased as well. Among the circled faces Mason recognized several who'd been arrested in Montenegro and were undoubtedly still in custody, which left the Dragon, his daughter, the woman seated on the table behind her, and the man kneeling in front of her without markings.

"The man in the front row is our operative," Zadorov said. "He is responsible for everything in this folder. It is not an understatement to say that it is because of him that the Kremlin still stands."

"Who's the woman at the table behind Valeria?" Layne asked.

"She goes by 'Sister.' We believe she was a nun before her conversion."

"What do the squares mean?" Layne asked.

"During the raid on Konets Mira, four members were taken into custody. We were able to turn two of them. They helped us track those who escaped into Montenegro."

"Where are they now?" Mason asked. "If they could help us find the Dragon—"

"They are dead," Zadorov said. "We received intelligence that Zmei was operating in Mexico, so we dispatched them to Mexico City to draw him out, but they were abducted—"

"'Here are your "faithful" followers,'" Mason said, the image of the butchered remains in the stall flashing before his eyes.

"Where did you hear that?"

The expression on Zadorov's face was one of anger and betrayal. He must have thought that someone in his department had leaked the information.

"We found the barn where they were killed," Mason said. "They weren't the only Russians there."

"That is why your friend asked about Mironov and Panarin."

"What were they doing in Mexico?"

"Their jobs, as far I know," Zadorov said. "I only familiarized myself with them after speaking with our mutual friend. All I know is that they worked for GazNat."

His expression showed no hint of deception.

"What about the Dragon?" Mason asked. "Do you have any idea where he might be now?"

"We do not know his current location," Zadorov said. His eyes widened when he recognized the gravity of the question. Fear momentarily shone through his otherwise impassive facade. "You think he is here. That is why you arranged to meet with me specifically, why you are in such a hurry."

There was no mistaking his surprise.

"You didn't know he was in the District," Mason said.

"If he is, then we are already dead."

50

Zadorov had abruptly stood, gathered his file, and left them to see themselves out. No one had said a word to them throughout the process of collecting their badges and guns from security and exiting the embassy. They'd simply walked out to the sidewalk, leaned against the fence along Wisconsin Avenue, and waited for Ramses to pick them up in the rental Ford Expedition.

The embassy had utilized signal-jamming technology so aggressive it had suppressed the feed from Gunnar's contact lenses. While most of the images had been lost, the final few pictures, including the group shot of Konets Mira, came through as they were driving away. It was a long shot, but with the full faces of the Dragon and his daughter, Valeria, there was a chance they might be able to find them using the vast network of traffic and security cameras throughout the city. Of course, a search of that magnitude was going to take time, which they could already feel slipping through their fingers.

"What kind of idiot cuts his teeth in the KGB and then loses the guy who made his career?" Ramses said. "Are you sure he wasn't blowing smoke up your ass?"

"He appeared genuinely surprised to find out that the Dragon was here," Mason said. "And with as quickly as he left, I wouldn't be surprised if he was heading straight to the airport."

"Speaking of which, why haven't they started grounding flights yet? The border's closed and they're in the process of relocating Congress, so why aren't there cops all over the streets? Where's the National Guard? The FBI? Either we got some bad intel and the Dragon isn't here or those fat fucking politicians are willing to let everyone in the city die in the hope that we'll go to war with Russia."

"Say that again," Gunnar said from the passenger seat beside him.

"The part about the bad intel or the fat fucking politicians letting us die so they can go to war?"

"You're brilliant, Ramses," Gunnar said, setting upon his computer with renewed vigor.

"If I had a nickel for every time someone said that . . ."

"You still wouldn't be able to buy a gumball," Layne said.

They passed the Naval Observatory on their way into Georgetown, where traffic on the tree-lined streets slowed. Flags hung everywhere. Children chased one another with water balloons and sparklers.

"'Never let a good crisis go to waste,'" Gunnar said. "Winston Churchill made that statement in regard to using the political climate following World War Two to create the United Nations. Those 'fat fucking politicians,' as you so eloquently put it, might not have any control over what's happening here, but they're sure as hell not going to let the opportunity to capitalize on it pass them by."

"Are you suggesting that people like my father are abandoning the city to its fate or that they're actively rooting for the entire population to be wiped out?" Mason said.

"Baron Nathan Rothschild is credited with saying, 'Buy when there's blood in the streets, even if that blood is your own.' He received word before anyone else that Napoleon had been defeated at Waterloo, so he made a fortune buying stocks while everyone else was pulling their money out of market. So, if I'm right—here we go. Since

opening bell this morning, more people have picked up the call options for a defense contractor named InnoVate than in the entire history of the company since its inception. That right there tells you
everything you need to know."

"How so?" Layne asked.

"A call option is a contract that entitles the investor to buy a spec-
ified amount of a stock at its current price. So if that price suddenly
goes up, the investor can still buy it for the lower price and resell it a
heartbeat later for its current market value. No risk, all reward. The
same thing happened with Raytheon during the days preceding the attack on the Twin Towers. It won weapons contracts used to arm the
military for the war in Iraq and went on to become one of the most
prominent private defense contractors in the entire world, making a lot
of people extraordinarily rich in the process."

"You're implying there were people who knew about the attack
before it happened?" Mason said.

"I'm just stating the facts."

"So if a nuclear device was detonated in the District and used as
justification to go to war—"

"Then whichever company landed the contract to arm and equip
all of those troops would become one of the most valuable companies
in the world, especially one that had already developed advanced tactical exoskeletons and non-line-of-sight cannons."

"You're talking about collusion between big business and the government."

"That's how dealings of this nature work," Gunnar said. "You
remember the predictive market the Thirteen used. There's always inside information being shared behind the scenes. I guarantee you that
any number of people with knowledge of the situation as it was devel-
oping tipped off the major investment firms. We just need to weed
out the opportunists from anyone who might have been forewarned,
which should point us in the direction of whoever's pulling the Dragon's strings."

"That's exactly what I was trying to say," Ramses said.

"Can you do it?" Mason asked.

"It'll take time," Gunnar said. "Any number of the big players
will undoubtedly be involved, which means I'll have to take a step
back and evaluate all of their potential motivations—"

"But how many of them will be going after what's left of Lang-broek's empire at the same time?"

Gunnar turned around and smiled at him.

"That should be a much smaller number, and provides me with the perfect segue to tell you what I was able to learn while you were in the embassy," he said. "I was right when I said the situation in the Middle East was about more than just the petrodollar. Natural gas is the key. Europe's consumption is expected to more than double by 2050, while its oil usage will drop to almost nothing."

"The caption of the picture of Mironov and Panarin in Ukraine mentioned something about a gas crisis between GazNat and the EU," Layne said.

"Russia, by way of GazNat, owns the natural gas, but Ukraine owns the pipelines through which it's pumped. Six European countries are wholly beholden to GazNat for their supply, which gives Russia an obscene amount of control over them. The Euromaidan Revolution and subsequent regime change were the result of Western powers sowing internal discord in an attempt to more closely align the country with European interests and limit Russia's economic influence over the region. As a sovereign nation, Ukraine can, in turn, apply an extreme amount of pressure on Russia and exact a hefty financial toll for the use of its pipelines, to the tune of ten percent of its total national budget."

"So Russia needs to find a way around it," Mason said.

"Exactly. They already control the Nord Stream pipeline, which runs beneath the Baltic Sea and services northern Germany and Scandinavia, but outside of that, there are really only two viable routes: underneath the Black Sea and into Bulgaria or through the former Soviet state of Georgia and into Turkey, all of which are on friendly terms with the U.S., which has its own interests in the region."

Ramses merged onto the Whitehurst Freeway, which offered a panoramic view of Waterfront Park and the Potomac River to their right. There were people everywhere, all dressed in their patriotic best.

"Why do we even care what Russia does in Europe?" he asked.

"Because the European Union is our largest trading partner. By far. Losing it to Russia would isolate us and diminish our global influence, not to mention threaten the reserve status of the dollar, which brings us back to natural gas. The largest single deposit in the world is trapped two miles below the Persian Gulf. It's co-owned by Qatar and Iran, who've proposed competing pipelines to carry that gas from different sides of the same field to Europe. And regardless of who ultimately builds that pipeline, it has to pass through Syria to get there."

"You're saying the Syrian civil war is being fought over who gets to run a pipeline through it."

"You have to understand the geopolitics of the area," Gunnar said. "Russia's support of the Assad regime enables it to pressure Syria to approve Iran's Shia pipeline, which would create the possibility for future expansion into Russia to the north, allowing its own supply to be pumped into Europe. To counteract this, the U.S. is forced to support the proposed Qatar–Turkey pipeline, despite our tenuous relationship with Qatar, which we consider one of the largest state sponsors of terrorism."

"Why the hell would we do that?" Ramses asked.

"The reasons are twofold. First, it would prevent the Russians from finding an alternate route into Europe by using the existing infrastructure built by a staunch ally like Iran. More important, to get from Qatar to Turkey, the line would have to be run through Saudi Arabia, allowing the kingdom to profit from both its share of the physical pipeline and the natural gas it could pump through it. Not only are the Saudis just about our only true allies in the region, they just happen to be the largest exporters of oil in the world, which means they could literally destroy the petrodollar all by themselves."

"So as long as we keep the royal family happy, they'll continue to support the petrodollar," Mason said.

"That would explain why we tend to overlook such inconvenient things as public beheadings and the oppression of women," Layne said. "Not to mention the war in Yemen."

"Say what you will, but the Saudis have us by the short hairs," Gunnar said. "They know the future looks grim for oil and they only rank sixth in natural gas reserves. As much as they hate the Qatari, they're willing to partner with them to make sure that theirs is the pipeline that reaches Europe, and we need to ensure that anyone receiving that gas pays for it in dollars, not rubles. The problem is you can't lay a pipeline in the middle of a battlefield, and the fighting in Syria shows no sign of abating. And as they say in the business world, time is money, which brings us to a third potential solution, one that involves gaining access to a different reserve with as much as a hundred million cubic meters of natural gas in a country with a historically strained relationship with Russia."

Mason could tell by the tone of Gunnar's voice that this was where things started to come together. His old friend looked at each of them in turn, as though waiting for them to connect the dots as he had.

"Just spit it out already," Ramses said.

"Azerbaijan," Gunnar said. "The same country Slate Langbroek was prepared to depopulate with drones filled with Novichok A-234 in order to reclaim the oil field stolen from his family by the Soviets just happens to be sitting on the second-largest natural gas reserves in the world, which would be easy to pump across Armenia and into the European pipeline passing through Turkey. Monopolizing both the country's oil and natural gas trade would have made Royal Nautilus Petroleum the most valuable company in the world, bestowing upon its chairman and chief shareholder a seemingly limitless amount of wealth and power. Perhaps even enough to assume control of the Thirteen."

"And considering Slate was the last of his bloodline, the Langbroek empire is ripe for the taking by another member looking to stage a coup within the organization," Mason said.

"One that could very well alter the course of mankind's future."

51

Ramses exited the highway near the Watergate Hotel and filtered into the congested holiday traffic, which crawled past the Kennedy Center toward the heart of the political complex. Red-white-and-blue decorations hung from every balcony, rooftop, and streetlight. An aura of power radiated from the buildings around them, growing stronger with every passing block until the Washington Monument appeared from the smog at the far end of Virginia Avenue, as though materializing from the mists of history itself.

"For all of their many faults, the Langbroeks were brilliant businessmen," Gunnar said. "They pioneered the field of liquefied natural gas—LNG—and turned it into an industry no one thought would ever be able to compete with oil, let alone surpass it. They recognized the potential market and set about controlling every aspect of the supply chain, starting with designing the technology to extract it from the earth, convert it into an inflammable liquid for transit, and then return it to its gaseous form to be piped to consumers. They expanded their tanker fleet to haul a full fifth of the global supply and commissioned the largest floating production facility in the world to access underwater fields impossible to reach by land. Not to mention the fact that they entered into joint ventures with the governments of some of the most natural gas–rich countries, including both Azerbaijan and Qatar, where they own thirty percent of the operation, including processing and liquefaction facilities, a fleet of carriers, and numerous offshore platforms and domestic pipelines."

Mason struggled to wrap his mind around the ramifications.

"So whoever gains control of Nautilus's assets would theoretically be able to control not only the future of the petrodollar, but the economy of the United States?"

"And, by extension, the entire world," Gunnar said. "Now imagine being able to dictate global economic policy."

"You wouldn't need the U.S. or the dollar anymore," Layne said.

"Precisely. You could set up your corporation as its own nation-state—the invisible power behind any crown or premier or president you wanted—and make sure that yours was the only currency you accepted for a commodity you controlled, from production through distribution. You'd enjoy a veritable monopoly over the trade and all the trappings of power that came with it, a fully realized energy-based economy like the Thirteen started planning nearly three decades ago at the Twentieth Assembly of the Society for Lasting International Peace in Copenhagen."

"So who are our prime suspects?"

"In addition to investment firms like AIP, who've already expanded their institutional ownership of Royal Nautilus Petroleum as a whole and have an eye on some of its more lucrative subsidiaries, there appear to be five dedicated energy exploration companies aggressively pursuing the acquisition of Langbroek's LNG assets, chief among them GazNat, which essentially functions as a straw buyer for the Russian government. Competitors like ExxonMobil, BP, Tectonic Energy, and Saudi Aramco have also become increasingly active over the past few months."

"So which one is it?" Mason asked. "Which one represents a member of the Thirteen?"

"That's what I intend to find—"

Gunnar's laptop chimed, cutting him off. Mason leaned over his old friend's shoulder to get a better look as he minimized his current window and enlarged his facial-recognition program. A blur of keystrokes and a picture of a kid who couldn't have been more than sixteen or seventeen years old opened on the screen. His bangs had been dyed red and hung past his eyebrows. He had dark eyes and a face still somewhat chubby with baby fat, unlike the subsequent photograph, in which he'd cut his hair short and wore a white shirt and black tie, but it wasn't until the third image that he bleached his hair and donned his trademarked round glasses.

"Meet Ronan Clark," Gunnar said. "His known aliases include Ronan Geoffrey Clark, Clark with the number four as the A, Quark, Quirk, Oddity, and Aberration, the latter three being synonyms for anomaly. Born October third, 1998, to a software developer and a former Miss California in Redwood City, California. Silicon Valley, USA. Enrolled as an undergrad at Yale at sixteen and promptly dropped out. He apparently went straight to work writing code for ransomware and hacking databases, with the intention of extorting the owners for seven-figure sums."

"He's just a kid," Layne said.

"A kid who at the ripe old age of twenty made the FBI's cyber-crimes most-wanted list. He was charged with economic espionage, theft of trade secrets, access device fraud, wire fraud, and accessing a computer without authorization for the purpose of commercial advantage and private financial gain. Two separate federal warrants were issued for his arrest. He was even sanctioned by a presidential executive order for his alleged role in compromising the voter registration systems in twenty-six states during the 2016 election. According to the NCIC, he was killed in a car accident three years ago."

"Or not," Ramses said. "How does he connect to the Thirteen?"

"If there's an ideological component, I don't see it," Gunnar said. "But you know who would . . ."

"See if you can get a hold of him," Mason said, staring at the young man on the screen. "Johan doesn't give up information without expecting something in return. There's a reason he wanted us to identify Anomaly and I'll be damned if I'm not going to find out what it is."

Gunnar grabbed his cell phone and started dialing.

Mason had known plenty of kids like Ronan Clark, bright kids from wealthy homes who viewed the world as their plaything. Many went through a rebellious phase on their way to assuming their birthright and conquering the corporate world, but he'd never met one who instinctively gravitated toward crime when fortune was already at his metaphorical fingertips. Something had happened to Anomaly to drive him away from academia and into the cybercriminal underworld, where the Thirteen had been waiting to recruit him. And whatever it was had to be the key to unlocking his motivations.

"Johan's logging into an encrypted virtual chat room as we speak," Gunnar said.

"That was fast," Mason said.

"I had the distinct impression that he was expecting our call."

"What happened to not trusting the Internet?" Layne asked. "Something about spiders luring flies with the scent of dead meat?"

"For him to take the risk," Gunnar said, tilting his computer on his lap so they could all see the screen, "we must have information he desperately wants."

Johan appeared a heartbeat later, his flushed face a stark contrast to his snow white hair and beard. The collar of his paisley pajama top stood from his robe. He'd obviously rushed to attend the virtual meeting. Gunnar's impression had been spot-on; they definitely had something the old man needed.

Ramses pulled to the curb in the shade of the trees across the street from Triangle Park so he could participate in the conversation, if only as an observer.

"It is wonderful to see you again so soon, my friends," he said. "To what do I owe this pleasure?"

"Ronan Clark," Mason said.

Johan leaned back in his seat, laced his fingers on top of his belly, and cocked his head. His eyes narrowed ever so slightly and the corners of his lips curled upward into the hint of a smile.

"Very good, James," the old man said. "Your ingenuity never fails to impress. I assume it is information you seek, presumably in relation to why this man would warn you of impending catastrophe when he would seemingly benefit more from your demise."

"I know exactly what he wants from me."

"Do you, now?" Johan said, smirking. His eyes sparkled with amusement.

"The two of you have a lot in common, you know," Mason said.

"We have nothing in common." Johan's face contorted with anger. *"Nothing!"*

"Outside of the fact that you're both trying to use me to eliminate your enemies."

Johan sighed, a placid expression settling upon his features, and again relaxed into his chair.

"It is not that simple, I am afraid."

"Then why don't you explain it to me?"

"Perhaps one day. When I am certain."

"Certain of what?"

"Where your loyalties lie."

"You can question a lot of things about me, but my loyalty is not one of them."

"And that is what frightens me," Johan said. "This is not a game we are playing, as this so-called Anomaly, the erstwhile Ronan Clark, understands all too well."

"You have a personal relationship with him," Mason said. "That explains how he knew we'd visited your archives."

"We do not have a relationship, personal or otherwise. He is the monster of my own creation, a nemesis borne of unintended consequences. His great-grandfather was Klaus von Kluck, an Oberscharführer in the Schutzstaffel responsible for the transport of prisoners to Dachau. He was arrested in Italy following the war and later fled to Chile, where my organization finally tracked him down in 1983. His picture hangs in my trophy room, much like that of his son, Bernd, who emigrated to the United States that same year, Americanized his name to Bernard Clark, and began organizing visas for war criminals like his father in hopes that they might escape our wrath. His son and Ronan's father, Peter, seemingly distanced himself from the transgressions of his bloodline and became a software engineer. We believed he had learned from his father's mistakes, but when we discovered someone laying virtual siege to Jewish-owned businesses, pillaging bank accounts and ransoming data, from a wireless band that we were able to triangulate to his neighborhood, we were forced to intercede."

"Only it wasn't Ronan's father who was responsible, was it?"

"Our intelligence said that the boy was still at school," Johan said. "My agent—Seraph's predecessor, Nimrod—had no idea the boy was in the house while he was taking care of the father. Not until months later, when Anomaly hacked into my system, acquired imagery from the security cameras inside my home, and sent the pictures back to me. Photographs of my children and grandchildren, doctored to look like they had been killed in the same manner as his father. Screen grabs from inside my archives. We tracked him to a warehouse in San Francisco, from which Nimrod sent a picture that appeared to have been taken after an accident of some kind." He held up a photograph Mason had seen before, the one with the lens of Anomaly's glasses embedded in his eye. "It was only later, when the body recovered from the ashes of the warehouse was identified as Nimrod's, that I realized the Thirteen had intervened and staged the boy's death. We photographed him in New York City just prior to the Times Square Massacre."

Mason knew all about Johan's so-called agents, who hunted and killed former Nazis on his command, but he had yet to fully grasp the sheer enormity of the old man's network of informants and spies. He remembered seeing a man who'd looked like Asher Ben-Menachem—code-named Seraph—on a crowded subway platform and understood the implications. Johan had been surveilling them, but now was not the time to let on that he knew. Their priority was finding the Dragon and it was obvious that both Anomaly and Johan knew more about who was ultimately behind the nuclear threat than they let on.

"Who is he working for?" Mason asked. "Rand Marchment seemed to think that I already knew."

"Be wary, young James Mason, for that is not a road you are prepared to travel."

"If you want me to end this, then you need to tell me everything you know."

"I believe Anomaly is attached to one of the less prominent members, a man who is patiently accumulating the assets he needs to win this civil war without ever stepping from the shadows." Johan leaned closer to his camera, his eyes boring through the screen. "As you said, he is attempting to use you to eliminate his master's competition, so his revealing himself at this juncture should tell you that the endgame will soon be at hand, and whatever it is will make the potential nuclear destruction of Washington, D.C., pale by comparison."

Gunnar glanced back and offered a nod of confirmation. He'd recognized the significance of the statement, too. Johan was obviously tracking them by their cell phones, but was there more to it than that? Had he intercepted Mason's conversation with Anomaly and that was why he'd been waiting for their call? It suddenly became clear what Johan hoped to receive in exchange for this information.

"You want me to lead you to Anomaly," Mason said.

Johan leaned back once more and offered a patient smile.

"I have no doubt that when the time is right, he will come to you, and I will be there waiting. But if, by some slim chance, you were to discover his location in the interim, I would expect you to volunteer those details"—Johan leaned so close to the camera that all Mason could see were his long teeth—"so I can show him how I deal with those who threaten my family."

The old man closed his laptop, terminating the connection.

52

Ramses was just about to merge back into traffic when his jacket buzzed. He removed his stealth phone from his pocket and glanced at the number of the incoming call.

"Allie," he said, answering on speakerphone.

"We identified several panel trucks leaving the abandoned neighborhood where we found the PUREX lab on satellite imagery," Alejandra said. "Six days ago, two of them crossed the border into McAllen, where the forensics department confirmed they were captured on the security camera of a convenience store, unloading their cargo in the alley behind a real-estate investment company."

"Lone Star Trust," Gunnar said. "I'll lay odds they were delivering cash to be laundered."

"We found the trucks in a dirt lot near the border, burned from the inside out."

"The cartel was in the process of dismantling the operation before you even found it," Ramses said.

"They left just enough behind to make us think we'd blown the whole case open when they'd already moved everything of real value," Layne said. "So the fuel rods in the lab are potentially only a fraction of the true number they harvested."

Mason felt sick to his stomach. He remembered all of the empty

DOE 3013 radioisotope shipping containers and realized there was no reason to have so many on hand for such a limited quantity of reclaimed plutonium.

"Then there's no way to predict how many nuclear devices the Dragon could have made," he said. "And every single one of them is inherently unstable, thanks to the presence of plutonium-240, which could potentially destabilize the fissile material and cause premature detonation."

"It gets worse," Alejandra said. "We picked up the other four trucks near Mérida, just across the Yucatán Peninsula from the Port of Playa del Carmen, before losing them in the jungle near where our sources inside Cártel de Jalisco Nueva Generación reported that they have established a base of operations. Satellite pictures show men massing for what appears to be an invasion. The president is calling for the military to be prepared for urban warfare in the streets of Cancún. I am on my way to the airport now."

Ramses cracked his neck and tugged his fingers through his hair.

"You anticipate a nuclear assault?" Layne said.

"The cártel would be signing its own death warrant," Alejandra said. "There is not enough money in the world to buy the politicians they would need to protect them from the fallout or turn public opinion in their favor. I believe it is their intention to take the shipping port."

"To what end?" Gunnar asked.

"I do not know, but I do not like coincidences. We were able to trace the movements of the Russians whose bodies we discovered inside the barn. Not only did they spend several days in Playa del Carmen in the days before their disappearance, they toured the power plants in Valladolid, Mérida, and Reynosa."

"What kind of power plants?"

"Natural gas."

Gunnar's fingers raced across his keyboard, and a map detailing Mexico's oil and gas industry appeared on the screen. Pipelines connected power plants in all of the major cities to refineries and production facilities in Monterrey and Mexico City. Oil fields lay just off the Gulf Coast, while the land surrounding Reynosa appeared to be one giant deposit of natural gas. He drew a straight line through all three of the plants the Russians had visited, connecting them across the Gulf of Mexico.

"It's possible we're ascribing ulterior motives to a perfectly benign proposition," Gunnar said. "The Russians could have merely been interested in investing in the infrastructure required to extract, refine, and pump the natural gas across the country. Considering they built the entire framework of pipelines in Eurasia, they definitely have the knowledge and experience to do so."

"That would explain why they met with Secretaría de Energía," Alejandra said. "Although I do not understand why they would do so without including representatives from Pemex. No one pursuing drilling rights in Mexico would be able to negotiate with the government and Cártel de Jalisco Nueva Generación without involving the state-owned petroleum company, which is at war with the cártel over billions of dollars in stolen oil. And Cártel de Sinaloa would see it as an act of aggression, one they would not be able to let stand. There has to be more to the situation than we are able to see. That is why the military is moving in such a hurry. And why I must now go."

Ramses killed the speaker, brought the phone to his ear, and climbed out of the car. Mason watched the expression on his old friend's face as he said good-bye, the lines of concern etched upon his face. Such an overt display of vulnerability was unlike Ramses, who apparently had a heart somewhere in that chest of his after all, despite his insistence to the contrary. He climbed back into the car, gunned the engine, and swerved into traffic.

Mason's federal cell phone vibrated. He saw the NO CALLER ID display and immediately picked up.

"I don't have a lot of time," Archer said, "so you'd better make it fast."

"I need to know what intel you received to trigger the evacuation of Congress."

"Damn it. You can't keep a bloody lid on anything in this town. I assume your father told you."

"No," Mason said. "You just did. Up until now, we only had our suspicions."

"I don't have the patience for games—"

"But you obviously do have specific and credible intelligence. You don't just enact what has to be a staggeringly intricate protocol on a whim."

"Ask him why he hasn't evacuated the general population yet," Ramses said. "Look around you. The streets are filled with people who don't have the slightest idea what's about to happen."

Mason covered the microphone with his hand and shot his old friend a look that could have stopped a charging rhino. Ramses winked back at him in the rearview mirror.

"No one's being evacuated," Archer said. "At least, not yet. The vast majority of congressmen—including your father—don't have the slightest idea what's going on, and we'd like to keep it that way. All I can tell you is that several dozen key figures have been assembled at a secure location for potential evacuation, should the order be given. There's no way five hundred and thirty-five elected officials could be airlifted out of here on the goddamn Fourth of July without causing a panic."

"You're waiting for the president to activate the continuity-of-operations plan," Mason said.

"We can't be having this conversation. Especially not over the phone. All I can say at this point is that our actions are precautionary. We have no reason to believe that an attack on the Capitol is imminent; however, that doesn't mean we aren't taking every conceivable precaution."

"What about your intelligence?"

"*The New York Times* received a video through its confidential tip line and passed it on to us. They receive threats all the time, and while they're certain this one's a hoax—some nutjob living in his mom's basement doing his best Cobra Commander impersonation, I believe were their exact words—after what happened in Times Square, they're not taking any chances. We, on the other hand, are taking it very seriously, but we need to make sure the media don't catch wind of our investigation or they'll compromise our operational capabilities on the ground."

"Were you able to trace who sent the file or where it originated?"

"It was submitted anonymously through SecureDrop, which strips all identifying metadata."

"So what leads are you following?"

"I can't get into that—" Archer was interrupted by another voice. He covered his phone to muffle their conversation. Nearly thirty seconds passed before he finally removed his hand. "I'll send you a link to the encrypted video. You ought to be able to figure out exactly what we're doing from there."

"Don't you want to know who's responsible for the nuclear threat?" Mason asked.

Archer paused, as though he'd already been in the process of terminating the call when he registered Mason's words and it had taken several moments for his brain to catch up with his ears.

"You have a positive ID?"

"His name's Zakar Borisovich Meier. The assassin from the hospital is his daughter, Valeria. They're Russian nationals associated with Konets Mira, the same cult the Scarecrow belonged to."

"I'll get back to you when I can," Archer said and, with a click, he was gone.

Mason opened his secure federal email program to make sure he saw Archer's link the moment it came through. The world darkened as the Expedition descended beneath an oversize American flag into the underground parking structure of the hotel Ramses had booked while he and Layne had been in the Russian embassy.

"What's the continuity-of-operations plan?" Layne asked.

"It's a set of protocols designed to make sure the government remains viable in the event of a nuclear war," Mason said.

"I know that. I was hoping that since your father is one of the more prominent senators you might have some insight into the actual procedures."

"Believe it or not, that's not the kind of thing we discuss in what little time we spend together."

"The president will be evacuated on either Air Force One or the National Airborne Command Center," Ramses said. "Critical personnel will be airlifted to a series of bunkers surrounding D.C. known as the 'relocation arc,' most likely either the Mount Weather Emergency Operations Center in Bluemont, Virginia, or the Raven Rock Mountain Complex near Camp David."

"So why not take the president there?" Layne asked.

"If you think that's where he should go, then that's the last place in the world they'd want to take him. Or, by that same logic, maybe that's exactly where they'd take him if they couldn't get him in the air in time. The truth is only a handful of people know the details of the plan, and they won't even share them with Congress behind closed doors. It's one big shell game designed to keep our enemies guessing while we relocate the key components of our government to command centers from which to reestablish continuity of government and launch a counterstrike."

The headlights constricted against the concrete wall of a parking place near the elevator. Ramses killed the engine and opened his door.

"Which is why they don't disclose the details," Layne said.

"Exactly. We can't afford for the enemy to know where we're taking our most powerful officials during our window of greatest vulnerability."

53

They'd reserved adjoining rooms at a hotel within walking distance of the National Mall. The view of the Capitol Building was magnificent, a reminder of the power the Founding Fathers had hoped to project with its creation. They'd barely had time to set down their bags when Archer's email came through.

"Are you ready?" Mason asked. He took a seat at the small table and clicked the link. Several interminable seconds passed while the site verified his credentials. It finally opened and revealed the video that had been sent to *The New York Times*. He glanced over his shoulder at the others, who'd gathered behind him to watch.

"What're you waiting for, a drumroll?" Ramses said.

Mason pressed the play button and the video started to roll.

A clattering sound preceded the appearance of a man wearing a silver CBRN suit. A reflective golden shield concealed his face. He was seated directly in front of the camera, a Russian flag hanging on the wall behind him. His tinny breathing through the respirator was so loud that it sounded like he was right there in the room with them.

"For years, I have stood by and watched you demonize my country," he said. There was no mistaking his accent or his failing physical condition. He seemed to labor for breath and didn't move in the slightest as he spoke. Mason had to admit he did kind of look and sound like Cobra Commander. "I will do so no longer. You must be made to understand that there are consequences for your actions. Your unfounded accusations and open hostilities have derailed any chance for peace between our nations. You hide behind your so-called moderate rebels and democratic revolutionaries and fight wars by proxy against us on every continent. You destroy entire countries so you can position your military along our borders. The time has come to face judgment for your crimes against my people, for the suffering you have caused and the starvation you have inflicted upon our children. Before the sun sets tonight, you will receive the prize you earned for winning your all-consuming arms race and become the first to experience the nuclear holocaust you so desperately crave." He paused and Mason could almost feel the weight of his unseen stare. "For Mother Russia."

A blur of movement across his face shield and the video ended.

Mason's breathing accelerated and he heard the rushing sound of blood in his ears. He glanced at the clock. 12:56 P.M. Exactly seven and a half hours before the sun set. They were running out of time.

"It's all bullshit," Ramses said. "He doesn't believe a word of the crap he's shoveling."

"I agree," Gunnar said. "He's trying to create the appearance of state-sponsored terrorism. A lone wolf, regardless of the enormity of his weapon, can't start a war all by himself. He needed to put a face to the enemy, flaunt its colors, and convince the world that his actions were on behalf of its people."

"I thought the whole point of starting a nuclear war was so that his group could usher in an age of enlightenment," Layne said. "With most of them either dead or imprisoned, his ideology falls apart."

"It's possible he hates the country he believes stole that future from him with such intensity that he wants nothing more than to see it destroyed by our inevitable retaliation."

"He was planning the Moscow attack before the raid scattered his cell. War with the U.S. had to be the goal from the very beginning."

Mason set down his phone and looked out the window at the Statue of Freedom adorning the crown of the Capitol Building while he composed his thoughts.

"This is about his daughter now," Mason said. "He knows he's dying and doesn't want Valeria to spend the rest of her life being hunted. Whatever deal he cut with the Thirteen benefits her. That's where their ideologies align. She'll be protected through the resulting crisis and help them build whatever utopian society they envision from the ashes."

"Forward the link to that video," Gunnar said. "Let me see what I can do with it."

"Can you send me the pictures from the embassy in return?"

Gunnar nodded, sat on the edge of the bed with his laptop on his thighs, and set to work. While he didn't have the proper security clearance, cracking the encryption didn't pose much of a challenge.

"Archer didn't want to discuss the details of his operation," Mason said, "but he was sure we'd be able to figure them out for ourselves after watching the video."

"That's what I'm working on right now," Gunnar said, swiveling his monitor to face them. "This is a screen grab of his face shield, or, more specifically, the reflection on it. If I zoom in and clean it up, you can clearly see the laptop computer he used to record himself on the desk in front of him, as well as the map hanging on the wall behind it." He zoomed in even further, applied a few more sharpening filters, and gestured toward it with a flourish. "Boom."

There was no mistaking Independence National Historical Park in Philadelphia, which was nicknamed "America's most historic square mile" for a reason. It encompassed what amounted to the entire history of the birth of the nation: from the First Bank of the United States to its earliest stock market, the Merchants' Exchange; Franklin Court to the Magnolia and Rose Gardens; the Library of the American Philosophical Society to the Tomb of the Unknown Revolutionary War Soldier; and the house where Thomas Jefferson wrote the Declaration of Independence to Independence Hall, where it was signed, smack-dab in the middle of it all. A red pushpin had been placed in the center, right on top of the statue of Commodore John Barry. In one fell swoop, the Dragon could obliterate them all.

"We're in the wrong place," Layne said.

"If we leave now, we can be in Philly in two and a half hours," Ramses said.

"It's too perfect," Mason said. "He has to know there's infrastructure in place to prevent an attack of that nature."

"You think he planted that map in the reflection?"

"What's the alternative? That he's not smart enough to realize that his mask is one big mirror?"

"It's always possible he thinks he's so much smarter than the rest of us that he can plant his bomb even with our best countermeasures in place," Layne said.

"For my money, this is a classic case of misdirection," Mason said. "He knows we're closing in on him and wants to show us what's in one hand, so we won't see what he's doing with the other."

"And just what do you think that is?" Layne asked.

"That's what we need to figure out."

Mason looked at each of them in turn. Their misgivings were written all over their faces.

"It's a huge gamble," Layne said.

"We have to trust the intel that brought us here," Mason said. "Besides, Archer has to be in the process of securing that entire area."

"But we know for a fact that the Dragon's daughter is heading west toward Pennsylvania. Surely there's any number of back roads leading into Philadelphia that don't pass through our checkpoints."

"If that's where the bomb is, then that's the last place in the world the Dragon wants her to be."

"I'll check in with Chris and see if they've figured out where she's going."

Layne grabbed her cell phone and ducked into the adjoining room. Mason sat on the bed beside Gunnar, whose face was still buried in his laptop. He'd been unusually quiet during their conversation.

"What do you think?"

"Remember that blur of movement across his mask at the very end of the recording?" Gunnar said. "I was able to isolate its source."

He again brought up a detailed image of the Dragon's golden mask, the upper half of which was eclipsed by a black shape, only it wasn't just a reflection on the mask.

"Something passed in front of the camera," Mason said.

"That's how I see it, too. And if you zoom in on it"—he manipulated the image as he spoke—"you can see the texture of the fabric. I'm willing to bet that it's the sleeve of someone reaching around the computer from behind it to stop the recording."

He scrolled the video forward, one frame at a time, until he reached the end, and then repeated the process in reverse until he suddenly stopped.

"That's not an ordinary sleeve, is it?" Mason said.

"No, it's not. Look at the way the fabric hangs, like it's draped over the forearm."

"Like a burka," Layne said as she crawled onto the bed behind them. "Or a nun's habit."

"The woman sitting on the table in the picture of Konets Mira," Mason said. "The one who's still at-large. Zadorov said that everyone called her Sister."

"Wait a second," Gunnar said, zooming in on the Dragon's mask.

"Look right there. You see the reflection of the monitor? Just to the left of it. See that shape leaning around the side, as though looking to make sure it knew where the right key was before reaching around to press it?"

"It's just a shadow," Layne said. "There's no detail."

"Have a little faith."

Gunnar's fingers flew across the keyboard. Different screens opened and closed and lines of code blurred past. He returned to the image and applied several different filters. With each pass, the image became more and more distinct, until it revealed a woman wearing a stiff black cap from which a veil descended, concealing her hair and everything below her chin. It was a *kalymafki,* the traditional head-dress worn by Eastern Orthodox nuns. A powder blue surgical mask hung from her neck.

"That's her," Mason said. "The woman who escaped from the Russians."

"If she's using that mask to cover her face in public, we have zero chance of finding her on any of the streetlight or security cameras."

"Not even with her eyes?"

"I need more points of comparison than that."

"We have to try," Layne said.

Gunnar was silent for a moment.

"Maybe if I treated that gap almost as though it were a smile, with the lower edge of the *kalymafki* and the brim of the surgical mask like lips, and the various points of reference between like teeth, I could create the facial equivalent of a dental X-ray. Between the eyes themselves, the distances between them and from the outer corners to the edges of the mask, the breadth of the nose, and the angle of the brows, I might have just enough . . ."

He scrolled through data so quickly that Mason couldn't keep up, so he stood and paced the room. They needed to catch a break if they were going to have any chance of stopping the Dragon before—

"Sometimes I amaze even myself," Gunnar said. He leaned away from the screen and released a long sigh. "I found our mystery woman."

The picture had been taken from a traffic camera at a busy in-tersection. While the subject was the Audi blowing through the red light, it had also captured the pedestrians on the sidewalk, including a spandex-clad woman jogging in place, a bearded man carrying a miniature dog, and a woman in a flowing habit, who appeared to be opening the door of a white building with green trim. She stood sideways to the camera, her face turned toward it as though checking to make sure no one was following her before entering, a surgical mask covering her mouth and nose.

Gunnar zoomed in on her face and cleaned up the image. There was no doubt in Mason's mind that this was the same woman.

"When was this taken?" he asked.

"Yesterday afternoon."

"Where?"

"The corner of North Carolina and Seventh Street."

"Here in the District? You're certain?"

"Without a doubt," Gunnar said. "It's maybe four blocks east of the Capitol Building."

Mason glanced back at Layne.

"Are you ready to end this?"

54

"Stay here," Mason said. He climbed out of the Expedition, slipped on the hooded sweatshirt he'd borrowed from Ramses, and shoved his Glock into the front pouch.

"Trust me when I say I never had any intention of going in there," Gunnar said from the passenger seat, where he sat with his laptop open, a live satellite feed on the screen. He fitted an earpiece into his right ear and positioned the microphone in front of his lips. "I'll be with you in spirit, though."

Mason nodded and closed the door. They were taking a risk by going in on their own, but they simply couldn't afford to waste time trying to coordinate the operation with Archer, who was convinced the Dragon was in Philadelphia, or Chris, who had his hands full supervising the search for Valeria and liaising between the DHS and FBI to secure Independence Square.

They were on their own.

"I have visual on all three of you," Gunnar said through the wireless receiver in his left ear.

Mason tapped his microphone twice in acknowledgment, but he refrained from responding as he passed a woman pushing a toddler in a stroller along the redbrick sidewalk.

"You sure you don't want me to go in there with you?" Ramses said from a step behind him.

"If things go sideways in there, I need you outside to make sure the Dragon doesn't get away."

"You just don't want me stealing your glory."

"If you shoot anyone, it's not glory you'll be charged with."

"You can suck the fun right out of anything, can't you?"

"Are you boys finished?" Layne whispered through the speaker. "I'm just about in position. There's a narrow opening off the alley, just wide enough to squeeze a car inside. Once I pass through there, I'll be visible from all of the windows along the back of the building."

"Then hold your ground for now," Mason said, slowing his pace as he neared the building. "I'll let you know when I'm at the front door."

"See you on the other side," Ramses said. He veered from the sidewalk, opened the gate, and ducked into the narrow gap between buildings, where he vanished into the shadows.

Mason leaned against the tree in front of the two-story structure and covertly watched for any sign of movement inside. The ground floor had been designed to serve as a retail establishment, the three bay windows positioned in such a way as to showcase the wares offered inside. Curtains had been drawn over two of them, while mannequins wearing sun-bleached, out-of-style clothes stood in the third. The sign in the window had been flipped to CLOSED, but there was no indication as to when, if ever, the store might open again.

"Who owns this building?" Mason asked.

"Give me a second," Gunnar said.

The front door was painted forest green to match the trim and the shutters beside the upper-story windows. Evaporative coolers jutted from two of them. White blinds obscured the view of the interior. They wouldn't be able to tell if there was anyone inside the building until they were in there with them.

"It's owned by a company called National Realty Trust, which is one of the largest publicly traded equity real-estate investment trusts in the country," Gunnar said. "It owns hundreds of commercial properties throughout the Midwest, primarily in rural communities, including processing plants, refineries, and facilities with industrial and agricultural applications. Plus, it owns a ton of land in the middle of nowhere and leases the mineral rights to various development and exploration companies who might or might not ever do anything with them."

"Why would a company like that invest in a place like this?"

"That's the thing, Mace. It wouldn't. A real-estate investment trust like NRT is designed to accumulate and manage income-earning properties within its dedicated sphere . . ."

His voice trailed off into silence.

"What is it?" Mason asked.

"Give me a second," Gunnar said. Mason listened to the clamor of keystrokes as he studied the building before him, searching for any sign that they were walking into a trap. "Here we go. National Realty Trust established a group of sister companies, ostensibly to help independent and minority-owned businesses enter the market in traditionally low-margin industries or lower-income areas. They operate at a net loss, which they're able to write off since they're technically performing a community service. It also allows them to transfer poorly performing assets from their main portfolio into accounts where any potential financial loss is turned right back into profit in the form of a tax write-off. The building in front of you was owned by a local sister company called Capitol Trust until three months ago, when the value of the land itself eclipsed the liability of the mortgage, necessitating its transfer to NRT's main portfolio, unlike the majority of its rural and agricultural holdings in places like Pennsylvania, where it operates a sister company called Liberty Trust, and in—"

"Texas," Mason said. "Where it goes by the name of Lone Star Trust, which bought the mortgage on the ranch where we found all of the dead bodies in the barn."

"Yeah," Gunnar said. He fell silent for several seconds. "Be exceedingly careful in there."

"That's the plan." Mason approached the entrance and tested the knob, which turned easily in his hand. "The front door's unlocked."

"You think they're expecting us?" Ramses said.

"Only one way to find out. Layne?"

"Ready on your mark," she said.

Mason's heart rate accelerated. This was the moment of truth.

"We go in on a silent three-count," he said. "Three . . ."

A surge of adrenaline kicked in. He attuned his senses to even the slightest sound.

Two.

He drew his pistol. Slowed his breathing.

One.

In one fluid motion, he turned the knob and ducked into the building. Surveyed the interior down the sight line of his pistol. Closed the door silently behind him. The smell hit him immediately, causing him to instinctively cover his mouth and nose with the back of his hand. Motes of dust glittered in the dim light, seemingly suspended in the still air of the tiled foyer. Straight ahead, a checkout counter with an ancient cash register perched on top of it. A doorway on his left; a blind corner around which he couldn't see on his right. He heard movement from somewhere beyond it and hoped to God it was Layne.

"I digitally removed the Dragon's scarring, re-created his original features, and fed the image into my facial-recognition program," Gunnar said. "It returned an immediate match. Zadorov knew exactly who he was the whole time and didn't say a word."

Mason tapped twice in acknowledgment, removed his mini Maglite from his pocket, and aligned it with the barrel of his Glock. Went around the wall. Low and fast. Swept his beam across the retail floor and nearly fired upon the mannequins leaning against the far wall. All of them were in various states of undress. Racks of dusty clothes had been shoved to either side to clear space for the bed in the middle of the room.

"He gave us his name," Ramses said. "What more could you possibly want?"

"It would have been helpful to know that his real name was Yevgeny and that he was the nuclear engineer responsible for implementing the safety protocols that might have prevented the Chernobyl disaster in 1986. He had a cousin named Zakar, who dropped out of circulation shortly after Yevgeny was released from prison, only to reappear, physically altered by scarring consistent with acute radiation exposure, in the files related to Konets Mira."

Mason shone his light onto the bed. The sheets were filthy and crusted with blood. A stack of unwashed bedpans rested on the floor. The TV tray beside them had been draped with a towel, on top of which was a handful of hooked needles and a spool of thick black thread.

Layne appeared from the back of the house and gestured toward the staircase. The stairs were wooden, the runner and railings smeared with blood. She reached them first and ascended with her flashlight shining upward toward the landing, beyond which they could see only a bare wall with rectangular discolorations where pictures had once hung.

"He was one of six men charged in the disaster," Gunnar said. "A farce of a trial was held in front of the whole country. They were convicted without the defense attorneys speaking on their behalf and received sentences ranging from two to ten years, based on their levels of culpability. Yevgeny got five years for negligence and was released in 1992 after serving his full term, despite a report issued the previous year by the State Committee for the Supervision of Industry and Nuclear Power, which acknowledged that the explosion had resulted from a design flaw in the control rods and not human error, producing a fizzle reaction that sent six tons of radioactive material into the air."

"Which is why he uses it as his calling card," Mason whispered.

The smell was even stronger on the second floor. Layne pressed her back against the wall beside the first open doorway and waited for Mason before going in fast. Their lights sliced through the darkness, illuminating the room where the bed downstairs must have once resided. In its place was a desk with a laptop computer sitting on top of it. A Russian flag hung from one wall, a map of Independence National Historical Park from the other.

There was no doubt in Mason's mind that the map had been a plant meant to mislead them.

"They dragged this guy in front of the whole country and made him believe he was responsible for killing all of those people," Ramses said. "And they didn't kick him loose when they learned he wasn't responsible after all? No wonder he joined a cult that wanted to see the whole damn world destroyed."

"Over here," Layne whispered.

Mason found her standing just inside the doorway of the room across the hall. He slipped in behind her and shone his beam onto a neatly made bed. The dresser was freshly polished and a curio cabinet displayed porcelain figurines that practically glowed in the dim light. An ionizer stood in one corner, a HEPA filtration unit in another. Essential oil diffusers were strategically arranged throughout. It was a scene completely incongruous with the remainder of the house, one that would have been jarring were it not for the walls, which were plastered with maps and photographs.

"We're definitely in the right place," Mason whispered.

The maps were of Washington, D.C., as a whole, and the National Mall specifically, and featured handwritten notes and distances measured in what could only have been steps. There were photographs of every structure from every possible angle. From the Lincoln Memorial in the west to the Capitol Building in the east, the White House in the north to the Jefferson Memorial in the south, and everything in between. He recognized the World War II and Vietnam Memorials, the American and Natural History Museums, the Smithsonian Castle, the statues and paddleboats and gardens and the security details assigned to each, including the exact times the photographs were taken. They'd been surveilling the area for what had to have been years. Every path, every blade of grass, every solitary inch was represented somewhere in the confusion of pictures, but it wasn't until he looked up at the ceiling and saw the Washington Monument that everything fell into place. The 555-foot obelisk stood at the very center of everything, a point from which a single detonation could wipe out the entirety of the American political infrastructure and erase its history.

If the goal was to trigger immediate and disproportionate reprisals, this was the surest way to do it.

Mason cleared the bathroom and met Layne beside the lone remaining doorway, the buzzing of flies emanating from within. They went in together, their flashlights scything through the darkness.

"Jesus," she gasped.

A workstation framed by gray bricks sat on the table just inside the doorway. A pair of lead gloves was draped over the clear shield in front of it. There were syringes in metal sheaths and a container with the radiation symbol on the side, but that wasn't what had caught Layne's eye.

A pair of legs rested on the small bed in a wash of congealed blood. They'd been amputated just below the groin, presumably by the chain saw leaning against the armchair. The decomposing flesh of the thighs had retracted from the femurs. He could still smell faint traces of burned meat and a hint of gas from the acetylene torch they'd used to cauterize the stumps.

"What is it?" Gunnar asked. "What did you find?"

Mason didn't have the slightest clue. He could only shake his head at the implications as he stared at what he had to believe were the Dragon's legs.

55

"Put me through to Secretary Archer!" Mason shouted into his phone.

He sprinted across the street toward the Expedition, with Layne hot on his heels as she called in what they'd found to the local division of the FBI. Ramses was already climbing behind the wheel when they caught up with him.

"Like I told you, Special Agent—" Archer's assistant started to say.

"I don't care if he's meeting with the president himself. Physically drag him out of there if you have to. He needs to know his team's in the wrong location!"

"The best I can do is have him call you—"

Mason terminated the call and speed-dialed Chris. The number rang through as he climbed into the backseat and slammed the door behind him. Layne's rear end had barely hit the seat when Ramses pinned the gas and peeled away from the curb.

"I have a live satellite feed of the National Mall," Gunnar said. "The whole place is positively crawling with people. It's a logistical nightmare."

"There have to be security cameras covering every inch of that place," Mason said. "See what you can do about hacking into them and finding a woman dressed like a nun."

Chris answered right before the call went to voice mail.

"This had better be important," he said.

"We found the Dragon's base of operations," Mason said. "The map of Independence Square was a plant. He's going to hit the National Mall."

"You're sure?"

"I'd stake my life on it, Chris."

"Considering where we're heading right now," Ramses said, "that's exactly what you're doing."

He weaved around a sedan waiting at the light and made a sharp turn onto Pennsylvania Avenue so fast that Layne was thrown up against Mason, pinning him to the door. The tires screamed and for a heartbeat Mason feared they were going to roll, but Ramses righted the vehicle and accelerated toward the Capitol Building. Layne scooted back into her seat and fastened her seat belt before the same thing could happen again.

"Have you talked to Archer?" Chris asked.

"He's 'currently indisposed' and I can't get past his assistant," Mason said. "I need you to see if you can use whatever clout you have to get him on the phone."

"He'll want to know what proof you have."

Mason turned and looked at Layne, who covered the microphone on her cell phone.

"How much do you want me to tell them?" Layne asked. "They already have a forensics team en route to the house. Are we prepared to cause a citywide panic?"

"Not yet," Mason said to her, and then to Chris: "He'll have all of the proof he needs in a matter of minutes. The D.C. field office has a crime-scene response team on its way to the Dragon's house, where they'll find a room filled with pictures of what has to be years' worth of surveillance imagery."

"And just what exactly do you propose we do about it?"

Mason hesitated. That was the real question. If the Dragon was already inside the mall with his nuclear device, then the moment he so much as sensed something was amiss, he'd detonate it on the spot. They couldn't risk tipping him off, and flooding the park with men in tactical gear was the surest way to do so.

"We're going to need plainclothes support," Mason said. "And they'd better be invisible. If I'm right, the Dragon's already in there somewhere and we can't afford for him to see us coming."

Ramses braked hard to avoid hitting a BMW slowing for a yellow light, jerked the wheel to the right, and blew through the red. The John Adams Building materialized from the branches of the trees lining the right side of the street.

"You're going in there after him?" Chris said.

"We don't have a choice," Mason said. "Just see what you can do about getting us some backup."

Mason terminated the call and braced for impact, but Ramses dodged a panel truck at the last instant and merged left as three lanes narrowed to two. The Library of Congress raced past beside them, its sidewalks packed with holiday revelers and children holding red, white, and blue balloons.

"I can't find anyone wearing a nun's habit," Gunnar said. "To disappear, all she'd have to do is take it off."

"Then focus on their faces and see if your program can find them."

"If they've altered their appearance in the slightest, it doesn't stand a chance. Our best option is to go back through the satellite footage, find them leaving the house, and hope to God we can catch up with them in real time."

Layne ended her call, chambered a round in her sidearm, and snapped the slide closed. Her foot tapped restlessly on the floorboard.

"There's too much ground for us to cover," she said.

"We're going to have to split up," Mason said. "We'll each enter from a different point and work our way toward the Washington Monument in the middle."

Ramses took a hard right onto First Street. The Capitol Building appeared on their left, the Neptune Fountain with its ornate statues frolicking in the water on their right. His eyes met Mason's in the rearview mirror.

"What's the plan, Mace?"

"Drop me off in front of the Capitol Building. Layne: You enter from the White House. Ramses: Park by the Lincoln Memorial and come in from the west. Gunnar: I'm counting on you to be our eyes and ears. Watch for anyone or anything that looks out of place, and for the love of Christ, if you see a man with no legs—"

Mason's cell phone rang, cutting him off. The incoming number was listed as NO CALLER ID. He picked up on the first ring and started talking.

"He planted the map of Philadelphia so we'd divert all of our resources to the wrong place."

"There's no way anyone's getting a nuclear device into the National Mall," Archer said. "We have an advanced radioactive threat detection system in active use. Very few outside of our security team know we put it into operation, and only DARPA knows how it works. There are a thousand mobile sensors capable of registering trace amounts of gamma and alpha radiation throughout the city, more than fifty within the mall itself, all networked via smartphones. You couldn't take a single grain of uranium ore in there without setting them off."

"There has to be a way to beat it."

Ramses slowed as he neared the intersection of First and Capitol Streets. The Capitol Building itself was enormous, the walkway leading up to it large enough to lay multiple football fields end to end. There were easily ten thousand people within his line of sight, all of them looking to the sky and applauding as a formation of fighter jets roared past, trailing slipstreams of red, white, and blue smoke.

"This is your stop," Ramses said, slowing only long enough for Mason to jump out.

Car horns blared as he suddenly appeared in the middle of the road. He braced his palm on the hood of a minivan to keep it from clipping his legs and darted across the oncoming lanes.

"I'm telling you," Archer said. "It can't be done. We've strategized every conceivable means of staging a terror attack on the mall and implemented countermeasures for every single one of them."

"But Marchment knew all about them, too."

Archer was momentarily silent.

"Look," Mason said. "If I'm wrong, all it costs you is wasted manpower, but if I'm right . . ."

He shouldered through the crowd and ran toward the Capitol Building, his eyes scanning the sea of faces.

"I didn't say I intended to do nothing," Archer said. "The president's already given the order to enact the continuity-of-operations plan. The First Helicopter Squadron's being dispatched to evacuate critical personnel as we speak. The National Capital Response Squad and the Joint Terrorism Task Force will have additional agents on the scene within a matter of minutes. And I intend to personally oversee operations in both D.C. and Philly. Believe me, Mason, wherever the Dragon goes, we'll be there waiting for him."

Archer ended the call.

Without breaking stride, Mason connected with the rest of his team and plugged the wireless transceiver into his ear.

"Can everyone hear me?" he asked.

"Loud and clear," Layne said.

A helicopter thundered across the sky, moving way too fast and coming in far too low. He caught a flash of navy blue from its belly, a

streak of yellow on its side, and the words UNITED STATES OF AMER-
ICA along its tail as it banked to the south. Three more followed in
rapid succession. The 1st Helicopter Squadron. The evacuations were
about to commence.

"I acquired the nun leaving the house this morning at 9:13 A.M.,"
Gunnar said. "Pushing a man in a wheelchair. He's buried under about
fifty blankets and wearing a baseball cap and a surgical mask. And he
definitely appears to have both of his legs."

"Then whose legs did we find?" Mason asked.

"Your guess is as good as mine. I'll try to catch up with them and
keep you apprised of my progress."

Mason ran past twin fountains, ornate lampposts that looked
more like ceremonial torches, and crowds posing for pictures in front
of the landmark. The lawns were packed with families staking claim
to their spots for the night's fireworks, lounging on blankets and underneath umbrellas. Twin paths led around the sides of the monolithic
Capitol Building: one past the Senate to the north, the other past the
House of Representatives to the south. Regardless of which one he
chose, there was an enormous amount of ground he simply wouldn't
be able to cover.

He went south on a whim and navigated the arched path paralleling Southwest Drive, angling around toward the rear terrace. There
were people everywhere, taking pictures of the fountain and the twin
sets of stairs leading all the way up to the congressional floor. He
studied them all as quickly as he could, but there were simply too
many of them. The security presence was readily recognizable. He
slowed and approached an officer wearing a baseball cap, sunglasses,
and black fatigues with a matching Kevlar vest. His nameplate identified him as HARRIS. He carried an M4 carbine and projected an air
of command.

Mason flashed his badge, held out his cell phone, and swiped to
the picture of the nun.

"Have you seen this woman?" he asked.

"Sister Anastasia?" the officer said.

"You know her?"

"Everyone around here knows her. She comes here every day with
Professor Vasiliev."

"Have you seen them today?"

"No, but between the building grounds and the mall itself, there's more than a thousand acres out here and we already estimate nearly a million people—"

"Let me give you my cell number. I need you to check with the other officers out here and find out if anyone's seen either of them today." Mason rattled off his number while the officer programmed it into his own device. "Call me the moment you know anything."

"Are they in some kind of trouble?" Harris asked.

"We all are," Mason said.

He turned and ran in the opposite direction, toward an oval-shaped lawn teeming with people. Two paths cut diagonally through it, one leading to the statue of James A. Garfield, the other to the Peace Monument, crowned with the classical female figures of Grief and History. Straight ahead was the Ulysses S. Grant Memorial, over the top of which he could barely see the spire of the Washington Monument in the far distance.

They were never going to find the Dragon in time.

56

Mason ran down the path paralleling the seemingly endless rectangular plots of grass, which were already nearly packed with people. Groves of elm and cherry trees obstructed his view of the sidewalks along Madison to the north and Jefferson to the south, both of which were lined with parked cars and sluggish one-way traffic that made it impossible to see the National Gallery of Art on one side or the National Museum of the American Indian on the other. For all he knew, the Dragon and the nun could have been inside any one of these buildings, lost in the throngs of tourists, hidden in their midst.

He sprinted across 4th Street, weaving through traffic moving in both directions, the distracted drivers looking at anything and everything but what was directly in front of them. Again, he hit the path and headed straight for the white spike of the Washington Monument.

"I picked them up again near Union Station shortly after eleven," Gunnar said through his earpiece. "If they're heading toward the mall, they're certainly taking a roundabout way of getting there."

Mason tapped his thanks. He couldn't afford to waste the breath answering. There was an insane amount of ground left to cover and his lungs were already burning.

The National Air and Space Museum passed on his left, its curbs bristling with tour buses and its front terrace swarming with people, none of whom had the slightest idea of the danger around them.

"I've passed the White House," Layne said. "They have the entire South Lawn and every possible ingress sealed up tight."

"I'm just now leaving the car," Ramses said. "There was nowhere to park, so I just jumped out."

Mason took in everyone around him from his peripheral vision, watching for black gowns and wheelchairs, both together and apart, knowing full well that if the woman shed her habit or the man abandoned his chair, he wouldn't be able to recognize either of them standing right in front of him.

"This is hopeless," Layne said. "I don't think I've ever seen so many people in one place in my life. And this place is so big that finding any single person is like looking for a needle in a field of haystacks."

Mason charged across 7th Street. A Lexus locked up its brakes with a screech. He barely had time to leave his feet and use his momentum to slide across the hood. Without missing a stride, he mounted the curb and hit the sidewalk on the far side.

He picked up a woman pushing a man in a wheelchair from the corner of his eye. Altered course to confront them. He was nearly on top of them by the time he recognized that the woman was too young and the man was too old.

"I have them at a Walgreens in Chinatown," Gunnar said. "Quarter after one."

"You're positive it's them?" Mason gasped.

"One hundred percent."

"Where are they going?"

"At a guess, I'd say the White House—"

"I could have walked right past them and not even seen them," Layne said. "It's one giant mass of humanity back there."

Mason's phone rang in his hand. He put his team on hold and answered before it could ring a second time. He took the opportunity to slow down, if only long enough to catch his breath.

"Special Agent Mason."

"This is Lieutenant Harris," the caller said. "We spoke at the Capitol Building?"

"Tell me you found them."

"Well, I can't tell you where they are now, but one of my men, Lewis, ran into them in Freedom Plaza a couple hours ago."

"Where's that?"

"About a block and a half from the White House."

"Thanks. And tell your men to keep an eye out—"

"I hate to say anything," Harris said, "but are you sure these are the people you're looking for? My officer said the professor looked so bad he could hardly sit up in his chair."

Mason switched lines and spoke to Gunnar.

"I have confirmation that they were in Freedom Plaza approximately two hours ago."

"That's about halfway between Chinatown and the Washington Monument."

"Then they have to be here somewhere," Mason said. He switched back to Harris. "Did he have his legs?"

"Pardon?"

"The professor. Did he have both of his legs?"

"I'm sure Lewis would have said something if he were missing them. That's the kind of thing you'd pick up on pretty quickly, especially since we've all kind of been watching him deteriorate. He's always been so outgoing and friendly, telling us all about how he nearly died in Chernobyl and how he had to start all over with nothing after the fall of Communism. The guy's lived a hard-enough life without having to go through what he's going through."

Mason quickened his pace to a jog and watched the people walking along the sidewalks flicker past beyond the trees, as though animated by a zoetrope.

"And what's that?" he asked.

"Don't you know?" Harris said. "He has terminal cancer. That's how we all got to know him. Every time the sister pushes him through here after one of his appointments, he's still radioactive from the PET scan and sets off all of our detectors."

"What did you say?"

"He gets these tests where they inject him with a radioactive isotope so they can see where all of his tumors are."

"So your man—"

"Lewis."

"You're telling me Lewis approached them because the professor set off his radiation detector?"

"Yes, sir."

"And he let him go because this kind of thing happens all the time?"

"We didn't do anything wrong, did we?"

"Have your men watch their sensors. The second he sets one of them off, I want to know where. But do not—I repeat, *do not*— approach him on your own. Are we clear?"

Mason terminated the call without waiting for an answer and toggled back to his team, catching Gunnar midsentence.

"—imagery of them in the plaza. It looks like they're just casually talking to an officer with a radiation detector attached to his utility belt."

"That setup we found in his bedroom," Mason said. "He's been using it to inject himself with a radioactive isotope for no other reason than to routinely set off all of the detectors. He's spent years conditioning the entire security team to let him walk right into the National Mall with a nuclear weapon."

"Then there's no talking him out of using it," Ramses said. "He came here with the sole intention of detonating it. You see that asshole's face and you'd better be prepared to put a bullet through it."

"But what if the bomb's somehow wired to him?" Layne said. "Like how the Scarecrow used Marchment's own blood to power the detonator on the subway?"

"Then I guess we're all going to find out how it feels to be vaporized, because I'm not taking any chances."

Mason accelerated and raced straight toward his destination, hurdling the chain-strung barriers along the sidewalks and weaving through a confusion of pedestrians and vehicles. He could see the ring of flags surrounding the base of the obelisk and the Washington Monument Lodge squatting at the foot of the grassy knoll leading up to it.

"Crossing Constitution now," Layne said. "I'm maybe a hundred yards from the monument."

"I'm roughly the same distance away to the west," Ramses said.

Mason crossed 15th Street, rounded the small stone building, and cleared the retaining wall. There was now nothing between him and the monument. He slowed his pace and gripped his pistol inside the pouch of his sweatshirt. His heart was beating so hard and fast that the edges of his vision throbbed.

The ring of American flags snapped on the breeze. Dozens of people were seated on the arched benches encircling the courtyard, where groups of tourists gathered in anticipation of making the journey to the top of the monument.

"I've got them," Gunnar said. "In the queue to enter the monument, about twenty minutes ago."

"Jesus," Layne said. "They're going to detonate it at the very top."

"How long is that line?" Mason asked.

"The tickets are sold in groups and by time slot," Gunnar said. "Depending upon the size of that group, it will likely take multiple trips with the elevator, and without knowing where they fall in the line, there's no way of accurately predicting it."

Mason ran uphill through the crowd and straight toward the entrance, an ordinary white stone cubicle with an unmarked door on its face and a line of people being admitted through a doorway on the side. He darted through a gap between benches and rushed—

A uniformed officer emerged from the building, his hand on the grip of the pistol holstered at his waist, and moved to intercept Mason.

The thunder of helicopters erupted in the distance, their silhouettes streaking across the horizon.

Mason flashed his badge, took the officer by the arm, and pulled him in close enough that he could speak directly into his ear.

"Did a nun pushing a man in a wheelchair come through here?"

"Yeah," the officer said. "Maybe fifteen, twenty minutes ago. They're still inside. Why?"

"I need you to listen very carefully and do exactly what I tell you."

57

A sensation of calmness washed over Zmei. All of the years he had spent reclaiming the plutonium from the exhausted fuel rods, converting it into weapons-grade fissionable material, and meticulously studying the physical and biological effects of unleashing such awesome power upon tens of thousands of unsuspecting victims . . . all of the sacrifices he had made for the cause, from letting the woman he loved walk away to pursue her own apocalyptic ends and throwing in his lot with the Thirteen to grooming his daughter as his replacement and selling his soul for her future . . . all of the decisions he had made along the way culminated in this singular moment in time. Here he sat, a dying man in a wheelchair, surrounded by teeming masses of people who had gathered to celebrate the birth of a nation, but instead would witness the beginning of its demise. And the first shot in a war that would destroy the world and allow people like his Valeria to rise from the ashes and usher in a golden age of humanity.

He watched the images scroll past on the video monitor beside the elevator. Photographs of the National Mall changed before his eyes from lush and green to desolate and gray, the Capitol Building and the White House dissolving into rubble, the Washington Monument becoming a crater, tourists littering the ground like autumn leaves scattered by a nuclear wind.

Zmei wiped the sweat from his pale face, so that it betrayed neither his discomfort nor his excitement, and rested his hands protectively on the blanket in what passed for his lap. Sister readjusted her grip on the handles to conceal a smudge of dried blood and prepared to push him one final time. In a matter of seconds, the golden doors of the elevator would open and he would commence his ascent to his grand destiny, the groundwork for which had been laid in the—

—hotel bar is largely empty this late at night. He sits in a booth near the back, little more than a shadow in the dim light. Valeria is seated across from him, her eyes restlessly roaming the room, searching for her prey. There is so much of her mother in her that it makes his heart ache, which only serves to fuel his anger and resentment for what could have been, and what he has to do now. What they both have to do.

The lone man at the bar raises a shot glass to his lips, his hand shaking so badly that the amber fluid dribbles down his chin when he tosses it back. He removes his ball cap and slicks the sweat from his comb-over into the fringe of hair, grown long in an effort to disguise his baldness. The cloying scent of fear radiates from him, although Zmei does not fault him for it. He recognizes the man from the barn earlier in the afternoon and remembers how he felt the first time he watched a man being butchered with a chain saw. That he had done it himself made it no less traumatic.

Valeria tenses and he follows her stare to the entrance. A godlike man with chiseled features, tanned skin, and hair spun from the purest gold strides straight past the distracted hostess and toward the man at the bar. Zmei rests his hand on his daughter's forearm when she starts to slide from the booth.

"Patience," he says, and she settles into the seat once more.

The man known as Tertius climbs onto the stool beside the man wearing the ball cap and speaks in a voice too soft to hear over the music. He produces a cell phone and proceeds to show the nervous man a series of pictures, which causes the color to drain from his face. The bartender pours a drink for the new arrival, but the other man waves him away with a hand trembling so badly that it appears palsied.

"Do you have the collection device ready?" Zmei asks. "We will only get one shot at this."

Valeria nods, the trepidation in her eyes replaced by a predatory hunger. She knows what she must do.

Tertius throws his arm over the shoulder of the other man, who shrinks beneath its weight. Zmei can almost make out the threats passing from the blond man's lips, for he has heard them himself and remembers them clearly. He looks forward to turning them around when the time is right.

He'd seen the way Tertius looked at his daughter when he entered the Mexican lab, watched his eyes rove over her body and the hunger rise within him. The blond man had wanted to demonstrate his prowess, to remind them who was in charge, which was why he had insisted that Zmei and Valeria join him on the other side of the tunnel, where he had set to work upon the Russians, who had been bound and gagged when they arrived. The image of the blond man, stripped to the waist, drenched in blood, and holding the severed head of his competitor was scored into the undersides of Zmei's eyelids. Along with the memory of the psychopath cornering Valeria, his slacks straining with need.

Zmei's first thought had been of what he would do to this man, but he had forced down his rage when the plan had taken root, a plan that would guarantee his daughter's safety after he was gone. He had driven straight to the nearest fertility clinic and sent in his daughter with a story about wanting to store some of her fictional husband's sperm in case they wanted to change their minds about *having children after his vasectomy. She'd come out an hour later with the collection device, which looked like an ordinary condom, and a signed contract for cryogenic storage.*

And now here they sit, waiting for the opportunity they know will soon come.

Tertius withdraws his arm and the balding man practically falls from his stool in his hurry to depart. He does not so much as look back as he exits the bar, leaving Tertius to drink with a contented smile on his face.

Zmei lifts his hand from his daughter's arm and leans back in his seat.

Valeria slides from the booth, adjusts her tiny black cocktail dress, and slinks up behind Tertius. She traces her fingertips up his arm and across his broad shoulders. He watches her reflection in the mirror behind the bar, a smug smile forming on his lips. She leans in close and whispers into his ear.

Tertius stands without a word, wraps his arm around her waist, and ushers her not upstairs as Zmei had expected, but rather into the narrow hallway leading to the restrooms. She is the help, after all. Inferior, unthreatening. A mere tissue to be used once and thrown away. He spins her around and forces her up against the wall, pressing his mouth to hers and sliding his hand underneath her dress. The collection device appears in her hand. She tears off the wrapper and reaches for him—

Zmei looks away before his temper boils over and he ends up hating himself even more than he does now.

The bartender appears at his table, a cordless phone in one hand, the mouthpiece covered with the other.

"Phone's for you," he says.

"Who is it?" Zmei asks. No one knows who he is, let alone that he is here.

"I don't know. All he said was he wanted to talk to the man in the back booth."

Zmei hesitantly accepts the phone and listens to the silence for several seconds before speaking.

"Who is this?"

"Who I am matters less than what I can do for you," the caller says. His voice sounds like any other, although power radiates from

his words. "I know what your daughter is doing and why. I can offer something far more valuable than her safety after you have . . . moved on."

"What is more important than that?"

"The child's inheritance and standing when its father is no more."

Zmei smiles and glances into the rear hallway as the man who believes himself to be a modern Adonis slams his daughter through the swinging door and into the restroom.

"I would appreciate that very much," he says. "What will it cost me?"

"Your revenge upon the country that sacrificed you will have to wait, at least for now, but rest assured that when the time comes—and I give you my word that it will—the fate you had in store for Moscow will pale in comparison to the nightmare I have planned for the whole country. For the entire world. The deaths I promise will make those inflicted by your devices seem merciful."

Zmei smiles at the thought, knowing the kind of suffering he has wrought. As long as his daughter remains alive, she will hold this man to his end of the bargain, or else she will execute the sentence he has imposed. He will see to that before he is gone.

"Say that I find your terms acceptable . . . what do you require of me?"

"You were working for Tertius," the caller says. "Now you're working for me."

"And who are you?"

"Call me Tertius Decimus and tell me about Konets Mira. More specifically, I want to know about something that you said long ago you could build. . . ."

Voices erupted from the opposite side of the elevator, where the tourists returning from the observation deck disembarked. Seconds later, the front doors opened and a National Parks ranger ushered the next group into the elevator. Sister had made their reservation a year prior, and even then it had taken plenty of sweet-talking to make sure they received the time slot they desired. He wanted the fireworks display to be just about to start, when he knew the mall would be as crowded as it was going to get. All eyes would be raised to the sky, only instead of a colorful pyrotechnic display, they would see the fiery breath of death preparing to wash over them.

Sister inched his wheelchair around the corner. He tried to count how many people were ahead of them to figure out if they would be on the next trip to the observation deck or the one after that. Not that it really mattered. He had waited a lifetime for this moment; he could wait a few minutes longer. Besides, he thrilled in the anticipation.

Zmei returned his attention to the video screen.

And his visions of what was to come.

PART 6

Well, first of all, the Federal Reserve is an independent agency, and that means, basically, that there is no other agency of government which can overrule actions that we take. So long as that is in place and there is no evidence that the administration or the Congress or anybody else is requesting that we do things other than what we think is the appropriate thing, then what the relationships are don't frankly matter.

—*Alan Greenspan, thirteenth chairman of the Federal Reserve,*
The NewsHour with Jim Lehrer *(September 18, 2007)*

58

"Start evacuating everyone from this area the moment that wheelchair's on the elevator," Mason said. "Do it as quickly and quietly as possible. And see what you can do about slowing down its ascent. Stop it only if you absolutely have to, but give me time to get past them on the stairs."

"What's going on?" the officer asked.

"There's no time to explain. Just do as I say."

Layne appeared from behind the bench to Mason's right. Her face was flushed, her forehead beaded with sweat. He didn't have time to wait.

"Show me where the stairs are," Mason said.

The officer led him through the security office and into a marble corridor crowded with people waiting to board the elevator. The last of a full load disembarked on the other side of the velvet rope before the golden doors closed upon a man wearing the gray uniform shirt and green slacks of a park ranger. He turned to face the doors on the opposite side of the car, where a new group prepared to board. The line snaked around the side of the elevator, where people lounged on benches and viewed ornate displays while they awaited their turn. He caught a glimpse of a woman in a flowing black habit rounding the far corner. If she didn't make it onto this load, she'd definitely be on the next.

"This way," the officer said, lifting the rope.

They passed beneath a frieze of George Washington in profile and entered a shallow recess to the right of the elevator, where the officer badged the sensor with a chipped card. Mason brushed past him, threw open the door, and started upward.

"Buy me as much time as you can!" he shouted.

The dim overhead bulbs cast a brassy glare onto marble steps lined with traction strips and bare stone walls that were polished and smooth in places, rugged and uneven in others. He gripped the railing and pulled himself around a tight spiral encircling the ductwork, which ran straight up the stairwell like a pillar. Willed himself through the fatigue, forcing his already sore legs to carry him higher, two steps at a time. Rounded landing after landing until the spiral opened to accommodate the elevator shaft, sunken straight down the middle of the obelisk. The car rumbled past on the other side of a wrought-iron divider that resembled a cage at the zoo. Gears clanking, motor whining, it rose into the darkness.

If the Dragon was on it, then they'd already lost.

The steps widened as Mason ascended. Walls stained with rust and scarred by the patches used to repair the damage from an earthquake blurred past. His footsteps echoed from the vast space, the acoustics of which amplified his harsh breathing. He could hear Layne coming up fast behind him. His head was already beginning to swim with the diminished oxygen flow and rapid increase in altitude. It felt as though a fire burned in his chest.

Gunnar started to say something, but his voice degenerated into static.

The observation deck was five hundred feet above the ground, near the top of the monument, which at one point in time had been the tallest structure in the entire world. Detonating the device up there would increase the spread of the fallout exponentially.

Mason tried not to think about anything beyond the next landing, clearing his mind of fear and doubt, ignoring the soreness and pain.

A thudding sound echoed from the bottom. Someone else had entered the stairwell and slammed the door behind him. Ramses, he assumed. The shaft suddenly fell silent as the elevator reached its destination at the top.

Mason pushed himself harder than he ever had in his life, his legs firing like pistons, driving him right up to the brink of his breaking point.

With a grumbling sound that sent faint vibrations throughout the structure, the elevator commenced its descent. Two flights later it blew past him, streaking straight toward the bottom, where he could only assume the Dragon waited. If he'd been on the last load, they'd have been dead already.

The stairs became wider and wider still, the inset stones larger and more precisely cut. Elaborate friezes and inscriptions passed in his peripheral vision, testimonials to the ideals upon which the nation had been built, memorializing history that might soon be lost forever.

A grinding sound preceded the arrival of the elevator at the bottom. The echo of their footsteps sounded increasingly labored in the resulting silence. He imagined the nun pushing the Dragon into the elevator and squeezing up against his wheelchair to make room for passengers who had absolutely no idea what the murderers in their midst intended to do when they reached the top.

Mason heard the grinding of gears, the rattling of chains, and the hum of the motor. He didn't need to look over the edge to know that the elevator was coming. The floor positively thrummed with its ascent.

Higher and higher he climbed, knowing full well the consequences of failure.

The racket increased in volume with every landing he rounded until he could sense the elevator mere floors below him. It abruptly stopped and light flooded the shaft so that those inside could view the decorative friezes surrounding them, buying Mason the critical seconds he needed.

The stairwell wended away from the shaft and once more the spiral tightened around the air duct. He heard voices, saw the movement of shadows. A heartbeat later he rounded the final bend and stepped onto the observation deck, underneath the aluminum pyramidion, where people were packed shoulder to shoulder in an effort to view the city far below them through the inset windows.

". . . on the elevator right now!" Gunnar shouted into his ear. The stairwell must have been blocking his transmission. "They'll be at the top at any second!"

Mason tapped his acknowledgment and fought through the throng of tourists until he found the National Parks ranger stationed outside the elevator. He held up his badge and struggled to draw enough breath to speak.

"Get . . . get these people . . . out of here." The ranger opened his mouth to protest, but Mason cut him off. "Take the stairs. We're already . . . out of time."

The floor shuddered with the impending arrival of the elevator. He approached the doors, his back to the window overlooking the ocean of humanity covering the endless lawn leading to the distant Capitol Building. If the Dragon decided to detonate his weapon inside of the elevator, there was nothing he could do to stop him.

Mason pressed his back against the wall, directly beside the door. Tried desperately to slow his breathing and steady his legs.

Layne battled through the herd descending the stairs and looked in both directions before she finally saw him. She staggered toward the elevator and assumed position on the other side of the door from him.

"How much . . . how much time . . . ?" she panted.

The wall behind them vibrated in answer to her question. On the other side, the elevator slowed and settled to their level. Any sound they might have been able to hear from inside the car was drowned out by the clamor of footsteps and panicked voices coming from the stairwell.

Mason drew his Glock, took a firm two-handed grip, and squeezed the trigger into the sweet spot, where the slightest application of pressure would cause the firing pin to strike.

"Good luck," Gunnar whispered.

A ding announced the elevator's arrival.

Time slowed to a crawl.

The doors opened, spilling light alive with shadowed movement onto the floor between them. There was no way of knowing how many people were inside. Innocents potentially standing between them and their targets, men and women whose lives were about to change forever.

". . . and enjoy the view," the guide said from inside the elevator.

Tourists flooded out of the elevator, focused solely on the breathtaking view straight ahead of them, oblivious to the armed agents standing to either side of them. The herd continued filing past until Mason saw a drab olive blanket covering the legs of a man in a wheelchair, who passed so close to him that he could positively smell the sickness radiating from him. He saw the burned texture of the skin behind the man's ear and along the slope of his neck before the woman's black form concealed him from view.

This was the point of no return.

Mason nodded to Layne, who stepped away from the wall, grabbed the sister around the neck, and pressed the barrel of her pistol against the woman's temple hard enough to make her release the handles of the wheelchair. Mason assumed her place and aimed his weapon squarely at the back of the man's head.

"Show me your hands!" he shouted.

"*Ne delay etogo,*" the woman said through bared teeth.

"She told him not to do it," Gunnar said.

The man slowly raised his hands from the armrests. They trembled so badly that he hardly seemed capable of controlling their movements. He obviously wouldn't be able to hold them there for very long.

Without altering his aim, Mason used a single handle to spin the chair around.

There, looking up at him through watery, bloodshot eyes, was the man responsible for the murder of Border Patrol Agent Ryan Austin and countless deaths in the Middle East on the orders of the Thirteen.

The man who intended to kill them all.

The Dragon.

59

"Keep your hands where I can see them!" Layne shouted. She tightened her grip around the nun's neck until she complied, her dainty hands protruding from wide sleeves that somehow remained in place and didn't slide down her forearms. A line of dried blood traced the contours of her left wrist to the base of her thumb. Her skin was pale, nearly to the point of translucence. It appeared almost blue in places, where the superficial blood vessels showed through. Her eyes were black, like jagged chunks of coal stomped into snow. "You even think about moving and I'll put you down."

Screams erupted all around them as the men and women who'd been on the elevator saw the weapons in their midst.

"Get them out of here!" Mason shouted.

The Parks Service ranger from the elevator couldn't have been out of his early twenties, but he didn't panic. He'd obviously been trained for this scenario. He held up his hands in the least threatening manner and spoke in a level tone.

"Everyone remain calm. I'm going to ask that you all follow me to the stairs."

"I am an old man," the Dragon said in a thick Russian accent. "You do not need those weapons."

Mason grabbed the blankets from his legs and threw them to the floor. The lower legs of a mannequin had been fitted with slippers and duct-taped to the leg rests. Where his thighs would have been was a lead case, approximately the size of a briefcase, only twice as thick, and scuffed from rough handling. The man himself was wedged behind it. A gangrenous stench emanated from the blood-soaked bandages covering his abrupt stumps. He wore a heavy sweater that bunched around the tape that had been used to bind his waist and torso to the back of the chair.

"I am not who you think I am," the man said. "I am a poor cripple inflicted with a rare form of cancer—"

"You were born Yevgeny Meier," Mason said. "You assumed your cousin Zakar's identity so people wouldn't immediately make the connection to Chernobyl. You became Z-Mei . . . *Zmei* . . . The Dragon."

The man removed his surgical mask and smiled. It was one of the most hideous expressions Mason had ever seen. His lips were thin and blistered, his gums gray and receded, and his teeth long and yellowed. The pallor of his face was shocking. It made the strandlike scarring look like peeled string cheese. And yet his eyes . . . there was a fathomless darkness within them, sheer malevolence given physical form, dark holes that offered a glimpse into the hell that awaited them all. This was no mere man; he was something else, an abomination the likes of which Mason hadn't seen since watching the Hoyl rise into the darkness, clawing bloody gashes into his own neck in an effort to remove the chain wrapped around it.

"Then let us set aside all pretense," the Dragon said in an entirely different voice. "You, and everyone within a two-mile radius, will die today. Hundreds of thousands more will be exposed to levels of radiation that will kill them slowly over the next few days. Everyone within twenty miles will breathe it from the air and absorb it into their lungs. Their deaths will be so painful they will wish they had been closer to ground zero. Many will take their own lives, just to end the suffering. Millions more will think they escaped unscathed, only to develop cancers and experience the latent effects of chronic radiation poisoning, as I have. They will give birth to deformed children and pass along mutations that poison the gene pool. And, most important, they will be made to pay for the crimes they committed against my people, against Mother Russia—"

"I thought we were setting aside all pretense," Mason said.

"That *Mother Russia* crap is nonsense," Layne said. "We know exactly why you're doing this. You're trying to start a war between our two countries, one you hope will destroy the better part of the world. We're not about to let that happen."

"My dear, how do you propose stopping me?" the Dragon said.

"You couldn't stop me from taking that case from you in your condition."

"How do you know it is not attached to a pressure plate that will cause it to detonate the moment you try to lift it?"

"Because this is the culmination of your life's work," Mason said. "Everything you've done has led you to this moment in time. You want the satisfaction of triggering the detonator yourself."

"So where is it?" Layne asked. She forced the woman's head even farther to the side. "Tell me now, or so help me, I'll—"

"You will do what?" the Dragon sneered. "You are an officer of the law. For as much as I imagine you would enjoy killing her, you will do no such thing. In Russia, our operatives are trained to set aside their scruples, their very humanity, in order to do what must be done. Here, you are soft, concerned more with public perception and your careers, you worry you will never be able to cleanse the stain from your souls."

Mason detected movement from the corner of his eye. A silhouette rising from the top of the staircase. Here one second, gone the next.

"*Pozvol' mne sdelat' eto,*" the woman said.

"She's telling him to let her do it," Gunnar said.

"*Nyet,*" the Dragon said, lowering his hands to the armrests.

"Raise them!" Mason shouted.

"I lack the strength to do so, I am afraid. It is all I can do to hold up my head under my own power. I want to be able to look into your eyes at the end. And I want you to look into mine. I want to witness the moment you realize that everyone you love is about to die and there is nothing you can do to stop it."

"What about Valeria?" Mason said.

The Dragon bared his teeth and sunk his claws into the padding of the armrests.

"Do not speak her name," he said.

"We have a bead on her. Our team picked her up via satellite switching cars near Round Valley Reservoir. We know exactly where she's going and have units in place to intercept her when she arrives. Are you prepared to let her die here with the rest of us?"

That awful grimace metamorphosed into a smug smile.

"Did you hear those helicopters a few minutes ago?" the Dragon asked. "They tell me that you are lying. You do not know where she is, let alone where she is going."

"You think the Thirteen will protect her? Do you honestly believe they care whether she lives or dies? They'd just as soon watch her burn with the rest of us."

"She is the Dragon now. The living embodiment of wrath and redemption. She will hold a place of prominence in the new world that rises from the rubble of this one. It will be from her womb that a new, enlightened incarnation of mankind is born. One free from the violence and suffering we insist on inflicting upon one another, one devoted to bringing about the next phase in the evolution of our species, the ascendency of the chosen few to a modern pantheon of gods."

"You've bought into the same nonsense as the rest of them. You're no better than anyone else. The willingness to slaughter millions doesn't make you a god; it makes you a monster."

"You would rather we kill each other over uninhabitable deserts where nothing can grow, that we bring billions more uneducated and impoverished children into the world to fight over limited resources, that we continue to poison the planet until no one can survive?"

Mason heard a scuffing sound from somewhere behind him, on the other side of the elevator.

"Keep him talking," Ramses whispered.

"They're manipulating you," Mason said. "One more useful idiot who believes he's important enough to the cause to dictate the terms of his involvement. The Thirteen won't even mourn you. And your daughter? They'll smile thinking about what she meant to you while they slit her throat."

"I have made sure she is taken care of."

"And you take them at their word? These men who would destroy both of our countries so they can protect the petrodollar and control the flow of natural gas into Europe? This so-called ascendency has nothing to do with your ideas about forming the foundation of an enlightened society. For them, it's all about cornering the world's resources and amassing all of the power for themselves. They already believe they're gods. In their minds, the ascendency is already complete."

"The Thirteen is an antiquated idea predicated upon the belief that a council can achieve what a single individual cannot," the Dragon said. "It has always been destined to come down to one, as Slate Langbroek learned. And as the others will, too, soon enough. A war the likes of which this world has never seen is coming, and you can either live on the side of the wolves or die with the sheep."

Mason visualized tightening the muscles in his trigger finger, the kick of expelled gases, the wet *thuck* of the bullet punching a hole through the madman's face, right between his eyes.

The Dragon wagged a gnarled finger at him.

"I see that look in your eye, Special Agent Mason. You want me dead so badly it consumes you, but you still do not know how I intend to detonate this device. Do you see a remote panel? Have I rigged it to a timer? Am I content to spend my last moments on this earth talking to you?"

"How do you know who I am?"

"Everyone knows your father," the Dragon said. "You look like him, you know. Speaking of the good senator, I trust they evacuated him in the first wave instead of leaving him to die with all of the lesser bureaucrats."

"What do you know about it?"

"My dear boy, you can learn all about the continuity-of-operations plan on the Internet. You Americans want so much to demonstrate your greatness to the world that you post all of your secrets online."

"*Pozhaluysta, Zmei,*" the woman said. "*Pozvol'te mne sdelat' eto, poka ne stalo slishkom pozdno.*"

"She's begging him to let her do it before it's too late," Gunnar said.

"I can take her," Ramses whispered.

Mason sensed more than heard his old friend easing along the side of the elevator toward him.

"Not yet," he said.

"Maybe you are right," the Dragon said. "Perhaps you have not yet revealed all of your secrets, but I can tell you that your president will be transported to a nuclear bunker in NORAD on board the National Airborne Command Center. The chiefs of staff and critical members of the various defense agencies will be taken to Raven Rock, where an underground version of the Pentagon has already been built. Four members of your congress will join them, while another four will be taken to Mount Weather. Between them, they will be empowered with the full weight of both houses, giving them the power to approve a retaliatory strike against their perceived aggressor, which, in turn, will reciprocate and start an escalation that will culminate in our mutually assured destruction."

"That's where your plan falls apart," Mason said. "You can't count on eight congressmen to agree on anything. Cooler heads will ultimately prevail."

"We don't need all eight," the Dragon said.

Again, he offered that horrible smile.

Mason suddenly understood everything.

He knew exactly where Valeria was going.

60

Mason studied the Dragon, from his false legs all the way up to his strapped torso and his hideous face. There was nowhere to hide the detonator on his person, at least not anywhere he could have reached it. No pockets, no odd bulges. He scrutinized the wheelchair itself, from the spokes of the gray wheels to the vinyl-padded armrests to the rubber grips of the handles. Nothing. He needed to be sure he was right about where the detonator was. If he guessed wrong, they were all dead.

He recalled the words of the Dragon: *You are an officer of the law. For as much as I imagine you would enjoy killing her, you will do no such thing.* And those of the woman, who'd spoken them in a language none of them would have understood had Gunnar not been with them remotely to translate: *She's begging him to let her do it before it's too late.* And he thought about the sleeves that didn't fall when she raised her hands, the dribble of dried blood on her wrist.

The Dragon had gambled that they wouldn't kill the nun, that even if someone recognized him and put a bullet through his head, she'd still be able to complete his life's work. Had there been no one waiting for them here when they arrived, he would have been able to do so for himself. All she would have had to do was hand him the detonator.

Mason picked up Ramses in his peripheral vision, a platinum-plated SIG P226 9mm semiautomatic pistol in his grip.

"Tell her to give us the detonator," Mason said.

The Dragon smiled that awful smile.

"You think you are so clever, but you do not understand anything. If you did, not only would you be as far away from here as possible, you would get down on your knees and thank me for what I am about to do."

"The detonator," Mason said. "Either she hands it over or I'll kill her myself."

Mason pivoted and aimed his Glock at the woman's face without taking his eyes off the Dragon.

"Do what you must. The bomb will go off regardless."

"You're bluffing."

"Am I?"

As if it were possible, his smile grew even wider, stretching the corners of his mouth nearly to his ears, like a crocodile.

"He's stalling," Gunnar said.

He was right and Mason knew it. The Dragon was buying time for Valeria to get into position.

Mason glanced over his opposite shoulder and made eye contact with Ramses, who'd ducked across the hallway and leaned against an interior wall where the Dragon couldn't see him. He hoped to God his old friend was prepared for what was about to happen.

"I guess we'll find out," Mason said.

He aimed squarely between the woman's eyes, the barrel a mere foot from the bridge of her nose, and tightened his finger on the trigger.

"*Proschay, moy drug,*" she said, closing her eyes. A sense of calmness settled over her. "*Uvidimsya na drugoy storone.*"

"She told him good-bye," Gunnar said. "That she'll see him on the other side."

When Mason faced the Dragon again, the monster's eyes were alight with what could have only been triumph.

"Since she has the detonator," Mason said, "I have no use for you."

He swung around his pistol and pulled the trigger. Blood exploded from the back of the wheelchair and spattered the panoramic window a split second after the bullet struck it, sending cracks racing through the glass. The wheelchair seemed to topple in slow motion as the Dragon grabbed for the wound in his shoulder, an expression of utter surprise on his face.

The report was deafening in such close confines and rolled through the structure like thunder.

The woman screamed and broke free from Layne's grasp. She pulled back her sleeve to reveal a homemade detonator that looked like a miniature effects pedal for an electric guitar. It had been sewn directly into the skin on the underside of her forearm with thick black thread, in a place where if she'd fallen it would have impacted the floor. She grabbed it with her other hand, tore the sutures straight out of her flesh, and raised it—

Mason brought his weapon around, but Ramses already had her in his sights.

A clap of thunder and her wrist shattered in a violent expulsion of blood and bone that nearly severed her hand, causing her to drop the detonator.

Mason dove and caught it before it could hit the floor. Slid his fingers underneath the pressure plate to prevent it from striking the contacts and triggering the bomb.

The woman shrieked and fell upon him from behind, tearing at his hair and clawing at his face with her lone functional hand. Layne struggled to pry her from on top of him, wrenching her torso into the air. He rolled out from underneath her as she turned her fury upon Layne, staggering her and knocking her to the ground.

Layne managed to raise her forearm in time to brace the chest of the woman, who continued to screech and slash at her, inflicting lacerations from her fingernails and the jagged tips of bone from her ruined wrist.

Ramses wrapped his arms around the nun's chest and lifted her just high enough that she couldn't reach Layne's face, so the woman went for her gun instead.

Mason crawled toward the wheelchair. It lay toppled on its side, the seatback torn from the frame, the case decorated with blood and resting several feet away.

The Dragon was nowhere in sight.

A roar of gunfire behind him and Mason turned to see the woman's face contorted with pain. Blood poured from her chest onto Layne's hands and the smoldering pistol clasped between them. Tatters of fabric hung from the exit wound on the nun's flank, right in front of Ramses, judging by the expression of surprise on his face as he released her and stepped backward, his jacket spattered.

Layne shoved the nun from on top of her and struggled to her knees. Pinned her sights on the sister, who sputtered blood and clutched at the entrance wound through the front of her habit. Her eyes widened in terror as she realized she was going to die.

"Where's the Dragon?" Mason shouted. He turned nearly in a full circle before spotting the trail of smeared blood leading across the floor and around the far side of the elevator. "I've got him!"

Mason raised his Glock and advanced in a shooter's stance, watching the bloody path from the lower edge of his peripheral vision. The stairs came into view as he rounded the elevator. The Dragon had managed to drag himself all the way to them and climb up onto the railing, where he rested, folded in half over it, the vinyl back of the chair still taped to his torso. He gripped the rail with his good hand, his injured arm dangling uselessly over the stairwell.

"Don't even think about it," Mason said.

The Dragon bared teeth pink with diluted blood. His lips and gums were scarlet.

"You have already lost," he said. "There is nothing you can do to stop what is about to happen."

Mason crept slowly toward him. No sudden movements. He needed to reach the Dragon before the monster could transfer his weight over the edge.

"I know where Valeria's going. I can protect her, but only if she doesn't go through with it."

"I have already ensured her safety."

"The Thirteen will discard her when they no longer have a use for her. I understand how they work—"

"You do not understand anything." The Dragon glanced down and then back at Mason. "And you never will."

He rolled forward and toppled over the edge.

Mason lunged for him, but his fingers passed through the empty air behind the bandaged stumps. He grabbed the railing and leaned over in time to see the Dragon's shoulder rebound from the ductwork, sending him cartwheeling toward the stairs several stories down. He landed on his head with a resounding crack. His body tumbled down the steps, leaving behind a crimson trail.

And then he was gone, taking everything he knew about the Thirteen with him.

61

There was no time to waste.

Mason ran back to the toppled wheelchair and grabbed the case, which was far heavier than he'd expected. The awesome power contained within it was staggering. In his hands was a weapon capable of turning the National Mall into a crater and wiping out the population of D.C. in the process. And then he remembered the inherent instability caused by the plutonium-240 and realized how little he wanted to hold it.

He rushed to the elevator and pressed the button. Hit Archer's number on speed dial. He needed to warn the secretary of the DHS that Valeria was on her way to Raven Rock and intended to take out the evacuation choppers when they arrived, but the call rang straight through to voice mail.

The doors were already sliding open by the time Ramses helped Layne to her feet. He practically had to drag her inside as she wiped the blood from her face with the back of her hand.

"What do you say we leave the case?" Ramses said. "I'm thinking the more distance we can put between us and the bomb inside, the happier we'll all be. Besides, I don't think either of those guys is in any condition to use it."

"It's a nuclear weapon. We can't just leave it here. Someone has to make sure it doesn't fall into the wrong hands."

"And just whose hands are the right ones?"

The doors closed and the elevator started its descent, granite walls blurring past through the inset windows. He tried Chris's number, but the call didn't even start to ring.

"Gunnar?" Mason said. "Can you hear me?"

There was no response from his old friend, either. The cellular signal must not have been able to penetrate the solid stone structure and the elevator at the same time.

Layne appraised a particularly nasty gash along her cheekbone in the reflection from a stainless-steel panel.

"How could you be certain the nun had the detonator?" she asked. "I get how what Gunnar said would lead you to believe so, but if his translation was wrong . . ."

"Her sleeves didn't slide down when she raised her hands, which meant she'd deliberately done something to hold them in place. The moment I saw the dried blood on her wrist, I knew exactly what they'd used the surgical needles and thread they'd left on the tray in the main room of that house for."

"That's one hell of an assumption," Layne said. "She could have been using them to stitch his amputation wounds."

"That's what the blowtorch was for."

"It was a dangerous risk to take. Had she so much as lowered her arm to her side, she could have killed us all."

"But, thanks to you, she didn't," Mason said.

Layne turned away from her reflection and looked at him with an unreadable expression on her face.

"It bothers me that he knew I wouldn't shoot her," she said. "And he used that knowledge against us."

"Had you, she'd have fallen on the detonator and we'd all be dead, so don't let it get to you."

The elevator slowed as it neared the bottom. Mason knew they were being watched through the interior surveillance cameras. The security forces could have easily killed the power to the elevator and trapped them on the uppermost floor. They'd undoubtedly already had time to activate their counterterrorism measures, which meant that the entire site had already been locked down. They would likely send one tactical team up the stairwell to evacuate the civilians and secure the observation deck, position another at various points along the stairwell should anyone on the elevator attempt to climb out while it was moving, and have a third waiting for them inside the main corridor.

"Ramses," Mason said. "Get behind me."

He set down the case and flipped open his badge jacket, knowing exactly what to expect the moment the doors opened. Layne followed suit, and just in time to face down a hallway packed with officers in full tactical gear, their M4s seated against their shoulders and aimed into the elevator.

"Federal agents!" Mason shouted. He held up his Glock sideways so they could clearly see his finger was nowhere near the trigger.

The officers swarmed them and bodily manhandled them out of the elevator and into the hallway.

"Be careful with that case!" Layne shouted.

"Talk to me, Mason," Gunnar said through the transceiver. "What's happening in there?"

"Get Archer on the phone," Mason said. "I don't care how. Tell him to reroute the evacuation choppers. We can't let them land at—"

"Down on the ground!" an officer shouted. "Hands behind your head!"

Impact to the backs of his legs and his knees buckled. He went down hard with the weight of two officers on his back. He could barely turn his head far enough to see Layne pinned to the floor beside him.

"I doubt you'll be talking to Archer anytime soon," Gunnar said.

Judging by the tone of his old friend's voice, Mason already knew the reason, but he had to ask the question anyway.

"Why?"

"There are reports of an explosion at a military installation in Pennsylvania, just on the other side of the state line from Camp David."

Mason closed his eyes and felt the world tilt underneath him. He heard the voices of the officers shouting at him from every direction at once, but he couldn't make out their words. A sensation of numbness passed through him even as his arms were wrenched behind his back.

"My dad . . . ?" he managed to whisper.

"I don't have any of the details," Gunnar said, "but I'll let you know the moment—"

The transceiver was torn from his ear, taking the microphone right along with it.

Mason shouted in frustration, which only served to cause the officer kneeling on his lower back to grind his face into the floor.

He closed his eyes and saw not his father's face, but rather that of the Dragon with his wretched, cadaverous smile as he toppled over the edge of the railing.

Despite everything they'd done . . . all of the lives they'd saved . . .

The Dragon had still outmaneuvered him.

62

The Sikorsky UH-60 Black Hawk streaked low over the treetops toward the Raven Rock Mountain Complex, known internally as Site R. Sparsely populated rural acreages boasting vast grazing lands and seamless rows of crops passed below them in the darkness.

Mason and Layne sat in the outer two seats in the back of the chopper so they could see out the windows. The contingent from the National Counterterrorism Center sat in the chairs lining the walls. They represented a multiagency task force comprised of CT specialists from every branch of the federal government—from the CIA and the FBI to the DOD and the NSA—assembled under the auspices of the Office of the Director of National Intelligence. While they were undoubtedly the most qualified to determine exactly what had happened and spearhead the resulting investigation, they knew next to nothing about the events leading up to the catastrophe, which was why the Black Hawk from the 12th Aviation Battalion had been ordered at the last second to land at the National Mall and pick up Mason and Layne, who'd gotten the team up to speed as quickly as possible.

Despite their physical proximity, they had to wear headphones and speak into the attached microphones to hear one another.

"You're certain we're dealing with a single individual?" Special Agent Amanda Wylie said. Mason had met her at Quantico, where she frequently lectured on counterterrorism methodology. Her hair was buzzed short on the sides and stood up in a peaked faux hawk down the middle. Like the rest of her colleagues, she wore combat boots, navy blue cargo pants, and an NCTC windbreaker over a bulletproof vest. "I find it hard to believe that a lone operative could pull off something like this. . . ."

She crossed the narrow aisle, took a seat between them, and held up her tablet so they could both see the screen, at the center of which was a blue helicopter with a horizontal yellow stripe and the words UNITED STATES OF AMERICA stenciled on the tail, just like Mason had seen earlier. A phalanx of armored vehicles and armed soldiers surrounded it.

Wylie tapped the screen and the footage started to roll.

A pair of men in camouflage fatigues and helmets ducked against the ferocious wind from the rotors and rushed to open the door. A balding man in a suit spilled out before they arrived. He hit the concrete and didn't even try to move. Another man attempted to crawl out of the chopper, his face a mask of blood. One of the soldiers reached for him, but suddenly recoiled, clapped his hands over his mouth, and fell to his knees. His partner rushed forward, shouting and waving his arms.

Without warning, the pilot lifted off, lurching straight up into the second helicopter, which had only begun to descend into the picture. The blades cut straight through the landing gear, and then the fuselage—

A blinding flash, an expulsion of flames, and the entire screen went out of focus as the aperture attempted to rationalize the sudden influx of light. By the time the view stabilized, all they could see through the billowing black smoke was a tangle of metal from which golden flames burned.

"She was alone when we last saw her near Round Valley Reservoir in western New Jersey about eight hours ago," Mason said.

"That's about a three-and-a-half-hour drive from Raven Rock," the woman across the aisle said. The ID badge on her lanyard identified her as K. TOMALTY. She had dark skin and eyes and wore her hair braided tightly against the back of her skull. "It could have easily taken her twice that long if she anticipated our checkpoints and managed to navigate the back roads."

"Regardless of how she got there, we should have seen her on the footage," the man sitting beside her said. He had a ruddy complexion, flat gray eyes, and a badge that read: C. SHARPE. "That base is under twenty-four-hour satellite surveillance and there are outward-facing cameras all along the perimeter. It's impossible to get inside that place without being seen."

"Go through it all again," Wylie said. "There has to be something we're missing."

"Watch for the greenish blue flash of the plasma laser striking the hafnium plate," Mason said.

Sharpe and Tomalty buried their faces in their laptops and set to work. The man seated across from them and closest to the barrier separating them from the cockpit appeared oblivious to the fact that the rest of them were even on the helicopter with him as he simultaneously networked via remote headset, cell phone, and laptop with any number of command centers. Mason didn't have to see the badge hanging around his neck to know he was CIA.

"How in God's name was she even able to get within range of those choppers?" Layne asked.

"We're still trying to figure that out," Wylie said. "The site was commissioned in the fifties, at the height of the Cold War, as an alternate joint communications center in the event of a nuclear war and later served as home base for various signal commands. It wasn't until after nine/eleven that it was designated an emergency operations center, so it's still in the process of evolving, although obviously not fast enough to keep up with advances in weaponry."

"Without knowing the energy level of that plasma laser, we can't even begin to estimate that thing's range," Tomalty said.

"There's your flash," Sharpe said. He turned his laptop so they could see the satellite image. He'd zoomed in on a grove of trees roughly two hundred yards from the helipad. A faint green glow emanated from the canopy. "Maybe fifteen seconds before the chopper set down."

"What do we know about that location?" Mason asked.

"Those trees line the ridge that serves as the western boundary of the base. If you look closely, you can see the perimeter fence just inside of them."

"Can you track her movements after the flash?"

"I can't even see her. The forest is way too dense through there."

"Find her," Wylie said.

Smoke stained the sky ahead of them and clung to the forest ascending a rounded mountain off to the right. A rural road appeared below them, cutting through the pastureland. It almost looked like it might intersect with the distant base. The acreages passing below them diminished in size, the houses growing larger and closer together.

"Are all of these private residences?" Mason asked.

"As far as I know," Wylie said.

"They practically back right up to the base."

"Especially this one right here," Sharpe said. He'd zoomed out on the satellite map just far enough to reveal a house with an aluminum roof in the middle of a broad expanse of grass. "This place falls on a straight line with both the flash of light and the helipad. Hell, it can't be more than a quarter of a mile away."

"Have you gotten a visual on the woman yet?"

"Negative."

"Then take us to that house," Mason said. "But first, I want to get a good look at what we're dealing with."

"Yes, sir," the pilot said. The Black Hawk banked to the east, passed over the fringe of forest lining the perimeter of the base, and circled around the helipad at a distance of maybe a hundred yards. "The area's still hot, so this is as close as we can get."

The fire trucks that had quenched the blaze were parked across the roadway amid the gathering of emergency vehicles with their lights twirling impotently. There were armed soldiers everywhere. The concrete platform was surrounded by portable spotlights on tripods and strewn with metal and debris. Investigators in yellow CBRN suits picked their way through it, collecting evidence and documenting the site. The bodies of the victims—or at least what was left of them—had been covered with lead-lined blankets.

Mason still didn't know if his father was among them. He'd spoken only briefly with Archer—who'd been evacuated on the National Airborne Command Center with the president and the majority of his cabinet—after Gunnar had finally reached him and insisted that he tell the agents in charge of the chaos at the Washington Monument to stand down. While the secretary had access to the passenger manifests of the four helicopters, he claimed he wasn't at liberty to share that information for reasons of national security. Mason tried not to infer anything from Archer's tone of voice or read anything into his decision not to tell him if his father was still alive.

He was just grateful that the secretary had been able to arrange to have them picked up so quickly. The director of national intelligence had already dispatched his top CT team from McLean, Virginia, and the National Mall had been right on their way, so the diversion had only been a minor inconvenience for the pilots.

Ramses, on the other hand, was likely enduring a lengthy and unpleasant decontamination and a debriefing he might have preferred to a fire-hose enema, but just barely. Mason would never forget the image of his old friend shouting, "Get to the choppa!" in his best Schwarzenegger voice as he was being led away by federal agents.

"They were lucky they had their own dedicated fire department just up the street," Tomalty said. "Otherwise this whole area would still be burning."

The helicopter thundered over the road connecting the helipad to the twin entrances into the underground facility, little more than rectangular concrete squares in the hillside. Neither offered so much as a hint as to the nature of the bunker concealed within, not that the guards would have let anyone get close enough to the gates to see inside.

They rounded the far side of the wreckage and the adjacent field. Veered south and descended rapidly. Landed right in the front yard of a single-level white house with a carport large enough for two vehicles. A prefabricated outbuilding had been erected flush with the back of it, as though to convert it into a garage, with a door and walls to protect the vehicles from the elements. The backyard hadn't been quite large enough to accommodate it, so whoever installed it had been forced to carve into the hillside to make it fit. The steep ridge-line towering over it was crowned with a thicket so dense it looked like it would take a machete to hack through it. Valeria could have easily concealed her movements beneath the canopy up there. Unfortunately, whatever trail she'd left was already growing cold.

Mason slid open the side door, ducked his head, and jumped down. He was suddenly acutely aware of just how exposed he was without a CBRN suit. If the woman who'd become the Dragon was still here, he wouldn't know he was within her sights until his skin started to blister.

63

Mason crested the ridge and advanced into the forest in a shooter's stance, his mini Maglite aligned with his barrel. He used his left elbow to part the branches before him. A haze of smoke had become trapped beneath the canopy. It smelled of fuel and metal and wood, the reason for which quickly became apparent. A trail of scorched tree trunks guided him to the east, the black bark still smoldering where the gamma rays had passed through them. The thicket abruptly gave way to a clearing contained behind a fifteen-foot perimeter fence coiled with razor wire. He couldn't have been more than a thousand feet away from the reinforced concrete barrier shielding the helipad from view.

Valeria hadn't even been forced to break cover. She'd simply aimed through the forest at the sound of the rotors and hit the chopper with a deadly barrage of radiation. The poor souls inside had never known what hit them.

"Mason," Layne called from behind him. "You're going to want to see this."

He retraced his footsteps and followed the sound of her voice to where he found her crouching over a circular impression in the earth. The detritus in the middle was disturbed where Valeria appeared to have stood when she fired her weapon.

"Look at the edges," Layne said.

Mason knelt beside her to better see. She traced the contours of the depression with her fingertips, causing a small amount of dirt to cascade through a narrow crevice.

He glanced up at his partner, and then started sweeping the dirt away from the widening crack until he exposed the edges of the piece of wood underneath. It was one of the ends of a spool of cable, more than large enough to conceal the hole in the earth and the ladder leading down into the darkness.

"Son of a bitch," Layne said.

Mason speed-dialed Gunnar's number on his cell phone and let it ring through while he hailed Wylie on the remote transceiver she'd assigned him.

"We found a hatch up here," he said. "It has to lead back to that house."

"We're inside now," she said. "No one's been here in years. Everything's covered with dust. There are timers on all of the lights and the heater and fridge are still running. Someone's been paying the bills to make it look like the place has been occupied the whole time."

"There has to be a reason for it. Keep looking. We'll go down and see where this thing lets out."

Mason's phone rang. He holstered his transceiver and answered immediately.

"Gunnar?"

"It's about time, Mace. What in the name of God is happening out there? All air traffic is grounded and there are preliminary reports of a foiled terrorist attack in D.C., but there's no mention of the helicopter crash and everything having to do with Raven Rock is vanishing from the Net as fast as I can find it."

"Both choppers were downed," Mason said. "There were no survivors."

"Jesus. What about your—"

"I don't know anything at this point, but that's not why I called. I need you to find out everything you can about the house at Two-seventy Harbaugh Valley Road." Mason shone his light down onto the dirty rungs of the ladder, which descended well beyond the range of his beam. "Call me the moment you know. There's something I need to do in the meantime."

He terminated the call and turned to Layne.

"You sure know how to show a girl a good time," she said.

"Shall we then?"

"Age before beauty."

"You realize that if she's down there, the gamma rays will pass right through me and hit you anyway, right?"

He held the base of his flashlight between his teeth and descended into the cool earth. The ladder shook and wobbled. His back grazed the wooden cribbing. The construction reminded him of the tunnel the Dragon had used to smuggle his nuclear device across the border into Texas. There was something about the way their confrontation had played out that didn't sit right with him. Destroying D.C. would have been the Dragon's crowning achievement, the culmination of his life's work, and yet in the end, his only thoughts had been of his daughter.

I have made sure she is taken care of.

Even after he'd lost the detonator and been forced to accept defeat, and even with a gunshot wound to his shoulder and the prospect of hurling himself down the stairwell ahead, he'd clung to his insistence that nothing would happen to Valeria.

I have already ensured her safety.

He had to have known that air traffic would be grounded, whether he succeeded in detonating his weapon or not. There was no way she would have been able to leave the country. If a retaliatory strike against Russia had been ordered, she would have shared the same fate as the rest of them when the Russians launched their reprisals. The very last thing she would have been is safe.

Mason paused when he reached the bottom of the ladder, maybe thirty feet down. His thoughts were firing in every direction at once. He sensed that he was on the brink of a revelation—

"Starting a war would only make the situation in Syria worse," he whispered. "No one would be able to build their pipeline. That can't be the only motive."

He lowered himself to his hands and knees and aimed his light into a tunnel that led roughly due west. Cribbing made from weathered sections of two-by-fours braced the rocky earth at five-foot intervals. He tucked his pistol down the back of his pants, against his lower back, and started crawling.

Despite the nature and the magnitude of the threat, they were only dealing with a single terrorist cell, not state-sponsored actors. Had the Dragon been successful in his attack on the National Mall, the powers that be would have been forced to evaluate his motivations solely by the missive he'd sent to *The New York Times*. The two in combination might have been enough to sell the country on a war with Russia while tempers were still flaring, but without the detonation of the nuclear device and the imagery of dead bodies in the streets and America's most recognizable landmarks in ruins, there's no way they would launch a strike that could very well lead to their own destruction, at least not without careful evaluation of all of the facts. While the attack on the helicopters was a tragedy, it wasn't nearly enough on its own, especially if they were able to catch Valeria and expose her for what she truly was: a slip of a girl ostracized from Russian society for her upbringing in a cult that had threatened a similar act against the Kremlin.

Whoever pulled the Dragon's strings had surely considered the possibility that he might fail. The Thirteen were nothing if not meticulous. Any of its members would have implemented a contingency plan, one that would still accomplish his primary goal, even if it didn't eliminate a third of the world's population in the process.

Everything suddenly came into focus as Mason emerged from the tunnel into the garage behind the house on Harbaugh Valley Road.

"Valeria knew who was going to be on those choppers," he said. "This wasn't an attempt to derail the continuity-of-operations plan and further cripple the government. It was an assassination."

64

Mason stood and turned in a circle. The tunnel had been cut through the back of the corrugated aluminum building and right into the hillside. A small boring unit that looked like a hot water heater with cutting wheels on one end rested beside the outer doors, nearly buried underneath excavated dirt. Footprints led back and forth along the narrow trail between mounds. He pushed open the doors and stepped out onto the driveway. Between the roof of the carport, the garage, and the tunnel, Valeria would have been invisible to aerial surveillance during the attack, but she had to have left the house somehow, and surely the satellite had captured her doing so.

"Sharpe," he said into his transceiver. "Run through the satellite footage. Unless she's attempting to evade pursuit on foot, she had to have parked a getaway vehicle somewhere nearby."

"I'm on it," the counterterrorism specialist responded.

Mason was just about to enter the house through the side door when his cell phone rang. He recognized the number immediately.

"I could use some good news, Gunnar."

"That house and the twelve acres attached to it are owned by Liberty Trust," his old friend said. "As you already know, Liberty is the Pennsylvania-based sister company of National Realty Trust, the company that owned the Dragon's lair back in D.C. What might surprise you, however, is that Tectonic Energy has been buying up NRT stock for the past five years, during which time it has somewhat quietly acquired a controlling share of the company."

"To what hypothetical end?"

"Nothing nefarious, it appears, at least superficially," Gunnar said. "It's a hydrocarbon exploration company based out of Oklahoma, with drilling operations from Texas and Louisiana all the way north into Ohio and Pennsylvania. Between all of its natural gas operations, it produces more than half a million barrels of oil equivalent per day. From a macroscopic perspective, it makes total sense for them to invest heavily in a real-estate investment trust seemingly custom-tailored to both their industry and their geographical range, especially if they could position themselves on the inside to influence the lease of facilities and mineral rights to themselves, which is essentially what your standard in-house corporate asset management firm does anyway."

"It can't be coincidence that we keep running into the real-estate investment arm of an energy exploration company that appears to be trying to hide its involvement with multiple properties tied to the Thirteen at the same time we're trying to unravel a natural gas conspiracy in the Middle East."

"Tectonic is also one of the most aggressive bidders on some of Langbroek's more lucrative LNG assets, although, again, such activity totally makes sense in context. They're obviously looking to expand, and acquiring assets and drilling rights directly from Nautilus would be the quickest and easiest way to make that happen."

"What do we know about whoever's in charge of Tectonic Energy?"

"If you're asking if someone involved in the business is potentially a member of the Thirteen, the answer's a definitive no. Tectonic's a hugely profitable corporation, but it's closer to the bottom than the top of the Fortune Five Hundred. It was founded in the late eighties by two geological engineers, who started with an initial investment of fifty grand and slowly grew the company, one drilling operation at a time, until they went public, cashed out, and stuck around in executive roles."

"No connection to old money?"

"Nothing even close. One of the partners left in 2006 to start a new company, while the remaining partner stayed on until he died in a car accident five years ago, at which time the board hired a more aggressive CEO, took out a monster loan, and started building up its holdings."

"Including National Realty Trust," Mason said. "There's something wrong with the timing, though. The founder and CEO dies and all of a sudden the company decides to become a player? Publicly traded companies don't suddenly decide to do anything, do they?"

"Not from my experience," Gunnar said. "I'll look into it and let you know what I find."

A click and he was gone.

Mason pocketed his phone and turned to find Layne staring at him with an unreadable expression on her face.

"I don't know if you noticed," she said, "but that boring unit back there is the kind an oil company would use to drill a pipe—"

His phone rang again. He recognized the number—or, rather, the lack of one—and started talking the moment he tapped the screen to accept the call.

"I need to know who was on those choppers," he said.

"Like I told you before, that's a matter of national security," Archer said. "I'm not able to—"

"The Dragon hated his country for what it did to him and he would have been happy to let us destroy it, but starting a war with Russia was his master's goal, not his. For him, it was always about the nuclear fizzle. He saw it as the source of all of his problems, an element of unpredictability that he needed to learn how to control. The disaster at Chernobyl cost him his career, his name, everything. It drove him into the arms of a doomsday cult that stoked the fires of his hatred and turned him into a weapon it could wield to achieve its apocalyptic ends."

"Get to the point, Mason. I don't have a lot of time."

"Destroying D.C. would have been his greatest triumph, and yet in his final moments his only thoughts had been of his daughter. Whether he succeeded or not, he had to know she'd never be able to leave the country. There'd be a national manhunt for her. Every officer would have a picture of her. And yet even after we had control of the bomb and the detonator, he'd remained defiant, because wiping out the District had only been part of the plan. He needed the president to enact the continuity-of-operations plan so Valeria could assassinate whoever was on that first helicopter. That has to be how he guaranteed her safety."

"Only a select group of people outside of those physically on those choppers knew who was being evacuated, and even fewer knew where those individuals were going."

"Then if I'm right, what does that tell you?"

Mason paced the driveway while he waited for Archer to respond. He understood he was asking the secretary to take in a lot of information all at once, and most of it on faith alone, but he could feel the truth of the words. He was right about this and if they didn't act quickly, whoever had ordered the deaths of the men on that helicopter would not only get away with it, he'd profit from it.

"The first chopper was the main target," Mason said. "The second was incidental. Had the first not flown straight up into it, it might not have been brought down at all."

"You realize what you're asking me to do, don't you?"

"I'm asking you to help me find out who's responsible for setting this whole thing up because he's still out there somewhere, which means we're all still at risk."

Archer growled in frustration.

"Davis Harper, Rudy Anderson, Theresa Powers, Aaron Carpenter, and Stan Ryder," he said. "You'd sure as hell better be right."

"I wish to God I weren't," Mason said, hanging up on the secretary of the Department of Homeland Security.

"He gave you the names?" Layne said.

"Now we just need to figure out who—"

A crackle of static and Sharpe's voice erupted from the transceiver.

"We picked her up leaving the house on foot an hour and thirteen minutes ago."

Mason opened the side door of the house, held it for Layne, and followed her into a mudroom that smelled of age and mildew. A short hallway led to the main room, where motes of dust glimmered in the moonlight passing through the gaps between the curtains. Wylie waved them over to where Sharpe had set up his laptop on the dining-room table. Mason leaned over the agent's shoulder in an effort to see the screen, upon which Valeria had been captured crossing the front yard, where they'd landed the helicopter. She'd already taken off her helmet and appeared to be in the process of shedding her silver CBRN suit as she ran.

Sharpe let the footage roll. Valeria sprinted across the street and disappeared into the forest on the other side. When she didn't immediately reappear, Sharpe zoomed out and fast-forwarded through the frames until she appeared again, only in a much different place than they'd expected.

"There she is," Layne said, tapping the screen where the woman passed beneath a gap in the canopy on a dirt bike, roughly half a mile to the southwest. "How long ago was this?"

"Fifty-six minutes ago," Sharpe said.

"If she continues on her present course, she'll cross the Maryland state line without passing through any of our checkpoints," Wylie said.

"What's out there?" Layne asked.

"The same whole lot of nothing we flew over on our way here."

Sharpe scrolled ahead through the satellite footage until he picked her up a mile south of the border, heading southwest toward a town called Sabillasville, where she pulled into the parking lot of a church, loaded the motorcycle into the back of a white pickup truck, and took off heading west.

"We've got her!" Wylie said. "How long ago was this?"

"Forty-two minutes," Sharpe said.

"Keep gaining ground. We need to know where she is right now."

"She's outside of the range of the satellite monitoring the base now. We're going to have to rely on traffic cams and there aren't a whole lot of them out there where she's heading."

"Coordinate with Christensen's team in New York," Layne said. "We need as many people looking for her as we can get."

"And once you have her, maintain visual contact at all costs," Mason said, running toward the front door and the Black Hawk waiting in the front yard. "We can't let her get away this time or we'll never find her again."

65

The chopper sped southwest over the heavily forested region and crossed the border into Maryland. Valeria could have easily vanished into the wilderness and they might never have found her. The only reason for her to take the risk of being followed was if she didn't have the luxury of time, which implied she needed to make it to a designated site at a predetermined time for extraction.

"I've got her heading south on Highway Four Ninety-one near Fort Ritchie forty minutes ago," Sharpe said through their headsets.

"That's barely half a mile from Sabillasville," Tomalty said. "We're losing ground."

"There just aren't enough cameras out there. There isn't another one along that stretch until Smithsburg and there are half a dozen rural roads she can take before she gets there."

"Stay on her," Layne said.

A crackle of static preceded the pilot's voice.

"I just received confirmation that the packages were delivered safely to Mount Weather."

Mason allowed himself a momentary sensation of relief. It wasn't much, but there was now a 66 percent chance that his father was alive. There was no time to dwell on that now, though.

He returned his attention to his cell phone, his open browser, and the search he'd initiated. If he was right and the victims on the first helicopter had been deliberately targeted, he needed to figure out why. He and Layne had broken up the list to expedite the process. He summarized out loud as he read through the information on his screen.

"Davis Harper was the undersecretary of Defense for Intelligence," he said. "He was in charge of the oversight of the Defense Intelligence Agency, the National Geospatial-Intelligence Agency, the

National Reconnaissance Office, and the National Security Agency. Retired from the Air Force with a rank of lieutenant general. His final assignment was military deputy commander of USNORTHCOM, the U.S. Northern Command. Exactly who the president would want inside that bunker to help coordinate the domestic response to a terrorist attack."

"Rudy Anderson," Layne said. "Undersecretary of Defense for Research and Engineering. Physicist and aerospace engineer. Worked for Lockheed Martin before moving on to NASA. In charge of the Missile Defense Agency, the Strategic Capabilities Office, DARPA, and the Defense Innovation Unit. On paper it might look like knocking this guy out of the picture would cripple our response to reprisals, but every one of those agencies is headed by someone with far more pertinent experience."

"New York picked her up at a traffic light in Smithsburg, heading south on Highway Sixty-four," Tomalty said. "Thirty-four minutes ago."

"The biggest town along that route is Hagerstown," Sharpe said. "Population forty thousand. Also the only place within an hour's drive with an airport."

"Which won't do her any good as long as flights are grounded," Wylie said.

"I can be there in under five minutes," the pilot said.

The Black Hawk banked to the south. Mason glanced down at the black carpet of treetops. A linear demarcation carved through them, too straight to be a road. Maybe buried power lines.

"Theresa Powers," he said. "Senator from Indiana. Sixty-three years old. Serving her eighth term. Married mother of two grown children. Worked for years as an assistant DA before moving briefly into corporate practice, which obviously didn't take as she joined the IRS two years later. She chairs the U.S. Senate Committee on Banking, Housing, and Urban Affairs and sits on the Judiciary Committee, including the Subcommittee on Crime and Terrorism."

"Aaron Carpenter was a senator, too," Layne said. "Montana. Also serving his eighth term. He chaired both the Committee on Homeland Security and Governmental Affairs and the Subcommittee on Federal Spending Oversight and Emergency Management. Distinguished service in the Marines. Practical experience in business management, community relations, and a volunteer firefighter to boot."

She paused. "I don't know about you, but I can think of any number of good reasons why every single one of these people should have been in that bunker."

Mason brought up the information on the fifth and final passenger and stared at an image of a man in his late sixties or early seventies. He wore spectacles, a gray suit, and his stringy white hair in a comb-over style. He was the definition of unimposing.

"Stan Ryder was a congressman from Arkansas," he said. "Serving his twelfth two-year term. Prior to his election, he was an accountant and comptroller for first the city of Little Rock and then the state. Gold-star parent. Lost his only son in Iraq. Ranking minority member on the U.S. House Committee on Financial Services and the Subcommittee on National Security, International Development, and Monetary Policy."

Mason set down his phone, closed his eyes, and tried to piece together the reason why any number or all of these specific individuals could pose a threat to the member of the Thirteen responsible for hiring the Dragon and trying to start a world war. Regardless of how much power he possessed, no man shy of the president of the United States would be able to make sure five specific individuals were assigned to a specific helicopter. They had to be looking at a subset of the five, but which one?

There were two high-ranking officials from the DOD, both of whom were political appointees in largely bureaucratic positions, but whose combined agencies were integral to maintaining the continuity of national security operations. While their deaths would disrupt the chain of command, they would by no means cripple the agencies under their charge.

The other three were career politicians, elected officials from both sides of the aisle, hailing from states most people couldn't find on a map. The Dragon had claimed that eight of them would be empowered with the full weight of both houses, but that they wouldn't need all of them to approve a retaliatory strike on their perceived aggressor. When the time came to vote, all they'd really need were three of the remaining five. Had these three been targeted because they would have voted against reprisals, or was there something about these three specifically that warranted their assassination?

"We lost her," Sharpe said. Mason opened his eyes. He felt as though he'd been punched in the gut. "We should have seen her entering

Hagerstown on Sixty-four roughly twenty-five minutes ago, but her truck never passed through the intersection."

"Where could she have gone?" Wylie asked.

"There are three possibilities: Highway Sixty-six south toward Mount Aetna, Sixty-two north into Leitersburg, and Robinwood Drive south into a residential suburb of Hagerstown."

"New York says she probably had another vehicle hidden along her route," Tomalty said. "That's been her MO so far."

"I can get us to the first in a matter of minutes," the pilot said.

"What's there?" Wylie asked.

"Cavetown," Sharpe said. "It doesn't appear to be much more than a fork in the road with a truck stop and a drugstore."

"That would be the perfect place to make a swap," Tomalty said. "It could easily buy her another fifteen minutes."

Mason closed his eyes again and attempted to visualize every possible connection between the congressmen. While nowhere near the most prominent or readily recognizable, they were three of the most experienced, tenured politicians who'd patiently worked their way up through the ranks of their respective parties and into leadership roles. They'd risen to positions responsible for implementing policy and overseeing critical aspects of the day-to-day operations of the federal government.

Through their service on various subcommittees, Powers, the senator from Indiana, had undoubtedly helped implement the domestic response to acts of terror, while Carpenter, the senator from Montana, probably knew more about Homeland Security and emergency management than any other elected official. It was the congressman for Arkansas who didn't seem to fit. Stan Ryder was a bean counter who'd been in the House for more than two decades. His only area of expertise appeared to be in finance, although he had served on the Subcommittee on National Security, International Development, and—

"Monetary Policy," he finished out loud.

"What about it?" Layne asked.

Mason tuned her out and attempted to follow that line of thought. Gunnar had used that specific term in regard to the function of the Federal Reserve, which implied that Ryder had been tasked with some amount of oversight of the central bank. Powers had chaired the senate committee responsible for overseeing the entire banking industry.

He opened his eyes, grabbed his phone, and initiated a search using both of their names and the term "Federal Reserve," which returned more than ten thousand results. The majority were articles from newspapers and major websites and featured titles like "Congressmen call for audit of Federal Reserve" and "Committee chairperson demands investigation of Securities and Exchange Commission" and "Representatives seek transparency in financial dealings." He searched each of their news feeds individually and found exactly what he expected. Powers had cosponsored the Banking Accountability Act and the Federal Reserve Transparency Act, while Ryder had proposed the Corporate Transparency Act and specific reforms to the Federal Bank Secrecy Act and anti–money laundering laws, all of which were currently working their way through various committees in an attempt to gather support.

Gunnar had been right from the start. It all came down to the petrodollar. He dialed his old friend's number and waited for it to ring through—

"There's her truck," Sharpe said. There was no mistaking the dejection in his voice. "She's gone."

Mason pressed his forehead against the window in an effort to see the ground. The helicopter hovered above a truck stop with a dozen fuel pumps hidden beneath a rain awning. There was a convenience store and a Subway restaurant inside the main building, beside which was a lot speckled with cars. Behind it was a dirt expanse where interstate truckers could spend the night if they got too tired, only it had been torn up and mounded with excavated dirt and gravel. Construction vehicles lined the thicket at the edge of the property. Parked among them was the white pickup truck.

The dirt bike was no longer in the bed.

66

The pilot landed the Black Hawk in a patch of grass the size of a baseball diamond. The few cars passing the truck stop pulled to the shoulder and watched the agents hop out of the chopper. They sprinted through the buffeting wind, past the convenience store and around to the dirt lot behind the building, where the construction vehicles sat idle. Plastic pipes as wide as a car's tire rested nearby, ready to be laid.

Valeria's truck was parked behind them, near a fenced enclosure housing pressurized gasses in tanks the size of cruise missiles.

Mason glanced to the north, toward the direction from which they'd come. This area fell in line with the scarring he'd noticed in the forest.

He switched on his mini Maglite and shone it onto the dirt behind the open bed of the pickup. It was impossible to miss the scuffed footprints where Valeria had struggled to lower the heavy bike to the ground or its deep tread leading toward the tree line to the south, on the other side of which were acres upon acres of orchards and pastures.

"She's heading south across the open terrain," Wylie said. "We need to get back in the air—"

"Hold up," Layne said. "Every move she's made so far has been a deliberate attempt at misdirection. We can't just fly off and hope we see her headlight out there in the countryside."

"She has to know we're coming up fast behind her."

"Which is all the more reason she'd try to throw us off her scent."

Wylie bared her teeth in frustration and paced for several seconds before grabbing her transceiver.

"Tell New York I need someone to access this place's security cameras," she said, heading around the side of the building. "I want to know if any of them picked her up. I'm going inside to see if I can find anyone who might have seen her."

Layne turned on her flashlight and followed the tire tracks in the opposite direction.

"If I'm right," she said, "I won't be gone for very long."

Mason's phone rang. Gunnar was already talking when he answered.

"—after the old CEO of Tectonic Energy died," he said. "The newly appointed CEO decided to expand drilling operations into the overseas market and courted banks willing to invest in the company's future. Within three months, he secured a loan from an investment bank for one billion dollars. That's *billion,* with a *b.* We're talking nine zeroes for a company whose total assets at the time weren't even a tenth of that amount. Now, as you can imagine, entering the natural gas market in the Middle East is easier said than done, which is why Tectonic was forced to renegotiate the terms of the loan when it fell behind on its payments. The bank agreed to exchange the amount in arrears plus future interest for enough stock in the company to become a solid minority shareholder, which it leveraged into seats on the board and ousted the CEO in favor of new leadership appointed from within its own ranks."

"So it could control the direction of the business to make sure it could recoup its investment."

"Precisely. The arrangement's not uncommon. Tectonic basically entered into a partnership with the investment bank, which directed it to sell the majority of its domestic assets and sign a lease agreement with the real-estate investment trust that bought them—National Realty Trust—and then set about acquiring a controlling interest in it. Suddenly, Tectonic was flush with liquidity, thanks to what amounts to self-dealing, and, with the help of its new business partner, ready to make a run at Slate Langbroek's natural gas holdings in Eastern Europe and the Middle East."

"It can't be coincidental that we're talking about an investment bank," Mason said. "Two of the congressmen killed on the chopper were Theresa Powers and Stan Ryder."

Gunnar fell silent. Mason could practically hear him trying to fit the pieces together.

"I found it," Layne said, wheeling the dirt bike out of the trees. Filthy water drained from the motorcycle's frame and exhaust pipe. "She rolled it down into the irrigation ditch back there."

"Make sure Wylie knows she switched vehicles," Mason said. "And try not to rub it in her face too much."

Layne smirked, leaned the motorcycle against a trencher, and headed into the convenience store.

"There haven't been two bigger thorns in the side of the banking industry since Ron and Rand Paul," Gunnar said. "Powers and Ryder champion accountability and transparency. They went to the mat back in 2008 in an effort to derail TARP and the bank bailouts. PACs come out of the woodwork every election cycle and contribute big money to the campaigns of their opponents. I guess if they couldn't find a way to unseat them—"

"A more permanent solution needed to be reached," Mason said.

"I can't believe I didn't see it. The Banking Accountability and Corporate Transparency Acts would have laid bare the investment bank's holdings, while the Federal Reserve Transparency Act and the proposed reforms of the Federal Bank Secrecy Act would have exposed its shady dealings, including whatever arrangement it had made with Cártel de Jalisco Nueva Generación."

"Who are we talking about?"

"The same investment bank that originally underwrote National Realty Trust's IPO—its initial public offering—way back in 1985. It buried Tectonic Energy in debt so it would be forced to cut a deal to remain in business. It used its own resources, under the guise of a series of loans, to acquire an energy exploration company and a real-estate investment trust holding the largest collection of mineral rights in the country, underneath everyone's noses. A successful bid on Langbroek's LNG holdings and it would control nearly all of the natural gas in America and the Middle East combined. It could exert its influence over the government to use the U.S. military to hold the Russians at bay while it laid its own pipelines to Europe from both Azerbaijan and Qatar, where Nautilus already has existing infrastructure in place."

"Tell me, Gunnar."

"American Investment Partnership, AIP, the most successful investment bank in the world, and one seemingly above reproach. The vast majority of its profits are derived from the sale of treasuries, which means that not only does its success hinge upon the creation of new debt to keep the printing presses running, its entire business model is predicated upon the perpetuation of the petrodollar. Only the Federal Reserve and the government itself have more at stake in making sure the dollar retains its reserve status."

"Surely they could just find other ways to invest if the government stopped printing money."

"You don't understand. At any given time, the investment banks responsible for financing trillions of dollars in new treasuries every year have tens of billions of dollars' worth of those IOUs listed among the assets on their balance sheets—like time bombs waiting to go off should the petrodollar fail—because the Fed doesn't buy treasuries from primary dealers every day. It utilizes, quote, unquote, 'open market operations' and a seemingly random schedule of its own design to force them to compete against one another to sell those treasuries, which simultaneously drives down the amount of interest the government has to pay and decreases the investment bank's profit."

"Who decides which primary dealer gets to sell its treasuries?" Mason asked.

"The Federal Reserve's board of governors," Gunnar said. "It determines how much the Fed will pay and who it will buy them from. Now let's say the majority of that board is comprised of governors allied with one of those primary dealers specifically, an unthreatening one with a reputation for being risk-averse and taking the 'slow and steady wins the race' approach to ensuring consistent long-term profits."

"Then that investment bank would have the inside track on the Fed buying its treasuries and could basically determine the amount of interest it makes from them," Mason said.

Layne ducked around the side of the building and waved him over. The rotors of the Black Hawk ramped up with a whine as he headed in that direction.

"It's a cash grab on a scale so ambitious it's amazing that anyone had the balls to even attempt it," Gunnar said. "The investment bank takes the government's IOU so it can print that hundred-dollar bill our elected officials so desperately want to spend and turns around and gets a digital transfer of a hundred and three bucks from the Fed, which essentially makes that money appear out of thin air on a balance sheet, passing on the tab to the American taxpayer."

Layne fell into stride beside Mason. The others were already climbing into the waiting chopper.

"The lady working the register said she saw Valeria leave here in a truck she thought belonged to the crew," Layne said. "One of those big numbers with logos on the doors, like an electrician's truck."

"Heading in which direction?"

"East."

"She doubled back?"

"We probably flew right over her."

"Keep going," Mason said. "I'm right behind you."

He stopped and covered his free ear so he could hear his phone.

"Our national debt is the face value of all of those treasuries," Gunnar said. "We're talking nearly thirty trillion dollars. At a three percent return, that's nine hundred billion dollars in unearned revenue for the primary dealers. Our debt increased by one point five trillion last budgetary cycle alone. That's forty-five billion shared between primary dealers and more than twenty-one billion for one in particular, one who would lose the lion's share of all of that free money if the government stopped running up its debt, one so integral to the global economy that the whole house of cards would come crashing down if it failed, one that has everything to lose if the oil industry—or the natural gas industry poised to replace it—starts trading in anything other than petrodollars and everything to gain if it takes control of that industry."

"You're saying that AIP is so powerful it can dictate foreign policy, that we invaded Iraq, Libya, and Syria to protect its financial interests?"

"So powerful that it can launder a drug cartel's money in the central bank of the United States of America with impunity and bring us to the precipice of war with Russia over a pipeline."

Mason tried to wrap his mind around the idea that countries had been destroyed and hundreds of thousands of people had been killed to protect a system designed to corner the world's wealth.

"All of this, just so an investment bank can siphon billions of dollars out of the economy."

"Try hundreds of billions," Gunnar said. "And a bank doesn't act without direction. In this case, one man has more at stake than anyone else, one man whose great-great-grandfather founded the company in 1869 and whose net worth makes him one of the twenty richest people in the world."

Mason's heart rate accelerated. They'd identified the man behind the nuclear threat.

"I was wrong about Avery Douglas," Gunnar said. "He's not just some pampered rich kid. He's a member of the Thirteen."

67

JULY 5

"She never reached the traffic camera at the main intersection in Smithsburg," Sharpe said. "There are only two roads she could have taken, both of which lead south into the middle of nowhere."

"She'll eventually reach I-Seventy and gain access to practically the entire country," Tomalty said.

"Not without popping up on every single camera along the way," Wylie said.

Mason glanced out the window into the darkness, the impenetrable canopy of South Mountain State Park racing past below him. His mind was still reeling at the revelation that Avery Douglas was a member of the Thirteen. He was one of the richest and most power-ful men on the planet and could have had anything his heart desired. Mansions, villas, entire countries. He could have cavorted with ce-lebrities or endowed universities, bought professional sports teams or funded the cure for cancer, and yet he'd plotted the ruination of coun-tries throughout the Middle East, instigated bloody coups that dis-placed millions of innocent people from their homes, and attempted to start World War III. And all for what? So he could make a fortune from European gas sales and cash out of the national debt business? Or was war exactly what he needed to get the printing presses rolling even faster?

The picture on Mason's cell phone showed a man with perfect hair, an easy smile, and a custom-tailored suit walking beside the president of the United States of America on the grounds of the White House he'd nearly destroyed. It was obvious which of the two wielded the most power, the kind that could have been used to change the world for the better, but that hadn't been enough for generations of Doug-lases, who'd been primary dealers of Treasury securities since the in-ception of the Federal Reserve more than a century ago. Men who, at some point during that time, had joined forces with the Langbroeks and eleven other families in their quest to rule the world.

"There has to be a natural gas operation somewhere nearby," he said.

"In Pennsylvania and West Virginia for sure, but there's no frack-ing in Maryland," Tomalty said.

"What about properties with mineral rights owned by National Realty Trust? Or maybe a liquefaction plant or a . . ." Mason felt everything come together. The real-estate investment trust with prop-erties throughout the Midwest. The natural gas company with drill-ing operations from Texas all the way north to Pennsylvania. The tunnel underneath the border. The boring machine at the house near Raven Rock. It was what the entire plot had been about from be-ginning to end, from the murder of a border patrol agent near the Rio Grande to the attempted destruction of the National Mall to the energy coup in the Middle East. ". . . pipeline."

Layne looked at him, and then at the picture on his phone.

"What do you know?" she asked.

"Later," he said. "I promise."

"There's a gas compressor station in Myersville," Tomalty said. "About ten miles due south of our current position."

"Get us there," Mason said.

The Black Hawk accelerated and thundered so low over the tree-tops that they could have stepped right out onto them.

"What kind of damage can she do at a compressor station?" Tomalty asked.

"It's her extraction point," Mason said.

"How the hell does she intend to get out of there?" Wylie asked.

"Through the pipeline," Layne said.

Lights materialized from the forest in the distance, lining the highway and the main streets, glowing from the windows of houses and the headlights of the few cars still on the roads.

"The plant's just south of the interstate," Tomalty said.

"There's a camera on the overpass leading into it," Sharpe said. "Ten minutes ago, it photographed a truck matching the description of the one we're looking for. The logo is clearly visible on the side."

"Tectonic Energy," Mason said.

"How'd you know?"

"Why didn't they report the truck as stolen?" Wylie asked.

"Because it wasn't," Mason said. He glanced at the picture of Avery Douglas one last time before shoving his phone into his pocket. "How close can we get without tipping her off that we're coming?"

"This beast was built to inspire fear," the pilot said. "Discretion was never part of the design."

"Then just get us as close as you can. If she so much as senses our approach, we'll be walking straight into the teeth of an invisible barrage of radiation."

"There's a clearing along Catoctin Creek, about half a mile to the northeast of the facility."

"That'll have to work," Wylie said, handing each of them a wireless transceiver. "Mason, Layne, and I will enter the complex on foot. Tomalty: Figure out where that pipeline goes and coordinate with local law enforcement to lock down whatever's on the other end. Sharpe: You're our eye in the sky. We're counting on you to let us know what kind of snafu we're walking into. And see if New York can access the security system inside that plant."

"You guys don't have any protection against that weapon of hers," Sharpe said.

Mason glanced at his partner and read the concern on her face. It was one thing charging into a situation where a bullet could end your life in the blink of an eye, but walking into the range of a DEW that could fire through the side of a building and cook you alive was another thing entirely.

"Then we'd better make sure we don't get hit," he said.

The Black Hawk descended through the canopy and alighted in a clearing enclosed on all four sides by trees, their branches tossing against the hurricane force of the rotors. Mason cast aside his headset, drew his Glock, and threw open the door. The wind battered him as he jumped down and sprinted toward the edge of the forest, through which he could see the flicker of headlights from the distant highway. He waited for the others to catch up with him before advancing into the thicket.

The chopper rose behind them and once more headed to the north.

"New York was able to hack into the security system," Sharpe said through their earpieces. "They have eyes on the grounds and along the perimeter. There are only a handful of cars in the parking lot."

"What about the satellite?" Wylie asked.

"It'll be in range within a matter of minutes."

Mason broke cover, scurried up a steep embankment, and crouched at the edge of a highway off-ramp. Vehicles sped inland along the westbound lanes of I-70, down the slope and through the trees. A steady stream of interstate truckers roared past along the eastbound lanes on the far side of the median, their tires buzzing on the asphalt. The compressor station was invisible through the dense wall of vegetation in the distance.

Layne and Wylie scurried up the hillside and knelt on either side of him.

"If we cut through those trees, we can cross the highway underneath the overpass," he said. "From there, we'll be able to take advantage of the cover of the forest all the way to the edge of the property."

"It's surrounded by an eight-foot security fence," Sharpe said. "The main road enters through a gate at the northeast corner."

"The Tectonic Transmission Pipeline originates at the Marcellus natural gas play in Western Pennsylvania and runs all the way to an export facility on Chesapeake Bay," Tomalty said. "What we're dealing with here is the early stages of construction on Tectonic's Eastern

Triangle Line, which branches from the main line just north of here and runs southeast to that compressor station in front of you. From there it heads east to a regasification plant in Columbia so it can be piped into Baltimore, Annapolis, and the District. Unfortunately, it's not scheduled for completion for another six years and I only have access to the blueprints, so I can't tell you how much of that line has actually been run."

"What's the closest town along the way?" Wylie asked.

"Frederick. Population sixty-five thousand. Twelve miles to the southeast."

"I can't imagine her trying to cover that kind of distance inside a pipe."

"We need to get moving," Layne said. "How's the view from that satellite?"

"The approach is clear," Sharpe said. "The first building you'll encounter appears to be the control center; the smaller one to the east houses the electrical works. The big structure in back with the smokestack has to be the compressor building. The Tectonic truck's parked right next to it."

"Then that's where we need to go," Mason said.

He hurdled the guardrail, ran across the off-ramp, and scurried downhill through the trees to the edge of the highway. Bolted along the shoulder and into the shadow of the overpass. He sprinted across the westbound lanes, the median, the eastbound lanes, and into the trees leading uphill to the off-ramp on the other side. Another twenty feet and he was safely concealed within the forest.

"New York patched me into the external security feed," Sharpe said. "There's no movement outside. No security guards or patrols. None of the pipes appear large enough for a person to crawl through, with the possible exception of the two exiting the rear of the compressor building."

"Any sign of recent construction?" Layne whispered.

"I detect a slight delineation where the one on the left might have been more recently laid."

"We need to know every location where it lets out along the way," Wylie whispered.

Mason raised his weapon and advanced through the trees. A chain-link fence emerged from the branches, the shapes of the buildings behind it defined by the lights mounted to their rooflines. Another few steps and he could see that the front gate was closed. The control center was maybe fifty feet straight ahead, across a fringe of grass and an asphalt parking lot.

"If we keep that building between us and her, she won't be able to see us until we're within twenty-five feet of the station," Mason whispered.

"But we'll be completely exposed after that," Layne whispered.

"We have to assume she's too busy trying to escape to be wasting time setting a trap for us," Wylie whispered.

"At least if you're wrong our families will be spared the decision of whether or not to have our bodies cremated."

Mason glanced at his partner. He couldn't tell from the tone of her voice if she was joking.

"New York's trying to get ahold of whoever's monitoring those security cameras to make sure they know to stand down," Sharpe said.

"They would have seen us coming long before now," Mason whispered. He darted out into the open and mounted the fence. "Either no one's watching or they're already dead."

68

Valeria shouldered through the door and headed straight to the back of the compressor building, passing massive rumbling machines that caused the floor to shudder. She ducked behind the last compressor in the series, where the final hurdle to freedom awaited. She'd spent the prior twenty-four hours on the run, switching from one vehicle to the next in a meticulously planned and carefully choreographed dance designed to keep her a step ahead of her pursuit. She had thought such extreme precautions overkill, but, as usual, Zmei had been right, just as he'd known that the father of the child growing inside of her would see to her ultimate escape, if only to make sure that it never drew its first breath. Although Tertius never threatened to do so out loud, she had seen the truth in his eyes, where the monster she'd watched set upon the Russians with a chain saw lurked. With the congressmen assassinated, her father likely dead, and the plot to destroy Washington, D.C., derailed, she'd become a loose end, one that Tertius undoubtedly looked forward to personally tying off, especially after how she'd manipulated him.

Fortunately, Tertius Decimus had promised to intervene on her behalf, and not only to save the life of her unborn, but to make sure that the child inherited its surname, and the trappings of wealth and power that came with it. All she had to do in exchange was arrange for the man who'd co-opted Tertius's plan to purchase specific aspects of the Douglas estate, alter the mechanism of exacting her revenge against the country that had betrayed her father and destroyed her family, and maintain certain financial arrangements with the cartel, who in turn would ensure that no one ever so much as thought about raising a hand against her.

And kill Slate Langbroek, of course.

After a lifetime of hard work and sacrifice, her father's plan was about to come to fruition. His dream would be realized and she would become the Dragon, a mantle he had worn with honor for so many years. Even better, she would soon become one of the Thirteen, regent until her child came of age, and help destroy everything that Avery Douglas and self-serving men like him had built.

Even though she hadn't seen her mother in years, she felt her presence now, and hoped her father was right there at her side, as he had always longed to be. A faint smile traced her lips beneath her helmet as she opened her case and set to work unscrewing the security plate that barred access to the gas pipe. She caught her reflection from the polished grate inside, her golden face shield—

—reveals a distorted image of her features. She turns the helmet over and over in her hands, tracing the smooth contours, the futuristic visor, the tubing of the respirator. Ever since she was a child, she has imagined how this moment would feel and yet the reality is beyond her wildest expectations.

Her father had weaned her on stories of how he used it to further the cause, weaving tales of eliminating his adversaries from up close with his directed-energy weapon and from afar with his fizzle devices. He'd taught her everything he knew about the power of the atom and the fury it contained, how to harness it for both energy and destruction, how to control it like a snake charmer summoning a cobra from a basket. He'd shown her how to harvest isotopic uranium and plutonium, reprocess them, and build them into weapons of all shapes and sizes, compressing the awesome power into increasingly smaller packages, some even light enough for aerial delivery, but he had never let her touch his suit, not like—

She realizes with a start that this is not his suit. The helmet is too small, the silver outfit too narrow. She glances up at him and reads the truth in his eyes. This is her suit, one that has been tailored specifically for her, and she understands the gravity of the moment, how it means every bit as much to him as it does to her.

Valeria tries to thank him, but the words will not form. She feels tears on her cheeks when she throws herself into her father's arms and hugs him for everything she's worth, willing him to understand that this is all she's ever wanted, that her life is now complete.

"Try it on," he says, wiping the tears from his own eyes.

She dons it over her clothes, just as she's seen him do so many times. It's hotter inside than she'd envisioned, the outside air unable to penetrate its impervious layers. She seats the helmet over her head and the world becomes gold, the vast expanse of shrubland appearing to burn with the sun's rays. Her father helps her shoulder the heavy backpack and hands her the aperture, her index finger instinctively finding the trigger.

"I have another surprise for you," he says.

He guides her across the gravel drive to the barn and opens the doors upon a space she knows well, although she's never seen the black truck before. At first she thinks he has bought it for her and finds the gesture confusing, at least until she sees the man and woman waiting for her in the stall, El Carnicero towering over them with his tattooed face and sharp-looking teeth. As usual, the blood on his clothing matches that of the people cowering on the straw-lined ground before him. She wonders where he's been, as she hasn't seen him in months. She's heard the rumors, though, spoken by the other sicarios, who claimed he'd betrayed Cártel de Jalisco Nueva Generación and joined forces with the Sinaloans, but this can't be true as he stands before her now, a smile on his face that only those who have known him for as long as she has can witness without losing control of their bladders.

"Are you ready?" he asks.

She nods and brushes past him.

The man on the ground pulls his wife behind him and tries to act brave. He wears denim from top to bottom and rattlesnake-skin *boots. She wonders how they'll smell when they start to burn, or if she'll be able to smell anything at all through the helmet.*

"What did they do?" she asks.

"Does it matter?" El Carnicero replies.

"No."

She braces her feet, raises the aperture, and presses the trigger halfway, until the pack begins to vibrate and hum. A green glow washes over the stall and the man utters a prayer. She pulls the trigger all the way and—

The last screw clattered to the ground at her feet. She kicked it aside and returned to her case, where the means of her escape was packed, the motor freshly fueled and primed. By this time tomorrow, she'd be on the other side of the world.

Watching the chaos unfold.

PART 7

I sincerely believe, with you, that banking establishments are more dangerous than standing armies.

—Thomas Jefferson, third president of the United States,
letter to John Taylor (May 28, 1816)

69

Mason took a quick mental snapshot from the top of the fence, jumped down, and hit the ground running. He crossed the parking lot toward a white building with a corrugated aluminum roof. There were no windows on this side, only a single access-controlled metal door. He ran right along its face, his shoulder brushing the siding, until he reached a blind corner.

His phone vibrated in his pocket, but he didn't dare pull it out to see who was calling.

He tightened his finger on the trigger, flexed his arms to absorb the recoil, and went around low, sweeping his sight line from left to right and back again, prepared to fire at the first sign of movement.

A cold sweat trickled down his lower back. He tried not to think about the fact that he wouldn't even know he was being targeted until his nerve endings suddenly lit up. Would he experience a wave of nausea or feel his outer layers of skin starting to heat up? Would he recognize the moment when the damage to his body passed the point of no return? Was he being irradiated at that very second? The mere thought of it was terrifying. The idea of death by acute radiation was no less horrific than the prospect of receiving a sublethal dose and spending the remainder of his abbreviated life suffering as the Dragon had.

Mason pressed his back against the building. Inched sideways toward the lone window. Risked a quick glance through the mesh-reinforced glass. The walls inside were covered with enormous banks of electrical components, digital readouts, and switches and dials. The chairs near the monitoring stations lay toppled on the ground. He caught a whiff of barbecued meat around the same time he saw the burned bodies on the floor and quickly looked away.

"What is it?" Layne whispered.

He shook his head. His heartbeat was racing so fast he had to concentrate on slowing it. He could feel every inch of his skin, as though not only suddenly aware of its existence, but its vulnerability.

A clanging sound echoed from somewhere ahead of them.

Mason crept to the edge of the building and looked past the Tectonic truck toward the compressor building. He was certain that was where the noise had originated.

Valeria Meier—the new Dragon—had to be inside.

"The approach is clear," Sharpe said through his earpiece.

Mason took a deep breath, blew it out slowly. Ran across the gap toward the lone ingress. Flattened himself against the wall. He gripped the knob and looked up at his partner, who'd assumed position on the opposite side of the door.

Layne nodded her understanding. She knew exactly what to do.

The moment he opened the door, she went in. Low and fast. Ducked to the right behind a massive turbine resembling the engine of a train, from which pipes protruded at odd angles.

Mason strode straight into the cavernous space, taking in everything around him down the sight line of his pistol. There were four churning compressor units to his right, the sources of the rumble that masked all other sounds in the lower range of hearing. To his left, metal stairs ascended to an elevated platform. Ductwork rose from the machinery on top of it and exited through a wall covered with a veritable jungle gym of gas lines and electrical conduits. The peaked roof was bare, the rafters exposed. Everything was either bolted to the ground or elevated on industrial springs to withstand the vibrations that made the ground tremble.

He detected motion and ducked to the side, behind a pipe thicker than he was.

Another resounding clang, followed by the clatter of a tool falling to the ground.

A shadow swept across the floor at the end of the main walkway, near the rear wall.

Mason glanced across the aisle at Layne, who nodded to confirm that she'd seen it, too. She turned away, ran in a crouch along the length of the compressor, and darted around the far end.

Wylie crawled out from behind the platform behind him and scurried across the gap to assume Layne's vacated position.

"Are you guys okay in there?" Tomalty asked.

Mason tapped that they were, stepped out from behind the pipe, and ascended the stairs on the other side, careful to alight as silently as possible on the metal steps. He ducked underneath the aluminum ductwork, squirmed behind a row of pipes, and advanced deeper into the building.

Layne flashed through his peripheral vision, darting from behind one compressor to the next in the narrow gap against the far wall. Wylie used the massive units as cover, picking her way through the machinery, working slowly toward the back of the building, where the pipelines Sharpe had noticed on the satellite imagery presumably exited from the final compressor unit in the series.

Mason contorted his body to slither underneath a pipe. Again, he detected movement among the shadows and caught a glimpse of a silhouette around the corner, just barely visible. The figure rose, shoved an enormous tool chest out of its way, and turned so that it appeared to be looking straight at him. The overhead lights reflected from the golden visor of the Dragon's silver CBRN suit.

He shrank deeper into the shadows so she couldn't see him, but he could almost feel the weight of her stare pass over him.

Wylie silently darted around the third compressor, crossed the walkway, and crouched just on the other side of the fourth from the Dragon. She held her pistol in a two-handed grip beside her cheek, her body tensed in anticipation.

Her eyes locked onto Mason's. He recognized her determination, her readiness to make her move.

Layne materialized from the corner of his eye. She momentarily leaned against the side of an electrical cabinet before sliding down to a crouch and disappearing from sight.

They had the Dragon cornered.

When Mason looked back again, all he could see of the Dragon was her shadow. A thumping sound, like a heavy object being dropped into a hollow space, reverberated throughout the building.

He held up his hand, fingers extended, to initiate the countdown.

Five.

Brought his thumb to his palm.

Four.

He met Wylie's stare as he lowered his pinkie.

Three.

An electrical crackle and a faint spark of greenish light.

Two.

Wylie paled noticeably. The corner of her mouth twitched and she furrowed her brow. An expression of confusion. Her eyes suddenly widened in panic. A blister formed on her cheek. Ruptured. She opened her mouth to cry out as her skin reddened and started to smolder.

"No!" Mason shouted.

He lunged out from beneath the pipe, dove across the aisle, and shoved Wylie as far away as he could.

"What's going on in there?" Sharpe asked.

A blur of movement behind him and the Dragon appeared, a square weapon held in front of her at chest level. It had handles on both sides and an aperture in the center, almost like an underwater diver's camera. A thick cable connected it to the power source harnessed to her shoulders.

He fired a shot to drive her back and scrambled to get his legs underneath him.

Wylie gasped in an effort to draw breath around her swollen tongue. Her eyes filled with terror, her face contorted into a rictus of pain.

Layne rushed out from behind the compressor, grabbed her by her arm, and dragged her out of the line of fire.

Mason ducked and ran low enough that the Dragon wouldn't be able to see the top of his head over the compressor. His instincts screamed for him to stop and check the aisle to make sure she wasn't waiting for him, but he couldn't afford to stand still for any length of time. As it was, he was likely already being exposed to gamma rays as she fired indiscriminately from behind the compressor.

He raced toward the back wall. Turned to his right. Came face-to-face with the Dragon. Saw himself reflected in her golden mask, his weapon pointed straight at her chest even as she raised hers toward him.

Mason shot first.

The impact lifted her from her feet, spun her sideways, and tossed her to the ground. She slid across the sealed concrete, leaving a smear of blood in her wake.

"Agent down!" Layne shouted.

Voices erupted in his ear. He pried off the earpiece and tossed it aside. Aimed his Glock at the Dragon and approached slowly. Cautiously. She still clutched the handle of the weapon in her right hand. He kicked it aside the moment he was within range. Stared straight down his barrel into his own distorted reflection, his weapon pointed back at him.

The fabric of her suit was punctured near her left collarbone. Blood welled from the wound, dribbled down her chest, and pooled on the floor. Sparks burst from her backpack. What looked like battery acid burbled from the hole left by the exiting bullet.

Layne approached from the opposite direction, her pistol aimed at the crown of the Dragon's head. She grabbed the helmet and wrenched it off. Valeria's eyes were tightly closed, her cheeks freckled with blood. She sputtered a mouthful of crimson and attempted to reach for the gunshot wound. The bullet must have nicked the top of her lung.

"Take care of Wylie!" Mason shouted. "I've got the Dragon."

He shoved his gun down the back of his pants and fell upon her. Tore off her backpack. Pressed his palms onto both sides of her upper chest in a desperate attempt to stanch the flow of blood.

She looked up at him with unadulterated hatred in her eyes and made a gurgling sound.

"Oh, no you don't," he said. "You're not getting off that easily."

70

Mason toppled onto his haunches when the paramedics arrived and let his arms fall to his sides. His palms were wet, his fingers sticky with congealing blood, but he'd managed to keep Valeria alive, which was all that mattered right now. Despite everything she'd done and all of the people she'd killed, he needed the knowledge she possessed, and if letting her live was the price he had to pay, then he was more than willing to pay it. Once he was through with her, however, he was happy to let events take their natural course. Assuming, of course, the Thirteen didn't find a way to kill her first.

His phone vibrated in his pocket again.

He looked around for something to wipe his hands on, but there wasn't anything suitable nearby, so he had to settle for his already soaked sweatshirt. He cleaned off the blood as best he could, dug his fingers into his pocket, and answered before the call could go to voice mail.

"Holy Hannah, Mace," Gunnar said. "I've been trying to get ahold of you for half an hour."

"You'll have to forgive me. I was a little busy taking down the Dragon."

"You got her?"

"Even better," Mason said. "We're bringing her in alive."

The paramedics strapped Valeria to a yellow backboard, lifted her onto a flattened gurney, and raised it to its full height. The waiting deputy from the Frederick County Sheriff's Department barely had time to cuff her wrist to the rail before they shuttled her down the aisle and toward the ambulance waiting outside. Its red and blue lights spilled through the open doorway and reflected from the floor.

"Excellent," Gunnar said. "Then I suppose it's not as urgent for me to tell you that I figured out where she was going."

Mason met the Dragon's eyes above the oxygen mask. The fury faded and a hint of fear appeared. She knew the consequences of failure. With any luck, she'd do a little soul-searching and realize that cooperating with them was her only hope for survival.

Another pair of paramedics wheeled Wylie out from behind the third compressor. Her eyes were closed and she appeared to be shedding the skin on her face like a lizard. A faint cloud of breath appeared on the inside of the mask over her mouth and nose with every labored exhalation. Her arms were tucked onto the gurney beside her. He reached out to give her hand a reassuring squeeze, but Layne intercepted it before he could. Upon closer inspection, he could see that Wylie's hand had been practically de-gloved of the outer layers of skin.

"They need to get her to the hospital," Layne said. "If she lives, it'll be because of what you did."

Mason hadn't realized the implications of jumping into the line of fire and shoving her out of the way until that very moment. He might not have felt anything at the time, but he'd hurled himself right into the path of the gamma rays that had nearly cooked Wylie alive.

While his dose was undoubtedly a fraction of what she'd received, he'd taken it all the same.

He watched them wheel her through the doorway and into the asphalt lot. The ambulance bearing Valeria sped away with the wail of sirens, making room for the Black Hawk to land. Transporting Wylie in a military chopper lacking medical supplies wasn't ideal, but it would save them valuable time. She'd arrive at the Johns Hopkins Trauma Center in Baltimore in less time than it would take for the Flight for Life helicopter to be dispatched.

"Are you listening?" Gunnar asked.

Mason realized he was still holding Layne's hand. He released it and headed back toward the rear of the building.

"Sorry, Gunnar. I didn't hear you. There's a lot going on here right now."

"I said I figured out where Valeria was going. Tectonic has a construction staging area about five miles southeast of where you are right now. I uploaded a screen grab"—Mason brought the phone away from his ear, opened the picture, and put the call on speaker—". . . believe what's there."

He zoomed in on a satellite photo of a vast swatch of dirt. The surrounding acreage had been razed to create a veritable parking lot for earthmovers and cranes of all shapes and sizes, not to mention stacks upon stacks of massive pipes easily as long as any of the vehicles. A trench had been cut through the forest at the top edge of the picture. He could see the point where the pipes coming in from the northwest terminated and the bare earth resumed. A row of trailers lined the bottom of the screen, where dozens of men had gathered around what looked like food trucks. In the bottom right corner was a circular patch of asphalt just large enough for the small helicopter sitting on it.

"When was this taken?" he asked.

"The last time a satellite passed over that area was two weeks ago," Gunnar said.

"Even if by some slim chance that chopper's still there, there's no way they're going anywhere with all flights being grounded."

"The FAA only controls the airspace above twelve thousand feet and within a certain radius of its towers. Everything below that ceiling and outside of those bubbles is considered Class G airspace, which means you can fly whatever you want, whenever you want to fly it, without having to file a flight plan. Why do you think there are so many drones everywhere now? Do you think the FAA has time to regulate all of their flight plans?"

It made total sense. Without any planes in the air, there would be no one to see the helicopter lift off from that landing pad, let alone be able to track where it was going.

"Who owns the helicopter?"

"I don't know about the specific one in that photograph, but I can tell you that the transponder beacon of a helicopter registered to Tectonic Energy is at that location right now."

The ramifications caught Mason by surprise.

"They were actually going to extract her," he said.

"What's going on?" Layne asked. "What's all this about a helicopter?"

"Keep track of that transponder, Gunnar," Mason said. He ended the call, turned to Layne, and showed her the picture on his phone. "This staging area is five miles southeast of here. Round up as many officers as you can find and surround it. And do so quietly. I don't want to spook whoever's waiting for her."

He brushed past her, but she grabbed him by the arm, halting his momentum.

"Where the hell do you think you're going?"

He turned around and winked.

"Don't worry," he said. "I'll meet you there."

Mason rushed to the area behind the fourth compressor, where Valeria had removed the security panel and grate granting access to the forty-two-inch pipe. Right there below him was the object he'd heard her drop inside. The contraption looked like a cross between a skateboard with rubber lawn-mower wheels and the kind of creeper mechanics used to slide under cars. There were two vertical handles on the front end, between which an LED light had been mounted.

He squeezed into the confines, lowered himself to his chest on the motorized sled, and gripped the handles. Squeezed the triggers. The motor whined and the tires squelched. He barely had a chance to switch on the headlight before he rocketed downhill and into the earth.

71

The two men were getting nervous. Something had obviously gone wrong. There was no doubt about it. The woman should have been there by now, but neither of them was in a hurry to tell their employer what had happened.

"She'll be here," a burly man with a bushy red beard said. He paced back and forth along the edge of the trench. "We'll give her five more minutes."

"That's what you said five minutes ago, Russ." The second man perched on top of a boulder the excavators had carved out of the ground. He was considerably smaller, both in height and girth. As usual, he wore his Orioles ball cap and his long hair in a ponytail, but even he knew he wasn't fooling anyone. There wasn't a person in the company who didn't know that Reggie Tyler had gone bald on top years ago. "I'm calling it this time. Five more minutes and we're heading back to the city. With or without her."

"Fine. Then you can be the one to tell him we left her behind."

Tyler flinched at the thought, but he quickly recovered.

"Fine. I will."

The truth of the matter was that while they were scared of their employer, they were terrified of his. There were men on this planet with whom you could reason, and there were others who didn't give a good goddamn and simply made their problems disappear. It was men like him, who hid behind their perfect smiles and polished veneers, that you needed to keep your eye on. They were the kind that snuck up behind you, buried a blade in your back, and left you to bleed out on the ground while they tracked down your family and everyone you ever loved.

These men were no different from the cartel bosses down in Mexico, these high-class executives with their million-dollar suits and better-than-you attitudes. They just did a better job of hiding it. Tyler knew both factions well. He'd flown cargo holds stuffed with bricks of cocaine across the border for Amado Carrillo Fuentes and the Juaréz Cártel back in the nineties after he lost his airline transport certificate, and then businessmen and oilmen for private companies like Tectonic Energy since he got out of the pen. They were all the same. They didn't care how many people got hurt, as long as they made their money, and he wasn't about to be one of those they casually discarded along the way.

"We could always go back to Baltimore and then just keep on going," Russ said.

He chuckled as though the suggestion had been meant as a joke.

Tyler and Jeremiah Russell had both been with Tectonic for close to a decade. While the former CEO had been a son of a bitch, he'd never claimed to be anything else. So he hadn't handed out Christmas bonuses and he'd gone out of his way to make sure that everyone around him knew just how replaceable they were, but at least he'd been partly human.

The guy who'd replaced him, Dave Lucas, was something else entirely.

They'd initially thought he was pretty special. He'd asked his employees about their families, talked about the previous night's ball game, and surprised his crews on the job sites with catered meals. He'd even invited a handful of the guys from their exploratory team to go to Mexico with him to scout out locations and negotiate a land-lease deal. That had been where he'd revealed his true self and shown them how he "negotiated" with reluctant business partners, right out the side door of the chopper and all the way down into the jungle. It had only taken two of the prospective partner's children before they'd struck a deal.

Worse, upon returning to Texas, Lucas had introduced them to his boss, a Greek god of a man named Avery Douglas, whose negotiating style made Lucas's look positively pleasant by comparison. Tyler and Russ hadn't had the slightest idea of how truly and deeply screwed they were until they watched him take care of those Russians who'd been trying to horn in on the Mexican deal.

That had been the night Tyler had gone down to the hotel bar to drink the memory away, only to be approached by the blond man with the deep tan, who'd been eager to discuss the merits of loyalty and the consequences of betrayal, starting with the pictures on his cell phone of Tyler's mother and younger sisters. His smile hadn't faltered as he'd described in sickening detail what he would do to them.

Not coincidentally, that was also the night Tyler quit drinking.

He glanced at his watch and pretended it was still two minutes earlier. Russ didn't call him on it.

A full minute passed before he heard a faint humming sound, almost like a cloud of mosquitoes in the distance, and hopped down from the boulder. It grew louder with every step until he got close enough to determine that it was coming from the pipe. He nearly sobbed in relief. For all his false bravado, he could only imagine what their boss—or, heaven forbid, his—would have done to them if he found out they'd left her here.

Russ skidded down the slope and into the trench beside him.

"Let's just grab her and get the hell out of here."

They knew next to nothing about the woman they'd been sent to escort back to Baltimore. Not her name, and not even a vague physical description. Only that if anything were to happen to her, the company would be in the market for a new pilot and production foreman.

The whine metamorphosed into a buzz and a light appeared from the depths of the pipe, faint at first, but growing brighter and brighter as it approached.

They stepped to either side of the orifice to clear a path. Five minutes from now they'd be in the air and this would all be a bad dream.

"It's not slowing down," Russ said.

"Get ready to catch her."

"Those things go like twenty miles an hour."

"You want to see her crash going that fast?"

Russ bent his elbows and knees in anticipation.

The buzzing continued to grow louder until the light burst from the pipe. The motorized sled rocketed past them before they could even attempt to make the grab. About the same time they realized that there was no one on it, a body slid out of the tunnel between them. Tyler looked down and found himself staring into the barrel of a semiautomatic pistol aimed at him by a man covered in dirt and what looked a whole lot like blood.

"I take it from the expression on your face that you were expecting someone else," he said. "Someone, perhaps, a little less"—the man pointed the gun at Russ and then back at Tyler again—"armed?"

Russ hunched his shoulders and clenched his fists. Readied himself to lunge. Tyler had seen him bowl right through half a dozen roughnecks in a bar brawl. There just might be a chance they could get out of this after all.

"I wouldn't do that if I were you," the man said.

"You think you can put me down before I get inside your arms and into your chest?" Russ said.

"Maybe, maybe not, but I know she can."

A spotlight snapped on behind Tyler, sending his shadow racing up the opposite side of the trench. He whirled around so fast he nearly lost his balance and looked uphill toward a woman with an FBI T-shirt, a shoulder harness, and a Glock aimed past his head and squarely at Russ's chest. She smiled, and for a second he thought that this was the woman they were supposed to pick up and someone was getting a good laugh at their expense. At least until the uniformed officers stepped out of the forest and converged in the clearing behind her.

"We're with the company laying this pipeline," he said. "We're just here to pick up a VIP."

"A VIP traveling through those pipes?" the woman said. "You realize how stupid that makes you sound, don't you?"

Unfortunately, he did.

"I'm going to need a lawyer, aren't I?"

72

BALTIMORE, MARYLAND

Valeria Meier had been stabilized at Frederick Health Hospital and transferred to a secure ward at the Johns Hopkins Trauma Center in Baltimore, where they could make sure no one was able to get to her, even someone as resourceful as she was. They'd kept her sedated the entire time to ensure her recovery and to make it impossible for her to communicate with anyone, at least until after they'd had a chance to interrogate her.

Mason and Layne had both slept the entire ride to the coast, grabbed breakfast and a change of clothes, and headed straight to the hospital, where Wylie had been admitted to their dedicated burn ward. They hadn't been able to see her, thanks to the sterile isolation tent in which she was housed, but one of her doctors had been kind enough to update them on her condition. While she wasn't out of the woods yet and she had a long and arduous recovery ahead of her—including the debridement of dead tissue and a painful series of grafts once they'd determined her immune system could handle it—he was optimistic that if they could stave off infection for the foreseeable future, she just might pull through.

With that conversation and the mental image it conjured fresh in his mind, Mason was more than ready to talk to Valeria. He'd been pacing the hallway outside of her room while he waited for the doctor to apprise her of her situation and evaluate her physical condition before letting them in. They'd flown in the physician from the Walter Reed National Military Medical Center in Bethesda specifically to treat her, in the hope that having a physician sympathetic to the best interests of the country might buy them a little extra professional courtesy when it came to her questioning.

Archer had arrived from Colorado less than fifteen minutes ago. He'd waited to make sure the president and his cabinet had been safely locked away inside a vault at NORAD, buried at the heart of Cheyenne Mountain, before immediately boarding a plane again. He looked like he hadn't slept in a month and he was more irritable than ever, but they were going to need the secretary to run interference for them, at least for the time being. Neither Mason nor Layne was entirely ready to face their debriefings. There were still questions they needed to answer and one big fish in desperate need of frying. The biggest problem was that in order to bring him in, they were going to need physical evidence, which was something they sorely lacked.

There was no doubt in Mason's mind that Avery Douglas was responsible for the nuclear threat, but he was insulated by so many layers of legal protection, accounting, and plausible deniability that they were going to need to find something irrefutable if they hoped to take a run at him. They'd only get one chance to do so before, like Slate Langbroek, he vanished into the wind.

"You need to stop pacing," Layne said. "You're making me nervous."

She leaned against the wall, a steaming cup of coffee in one hand and her cell phone in the other, her eyes fixed upon the doctor through the gap between the curtains in the hospital room's interior window. As soon as he stood from the foot of the bed and headed for the door, she set down her cup and crossed the hallway to meet him.

The doctor was a tall man in his early fifties, solidly built, cleanly shaven, and only starting to gray at the temples. He tucked his stethoscope into the pocket of his lab coat and braced himself for the conversation to come.

"She's awake and alert," he said, "but that doesn't give you license to abuse her. Regardless of her alleged involvement, she's endured a difficult ordeal. Not to mention the fact that she was shot in the chest and had to have emergency surgery to drain the blood from her thoracic cavity and repair her lung. As her physician, it's my job to make sure that no harm comes to her. If I feel that you're harassing her in any way, I'll terminate the interview. If she asks you to leave, I'll see you out myself. And if she requests a lawyer, we're done. Are we all clear on the terms?"

Mason nodded, squeezed past the doctor into the room, and immediately met Valeria's stare. Her head was propped on a pillow, her bed raised just high enough that she could look at him down the length of her nose, past the tubes snaking out of her nostrils. The corner of her mouth twitched, but otherwise she showed no appreciable reaction to his presence.

"Do you know who I am?" he asked.

Mason glanced at the monitor beside her bed, which displayed her vital signs as relayed by the cords running under her blanket and beneath her hospital gown. He gauged her baseline heart rate and blood pressure, watched for any sudden changes in either from the corner of his eye as he dragged over a chair and sat near the foot of her bed.

"Yes," she said with no trace of an accent. "You're FBI."

Mason recalled the group photo of Konets Mira and the Dragon's blurred hand as he reached for Kameko Nakamura's. Valeria was physically stunning, the best of both of her parents. She had her father's facial architecture and her mother's skin tone and almond eyes. As the daughter of the Dragon and the Scarecrow, she'd never stood a chance of having a normal life.

Her eyes twitched toward the door when the others entered. Layne walked past him and leaned against the bulletproof screen in front of the outer window, while Archer and the doctor hovered at the back of the room.

"I need to ask you some questions and I need you to answer them honestly."

"Only if you answer some for me first," she said. "Perhaps if you are honest with me, I will show you the same courtesy."

"That's not how this works."

"It is if you expect me to say a single word."

Mason didn't speak for several seconds. He made a rolling motion with his hand.

"Is my father dead?" she asked.

Mason glanced at Layne before answering.

"Yes," he said.

"Did you kill him?"

"No."

"How did he die?"

"He threw himself down a stairwell."

Valeria closed her eyes and nodded to herself.

"We need to know about the man who hired your father to build the nuclear device," Mason said.

When she opened them again, there was no sign of emotion. She stared straight through him with eyes that might as well have been dead.

"I know nothing about him," she said.

"What happened to honesty?" Layne asked.

"We can protect you," Mason said.

"Like you protected your congressmen?"

Valeria laughed and immediately regretted it. She looked down at the tube protruding from her chest, right above her dragon tattoo, to make sure it hadn't suddenly filled with blood.

"You'll be tried for multiple counts of first-degree murder, but there's no point in threatening you with the death penalty. We both know you'll never see trial. The Thirteen will make sure of that."

She smiled at him as though he were a small child.

"If only you knew how right you are."

"You think Avery Douglas is going to get you out of this?"

Her eyes hardened and her smile momentarily faltered. Her heart rate accelerated on the monitor.

"I have no idea what you're talking about, Special Agent Mason. That is your name, isn't it? It's my understanding you recently lost your wife. Allow me to express my condolences."

She was baiting him, which meant he was on the right track. He needed to press harder.

"Even as we speak, Mr. Douglas is calling in favors and promising others in return. He's trying to find the perfect person to make his problem go away, because right now, Valeria? Right now you're more than a headache; you're a threat that needs to be eliminated. Permanently."

Valeria's pulse quickened and her monitor started to beep. Her impassive facade cracked, revealing a hint of the monster hidden underneath.

"Special Agent . . ." the doctor said.

"What about those poor people in Times Square?" Valeria said. "I watched them on TV, you know. I couldn't believe how terribly they suffered."

"You mean like your mother? I heard she went out hard, just like your father. Do you know the sound a head makes when it hits a marble staircase from three stories up?"

The bedside monitor beeped faster and faster. She bared her teeth like an animal and jerked at her cuffed wrist.

"That's it," the doctor said. "I want you all out of here."

"How do you think they'll do it?" Mason asked. "Will it be one of your nurses? Maybe a police officer or special agent like me? Someone will come when you least expect it and inject something into that IV over there. Or maybe smother you with a pillow—"

"Enough!" the doctor shouted.

He grabbed Mason by the shoulder and attempted to pry him from the chair.

The monitor alarmed and lit up with flashing lights.

"We can protect you," Mason said. "Tell us everything you know about the Thirteen and I'll make sure no harm comes to you."

The doctor yelled for security and finally succeeded in hauling Mason out of the chair.

"You need to try to relax," he said to Valeria. "Your body can't handle this kind of stress right now. Not this soon after surgery, and especially not with—"

He cut himself off before he finished the sentence.

Mason stopped struggling and looked into Valeria's eyes. Read the truth in them. And he knew . . . positively knew . . .

He heard her father's voice . . .

I have made sure she is taken care of.

. . . And recalled something he'd said, which at the time Mason had assumed was just a turn of phrase, but he now realized was in fact quite literal.

It will be from her womb that a new, enlightened incarnation of mankind is born.

Valeria must have known he'd figured it out. She frantically shook her head back and forth. Screamed at the top of her lungs.

Mason straightened his shirt and headed for the door. He had everything he needed, at least for now.

"They'll come for you, too!" she shouted after him. "You can't stop them!"

Mason had barely stepped out into the hallway when Archer grabbed him and shoved him up against the wall.

"What the hell was that in there? She's burned as a witness now. You know that, right?"

"We don't need her to get Douglas," Mason said. "All we need is a sample of her blood."

"You think that even with a subpoena we'll be able to get that now?"

"No, but I'd be happy to give you my sweatshirt without one."

73

"It's a gamble and you know it," Layne said. "All Douglas has to do is deny it and we've lost. Valeria's not about to let us anywhere near that fetus."

The forensics lab had been able to collect a large enough sample of the blood from Mason's sweatshirt to confirm their suspicions without having to subpoena Valeria's medical records, which would have taken days, if not weeks. She'd suddenly developed simultaneous cases of amnesia and laryngitis, presumably contracted from her legal counsel. Fortunately, she wasn't their only potential source of information.

Mason stared through the two-way mirror at the man with the ponytail hanging down his back from his bald head. If ever a human being had looked like a rat, it was Reginald Tyler. They could only hope that he possessed the same survival instincts.

They'd separated him from his partner, Jeremiah Russell, who at this moment had to be crapping himself in lockup thinking that his friend here was going to be the first to cut a deal and he'd be out of luck when it was his turn. He'd talk, but Mason had a hunch that Reggie would do so first. He was the weak link. He'd served time in federal lockup, so he knew better than to risk going back. They just needed to get to him before he could call a lawyer, which, surprisingly, neither of the men had attempted to do so far, an interesting development that all but confirmed Mason's speculations. They were so afraid of what their boss would do to them that they were happy to simply disappear into the penal system and hope they never saw him again. A recidivist like Reggie, however, had to know that there wasn't a reward for carrying someone else's weight. No one was safe on the inside, not even guys who'd taken the fall honorably.

"This won't take long," Layne said. She broke away from the mirrored glass, activated the recording device, and headed for the door. "Are you coming or what?"

Mason followed and entered the interrogation room behind her. He was content to be the good cop in this scenario, because when it came to playing bad cop, Layne had been born for the role.

"Sorry to keep you waiting so long," she said, taking the seat across the table from the prisoner. He instinctively drew his arms away from her, but the chain between his cuffs caught on the O-ring bolted in the middle. "We know you've been through this before, so why don't you save us all a lot of time and get to the part where you tell us what we want to know."

Tyler hung his head and mumbled something unintelligible.

"I'm sorry, Reggie. I didn't catch that."

"I said I don't know anything."

"Then maybe we should switch roles and I'll tell you what I know." She craned her neck so that she could look up into his face. "I know you've been flying that helicopter for Tectonic Energy for close to a decade. They have you running all over the East Coast. The transponder on that chopper says you've landed at just about every drilling operation throughout the Appalachian Mountains, isn't that right?"

He nodded, but he couldn't seem to raise his eyes to meet hers.

"Are you looking at my breasts, Reggie?"

His eyes widened in sheer terror and focused like lasers on her face. Mason had to turn away to keep from smirking.

"They have you flying so much I didn't think they ever gave you a vacation, which is why I was so surprised to see your name attached to a rental agreement as the pilot of a private helicopter based out of Rio Grande City, Texas. You'd think that flying would be the last thing you'd want to do on your own time, or at least I would. It's a lot harder to cross the border down there than it used to be, which is why I imagine you filed your flight plans with the FAA. Don't want to have to serve any more time in Texas, do you? At least not while you're on vacation and not doing anything illegal. And you weren't doing anything illegal, were you, Reggie?"

His face paled before their eyes. He tried to shake his head and only ended up quivering.

"That's good to hear, because we found it awfully interesting that you were there at the same time as your employer, David Lucas, who just happened to be in Mexico negotiating a land-lease deal with a gentleman named Jorge Trujillo, who took his own life shortly after signing said lease. And the disappearance of his two eldest children, of course. You don't know anything about that, do you, Reggie?"

This was the part where people who knew they'd been caught generally either started denying everything or actually looked relieved that the secret that had been eating them alive for however many years was finally out in the open. Reggie, on the other hand, looked like he was about to pass out, which meant they hadn't even scratched the surface of the full extent of his involvement. And there was only one thing Mason could think of that was worse than being party to the disappearance and possible murder of two children.

He took out his cell phone, scrolled through his gallery until he found a specific picture he'd taken in one of the stalls in the barn at the end of the drug tunnel in Texas, and set it down in front of Layne. She stared at the image for several seconds before glancing back at him. He nodded for her to proceed, which she did with a flourish. She spun the phone toward Reggie across the table. It came to rest right in front of him. He cocked his head to better see the picture, and quickly closed his eyes, pinching tears from the corners.

"Do you know what the message on the wall says?" Layne asked. "It says, 'This is not a game.' Those men were taken apart by an animal. Literally taken apart while they were still alive. He used a chain saw on their arms and legs. I don't even want to think about how much they bled. He saved their heads for last, didn't he? He waited until that last spark of life was about to fade from their eyes, and then he—"

"He said he'd do the same thing to my mom and sisters," Tyler said.

"We can keep you safe," Mason said. "It's not you we want. It's your employer. We want to connect him to—"

"Lucas threw those poor girls out of the chopper, but he didn't do . . . *that*."

"Then you should really tell us who did," Layne said.

"If I say a word, he'll do exactly what he said he would. I don't doubt it for a second. What about my mom? My sisters? Who's going to keep them safe?"

"That's what the witness protection program is for," Mason said. "To protect innocent people who get caught up in events outside of their control. It's a second chance, Reggie. A second chance to not only have a life, but to keep your family alive."

"You don't understand how much power he has. He's wired into everything. There's nowhere I can go that he won't be able to find me." Tyler positively shook with fear, the unmistakable scent seeping from his pores. "You didn't see him. You didn't see how much he enjoyed doing it, how he took his time with those Russians while they begged and pleaded for him to stop."

"Why the Russians?" Layne asked.

"They wanted to be the ones to lay the pipeline."

"Into Mexico?"

Tyler looked momentarily confused.

"No," he said. "Through it. That's why CJNG was there. He needed to work with them to get his line across the Gulf of Mexico. Those Russians were trying to beat him to it, so he wanted to send a message back to their employers, and, in the process, let the cartel know that he meant business."

"Who are we talking about, Reggie?" Layne asked.

"Don't make me say it," he whispered.

"We already know who you're talking about. We just need you to say his name. Then we can start working on protecting your family."

If they didn't seal the deal right here and now, they might lose him. Mason spoke as calmly and softly as he could.

"We know you're not a bad guy, Reggie. This whole thing has to be eating you alive. You messed up back in the nineties and served your time. We all make mistakes. You just wanted to start over and make a life for yourself. We both get that."

"I swear I didn't know what they were going to do to those little girls," Tyler said.

"We believe you," Layne said. "You probably thought Lucas was a decent guy right up until the point that he wasn't anymore."

"You might even have thought he was a little naïve," Mason said. "After all, he didn't have any practical experience with natural gas before he took over Tectonic, but I assure you that wasn't the case. David Lucas was a prominent member of the executive council at AIP and sat on the board of directors for Royal Nautilus Petroleum. He knew exactly what he was doing, especially when it came to what he did to the Trujillo children. And for that we'll be able to put him away for the rest of his natural life."

"And not just him," Layne said. "We're going to take down the man pulling his strings, the man who did such horrible things to those Russians. With or without you, Reggie. But we can't help you if you don't tell us his name."

"You promise you'll protect my family?"

"I give you my word."

"What about Russ? He's in the same boat as I am."

"We won't hang him out to dry," Mason said. "We'll make sure that he and his family are taken care of, too."

Tyler closed his eyes and remained silent for several seconds.

"Tell us his name, Reggie," Layne whispered.

When he finally spoke, it was in a tone of determination.

"I can do better than that."

74

NEW YORK CITY
July 6

Avery Douglas owned personal property on every continent and in practically every country around the globe, from mansions in Greenwich and Palm Beach to the French Riviera and London, where his office claimed he'd been living for the past several months, ostensibly to acquire a Premier League soccer franchise. They found him in his penthouse on Central Park West by triangulating the GPS beacon on one of his personal cell phones.

Mason didn't care where he was. He'd track him to the ends of the earth if he had to and drag him back here, kicking and screaming, but he was confident it wouldn't come to that. Douglas already knew he was beaten. The lawyers he'd provided for Valeria through an offshore shell company had undoubtedly already informed him of everything that had transpired, which meant he also knew they'd discovered that she was pregnant with his child. The Dragon had devised the perfect contingency plan to guarantee the safety of his daughter, whose child carried the proof of Douglas's involvement in the nuclear plot in his or her DNA.

Mason and Layne waited patiently for him to emerge from the golden revolving doors of his building and intercepted him before he could reach his waiting Town Car.

"Let's take a walk," Mason said.

He gripped the investment banker by his left arm, while Layne more casually looped her arm around his right, as though they were a couple out for a stroll. They crossed at the light, entered Central Park near the 65th Street Transverse, and headed downhill toward the arch underneath West Drive. He was easily able to identify the plainclothes agents trying to blend in with the other people out for a walk on this sweltering day.

Locker and his team were serving search warrants for Douglas's office and his various houses at that very moment, knowing full well they'd find nothing, but going through the motions on the off chance they just might get lucky. Based on Douglas's demeanor, however, Mason didn't hold out much hope.

The CEO of American Investment Partnership looked older in person. Up close, Mason could see where the crow's-feet had taken root and the smile lines around his mouth had formed permanent creases. Or perhaps they just stood out more because of his tan, which made his blond hair appear even brighter, as though it were spun from gold.

"My grandfather used to bring me to this park when I was a small boy," Douglas said. He spoke in a surprisingly deep voice and wore a wistful smile. "'Avery,' he would say to me, 'I want you to always remember moments like these because they're worth more than all of the money in the world.'"

"And you believed him?" Layne said.

"Not for a second. I would have rather been anywhere else and with anyone other than this stuffy old man I hardly knew." He switched subjects without missing a beat. "How do you foresee this playing out?"

"When we're finished with our little chat, we're going to cuff you for the entire world to see and take you into federal custody," Mason said.

"And my lawyers will have me out before you've even finished patting each other on the back. So, again, I ask: How do you foresee this playing out?"

"You know we have you dead to rights. There are a lot of things we might not be able to prove. At least, not yet. But we'll have plenty of time to find the evidence while you're incarcerated for the murders of Kostov Mironov and Patrushev Panarin. We'll eventually be able to connect you to Valeria Meier and, by extension, her father—whom you hired to build the nuclear device you intended to detonate in Washington, D.C., and assassinate Rand Marchment, Theresa Powers, and Stan Ryder—through the DNA of your shared child. And it's only a matter of time before we can prove that you used your investment bank to launder money for the Jalisco New Generation Cartel and wrest control of Tectonic Energy from its board of directors so you could stage a natural gas coup in the Middle East, starting with the pillaging of Slate Langbroek's holdings."

"Don't forget stealing billions of dollars from the American people through the Federal Reserve," Layne said.

Douglas chuckled. It was a carefully rehearsed affectation honed through years of repetition.

"My bank provides a valuable service to our elected officials," he said. "If you have a problem with the way they do business, I recommend taking it up with your senator."

The man winked at Mason, who somehow managed to keep from dropping him right there on the concrete path. He still hadn't heard from his father and Archer, maddeningly, hadn't even been willing to confirm that he was still alive.

"I grow weary of this conversation," Douglas said as they emerged from the tunnel. "You can no more prove intent to harm with a business loan than you can with a feather duster, especially considering the lengths to which I've gone to ensure Tectonic's viability, not least of which is placing one of my most trusted financial advisers in its primary leadership role. I highly doubt that Ms. Meier is pregnant with my child or even that her pregnancy will go to term. And I have no knowledge of these individuals you've accused me of murdering or any relationship to the officials I supposedly conspired to assassinate, so if all you have on me is an attempt to outbid my competition to secure the prime assets of a company ripe for the plundering, then I suppose I stand guilty as charged."

He held out his wrists as though daring them to cuff him.

Mason removed his cell phone from his jacket and placed it in Douglas's open palms. One glance at it and the smug grin vanished from his face. It was the picture that had been posted to the *La Prensa* website, of the group of men posing behind the butchered remains of the two Russians. While everything above their midsections had been cut off, the blood-drenched stomach and slacks of the man in the middle were clearly visible.

"Hang on," Mason said. "That's the wrong one. Give me a second."

He grabbed his phone, swiped the screen, and set the phone back in Douglas's hands.

On the screen was an image of Avery Douglas, stripped to the waist, his bare chest and slacks soaked with blood. A chain saw dangled from one hand, the severed head of Patrushev Panarin from the other. The look in his wild eyes, leering out from a mask of blood, would haunt Mason for as long as he lived.

Douglas licked his lips, shot his cuffs, and returned Mason's phone. Reggie Tyler hadn't been your average recidivist. Having worked with and served time for the Juarez Cartel, he understood the value of leverage, while Douglas had been so confident in his superiority that he'd underestimated a man he'd thought of as the hired help. With any luck, good old Reggie and his mom and sisters would enjoy the heck out of their new lives.

"A pathetic attempt at a shakedown, Special Agents." He freed his arm from Mason's grasp and turned to leave. "You can deal with my lawyers. We're done here."

Layne had his hands behind his back and cuffed before he knew what was happening. She spun him around to face them again.

"We get to say when we're done," she said.

"Listen carefully," Douglas said in a voice that sounded as though it came from someone else living inside his skin. "You can't hurt me.

You could have a picture of me blowing up the White House myself and no one—not even the president himself—would do a damn thing about it. And do you know why? Because without my investment bank to lend the government the money it needs to spend on endless wars and provide sustenance for the dregs of society who suckle at its teat, the American dream would die a miserable death. I have as many politicians on my payroll as I do brokers, and I guarantee you they'll make that picture go away in less time than it takes you to lose your badges. They know that without me, they lose everything, and not just their pathetic little fortunes. The bottom would fall out of the entire global economy. The civilized world as we know it would end and we would revert to the savagery of our ancestors, fighting over scraps and killing each other just to be able to feed our families."

"I thought that was the whole point," Mason said. "Then the Thirteen can step in and establish the global rule it's always wanted."

Douglas laughed. It was a horrible sound, full of loathing and contempt.

"In case you didn't notice," he said, "it already has."

A line of blood trickled from his nose and passed over his lip. He instinctively licked it. His momentary expression of surprise was replaced by one of genuine panic. Both sides of his face drooped at once, like melting putty. The vessels in his left eye ruptured and flooded the sclera. He started to twitch, and then outright convulse.

Mason grabbed his arm and tried to hold him upright, but Douglas jerked out of his grip. Fell. Landed on his back, his arms pinned underneath him. He sputtered a mouthful of vomit and appeared to deflate. He settled to the ground, motionless.

"Uncuff him!" Mason shouted.

He threw himself to his knees on the sidewalk and immediately started giving chest compressions.

Agents converged from seemingly everywhere at once.

A woman screamed from the bridge above them.

"Someone call an ambulance!" he shouted, but he knew it was already too late.

The Thirteen were now eleven.

EPILOGUE

WASHINGTON, D.C.
July 7

"The medical examiner found this implanted in his frontal lobe," Chris said. He slid the small sealed plastic bag across the desk. "It's a miniature electrical device that triggered a small burst of voltage. Just enough to pop every blood vessel within about an inch of the central sulcus of his brain."

Mason raised the bag and appraised the small device. It looked like a resistor from a circuit board, with wires trailing from either end of a black body about the size of a grain of rice, the center of which had erupted. He passed it to Layne, who held it up to the window to better see its contours.

"They found remnants of its antenna embedded in the gray matter," Chris said.

"It was remotely activated?" Mason said.

"Forensics is still working on its range, but based on its size and the theoretical level of interference caused by his skull, they don't think it could be more than a block, if not direct line of sight."

Mason imagined someone sitting on a park bench or watching from the window of his apartment, driving past in a taxi, or, heaven forbid, even one of their own agents, activating the device when they put the cuffs on Douglas. Were the Thirteen so paranoid as to have spies watching one another at all times? Or had they already been in the process of eliminating Douglas, like Langbroek, when they realized he'd been exposed? Either way, it was only a matter of time before a criminal investigation compromised Douglas's holdings, assuming the IRS investigators decided to dig deeply enough.

"How did it get inside his head?" Layne asked.

"We had a team of physicians examine his medical records," Chris said. "They discovered that he suffered a traumatic brain injury in an MVA twenty-some years ago. It's possible the implant was placed during the surgery, but we'll likely never know for sure as every doctor, nurse, and surgical tech listed in the operative report has been dead for at least two decades. Convenient, right?"

"What about manufacturer markings on the device itself?"

Layne set the bag on the desk and slid it across to Chris.

"Microscopic evaluation revealed nothing of any potential significance, and it's not like we have another device like it for comparison."

"Speaking of devices . . ." Mason said.

"DARPA has the gamma ray weapon squirreled away somewhere."

"That's what worries us," Layne said. "You didn't see that thing in action. I've never witnessed anything so terrifying in all my life."

"I've been assured that while they're excited to study it, they have no plans to share it with the military directly, and they certainly have no desire to contribute to putting it into mass production."

"And what about the Dragon's nuclear weapon?" Mason asked.

"Safely disarmed and disposed of."

Chris leaned back in his chair. His new office was a lot bigger than his old one back in Denver, and even more sparsely decorated. As the first director of the Special Projects Initiative, a joint venture between the Federal Bureau of Investigation and the United States Departments of Defense and Homeland Security, he was just beginning to feel his way into a job that had yet to have its duties clearly defined.

"You two should be proud of yourselves," he said. "A lot of people are still alive because of you."

"Don't forget Ramses and Gunnar," Mason said.

"I couldn't if I tried. And believe me, I have."

For his contributions to saving the National Mall, its irreplaceable monuments, and the population of Washington, D.C., Ramses had been rewarded with a plane ticket back to Colorado that he didn't need and the promise of a Presidential Medal of Freedom that he didn't want. Of course, when he told Mason about it, the expression on his face had been one Mason had never seen there before. Whether or not he ever admitted it to another living soul, the honor obviously meant something to him.

Gunnar had already found himself with a slew of new government contracts thanks to the various loopholes he'd revealed in the country's financial and political infrastructure, the cracks in the foundation of their very republic, although it remained to be seen if anyone actually did anything with the information he provided or if, like everyone else in the business world, these politicians were simply looking for leverage over their rivals.

They could cannibalize one another for all Mason cared. There were still eleven members of a secret cabal committed to culling the human race out there, and he fully intended to track down each and every one of them. No matter the cost, and no matter how long it took. He was going to put an end to the evil machinations set into motion behind the backs of the Founding Fathers and the inheritors of their power ever since.

"Why don't you take a few days for yourselves," Chris said. "Get your affairs in order. We have our work cut out for us when you're ready to dig in again."

Mason rose from his seat, reached across the desk, and shook Chris's hand. For the first time, it felt like the tide was finally starting to turn.

They were halfway out the door when Layne stopped and turned around.

"What about Tyler, Russell, and their families?" she asked.

"They've been placed in protective custody pending the assignment of their new identities. From what I understand, a concerted effort was made to give them new lives that might actually be an improvement."

"And Valeria?"

The way she asked the question suggested she didn't really want to know the answer.

"I know what Douglas told you, but that woman's not about to let anyone near her child as long as it's still inside her. I pity whoever's job it is to take it from her once it's born."

Layne nodded and closed the door behind her. Mason thought for a second he might have seen her wipe a tear from her eye.

The second-floor hallway of the Nebraska Avenue Complex was in a state of transition as many of the departments were in the process of relocating to the St. Elizabeth Campus, freeing up the majority of the thirty-two buildings and 650,000 square feet of space for the Special Projects Initiative, which was still in its formative stages. It was the brainchild of the secretary of the Department of Homeland Security, Derek Archer, whom Mason was more than a little surprised to find waiting for him on the terrace outside the elevator.

"I was starting to feel badly for you," Archer said. "So I figured, you know, it's the least I can do. . . ."

"Hello, James."

Mason would have recognized that voice anywhere. He turned and saw his father exiting the vending area with a can of ginger ale in his hand. He strode right up to his old man and hugged him.

"Had I known that was all it took to get a little affection out of you, I'd have let you think I was dead a long time ago."

Mason released him and stepped back.

"Mount Weather?"

"I'd love to say it was the luck of the draw, but they wanted the chairman of the Federal Trade Commission in a position of being able to supervise the chairman of the Federal Reserve. For whatever reason, the president doesn't seem to trust that man."

"Unfortunately, that's just about all the catching up we have time for today," Archer said. "We're down four congressmen and a good chunk of the leadership at the Pentagon, so we have our work cut out for us."

"Who was the fourth?" Layne asked.

"Excuse me?"

"You said four congressmen. We only knew about three."

Mason's father looked crestfallen when he faced him.

"Do you remember Owen Royer?"

"Jesus," Mason said. "He used to come to our house when I was a kid."

"He was my mentor and probably my best friend in this snake's den we call a capital."

"Wasn't he the Senate minority leader?"

"Your father will be taking over his duties on an acting basis," Archer said. "Speaking of which . . ."

The two men entered the elevator and turned to face them once more.

"I'm told that millions of people would have died were it not for you, son," the senator said.

Layne cleared her throat.

"And you too, of course, Special Agent Layne." He smiled, but it was an expression tempered by sadness and exhaustion. "I hope you both know how grateful this entire country is for what you did, even if it will never know what happened. And James? As your father, I couldn't be prouder."

The doors closed between them and the elevator started its descent.

"Is there a reason we couldn't ride down with them?" Layne asked.

Mason smiled and nudged her shoulder.

"My father has a flair for the dramatic. Always leave them wanting more. It's funny how the longer you know someone, the less you notice things like that about them."

DENVER, COLORADO
July 8

Gunnar had just finished upgrading the operations center in Ramses's penthouse so that it formed an approximation of the most-wanted section of Johan's archives. He'd hung flat-screen TVs on the walls and networked them to a series of hard drives air-gapped from the mainframe, so that whatever information they learned about the men and women on the screens never left this room. Outside of the hourly backup to encrypted off-site cloud storage, anyway. The main console tracked the assets of AIP, Royal Nautilus Petroleum, and their respective deceased owners in real time. For as aggressive as companies had been in scavenging Langbroek's holdings, they were equally hesitant to attack Douglas's. The remaining members of the Thirteen had to be watching for signs that one of its own was preparing to make a move against the others, and when that happened, Mason and his team would be waiting, only this time with the full weight and resources of a newly minted federal agency behind them.

"It's starting to take form," Gunnar said.

"Not nearly fast enough," Mason replied.

The rolling white boards in the middle of the room were covered with names, notes, and markings. One contained modern information, the other historical, and each had a pyramid in the center that served as a template for the theoretical hierarchy of the Thirteen. The names Langbroek and Douglas appeared on both sides, as well as their lines of inheritance, known affiliations, and points of intersection. There was a section devoted to the analysis of the Twentieth Assembly of the Society for Lasting International Peace in 1994, at which Stephen Douglas had delivered the keynote address to an audience consisting of Slate Langbroek's Nautilus contingent, the Scarecrow and her brother, and quite possibly even a young Avery. They were beginning to suspect that the conference had been used to create something of a blueprint for the Thirteen's global conquest, an event signifying the commencement of an endgame centuries in the making.

"It starts to feel like looking into the sun after a while, doesn't it?" Layne said.

"That's why you don't just stand there staring at it," Ramses said, grabbing a beer from the six-pack and offering the remainder to the others. "At least not without one of these in your hand."

He glanced at his stealth phone for what had to be the hundredth time. Alejandra had been scheduled to call nearly half an hour ago. Although satellite surveillance confirmed that the bulk of Cártel de Jalisco Nueva Generación's men were still at the staging ground in the jungle near Valladolid, southeast of Mérida, there were reports of scattered firefights on the streets of Cancún.

"She'll call," Mason said.

Ramses nodded and looked away.

"There are unresolved aspects of this case that I still find troubling," Gunnar said.

"It's kind of like nothing's changed with Douglas out of the picture," Layne said.

"The global economy depends upon the services his bank provides."

"Services that almost started World War Three," Ramses said.

Mason hoped no one ever found out how close the Dragon had come to successfully pulling off a false-flag operation that could have destroyed a third of the world and enriched Douglas in the process.

"I'm talking about the fact that Valeria knew who was going to be on that chopper," Gunnar said. "That alone proves that the highest levels of our national security apparatus have been compromised, but there's more to it than that. Assassinating the congressman threatening to lift the cloak of secrecy from the Federal Reserve creates more problems than it solves in the long term."

"What's your thinking?" Mason asked.

"There's more to it than just maintaining the system from which the investment banks profit from the creation of government debt. The Federal Reserve is like a cartel in many ways; it functions out in the open for all to see, and yet its business dealings are opaque, even to the agencies tasked with its oversight. It controls the production and distribution of its product and dictates its value, but it's faced with the challenge of either diversifying its operations to maintain its profitability or riding the dollar to its inescapable hyperinflationary demise. Factor in the rise of cryptocurrencies, the fact that every major government—our own included—is suddenly amassing significant quantities of gold again, and the eventual crowning of a winner in the Middle East pipeline race, and I fear that someone with a vested interest in both the Federal Reserve and natural gas is on the brink of making a major move."

Mason nodded as he surveyed the boards. He could feel something building, too, something far worse than anything they'd encountered so far. There was a power struggle occurring within the ranks of the Thirteen, an internal battle being waged as though it were a game of chess, using real-life players as pawns, including the four of them and monsters like the Hoyl, the Scarecrow, and the Dragon, who spread death wherever they went.

"Speaking of cartels," Mason said, "why would someone like Douglas even attempt to negotiate with them?"

"That pipeline must have been pretty important to risk entering into a partnership with those CJNG butchers," Ramses said.

"Especially for the Russians. Setting up operations for a nationalized natural gas company right on our border is an aggressive move with potential political and military consequences."

"GazNat isn't invested in North American energy resources," Gunnar said. "In fact, they're in direct competition, which suggests they were attempting to build a pipeline not just to carry resources to Mexico, but potentially through it and into the United States, to undercut the prices at which we distribute to our own people in an effort to destabilize our economy."

Ramses's phone buzzed in his hand. He blew out his breath and ducked from the room to answer.

"Where could they possibly find natural gas for cheaper than we can get it out of the ground beneath our feet?"

Gunnar took a seat at the console, spun around the chair, and brought up the map of Mexico's oil and gas industry. He zoomed out and drew a straight line through the natural gas facilities the Russians had toured—from Reynosa, across the Gulf of Mexico, and through Mérida and Valladolid—and extended it all the way across the Caribbean Sea to the point where it intersected land again.

"Venezuela," Layne said.

"Exactly," Gunnar said. "It has some of the largest energy reserves in the entire world and a ruinous state of internal affairs that makes it vulnerable. I fear it's only a matter of time before it becomes the next Syria. There's more at stake than mere energy, though. I can feel it. Something's going on down there that I just can't see."

"But what could that possibly be?" Mason asked.

Ramses rushed back into the room and transferred the video call to the main monitor, replacing Gunnar's map. Alejandra appeared on the screen, a bare plaster wall behind her. She simultaneously looked wide awake and like she hadn't slept in a month. Something must have been going down.

"Show them what you showed me," Ramses said.

"An undercover operative within Cártel de Sinaloa took this picture outside Culiacán," she said.

She turned the camera toward her laptop's monitor, which

displayed an image of three distant airplanes in tight formation, rising above the treetops, silhouetted against the red sun as it prepared to descend behind a densely forested mountain range. They were smeared by motion, but it was still apparent that their noses were oddly helmet-shaped, their wings were curiously long and thin, and their tail fins pointed diagonally upward. Their slender landing gear remained extended and propellers blurred on their tails. Camera turrets bulged from their undersides.

Mason's chest tightened with the realization of what it was. He recalled Gunnar's words: *We can only assume they're still devoted to the apocalyptic teachings of Hayakawa, who, at the time of his arrest, had in his possession the schematics for a directed-energy weapon . . .*

"When was it taken?" he asked, his mouth suddenly dry.

"July fourth," Alejandra said. "6:26 P.M. local time."

"That's 8:26 eastern standard time," Layne said. "The same time as sunset in D.C."

"And the moment the Dragon was supposed to detonate his nuclear device," Mason said. "They intended to use the attack to conceal the launch."

. . . technical drawings of a fission device small enough to fit in a suitcase . . .

"It took several days for the intelligence to reach us," Alejandra said, "but we immediately started combing through satellite footage and found a makeshift runway cleared from the forest near a suspected cártel stronghold."

Mason's heart rate accelerated and his pulse thundered in his ears.

. . . and blueprints for a nuclear-powered HALE UAV—a high-altitude, long-endurance unmanned aerial vehicle.

He pulled his cell phone from his pocket and speed-dialed Archer. Someone needed to warn him, although it was probably already too late. Alejandra's words returned to him, reverberating in his head.

I can see Ismael Zambada or the sons of El Chapo negotiating with the Thirteen on behalf of Cártel de Sinaloa. They are practical businessmen who know how to play the long game, which is the reason they have been able to survive for four decades, while so many rivals have come and gone.

Someone within the Thirteen had outmaneuvered both CJNG and Avery Douglas, whose plan had been co-opted by another of its number, a fellow member who'd set them up to take the fall while he enacted his own machinations. He'd murdered Douglas while in federal custody and was now on the brink of achieving his goals, not to mention those of the Dragon.

No one pursuing drilling rights in Mexico would be able to negotiate with the government and Cártel de Jalisco Nueva Generación without involving the state-owned petroleum company, which is at war with the cártel over billions of dollars in stolen oil. And Cártel de Sinaloa would see it as an act of aggression, one they would not be able to let stand.

The image on the screen cut out, the photograph of the drone slicing across the horizon vanishing. A man materialized from the darkness, his face masked by an algorithm that made his features appear to be made of mercury, his voice that of several people all speaking the same words at once.

"I must congratulate you on seeing through our deception," Anomaly said, "but you're too late to do anything about it. The drones are preparing to deliver their payload to the targets as we speak."

Mason lowered the phone from his ear.

Black-and-white aerial imagery appeared on the monitor, crosshairs sweeping across ground so far down that the seamless canopy of the forest resembled cottage cheese. Azimuth and elevation markings framed the screen, while geolocational coordinates and altitude readings filled the corner. A village whipped past, little more than a cluster of black rectangles, before the forest resumed once more. The drone suddenly tipped forward and commenced a rapid descent, the trees rising toward it, the elevation numbers dropping so quickly that it was impossible to visually keep up.

Mason waited for buildings to come into view, for the bull's-eye shape of Moscow to form, and the Kremlin to emerge from the center. He heard Archer's voice from the phone in his hand as he helplessly watched the forest rise, closer and closer, until he saw a clearing filled with tents and vehicles and thousands of men. He'd barely registered the thought that he was looking at the CJNG staging ground in the Mexican jungle when the screen went white, and then the feed turned to static.

The member of the Thirteen who'd usurped Douglas's plan had manipulated the cartel into assembling at a single location and eliminated the only force standing in the way of a pipeline running from

Venezuela to Reynosa. He'd cut a deal with the Sinaloa Cartel, who, in exchange for wiping out their competition, had undoubtedly agreed to leave the natural gas operations alone and launder their money through the financial machinery of whoever inherited Douglas's empire. In one fell swoop, he'd cleared the way for his pipeline and assumed a percentage of Mexico's multibillion-dollar drug trafficking industry in the process.

"Allie!" Ramses shouted.

Mason glanced at the screen of his old friend's phone in time to see Alejandra shoulder through a door and burst out onto a balcony. She turned her camera upon the jungle in the far distance, where a dark cloud spread across the horizon. Car alarms blared and people took to the street below to see what was causing the commotion.

A satellite image appeared from the static on the main monitor, revealing a massive crater, just like the one in the photograph of the Dragon's handiwork in Libya, only surrounded by burning trees and bodies, which brought to mind a question Mason couldn't help but ask.

"What about Russia and the Syrian pipeline?"

"I don't think you need to worry about that anymore," Anomaly said.

"Jesus," Gunnar said. He brought up a map of the Middle East on one of the other monitors. Red beacons radiated from the Iranian coast of the Persian Gulf and the Syrian border with Iraq. "They hit Asalouyeh and Abu Kamal, the site of drilling operations and the point where the pipeline enters Syria, killing the Shia line and paving the way for the Qatari line."

"And making it impossible for them to rebuild their operations for the foreseeable future," Anomaly said. "Or at least not without full radiation protection gear."

"What about Moscow?" Mason asked.

The hacker leaned closer to his camera and a knifelike smile cut across his liquid silver face.

"Its time will soon come," Anomaly said, the screen once more going black. "And the war to end all wars will follow."

ELSEWHERE

"How close are you?" the man seated at the desk asked.

His computer screen displayed an encrypted virtual chat room. On the left, the digital features concealing his face moved with a slight delay. They shifted and morphed thanks to an artificial-intelligence algorithm that made him appear to be completely different people from one second to the next, a constantly changing mask plucked from the imagination of a machine.

The man on the other side of the screen took no such precautions, for he had no reason to hide his true identity.

"Mere months," he said. "The trials have gone even better than I could have hoped."

"That's what I was hoping to hear. Our window of opportunity is fast approaching and we need to be ready to act the moment it opens."

"I'll be ready, but I should remind you that even I have never attempted anything on this scale before. There are factors outside of our control. This is no mere virus. There will be considerable"—the man leaned closer to the camera until his stunning blue eyes, a shade of blue unique in all of nature, eclipsed the screen—"casualties."

"I'm counting on it."

ACKNOWLEDGMENTS

I'd like to extend my sincerest thanks to my team at St. Martin's Press/Macmillan: Pete Wolverton, my friend and incomparable editor, who challenged me to raise the stakes and my own game; Lily Cronig, who does all the work behind the scenes; Ryan Jenkins, copy editor; Michelle Cashman and Sarah Bonamino, marketing and PR; Ken Silver, who's responsible for the stunning book you hold in your hands; and Young Jin Lim, who absolutely nailed the cover.

To my away team at Trident Media Group: Alex Slater, who's pulled off a miracle or two for me (hopefully this won't be the last); Nicole Robson, who knows just about everything about everything; Caitlin O'Beirne, queen of graphic design; and Robert Gottlieb, the man behind the curtain.

To my home team: my wife, Danielle, and my kids, who make life worth living; my mom, for her unwavering support; my dad, whom I miss every day; and the Bannigans.

Special thanks to: the Bedard family; David Bell; Richard Chizmar; Liza Fleissig; Mark Greaney; Michael Patrick Hicks; Gus Isuani; Michael Koryta; Jennie Levesque; Jonathan Maberry; Jim Marrs; Tom Monteleone; Ron and Rand Paul; Andi Rawson; Justin Robbins; James Rollins; Michael Marshall Smith; Jeff Strand; The Tattered Cover; Thomas Tessier; Paul Wilson; Kimmy Yerina; and to everyone else who's contributed to my success on a personal level: You know who you are and how much you mean to me.

My most sincere admiration and respect to all booksellers and librarians, who keep the torch of literacy burning.

And, most important, to all of you, my readers, without whom this book wouldn't exist.